# HOLDING ONTO LOVE

The Taverstons of Iversley
Book 2

By Carol Coventry

© Copyright 2024 by Carol Coventry
Text by Carol Coventry
Cover by Dar Albert

Dragonblade Publishing, Inc. is an imprint of Kathryn Le Veque Novels, Inc.
P.O. Box 23
Moreno Valley, CA 92556
ceo@dragonbladepublishing.com

Produced in the United States of America

First Edition December 2024
Trade Paperback Edition

Reproduction of any kind except where it pertains to short quotes in relation to advertising or promotion is strictly prohibited.

All Rights Reserved.

The characters and events portrayed in this book are fictitious. Any similarity to real persons, living or dead, is purely coincidental and not intended by the author.

**ARE YOU SIGNED UP FOR DRAGONBLADE'S BLOG?**

You'll get the latest news and information on exclusive giveaways, exclusive excerpts, coming releases, sales, free books, cover reveals and more.

Check out our complete list of authors, too!

No spam, no junk. That's a promise!

**Sign Up Here**

www.dragonbladepublishing.com

———⟫⟫⟫⟪⟪⟪———

*Dearest Reader;*

*Thank you for your support of a small press. At Dragonblade Publishing, we strive to bring you the highest quality Historical Romance from some of the best authors in the business. Without your support, there is no 'us', so we sincerely hope you adore these stories and find some new favorite authors along the way.*

*Happy Reading!*

*CEO, Dragonblade Publishing*

## Additional Dragonblade books by Author Carol Coventry

### The Taverstons of Iversley Series
Counting on Love (Book 1)
Holding Onto Love (Book 2)

# PART 1
## Time to Move On
### November 1812
### London

# CHAPTER ONE

*Dearest V.—My father had another apoplectic fit—we think—so I must return to Chaumbers. Leaving tonight. The devil—I dashed out of Lady Andini's ball like some sort of reverse Cinderella. I'll write as soon as I know more.—J.T.*

*Darling—I am so, so sorry. I pray it isn't that. Or if it is, that he recovers quickly. The earl is a good and gracious man. Is Reginald with you? Have you sent for Crispin? Oh, I don't mean to fire questions at you. I'm concerned is all, and I feel so for your worry. God bless.—V.*

*Dearest V.—The earl is very ill. Reginald is here, thank God. Crispin has been sent for. The physician is being very guarded. Father fooled him last time, so he doesn't want to say. I'm afraid I won't be back to London anytime soon—I'm sorry to abandon you—again—with the social Season getting underway. I know how uncomfortable it is for you.* ~~I wish~~ *I'll write more soon. Father has left a devil of a mess.—J.T.*

*Jasper, dear—Don't worry about me. For Heaven's sake. I'm fine. I'm sorry your father is suffering. Surely Reginald is a comfort? What do you mean by a mess?—V.*

*Dearest V.—Reginald tries. God—I mean, yes, he's a great help—more practically than spiritually, but in truth, I need the practical more. The mess is my fault, not my father's. I thought him better recovered from his last attack than he was. Moreover, the steward was ill and now has passed. The accounts are a jumble. There are stacks of correspondence my father never even opened—the tenants rightly have been feeling neglected—this must all sound so cold. I'll write a better letter when I can think straight. I am missing you so.—J.T.*

*Dear Jasper—I miss you too. You don't sound cold. You sound overwhelmed. Please remember that you don't have to fix everything all at once. Cherish this time with your family. And please don't worry about me, about writing "better" letters to me. Darling, I know how your mind works. Don't put writing to me in that "duty" pile. This is a terrible time for you, and you know I understand that. All my love, V.*

Mrs. Vanessa Wardrip handed her coat to the butler, took a deep breath, and joined Mrs. Lowry's party's receiving line—a sad collection of almost-acceptable ladies of gentle birth and cast-off once-acceptable ladies. They were the unchosen and their desperation was palpable. This ill-furnished townhouse, leased for the Season by the widowed Mrs. Lowry, depressed Vanessa as much as the guest list. She wouldn't have come, except that she wanted to be able to tell Lord Jasper Taverston that she was not hiding away like a hermitess. Last year, after the earl's previous attack, when Jasper had spent so much time at Chaumbers, she had done just that. Jasper had enough to worry about without guiltily envisioning her sitting at home lonely and bored. An invitation to Mrs. Lowry's musicale might not be anything to boast about, but Jasper would see she was still being included, at least on the fringes.

Naturally, Vanessa could never attend high Society's more exclusive balls and parties. Held during the height of the Season, those events were meant to bring out debutantes and to reinforce connections between aristocratic families by facilitating advantageous marriages. Vanessa didn't care that she was excluded. She had never wanted to claw her way into places where she did not belong. The trouble was that Jasper did belong. He enjoyed the company of his peers. And when the debutantes and their mamas surveyed those exclusive balls and parties seeking out eligible gentlemen, they saw Lord Jasper Taverston, heir to the Earl of Iversley—a very eligible gentleman indeed.

Mrs. Lowry, a lowly second cousin to someone important, was trying to scale society's ladder and had no doubt invited Vanessa in order to weasel her way into Lord Taverston's good graces. Vanessa did not like the woman, a conniving gossip, but with Jasper away, invitations were few and far between. She had hoped at least one of her London friends would be attending, but saw none in the reception hall.

She reached the front of the line.

"Mrs. Wardrip," Mrs. Lowry said, opening her eyes wide. The woman did not only powder her face but painted it. "I am surprised you've come!"

"Did you not receive my card? I'm so sorry." *How awkward.* Her invitation had only arrived that morning, but she'd sent a response at once.

Now other ladies were staring. Vanessa heard a few giggles. A few snickers. Just like this afternoon at the milliners, though she had convinced herself then that she was imagining things. She forced a smile. She was here now; she would have to make the best of it.

"I've heard a great deal about the harpist you've hired."

Mrs. Lowry lifted her chin and looked down her nose. "Hmm, well, do take some refreshment before going to the music room. The program will begin in a quarter hour." She turned to the next woman in line. "Lady Grayson! I'm honored you've chosen to attend."

Vanessa moved on. She didn't know Lady Grayson. She recognized several of the others—she'd seen their faces in shops and occasional drawing rooms. She could put names to a few of the faces. She ought to approach someone. She wasn't afraid to do so, not exactly. After all, it had been more than three years since anyone had given her the cut direct. But it was *not* her imagination to think ladies were sliding their eyes toward her and whispering behind their hands.

Too uneasy to eat, Vanessa avoided the refreshments and went straight to the music room. Several rows of rosewood saber-legged chairs, five to a row, had been arranged facing a large bay window, in front of which sat a harp and a pianoforte. There were other guests, but no one with whom Vanessa could claim an acquaintance. She chose a seat alone in the middle row.

Almost at once, three overdressed matrons entered the room, dragging daughters. The girls wore pale-colored frocks and insipid expressions. Debutantes. They sat in the row behind Vanessa.

"Oh!" one of the women exclaimed. "For pity's sake. Adela, come."

Startled, Vanessa glanced over her shoulder to see the plumpest matron rise, clench her daughter's shoulder, and move another two rows back.

"What is it, Mrs. Greaves?" A second woman stood, hand on her fleshy neck, to look around in confusion. "Are we…?"

She looked so confused and so out of place that Vanessa was ready to pity her. Until the first woman said, in a whisper that could have been heard across the room, "That is Lord Taverston's lightskirt."

"Good Heavens!" the woman cried, aghast.

Vanessa's face flushed hot. She looked forward and sat rigidly while the women and their daughters scrambled to distance themselves from her, gabbling all the while.

"She must know, don't you think?"

"What will she do now, do you suppose?"

"What do you mean, Mama? Who is it?"

"Hush. Hush. Go get some cakes, dear."

"But—"

"Get along with you."

When the debutantes scampered away, the whispers flared

again.

"Someone else will take her. That's how it works. Until she loses her looks altogether."

At that moment, a shadow fell across Vanessa, then Lady Rose Posonby sat down beside her. A friend, thank God. Her no-nonsense blue broadcloth day dress matched the businesslike expression on her face.

"Mrs. Wardrip," Rose said. Loudly. "How good it is to see you."

Vanessa gave her a nod. Lady Rose's pedigree was impeccable, which saved her from the ostracism that her bookishness and disdain for convention would otherwise condemn her to.

"Have you had any ratafia? Oh, you must," Rose continued, touching Vanessa's arm. "The music won't start for a while. Come with me. I'm about to expire of thirst."

Vanessa stood and followed Rose from the room. As they walked down the narrow hallway toward the refreshments, Rose leaned closer and said, "You haven't heard?"

"Heard what?"

Rose's face sagged. "Then you haven't. About Lord Taverston. Leave it to Jane Lowry to stoop to something like this. She wants her little party to be the talk of London. Vanessa, I will spill on my gown, and we will leave together."

"Leave?" Vanessa felt sick. Had the earl died? Her letter must be in the post, such a difficult letter to write. "Oh, poor Lord Taverston."

"*Poor* Lord Taverston?"

"To lose his father—"

"His father is not lost. Not yet." Rose tossed her head and scowled. "Honestly, I don't know what Lord Taverston is thinking. His haste is very bad form."

They stepped into the refreshment room. Conversation ceased. Hands holding glasses or pastries stopped before reaching mouths. All eyes focused on Vanessa. Little ripples of laughter started, then stopped. Mrs. Lowry spoke up. "We were only saying it all makes sense now. Lady Georgiana was waiting for him."

Lady Georgiana? Vanessa scoured her brain for half-forgotten gossip; Lady Georgiana, the Duke of Hovington's daughter, had taken the ton by storm last year when she made her debut. Vanessa had never met her, of course, but she was said to be exquisite in every way. A diamond of the first water. She had received—oh, more than a dozen proposals and turned them all down, to the amusement and then the consternation of the ton.

Rose gave her a small nudge. Then, quietly, she said, "Lord Taverston is courting her."

Vanessa froze. She felt lightheaded. The room began to spin.

*No.* She would not faint in front of these women. She stiffened her spine and stretched a smile across her face.

"How lovely."

And how ridiculous. Jasper was not even in London. He was out at the family's country estate, tending his sick father, just as he had been nearly all of last Season while Lady Georgiana was making such a splash. If the lady had been waiting for Jasper, she would just have to wait longer.

Vanessa fetched a glass of ratafia, did *not* spill it on Rose, and made her way back to the music room, Rose right behind. She sat and took a gulp, wishing it were brandy.

Rose squeezed her arm. "That was brave," she whispered.

"Oh, not so very. How do these silly rumors start?"

"Rumors?" Rose squeezed again. "Vanessa, I'm afraid it is the truth."

"Lord Taverston is at Chaumbers."

"And so is Lady Georgiana. Or she will be by nightfall. Lord Taverston invited her." Rose bit her lip. "I am so sorry. Lady Georgiana and her mother left for Chaumbers this morning. Everyone knows. We've all been expecting this, something like this, ever since he danced with her to open Lady Andini's ball."

Vanessa curled her hands into fists and blinked rapidly. Jasper wrote that he fled that ball. He said nothing about dancing the first set with the exquisite Lady Georgiana.

More guests filtered into the music room. Filling seats. Murmuring. Cutting their eyes toward Vanessa. It couldn't be true. It couldn't be.

But she was one hundred percent certain that it was.

*J.—Did I miss a letter?—V.*

*Dear V.—Sorry. No, ~~I've been so ungodly busy~~—I've been trying to write for a week now—Father is improving, slightly—Crispin just arrived. It's all so very hectic. ~~I need to write~~ I want to steal home for a few days to see you. I don't know when I can get away. The devi—if I can't get away in a day or two, I will write ~~the~~. ~~Please~~ I will write as soon as I can.—J.T.*

*J.—Do not bother.—V.*

*Dearest V.—Don't be like this—~~you~~ I meant to tell you. ~~I tried~~ But this is not something one puts in a letter. You must see that I needed to tell you in person. You deserve that much. And my letters are terrible—I know that. He's dying and I have responsibilities—but you know this.—J.T.*

*J.—You may not dictate how I can "be." Nor may you decide what I "must see." You have broken every other promise you made to me. I don't know why I expected you to keep this one. I don't deserve "that much," I deserve better.*

*V.— ~~I'm so sorry~~*

*V.— ~~I never meant to hurt you~~*

*V.— ~~Please wait for me to explain. I'll come home as soon as~~*

*V.—You know how much you mean to me. I don't want to lose you. Tell me what you want from me.—J.T.*

*J.—How dare you? We both knew you would eventually court someone respectable. And then you would lose me. You cannot change the terms of our agreement. I asked one thing from you. One. You promised me that. And reneged. You, who pride yourself on your honor. You have none, Jasper. None.*

*V.—And you pride yourself on being sensible. Where is that sense? For God's sake. I am a full day's ride away, up to my neck in neglected duty. If I could have come back to London, you know that I would have. And you cannot tell me that if I had written to say that I must needs begin courting my countess, all would be fine. You would not have accepted that either. You would have wrung my neck for cowardice for putting it in a letter. You cannot say you were blind-sided. The earl is dying, Vanessa. Dying. I've put off marrying as long as I could. Too long. I'm sorry you see me as dishonorable. I have always tried to be honest with you.—J.*

*J.—Do you even care how I found out? Do you know who told me?*

*V.—Does it matter? It was not me. It should have been. I know that. I suppose Hazard told you. I'm sorry. I wish it had been me. I swear to you, I wish it had been me.—J.*

*J.—Doesn't it matter? It was not Hazard. Common gossip, that is all. But according to you, I cannot say I was blind-sided. I suppose I should not have been.*

*V.— ~~I'm so sorry. This is killing me, Vanessa. I can't bear to think~~*

*V.— ~~I never wanted things to end this way~~*

*V.— ~~Rose Posonby wrote to me. The devil. I'm sorry. But I cannot stop the mouths of gossips~~*

*V.—Can you not grant me a little grace? I would never intentionally hurt you. I've dreaded this—God knows how I've dreaded this. I would have told you that I had decided to court Hovington's daughter, but I received word of my father's relapse and I had to race away. Everything has happened so quickly. Too quickly. Can you not forgive me?—J.T.*

*J.—You decided to court Hovington's daughter and then you were called away? Jasper, you were with me the morning before Lady Andini's ball. Are you telling me you danced with the girl once and decided she would be your wife? Or are you telling me that you held me in your arms, you made love to me, AFTER you had decided to woo someone else? We both know the answer. And no, I cannot forgive you.*

*V.—Just let me come speak with you.* LETTER RETURNED UNOPENED.

*V.—We can't end like this. Not after all we've had. Darling, I'm wrong. I know. But you misunderstand. This is nothing I ever wanted. We both knew we would have to part, but we can't part like this.* LETTER RETURNED UNOPENED.

*Damn it, Vanessa. Answer me. You're being childish. We have to speak. We have too much to discuss. Practical things. If you can't forgive me, fine. I don't deserve forgiveness. But you must let me see you. At least to say goodbye. And to be sure you are taken care of. Vanessa, answer me.* LETTER RETURNED UNOPENED.

## Chapter Two

So, it was over. Time to move on.
*Travel light.* That was rule number one. Of all the lessons Mrs. Vanessa Wardrip had absorbed from the other wives while "following the drum" on the Peninsula, this was the one she still took most to heart. She did not need things. Yet for all that, over the last four years she had accumulated quite a lot of them. They had to be jettisoned.

She chose only a few serviceable dresses to keep and allowed her lady's maid and her cook each to choose two. The rest she bundled up and sold to a rag-and-clothing shop. Things might not be important, but money was.

She kept her jewelry. Jewelry was portable. The necklaces, rings, brooches, and bracelets had never been payments; they were gifts. Now they would serve as her pension. She had always known that she would have to part with them, so she had not allowed herself to become attached, despite the giver's exquisite taste and thoughtfulness. She knew he had chosen each piece himself.

Everything else, she would leave behind. It was his property. She was not being petty by leaving it all for him to dispose of. The furniture, the pianoforte, the bedding, the kitchen implements, this too-large-for-her house that he leased—they had never been hers.

Even her cook and maid were his. References provided by his hand would serve them much better than any from hers.

She burned all his letters. Memories were too burdensome to carry.

*Be prepared.*

That was the second rule, and it was subordinated to the first. Preparation was not synonymous with stockpiling. Preparation meant having a plan. Ever since the beginning of their arrangement, she had been planning for its ending. The inevitable ending when Jasper became the Earl of Iversley.

Jasper's father had passed nearly two weeks ago. The funeral had been held in Iversley just before Christmas. Vanessa didn't know when Jasper would return to London, but as it was now New Year's Day, she suspected it would be soon. She intended to be gone long before. Last week, she'd put the final signatures on the papers needed to purchase the cottage in the lake district where she would disappear. Poor Henry's death, four long years ago, had given her a widow's freedom to sign her own papers.

She packed her trunk and hired a coach to transport her to Cartmel. The coach would be in her drive within two hours.

Sitting in the drawing room of the Bleeker Street townhouse, Vanessa closed her eyes for just a moment and let sadness wash over her. She would miss him. Angry as she was, she would always miss him.

She heard Madeline's light footsteps in the hallway and prayed she was not coming to announce a visitor. She had told her maid that she was not at home to anyone.

"Ma'am?" Madeline appeared thinner and plainer than ever. Uncertainty did not sit well with her. Vanessa hated that she could not take the poor girl along, but she had to cut all ties, and Jasper would see to it she would be re-employed.

"Yes, Madeline? What is it?"

"There is a caller. Lieutenant Taverston."

*Crispin.* If she'd thought Jasper could not infuriate her more, she was wrong. Sending his brother was the worst thing he could have done.

"I am not at home."

"Yes, I told him so, ma'am, but he wouldn't be put off. He says he will sit on the front stoop until you admit him."

She would let him do just that if not for the scandal it would cause.

"Oh, show him in." None of this was Crispin's fault, but she had wanted to avoid any painful scenes. Surely he had the sense to know that.

She stood up, hoping he would recognize he was unwelcome and would not stay long.

"Lieutenant Taverston," Madeline announced, then backed out of the room.

Crispin came forward, such an absurdly skinny man, yet there was steel in every sinew. He looked sharp, dressed in his officer's uniform, greatcoat slung over one arm, but he carried the mud and slush of the road with him. Had he come straight from Chaumbers without bothering to rest or change his clothes? How like him.

"Good afternoon, Lieutenant."

He put his heels together and gave a small bow.

"Mrs. Wardrip."

He took in the room at a glance. Nothing was out of place. The drapes had not been taken down; the rug had not been rolled up. Knickknacks remained on their shelves. But he would not be fooled. It had the empty atmosphere of a leased house about to be abandoned.

"I'm not here to make excuses for Jasper."

"No?"

"I will not plead his case."

"Good."

He gave her the weakest of smiles. "So will you be good enough to offer me tea? I'm parched."

Her resolve to quickly see him off crumbled. She owed him far too much to refuse him a cup. She pulled the bell for Madeline to return. "Tea, please, and biscuits for Lieutenant Taverston."

"Just tea," he said. "Please don't go to any additional trouble."

When Madeline left the room, Vanessa gestured to a chair.

"May I offer my condolences again?" She had written to him. To him, but not to Jasper.

"Thank you." He sat with an officer's straight-backed rigidity. That gave him away. He was uncomfortable too. Otherwise, he had a terrible tendency to sprawl. She sat in the nearest chair. With his long legs, their knees almost bumped.

"Why have you come? Did you think to rescue me again?"

"Do you need rescuing?" he asked in a flat voice, betraying no expectation and no condescension.

"No."

"I thought not. Despite the difficulties at Corunna, I have always thought there was no creature in the world more resourceful than a British soldier's wife."

It was good of him to say that. To prop up her sagging pride. Even so, she knew if she were to have said yes, he would determine what she needed and provide it, without question.

He breathed deeply, then got on with it.

"I have a bit of news to share with you. Something I'd like for you to know *first*."

He emphasized the word. So he knew of Jasper's betrayal. Moreover, Jasper had evidently compounded the error by discussing it with his brother. *Good God, Jasper!* She shook her head.

"Whatever it is, I don't care. And if you are carrying back a report, you may tell him that. Since apparently nothing between us was private."

"I'm not doing his bidding. In fact, he would be furious at me for interfering. Nevertheless, I've come to give you this: the lady refused him."

For a moment, his words made no sense. Then they did. Vanessa gaped. "Hovington's daughter? Refused Jasper?"

Crispin was nodding, amused, but Vanessa was not. Jasper

was the *perfect* catch. Titled, moneyed, courteous, and the most handsome man in the ton. By far. Strikingly blue eyed, with well-behaved, thick blond hair, and a dimpled cheek accompanying an array of beautiful smiles, he was almost a caricature of male perfection. It had taken her months to finally discover that one earlobe hung lower than the other. "What is *wrong* with her?"

The near-grin left Crispin's face. His eyes narrowed, only slightly, but a darkness entered behind them. Her mouth dried. She recalled Henry saying that men under Lieutenant Taverston's command claimed they would rather be captured by Boney's soldiers than fall on the wrong side of their lieutenant.

"That was unworthy of me and, I'm sure, of her," she whispered. How horrid to blame Lady Georgiana for exercising the one small concession granted to her: the right to refuse. If Vanessa had been allowed as much, how different her life would be.

The disapproval disappeared from Crispin's expression. She would have thought she'd imagined it if she didn't still feel a bit queasy.

He said, "Lady Georgiana is a gem. I gave you that information because I expect you will hear it soon enough elsewhere, and I wanted you to be prepared."

Be prepared. Of course, he knew the rules too.

"Thank you. I will not gossip."

"I know. I have trusted you with worse."

She swallowed hard. Then, because she also trusted him, she let her hurt show.

"Nevertheless, your news has no bearing. I will not be here when Jasper returns. This lady may have rejected his suit, but the next will not. I won't wait around to be discarded a second time."

Crispin winced. She read in his expression that he knew she was right. Marrying well was Jasper's duty. He would do it—once he got over the shock of being refused.

She tossed her head, still unbelieving. "How could she have said no? She may be a duke's daughter, and beautiful, but Lady

Georgiana has spurned half the ton! How much does she believe she is entitled to?"

"Love, I suspect."

She sniffed. Lady Georgiana must have someone unsuitable in mind. She was testing her parents' resolve. "I hope she does not plan on running off with a soldier."

Crispin laughed, making Vanessa flush. "Oh, Crispin, I don't suspect you." She recalled how very careful Jasper had been to make sure there was nothing between her and Crispin. "You would never approach a lady Jasper meant to court."

"No." He smirked. "But Reg is evidently not so scrupled."

"Reg? Reginald? Your *brother*, Reginald?"

Vanessa had met him twice, briefly each time, more than a year ago. He was very young, quiet, and very polite. He was going to be a clergyman, so Jasper had told her. He hadn't needed to tell her; she could have guessed. Who on earth would choose Reginald over Jasper?

Crispin nodded, a crooked smile on his face.

"I expect he'll be speaking with Hovington in a day or two. I hope the man is smart enough to see what a prize of a son-in-law Reg will be. But Reg's suit is disadvantaged by his being a third son. That might matter to the duke."

"I suspect if you think they should be together, they will end up so. You would realign the stars if a constellation did not suit you."

"Stars are easier to budge than dukes."

Madeline returned with tea. Vanessa dismissed her and then rose to pour.

"Sugar? Cream?"

"A little sugar, if you please." He waited for her to bring it to him. "Thank you."

She poured her own cup, too, then returned to her seat.

"Vanessa, Jasper worries me. I fear he will stop living his life. He courted Georgiana as though sleepwalking through it."

With or without enthusiasm, she didn't want to picture him

courting. It hurt too much. "Jasper is no longer any of my concern."

"The only thing that pierced his armor was whatever correspondence you two were carrying out. It befouled his mood. Truly befouled it."

"I hope you are not fishing for what we wrote to one another."

"Of course not. However, I did take note that more recently he has received no letters from you other than his own, returned unopened." Crispin shook his head. "A masterstroke, Vanessa."

"It was not a scheme. I simply saw no point in repeating hurtful recriminations and apologies that meant nothing."

"I'm not accusing you. Nevertheless, it was masterfully done. Frustration is oozing from his neatly buttoned edges."

"Crispin, please." A chasm opened in her heart. "I don't know what you want from me. I have nothing to give. You know that. The kindest thing I can do is disappear gracefully."

"I don't agree. But before you point out that I am no expert in affairs of the heart, I will draw my unwelcome visit to a close. I have to speak with Bathurst this evening and board a transport in the morning. I should have been in Spain a week ago." He drank the last of his tea and set down his cup. He stood. "The real reason I came was to extract a promise. If you find your advance preparations in any way lacking, get word to me."

"I won't need anything."

"If it's urgent, and I cannot be located, get word to Reginald."

She started. "Reginald? I couldn't! He barely knows who I am."

"He's a Taverston. And as far as I'm concerned, so are you. In every way that matters."

"Crispin! Enough!" If she started to cry, she would never forgive him. "Please go."

"Not until you give me that promise."

"Fine. If I need rescuing I will count on you. But I won't need rescuing."

He smiled at her. His smiles often held a touch of sadness, she thought. As well as she knew him, she didn't know him at all.

"Will you tell me where you are going?" he asked.

"No."

"I won't tell Jasper."

"Perhaps not," she allowed, "but it would be unfair to put you in that position." She had made the same excuse to Rose Posonby, her first London friend and her fiercest, and to Lady Effie Andini, her truest friend, who had known similar loss.

He gave her a long, studying look. "You truly do not wish to be found?"

A significant question. Vanessa knew Crispin. What he did. How well he did it. She could not flee far enough to hide from him if he chose to find her.

"This is not a game to me."

He blinked and looked away. Then he shrugged. "And so, farewell, Vanessa. I will see myself out."

# Chapter Three

The Taverstons' home at 8 Grosvenor Square was palatial as were most all of the homes rounding the square. Lord Jasper Taverston, the fifth Earl of Iversley, had been born there and had grown up running up and down its halls. He loved this house. He appreciated its comforts, luxuries, and pleasant memories. Even so, he could not inhabit the entire monstrous dwelling by himself. Having plentiful staff was not the same as being surrounded by family. The emptiness echoed.

Even the designed-to-appear-intimate morning room felt cavernous. Jasper pushed aside his untouched plate of kippers, snatched his coffee cup, and headed for the stairs. The clacking of his shoes on the marble floor sounded very nearly ear splitting.

Ascending the long, wide, central staircase felt like climbing a mountain. He nearly had to grab the banister and haul himself up. It was depressing to look out over the next several days, weeks, and months, and know there was nothing to look forward to. Crispin had gone back to his regiment. Reg was squirreled away with his new wife. And Vanessa had vanished into thin air.

In the last six weeks, he had made three trips back and forth between London and Chaumbers, his father's—no, the bloody devil, it was now *his*—country estate, trying to see to the myriad things that had to be done. And mostly failing. *Damn it.* He was still without a steward and couldn't hold the position for the man he wanted much longer.

At Chaumbers, at least he'd been allowed to grieve; mourning his father, of course, but also using that acceptable grief to mask his unseemly pining for his mistress.

That was in private. In London, in public, he must move on. He had dutifully taken his seat in Parliament, listened to speeches, and met with numerous lords on both sides of the aisle, partly for political purposes but also to receive their condolences. When men started to treat him more as a young peer than a bereaved son, he saw that it was time to curtail those comforting visits to the countryside and trust that Mother and Olivia, his sister, were coping on their own.

Well, they had each other.

Father's—*his, damn it*—second-floor study, with its small windows and funereally dark décor, had become his breakfast parlor of choice. He set his coffee cup on the desk, an overlarge boxy piece made of mahogany. It had been Grandfather's. Father had always hated it but would not get rid of it. And now, Jasper sighed, he would keep it as well.

He sat, picked up the morning newspaper, failed to read anything, and finally laid it back down.

The one bright spot had been Reg's wedding to Georgiana. His youngest brother looked contented. One might even say that he looked happy. And Georgiana was radiant. Jasper had once imagined she would make him a perfect countess, but she was a more perfect sister-in-law. A fortunate turnabout, really. She was too chilly for his taste.

Naturally, his friends had ribbed him for the ludicrous failure of his courtship, but it was kindly meant since ignoring the farce would have been awkward. And since no one in the world could think badly of Reg, those who knew them accepted it for what it was: an unexpected love match.

No. All well and good to tell himself that. The truth of it was that he was sick to death of arses slapping his back and telling him his botched suit caused them financial ruin. They had all laid their wagers at White's upon expectations of his success. *Har-har-har!*

Good God! How could he be both desperate for company and yet sickened by it?

At least the matchmaking mamas were biding their time. Or perhaps he was simply adept at avoiding them. He accepted no dinner invitations and attended no ton functions. He was not only in mourning but had soured on the prospect of marriage.

He rose and paced. His footsteps fell along worn spots in the carpet. Apparently, his father had been a pacer as well.

What he needed was to see Vanessa. Not to beg her to take him back. He wouldn't put her through another parting, not for all the world, not even to do it correctly this time. But he needed to see her for practical reasons. To settle things.

He had been to the house, the one they'd shared for four years. Four years! Though "shared" might not be the correct word. He'd leased it for her, but when in London, he spent most of his evenings with her and was often, usually, still there in the mornings.

Once he'd established that she left no letter for him, and no indication of where she had gone, he told his man of business to dispose of everything and cancel the lease. He wanted no reminders. He had to let go. But how ridiculous of her to disappear like this! Almost...spiteful. She knew how worried he would be.

Well and so, he was bringing to bear the full force of his newly enhanced authority. He'd sent a card to Vanessa's solicitor, asking him to come around to the house for a meeting. Summoned by an earl, Mr. Collingswood had no option but to come.

Jasper piddled away the morning perusing the newspapers, still retaining nothing from them. When his stomach began rumbling, he rang for sandwiches. Thus fortified, he studied the text of a speech that his friend, Viscount Haslet, would be reading on the floor sometime in the next few weeks. Nitpicking about a new tax on leather. Hazard was a Whig. Jasper was a Tory from a long line of staunch Tories. Sparring over politics could prove diverting.

Jasper had taken off his jacket and shoes and was sipping tea and marking a few points on Hazard's speech when Finley appeared at the door. Finley, the under-butler, was in charge since Peters was still at Chaumbers. Finley did a fine job but had a nervous edge that could be irksome.

"Yes?"

"Mr. Collingswood is here, my lord."

"Good. Bring him up."

Jasper slipped his shoes back on and pulled on his jacket. He checked the small mirror mounted on the side of the shelves behind the desk to be sure he looked intimidating enough. Then he stood beside the liquor cabinet and waited.

"My lord." Mr. Collingswood entered the room and bowed. Soberly attired and straight-backed, he was the very picture of professional respectability.

"Good afternoon. I won't keep you long. I have just a few questions."

"Which I will be happy to answer so long as they do not involve clients of mine."

Jasper scowled. "In fact, the questions regard Mrs. Wardrip. I do not ask you to betray client privilege, I merely wish to know how to reach her to be sure…" He stalled, then carried on, "that sufficient financial arrangements for her are in place."

"I'm afraid that is confidential." *The devil.* The man looked smug.

"Her whereabouts? Or her financial situation?"

"Both."

Jasper changed tack. "I have in mind establishing a trust, through your office, from which she can draw funds as needed."

"Through your office" was a tactful promise of a percentage. A bribe.

Mr. Collingswood's mouth hardened. "I believe if she wished you to know her address, she would have provided it. And had she wished for a trust of some sort, one would have been previously arranged."

Bloody hell. Of course, Vanessa would have availed herself of one of the few incorruptible solicitors in all of England.

Peers of the realm were supposed to command respect. Jasper had spent his life acquiring the trappings of his position: the tone of voice, manner of carrying himself, style of dress. He knew when to give an order and when to make a request. He knew how to be courteous and how to charm. He had imbibed the very essence of lordliness so that it was second nature to him now. And yet, what a sham. Crispin possessed more natural authority in his thumb than Jasper did in his whole body. The devil of it was, one could not beg a solicitor for information he was not allowed to give.

He thought of one last thing he could try.

"You could deliver a letter to her without compromising your integrity, one would think."

Collingswood hesitated, then said, "I suppose I could."

Gudgeon that he was, he had not prepared one. Letters had not been successful in the recent past. But this was the best he could do.

He went to his desk and pulled out a sheet of foolscap. He dipped his pen into the inkpot and thought for a moment. He could hardly offer her money outright. Nor could he beg forgiveness. Not in writing. And Collingswood was waiting.

He put pen to paper and wrote the only words he had.

He folded the paper, sealed it, and gave it to the solicitor. It felt as though he were handing over the heart from his chest.

As Collingswood took the letter, Jasper said quietly, "I hope that any investments you advised have been sound."

Contempt flashed in the solicitor's eyes. "My advice is always sound."

Jasper supposed he would have to content himself with that. He pulled the bell for Finley, who appeared quickly and appeared to fidget. "My lord?"

"Mr. Collingswood is leaving."

"Yes, my lord. And Viscount Haslet has come. He is awaiting you in the drawing room. Shall I bring him up?"

Hazard was here? They'd made no plans that he recalled.

"Yes, do. No, wait. I'll come down."

Finley escorted Collingswood out. Jasper lagged, preferring not to walk down with the butler and the solicitor. After a decent interval, he picked up the copy of Hazard's speech and went down.

The drawing room was located near the front entrance. It was a pleasant, airy room entered through two tall doors that were almost never closed. As Jasper approached, he could see Hazard standing inside. If he could see Hazard, it meant that Hazard would have seen Collingswood leaving.

Still, that was no cause for alarm. Hazard might recognize the man, but should have no reason to connect the call to Vanessa.

He drew himself up and walked into the room. Hazard's bright yellow waistcoat was unusually foppish. If things became awkward, he would tease him about it.

"Good afternoon, *Iversley*," Hazard said, teasing *him*. He was no longer simply Lord Jasper Taverston. He outranked Viscount Haslet.

"Haz. I'm sorry to have kept you waiting."

"Not at all. I haven't been waiting long." Hazard nodded toward the hall. "Wasn't that Collingswood, the younger? Has Wilkerson let you down? If you need a new man—"

"Yes, it was Collingswood. No, I am perfectly content with my own solicitor." He offered nothing more. He watched his old friend consider digging, then letting it go. Jasper pulled the folded speech from his pocket. He held it out. "Very nice. It won't get the votes, but I applaud the effort."

"Oh, I'm not expecting anything this go around. I'm laying the groundwork. I hoped you would argue something specific so I can shore up any glaring weaknesses before I speak."

"I marked a few places. Our argument is always the same. Cost. The wars have sapped the treasury."

"Which means our priorities are wrong." For a moment, Hazard sounded harsh. But then he shrugged, and his more usual good humor replaced his frown. "But I didn't come here to harangue you. I came because it is past time for you to get well-foxed and bemoan your lost days of wild irresponsibility."

Jasper would have joked that he had never had wild days, but that would not sit well with Hazard, who knew better. Still, his days of wild irresponsibility were already far in the past. He'd been more faithful to his mistress than most men were to their wives.

"I'm in mourning," he pointed out. "It would be disrespectful to my father."

"Bollocks. I'm not suggesting you drink a wheelbarrow at White's and start tossing insults at peers. I'm talking about a seedy place in Southwark where no one will know you if you start singing bawdy songs."

Jasper recoiled. "I won't go to a brothel—"

"With me?" Hazard laughed roughly, showing teeth. "Believe me, I would not take you anywhere I would be interested in going." He shook off his annoyance and added, "This is not a brothel, merely a pleasantly disgusting drinking establishment."

Jasper hadn't meant to scorn Hazard's company—even if rumors of his predilections were true. But he had no interest in running to light skirts. On the other hand, drowning his sorrows did hold some appeal.

"I have a better idea. We'll drink here. The liquor is better and the entertainment more refined."

Hazard looked at him narrowly, then said, "I suppose I'll be spared having to carry you home. Billiards or cards?"

"Billiards. Crispin had me practicing."

"Did you win?" He sounded skeptical of the possibility.

"Once." Jasper turned to the door, gesturing for Hazard to accompany him. "Will brandy do or will you want champagne?"

"I wanted gin. But brandy will do."

They climbed the stairs and then strolled the hall toward the billiards room. Jasper searched for something to say, something innocuous. "I'm thinking of having the walls painted."

"Eh?" Hazard pulled a snuffbox from his pocket. He offered it, out of habitual politeness, Jasper supposed, though he must know by now that Jasper would wave it away. He'd never seen the appeal of that particular vice. Hazard took a pinch and put it back, waiting for Jasper to continue.

"Yes, they look rather dingy. If I'm going to undertake such a project, it would be best to do it while the place is empty."

Hazard snorted, rejecting the conversational topic for the feint it was.

Jasper stopped to speak to a footman. "George, have a bottle of brandy and a couple of glasses brought to the billiards room."

"Yes, my lord."

They walked the rest of the way in silence. The billiards room was dark and dreary. The air smelled stale. Jasper crossed the room to push open the curtains. When he turned around, he saw Hazard leaning a hip against the table, arms crossed over his chest, looking at him with an amused irritation.

"Are you going to tell me, or do I have to wait until you are drunk and weepy?"

"Tell you what?"

"Why you were meeting with Mrs. Wardrip's solicitor." He smirked. "Are you about to be sued for breach of promise?"

Breath left Jasper's chest as if he'd been struck. "I'd concede in a heartbeat."

Sympathy washed across Hazard's face. He must have expected Jasper would lash out, not crumple up in a heap.

"Collingswood refused to tell me what I wanted to know. He agreed to deliver a letter, but it won't change anything."

"Would you want it to?"

"The devil. No. I should leave her alone." He drew in a deep breath. He was not going to lose any more of his self-control. "I'm worried about her. There is, of course, no widow's jointure. And our contract was one between two young fools who were not looking ahead."

"She wouldn't accept a settlement from you?"

He shook his head. "No."

"Well." Hazard unfolded his arms and stepped to select a cue from the row against the wall. "She has family, does she not? She can't still be that estranged from them if she's using her father's man."

And that, Jasper saw, was how Hazard had made the connection. The elder Mr. Collingswood represented the Culpeppers.

"Young Collingswood is not her father's man. He is hers. Culpepper is unaware and is to remain so."

"Is to remain so" was enough. Hazard would not gossip. Nevertheless, Hazard was still regarding him with an intensely questioning look on his face. And Jasper realized it would not take drunkenness to unburden himself.

"When I asked Vanessa to…to have a relationship with me, I told her I'd have a contract drawn up to protect her interests." He snorted. Remembering. "I suppose I thought she'd say there was no need. That she trusted me. All the things one expects a woman to say. But she answered that my solicitor would hardly be putting her interests first, and she would have her own man speak with mine." He saw Hazard bite back a smile. "I thought she'd resort to some pettifogger. I was shocked to my toes when she pulled out Collingswood. It seems she and *Will,* as she called him, have known each other since they were children. He would not say anything to her father or to his."

Naturally, word of his daughter's sordid affairs returned to Culpepper despite her solicitor's discretion, but Vanessa already considered herself cut off from her family. And, apparently, so did they.

He sniffed. Collingswood was married, but that didn't mean he wasn't half in love with her also.

"Will Collingswood despises me." If there had been any opportunity for a reconciliation with her family, her acceptance of Jasper's proposition quashed it. Jasper considered that a good thing, but others might not.

Hazard began to fussily line up the billiard balls. "Yet you think he will deliver your letter?"

"He said he would, so I'm certain he will. I'm less certain she will read it. And I'm positive it will make no difference if she does." He should have written something else. Although nothing would have been adequate.

Finley appeared at the door with a tray. "Will this do, my lord?"

Jasper beckoned and Finley brought forth the tray. Anything from Father's cellar would do. The man had always said life was too short to drink bad liquor. He heard the tap of cue against ball and the clicking of balls connecting.

"Cognac, Haz?" His voice sounded rough. His father's life had been far too short.

"Start pouring, Iversley. Start pouring."

# Chapter Four

The cottage Vanessa had purchased was in Cartmel, near the lake district. She chose the location for its beauty and because it was a solid three days away from London, but mainly because she would be near to Mrs. Lydia Compton, a campaign-forged friend, the most pragmatic woman she had ever known.

Lydia was a war widow twice over. Her third husband, Corporal Compton, had not died, thankfully, but lost an eye and an arm in one day's battle, injury enough to see him sent home. And Lydia—who had taken each new young soldier's wife under her wing and taught her how to survive come what may, how to prevent pregnancy, sometimes successfully and sometimes not, how to supplement her husband's meager rations, cook over an open flame, clean and mend his clothes and her own, bandage his wounds, and eventually search for his body among the dead—Lydia, too, had been ready to retire from the fight. Fortunately, Corporal Compton had a brother, a bootmaker in Cartmel, who welcomed them into his household. Lydia wrote that Brother Jon had put them both to work, and she had never been happier. If Vanessa ever found herself in need...

Vanessa couldn't see herself a bootmaker. She had not wanted to live in Cartmel, only near it. But her attorney friend found her the perfect cottage on the outskirts of the village. It was small: one story, four rooms, a bit of a garden. A twenty-minute walk would bring her to church, forty and she would be at Lydia's door. The previous owner had died six months earlier. Vanessa suspected Will had reserved the property then, anticipating her need, but to accuse him of that would serve no purpose. It was perfect, and he knew it, and that was that.

On this unseasonably warm February day, she knelt on a split log in her garden, examining the tangled mess of brown stems and rotten vegetables that had grown as volunteers and then died on the vine. The garden had not been properly tended in a long while, though it was difficult to say how long since Vanessa had never tended a garden before. Her neighbor, Mrs. Charlotte Gowe, had given her a few pointers, peering over the fence. They were becoming friends. Charlotte was acquainted with Lydia, who corroborated Vanessa's story, that of a war widow with just enough means to purchase a cottage and live quietly. *Even now, she leaned on Henry.* No one need know she was the daughter of Frederick Culpepper. No one need know she had been the mistress of a lord who was now an earl.

Vanessa turned at the scuff of boots coming up the road, an uncommon sound so far from the village center. Will Collingswood was walking toward her cottage as if her thoughts had summoned him. She stood up, fighting the urge to wring her hands. What in God's name could bring him all the way out here?

She met him at the gate.

"Mrs. Wardrip, good afternoon," he said, removing his hat and tucking it under his arm. His sandy hair was already thinning. He would soon be as bald as his father.

"Good afternoon." She studied him nervously. "Why are you here? Is something wrong?"

He frowned. "Must something be wrong? I told you I would check on you after you had a few weeks to settle in."

"I thought you would write. It's a long way to come." His concern felt condescending. "I'm sorry, but you know I can't ask you in."

"Of course not," he said, his scowl deepening.

She had nothing to fear from Will. He had always treated her respectfully, even though she was no longer respectable. But she could not bring a man into her house. Already villagers regarded her differently because she was young and without a male guardian or female companion. She should have realized people in a small town would be even more suspicious and narrow minded than those in London. She had to be very careful. Still, she could not be rude to Will.

"Are you thirsty? Hungry? I can bring something out."

"No. There's no need."

She wiped her hands on her apron. "And you've come all this way. Thank you. I-I'm doing well. Truly, I am. This house is perfect. And Lydia has been so very welcoming. I've met a few people." She trailed off. He looked disturbed. "What is it?"

"I brought you something. I don't know that I should have. I hesitated to put it in the post with no explanation."

He pulled a folded paper from his pocket. She recognized the seal and winced.

"Will—"

"I told him nothing. That's why he asked me to bring this." He held it out. "He had no other way to reach you."

"Because I don't want to be reached."

He let his hand fall. "Should I give it back to him? Tell him you refused it?"

"Oh, for Heaven's sake." It seemed inordinately cruel to subject Jasper to that humiliation. "No, give it here."

She took the letter and tucked it into the waistband of her apron.

"Is there something else?" Will's pained expression suggested there was.

"Iversley wanted to set up a fund for you to draw from. I refused on your behalf. And I've been worried that I shouldn't have."

"You did right."

"Vanessa." His voice was a groan. "It would make things

easier for you. You could hire a companion. You really should have one."

She laughed, more irritated than amused. "I'm not sure I can purchase respectability with my ex-lover's money."

"Don't talk like that. You deserve better."

"Will, there is no question of deserving. None at all."

"But to punish yourself—"

"Punish? This?" She gestured to her home. "I have more than I need. This is heaven on earth."

He had never seen a soldiers' camp. He had never slept on wet ground after walking an entire day wearing shredded boots that did not fit, stripped from a corpse. He had never marched two days straight with half a bread crust for sustenance. He had not... He had not. Vanessa had. Lydia had. The others, too. They'd borne all that and worse.

"All right," Will said, holding up a hand. "If you're content, that's all that matters. I delivered the letter. Answer him or don't. But I won't serve as a go-between."

"I would not ask it of you."

He nodded, holding himself very stiffly. "But he did. If he asks again, I will tell him no."

"Thank you."

He gave her a doubtful look, then said, "Keep me informed of any changes."

"Changes? What changes?"

Could he think she would go back to Jasper? Did he think the letter was a request to come back? Oh, Lord. Was it? Could Jasper imagine she would return?

"*Any* changes. I'm still your solicitor, Vanessa. I have an obligation to my clients."

"Yes, of course." If he wanted her to believe that was all he meant, she would. "But you are aware that it is not good for me to be seen talking at length with a stranger."

He glanced down the long, empty road to the Gowes' cottage, then nodded.

"Goodbye then." He sounded annoyed, having come all this way for such a poor welcome, but what did he expect her to do?

She watched him walk down the street until he looked very small. Then she went inside. She paused a moment to drink in the space. The white walls were scrubbed clean, devoid of ornamentation; no memories there. The parlor had a rag rug, but elsewhere the floors were bare wood, worn smooth. With the shutters open, a breeze swept through, and the home had a comforting scent of clean English air. She would be happy here. She *would*.

For this escape, she had saved, and Will had invested for her nearly every penny of her pin money, as well as the proceeds of the sale of a particularly lovely bracelet that Jasper had given her as an apology for an offense she no longer remembered. No one could say she had not been preparing all along.

She went all the way to the back, into her small kitchen. She pulled the letter from her waistband and laid it on the table in the middle of the room. Then she untied her apron and draped it over the back of a chair. She stared at the letter. If the stove had been lit, she would have fed it into the fire. But the stove was cold.

*Jasper, why?*

It had been two months since she had returned his last letter unopened. She supposed they had both had sufficient time to reflect. She had, in her heart, forgiven him for failing to tell her he intended to court Lady Georgiana. She understood his decision to do so had only been half-made when he rushed off to attend to his dying father. She recognized as well that it was time for him to find a suitable lady to wed. The truth was, prepared though she may have been, she hadn't been ready.

*What could he have written?*

He was thinking of her still. That shouldn't please her, but it did, since she thought of him constantly. How could she not? They had been lovers for four years. Three years longer than she had been married to Henry, and she still thought of *him* often.

Of course, she had known Henry her whole life. And it was a different kind of knowing once they were wed—she could never forget that. She had been surprised by the act of love. Surprised that she could share such sweetly intimate joys with someone as awkward and familiar to her as Henry. Maybe if he had lived, that would have been enough.

Lord Taverston had been neither awkward nor familiar. They were strangers, thrust together by circumstance, both caught off guard by what happened between them. She could not have anticipated her body's capacity for pleasure so intense. Or that over the course of four years, she would grow to love him with a strength even greater than their passion.

Vanessa swallowed a sob.

And now he wanted to pay her off. Clear his conscience. That was surely what the letter was about. Will had implied as much, hadn't he?

Or was he writing to inform her of his betrothal?

She picked up the letter. She should not read it. He must know that she would not respond. Nevertheless, she broke the seal.

*I love you. Always. C J.T.*

She traced her fingers over the letters.

*Oh, Jasper. Why?*

He'd had four years to say the words and had been very careful not to.

She shoved the letter into the cold stove. She would burn it later.

# PART 2
## This is an Arrangement
### Late February 1809
### London

# Chapter Five

It was Vanessa Culpepper Wardrip's twentieth birthday. She had been living in Lord Jasper Taverston's rented townhouse for one month. Since he was an earl's son, she was reaccustoming herself to life's creature comforts. She sat in front of a roaring fire, wrapped in a heavy wool blanket, lamps lit along all four walls. Nevertheless, she felt cold, frightened, and very much alone.

One week ago, she and Lord Taverston had put their signatures to the contract. And now, listening to sleet pattering on the windows, she wallowed in regret.

She had justified her decision with the fact that Lord Taverston made her feel safe. To live under his protection meant financial security and physical comfort. The arrangement gave her the independence she had always believed she craved.

Yet it had occurred to her tonight, sitting here alone, surrounded by paintings of people and places she did not know, that they were strangers. She had signed away her good name, what was left of it, irretrievably, to a stranger.

Moreover, she had an inexplicable knot of worry in the pit of her stomach that what they had done would disappoint Lieutenant Taverston. She didn't care to disappoint him. He frightened her, kind though he'd been.

On the Peninsula, ranking officers did not concern themselves with the welfare of the common soldiers' wives and children, but

Lieutenant Taverston was different. He knew them by name. And he'd known Henry. In Corunna, he'd brought word of Henry's death to her himself. He'd recognized something in her grief that told him she would not avail herself of a widow's best chance for survival: marrying one of her husband's comrades. That made her useless to the army. Dead weight. Yet rather than abandon her to the advancing French, he wasted precious time finding room for her on one of the British evacuation transports, no doubt through bribery. He paid a fleeing clergyman to watch over her during the voyage. And he gave her a sealed letter to present to his brother in London. An introduction, he said, and she trusted him.

By the time she'd met Lord Jasper Taverston, she had known what it meant to be hungry, to be cold to the marrow, to have scabbed feet and dirt in the creases of her skin, to be so sick and exhausted and frightened that devastating loss was experienced as just one more nightmare in an endless series of horrors. After reading his brother's letter, Lord Taverston had surrendered to her use of the townhouse he had recently leased. He'd hired a maid to tend to her, even tasking the girl to buy her some decent clothes. Then he'd left her alone. A week had passed. When she'd found herself wakening from her nightmares to find herself safe and clean, warm, and full bellied, she had been able to hold in her heart two feelings at once: pride that she had endured such challenges and survived, and determination never to find herself so desperate again. She'd needed a plan.

That was when Lord Taverston had returned. To assure himself she was reviving. To see what else she needed. To be able to send a report to Lieutenant Taverston.

What followed over the course of the next fortnight was not a seduction. Or perhaps it was. What did she know of such things? All she knew was how he made her feel. Cared for. Cossetted. Safe. Admired. Desired.

And how he made her *feel*.

She had loved Henry in a quiet way though it was wrong to

have married him. She mourned a friend, a champion, not a husband. True, she had enjoyed their special nights together, few and brief though they had been. They'd been a gift. But lying with Henry was nothing like lying with Lord Taverston. With Jasper. He'd told her to call him by his given name; she was trying to remember to do so.

To be truthful with herself, it was for the lying together that she agreed to be his mistress, not the security, comfort, or independence. And now she worried he'd tired of her already. Where was he?

Somewhere safe, of course.

When in London, he lived at his parents' home in Mayfair. He'd leased this house as a hideaway, as peers' sons often did, to get out from under their mothers' noses. But he'd yielded the house to her at once, exclusively, for propriety's sake, since he understood her to be, in some way yet to be defined, under his brother's wing—a way that, she assured him, was not what he was thinking.

Before the previous week, they'd been discreet. He'd spent only one full night with her in his own townhouse and that by accident. Afterward, perhaps expecting such accidents to occur more frequently, they'd agreed to formalize what they had informally begun.

Their contract was detailed but not lengthy. She would have adequate "pin money"—she supposed she was not to be cheapened by calling it the salary that it was. She would have a lady's maid. The house would be staffed with a butler and housekeeper-cook, as well as a groundskeeper who could also serve as a groom. Lord Taverston offered a riding horse, but she did not care for riding, so he provided the use of a carriage and coach horses. The contract also transferred the lease on the house to her name. Will had said that was to ensure that Lord Taverston would not bring other women into it—*good Lord*! In situations mutually desirable, she could be asked and could agree to serve as Lord Taverston's hostess. However, she was not permitted to entertain men in his absence and was not *required* to entertain his friends in any capacity. She didn't dare ask Will what that meant. She was granted the right to refuse Lord Taverston access to her bed ten days each month wholly at her discretion. It galled her to think these were considerations to be negotiated. But it had reassured her, somewhat, when Lord Taverston—Jasper—had agreed to all of Will's stipulations with no more argument than a superior look down his nose.

But Will could not stipulate that Jasper *must* spend his nights with her. The fact that he had done so every night since the ink was dry did not guarantee he would always come home. She suspected, by the lateness of the hour, that he had supped with his parents, and then gone to his club. He hadn't said. She was his mistress, not his wife; she could not expect him to say.

Perhaps peers' wives had no such expectations either.

Vanessa shifted in her chair, drawing her blanket closer. Gooseflesh rose as rivulets of fear rolled down her neck and shoulders, causing her arms to tremble. She did not like being alone.

She could wake her maid, Madeline, but the poor girl was bone tired, and Vanessa was not careless of servants as she had once been. Besides, it was not Madeline's company she wanted.

She wanted Jasper. And she missed Henry. This fear she felt was too much like fearing for her husband, a fear that had proved all too valid.

The quality of the noise beyond her windows had changed. In addition to sleet, she heard the clicking of feet on cobbles and men's voices. She strained until she picked out Jasper's. There was much laughter, but she didn't hear his, only his rumbling. As the voices drew closer, she pulled out a few words. They had been gambling. Drinking. There was a horserace...tomorrow? She heard the name "Bathurst" twice, sworn like a curse. Then Jasper was saying goodbye. Sending them off. The front door groaned open, and she heard Bremont's deferential murmur.

Jasper said, "The sitting room?" He sounded surprised. A bit slurred. She couldn't make out Bremont's question, but Jasper's answer was loud. "No. But coffee would be welcome. And toasted bread if Cook is…no, don't bother her. Van—Mrs. Wardrip will fuss at me." He chuckled. "Just cold bread."

Footsteps came up the stairs, then he swept into the sitting room.

"Vanessa." He reeked of tobacco and brandy. At least it was not rum. "You don't have to sit up for me."

"I was not waiting for you," she said carefully, wanting to strike the right tone. Not accusatory, certainly. But not apologetic either.

He stepped closer. He was not unsteady on his feet and his eyes did not demonstrate that sheen of drunkenness she had learned to recognize all too well. Ah, but perhaps gentlemen held their liquor better than soldiers.

Rather than squashing into the chair beside her, he drew another one up close. His movements were all graceful, not sloppy, and not overly controlled. He might have bathed in brandy, but apparently, had not imbibed too much of it.

He gestured toward the window. "It's very late. Is there something bothering you? Keeping you up?"

She bit her lip, then said, "Just thoughts. Hard to banish thoughts."

He nodded. "I'm sorry." He let out a long sigh. Then he pressed her. "Past thoughts? Or are you having regrets?"

"Regrets?"

"About…" He swept a hand in the air, indicating everything but nothing in particular. "This." Then he leaned forward, lifted her hand from the blanket she was clutching, and squeezed it. "Did I pressure you into something you were not ready for?"

She thought yes but answered, "I am not a green girl." His gaze was so steady, it made her ask, "Are *you* having regrets?"

He planted a quick kiss on her hand, then dropped it. He rose, paced a few steps, then turned to face her.

"Not regrets. One might call them 'concerns.'" He waited for a response, but she gave none, so he went on unprompted. "I've never done this before, and I fear I am doing it wrong."

"This? Wrong how?"

"Well, for example, this evening. I *thought* that I was looking forward to it." His tone changed to musing, irritated musing. "First, I had planned to sup with an old friend from Oxford. A scholarship boy, but well brought up, and we'd always gotten along despite his lack of breeding."

That stung, but she did not point out she also lacked what he called "breeding."

"I brought him around quite often in our college days, but I haven't seen him in a long while. I heard he had a business opportunity in Canada and might be going." He smiled. Embarrassed. "That isn't the point. The point is, I had been looking forward to seeing him again."

"Why haven't you? Because he is no longer in your social sphere?"

"Partly. But also Olivia. My sister. She had an adorable infatuation with him. My brothers and I used to tease her. But she is fourteen now. Past adorable. Her blushes became insupportable for everyone. Mostly for Benjamin, I'm afraid. And, of course, Olivia."

She felt for the girl. And respected the man for absenting himself at the cost of distance from an influential friend.

"Did you not enjoy your supper?"

"I did, to a point. Less so the gathering afterward. An evening with my usual set. The exact same evening I've enjoyed hundreds, if not thousands, of times." He sagged. "Vanessa, I spent the whole night looking at the clock, wishing I were here." He let out a breath of laughter. "I don't think that is normal."

The butler knocked, then came in with coffee and thin slices of bread. Jasper did not speak until Bremont left. Then he picked up where he had left off. Or close to it.

"I am concerned that I have been overly…" He cleared his throat and transferred his gaze to a spot on the wall. "Overly demanding. I thought that you might appreciate an evening to yourself."

She was afraid to laugh because he was so serious.

"I have not found my duties onerous," she assured him.

He must have sensed she was biting her cheek because he turned to her and grinned.

"Well, that, at least, is a relief. But promise me you will tell me if they become so."

"I will. But it is not something I can imagine coming to pass."

She wondered if they would now go to bed, but his grin fell away, and he reclaimed the chair beside her. He was silent a long moment, then he blurted, "Is it the newness, do you think? I swear Carleton and Perry knew I was chomping at the bit to be rid of them. They mocked my distraction."

"Are you embarrassed by me?"

"Not by you."

"Are you embarrassed to have a mistress?"

He fretted a little, then said, "I don't know. Perhaps. I know I have no reason to be." He shot a sideways glance at her. "Are you—please, I don't mean to be insulting—are you embarrassed to be one?"

"Yes."

"God." He groaned.

"But embarrassment is a frivolous emotion. I thought myself shed of it. Now I recognize there is an element of privilege in feeling it again."

He frowned. "That is too much for my brandy-soaked head."

"Are you brandy soaked?"

"Enough to be confessional. I confess the decision was more impetuous than is my wont. And that I am too often swayed by the opinions of my peers."

"You fear they will disapprove? Of your taking a mistress?"

"Not rationally fearful. Not of them." He shook his head. His face reddened. "The sobering thought is facing Crispin."

Vanessa puffed out a breath. "More than sobering, I think.

Frightening."

Jasper started. He turned widened eyes upon her. "You said there was nothing between you."

"And there isn't. I scarcely know him. I have no idea why he took it into his head to rescue me."

"That is easily explained. He was just being Crispin." He sighed. "Always the better man. The letter he wrote, do you wonder at it?"

"He said it was an introduction. I suppose a bedraggled miss showing up at your doorstep would need one."

"He wrote that you were the widow of a fine British soldier. He asked me to give you whatever support you needed. Give you space to mourn your husband. Then help you back onto your feet, when you were ready. Little enough to ask of a man in my position. But Vanessa, I did exactly the opposite."

"What could he have expected? From me, I mean. Not from you."

"He said—" Jasper made a sound like a cough—"you might decide to return to your family. Or to your husband's. But if those were not options, he hoped I could find a position for you."

She laughed a little hollowly. "That you did."

"God."

After a moment, she pushed aside her blanket—it was too warm in the room now—and stood. "I don't suppose we need live our lives in fear of Lieutenant Taverston's disapproval. Or even if we do, the mistake is made. Tearing up the contract will not undo it."

"I never suggested that!" He jumped to his feet and caught her by the arm. "Vanessa, the very last thing I want is to lose you. I want to do right by you. Insofar as I can after all this. Crispin mentioned family, yet I didn't even consider them. I never asked who they—"

"There is nothing to consider. We were estranged from both sides." She shook off his hand. "I'm sorry, but I am not ready to discuss my past with you."

He stepped back. She saw hurt in his eyes and softened her voice. "But I will discuss my current concerns. Our contract laid out the framework for a commercial transaction. A necessary framework, but we both recognize there is more to it than that. Things that cannot be codified should nevertheless be understood."

He nodded. "Yes. Yes, thank you. That is what I have been trying to get at. I want to know your concerns."

He drew her back to the chair.

"Would you like coffee? I need some."

"No, thank you."

He poured himself a cup, then sat beside her, an expectant look on his face. Outside, the sleet had stopped falling. If she were not mistaken, the sky had lightened a shade.

"Well, for one, I don't like to be left alone."

His cup rattled but he steadied his hand and said, "Oh?"

"That is not meant to alarm you. I don't expect you to tie yourself to my apron strings. I am not, by nature, a nervous woman, but in Portugal and more particularly in Spain—" She held up a hand to keep him silent. "I know there is no danger here. But even over there, my concern was not so much for myself. I wasn't strictly alone. I was always with other women." She shuddered, voice dropping. "Even on the retreat, when I was…sick, and fell behind, Lydia would not leave me."

"Where was Henry?" he demanded. "If you were sick—"

"Soldiers' obligations are to their units. If Henry had abandoned his post to look after me, he would have been shot. We looked after ourselves."

Jasper turned pale. "That isn't right."

"That is war. Jasper, every time I said goodbye to Henry, I knew it could be the last time. Every time, until it was. I have spent far too much of my life waiting to hear reassuring footsteps. That's what I mean by being left alone. It isn't my place to ask, and logically I realize you are in no danger, but if you know you won't be returning at night, will you tell me beforehand?"

"Yes. Yes, of course, I will. And if I am ever detained and you are expecting me, I will send word."

She felt a wash of relief and laughed shakily. "I will outgrow this, I expect. I know it is a great deal to ask—"

"It is not. In truth, it's basic courtesy. What else?"

"You must ask one of me first."

"Is that how we will do it?" He *hmmmed* and regarded his hands. "All right. But this one is delicate."

"Go on."

"I noticed you have been using..." He clenched and unclenched his fingers. "A vinegared sponge."

She nodded, willing herself not to blush. She needn't justify herself.

He said, "It is only that—as I understand it—the efficacy of that measure is unreliable."

She knew that. "But it is better than nothing." So Lydia had told her.

"French letters are a better option."

"But difficult to obtain. And impossible to afford."

"Ha! Well, no. On both counts, no." He reached out to touch her arm lightly. "If you'll permit me, if you trust me, I'll take care of that. You needn't."

"I trust you."

She had more to fear from an unwanted pregnancy than he did, but perhaps *he* did not trust *her* to always take the necessary precautions. Which steered them toward the inevitable. The question that must loom largest before them both.

"Your turn," he said.

So she must raise it.

"You are heir to an earldom. I know that means you will one day need a countess to bear you an heir."

"I—"

"No, don't interrupt. I know how your world works, Jasper. There are some things I cannot abide. I will not engage in adultery. Our contract ends when you take a wife."

He nodded, jaw tense, pale, looking at the floor. He said quietly, "I agree."

"All I ask is that you give me fair warning. When the time comes, when you are ready to start courting in earnest, will you promise that you will tell me first? Will you allow me the dignity of my retreat?"

"Yes, of course." He sounded choked.

"All right. Your turn, Jasper."

"I'd like—" He grimaced. Then, though his chin was down, he lifted his eyes to her. "This may be too much for *me* to ask. But, for example, those thoughts that kept you up? Those difficult-to-banish thoughts? If sharing them would help to banish them…" He shook his head. "The devil. We jumped into this so very quickly. I'm trying to say I'd like to know you better. I'd like for you to know me."

She hesitated. There was a measure of protection in remaining strangers. Still, she answered truthfully. "I'd like that too."

# Chapter Six

Jasper knew a few things about his new mistress and was learning others.

First, she was very, very pretty. She was not beautiful. At least, she was not startlingly beautiful; not, for example, like Earl Darlington's look-alike twins. Their alabaster skin and bow lips disadvantaged them, as gentlemen could not decide which of the beauties to court, so ended up courting neither. Or both. He himself had decided upon neither.

Or, at the opposite end of the social spectrum, there was the groin-tightening beauty of the queen of the demi-monde, Henrietta Pindar. He'd gone so far—this was well over a year ago—as to make inquiries. He learned that he could, by spending a year's allowance in one fell swoop, bed her once. To his embarrassment, he'd actually considered it. She was said to know *secrets*. But thankfully Crispin, whose regiment had not yet been posted and was still in London, smacked him on the side of the head.

"Her secret is a mirrored ceiling. She will straddle you so that you can watch yourself be taken by 'the most beautiful woman in the world.'" He snorted.

Jasper had envisioned something more mystical. His interest flagged. But rallied. "How would you know that?" His brother's funds were nonexistent after he'd purchased his own commission.

Crispin sneered. "Sources. Save your blunt. Hire a doxy, close your eyes, and use your imagination."

Jasper never learned Crispin's sources, but he recognized sense when he heard it.

And, everything considered, had he not "saved his blunt," he would not have taken the lease on his townhouse. Things would not have sorted as they had. The thought made him inexpressibly grateful. Vanessa's skin might sport blotches of freckles, darker on her left cheek than the right, her chin might be a little too severe and her eyelids a little too heavy—but only if one analyzed her individual features. To gaze upon her face as a whole was to see its rather sublime prettiness. He gazed upon it a lot.

He did so now, while she remained sleeping. Sunlight streamed through the window, illuminating her side of the bed. There was nothing he would rather look at than her form beneath a tangled white sheet. One perfectly shaped arm flopped at her side; the other, under her head, propped her splayed chestnut-brown tresses. Her hair carried a scent of tree bark. Not flowers. Bark. He couldn't explain it, but it was the headiest fragrance he'd ever inhaled.

The second thing he knew was that Vanessa was an energetic lover. Not in the performative way of women paid to please, thank goodness; he'd always found that off-putting, after the fact.

Before Vanessa, he had indulged in a few very brief affairs with women interested in such. Sex was hurried and furtive and while there was a certain allure to that sort of energy, it could grow tiresome. Hence the brevity of the affairs.

Sex with Vanessa was an altogether different experience. They shared a togetherness, a coequal desire to please and be pleased. He felt it also in his heart, if that made sense. "Energy" might not be right; perhaps he meant *passion*.

But how ridiculous to try putting it into words.

The third thing he knew was that she was brave. Following the drum was not for the faint of heart. Before Vanessa—it seemed his life was now divided into "before Vanessa" and "now,"—he hadn't ever questioned the day-to-day reality for soldiers' wives. After formalizing their arrangement, as she still seemed reluctant to speak of those days, he'd made discreet inquiries elsewhere.

Most soldiers did not bring their wives. They could not. Numbers were restricted and there was a lottery of a sort. Those chosen were told at the last possible moment so as not to create dissent in the ranks before ships were even boarded. Women were afforded no official military protection. No allowances were made for children, even though they inevitably arrived. Wives were given some food, but only a mere fraction of the soldiers' meager rations. In truth, a good part of the reason that any women were permitted to accompany their husbands was for the role they played in foraging for extra sustenance. Not to mention all the other tasks they performed without maids or cooks or laundresses. They slept on the ground. They traveled on foot all the miles the men traveled and then some. It all strained credulity. Especially the fact that when a soldier died, his wife's rations were cut off. There she would be. On the damned Peninsula. With no way to return home and no means of support.

Yet wives were assets. They provided comforts. A soldier would not be cold in his grave before his friends lined up at his widow's "door" and awaited her choice. Jasper thanked God that Crispin had extricated Vanessa from that.

Why did women go? He'd asked that one night—naïve earl's son that he was—of the tavern bawd who'd brought him his ale. He paid with a crown to loosen her tongue, then had to refuse other favors, to the amusement of Carleton and Waverly. Because, she explained, the government provided nothing at all for the wives left behind. Not a farthing.

These were not women who had other resources. Their husbands joined the army because they had no choice. They *needed* to take the King's Shilling. They might have intended to send their wages home, but most found a pittance could not stretch that far.

What Jasper could not understand, what Vanessa had indicated she was not ready to discuss, was why *she* had gone. Wives of common soldiers were undoubtedly common women. Vanessa was no aristocrat. She was not even gentry. But she had the manners and mannerisms of a lady. Her voice and vocabulary were cultivated. She played the pianoforte. That fact slipped out one evening and now he was determined to provide one for her, as soon as she acquiesced. Her husband could not have been a laborer or some bumpkin. Jasper could not, would not, believe it. There had been money there somewhere.

So why had they gone to war?

He didn't know. All he knew was that she had been brave enough to do so. Now he needed to learn if any of that bravery was left.

A bit of a breeze rippled the sheet and Vanessa stirred. She opened her eyes and gave him a lazy smile. He trailed his finger down her exquisite arm.

"I fear I miscalculated."

She propped herself on her elbow. "What do you mean?"

"I skipped Tattersalls out of impatience. But now it is a mere three o'clock in the afternoon."

They'd spent themselves, then napped. He supposed he'd envisioned making love to her for hours on end. He'd felt so amorous he thought cavorting would carry them through until a late supper. But it was only teatime. So he was rather nervously considering asking if she played cards.

That was not true. He wanted to ask her something else. If she would assent to something. If she were brave enough.

She murmured, "Is it too late to meet up with your friends at Tattersalls?"

He shrugged. He'd rather spend time with her. "If I did, what would you be doing?"

She paused, glancing away, then back to him. "I have some sewing to do."

"Sewing?"

"Seams to let out. I am too well fed."

He felt a growl in his throat. When this had started, the base of her neck showed deep hollows and his fingers could, with very little pressure, trace her ribs. He'd found it worrisome. Now she was gaining a pleasing softness. A *very* pleasing softness.

Her words registered.

"Wait. You are *sewing*? Fixing clothing?" That irritated him beyond measure. He sat up, the sheet slipping down to his hips. "You have a maid. And if she has not the skill, hire a seamstress. I'm not a pauper."

She sniffed, as if to jolly him out of his temper. "It's not your dress."

"It's a reflection on me."

At that, she laughed outright. "How? How will your set know that I am mending my own clothes?"

He had no answer for that. Instead, he considered a moment, then said, "I am wrong. If you wish to do it yourself, by all means, do it. But you don't *have* to, do you see? I know ladies have expenses. I want to be generous. It hurts me to think you would scrimp rather than ask for something."

"Still, you must see that it bothers me to ask."

If she didn't ask, he wouldn't know.

"But I can't read your mind. I can't anticipate your needs."

"It's not a game I am playing."

"I didn't say that it was!"

Vanessa rolled from him, tucking the sheet about her, shielding herself from his gaze as she sat up and settled her feet on the floor.

Was this to be their first argument? How ridiculous.

"Vanessa, I refuse to quarrel over something so insignificant."

"It is not—"

"Why don't I simply increase your pin money?"

"We have a contract, Jasper. If I don't abide by it, how can I expect you to?"

"What do you think I will do? Refuse you your ten days?"

She scowled. Rightly. He didn't know why he'd said that. She had turned him away only five. By his reckoning, it would soon be five more. But that was all. There were a few nights he had not come to her. He informed her first that he had to spend time at the parental home because they were insistent. But those nights should not count against her ten because she had not turned him away.

"I mean," he blurted, "that there are still ambiguities in the contract. And this is not what I wished to argue about."

The annoyance fell from her face, and she teased him. "Do you mean you had a separate argument planned?"

"Don't laugh. I did."

She laughed.

He made himself smile. "Vanessa, I'm terrified that you're bored all day long. And don't tell me you have plenty of sewing to occupy yourself."

"If this is about the pianoforte—"

"It is not. But we can take that up again also."

"Well, then, I have decided to accept your generous offer. I would like one."

"You are bored during the day."

She was quiet a long moment, then admitted, "Sometimes I am. I'm sorry."

"For God's sake, don't be sorry. How could you *not* be bored? You rarely leave the house."

"I have nowhere in particular to go. Jasper, it hasn't been terrible. You mustn't think so. I have been...recuperating."

That shook him. "Mourning?" Her husband was only a few months in his grave. He shouldn't keep forgetting that.

She nodded. "Yes. But not only Henry. I–I lost others too. In truth, I lost all my friends. So many are still there. And I worry about them. Can you understand?"

"I'd be a beast if I could not." He drew a breath. Blew it out. This was not the time to ask her to attend the theater. That much was obvious. But she was bored. His greatest fear was realized.

He was a boring man. "What can I do? The pianoforte, certainly. Would you like…" He wracked his brains for something to offer. "A companion?"

"A companion? Do you mean a paid friend? A chaperone for your mistress?"

He groaned. "I'm at a loss."

"You're sweet. And I appreciate that you care. But it is *time* that I need. Time that I don't mind spending doing mindless things. Tell me this: What did you intend to argue about?"

"It doesn't matter. We may leave it for another day."

"It does matter. And not because I am paid to be biddable. I want to know because *I* care."

His heart actually ached. He spoke from it.

"I feel, sometimes, when I am going about in town, that I am your jailor." He waited for her protest. Then hurried on when she made none. "I want to be with you. But I want the rest of my life as well. And I know you don't like to be left alone—"

"I don't feel imprisoned. And I certainly don't wish for you to feel imprisoned alongside me."

"I'm not expressing myself well."

He threw off his part of the sheet and rose from the bed. He stepped to the washstand to splash water on his face. He avoided the mirror, fearing he would look dissipated, but then glanced anyway and saw he did not. Well, he had not been drinking. And he'd slept well. This was ridiculous. He was standing naked, worrying about how his *face* looked.

He turned to see Vanessa's eyes fixed upon him. He snatched his banyan from the bedpost and put it on. He could be tempted again, but did not wish to be. He sat on the edge of the bed. Cleared his throat.

"You don't eat fish unless there is nothing else. Because once, long ago, you ate a piece of fish that had turned."

A little smile curved her lips. "You can, if you must, wear a poorly turned neckcloth but you will not abide one with a smudge."

He chuckled. "You hum in your sleep."

"You snore. Not often. But like this." She made a snorting sound that was convincingly piglike.

"You have a wart on your left big toe."

"I certainly do not!"

"Why do you think I am so enamored of your right foot?"

"It is a callous. My left shoe fits poorly."

"Then I will buy you new shoes."

She swung her feet back onto the bed and settled back against the propped pillows.

"I will graciously accept."

He felt his smile grow. "You eat your eggs unsalted. You are a madwoman."

"Are those two things?"

"No, just one."

"You always say goodnight twice."

"Do I?"

"Always."

"Now I will catch myself doing it."

She giggled. Giggled like a little girl. He sighed. He loved this game that they played, learning the small things about one another. But he wanted more. "Vanessa."

"Jasper?"

"You are a social woman who misses the company of her friends."

She was silent a long moment and he was afraid he'd misstepped. At last, she answered quietly, "I am. I do. Though I had very few playmates as a child. I learned late the value of friendship. If there was anything good about that year…" She tossed her head. "And you are a gregarious man with many friends."

"I like people. I like being around people."

"Of course you do. And people are drawn to you."

"You cannot know that."

"It's easy to guess." She reached across the bed and squeezed his arm. "Jasper, what are you fishing for?"

"We have established, I think, that I like my life. What I have been trying to ask is if you would be willing to share in it a little more."

She pulled back her hand. "A little more?"

"Only as much as you are comfortable doing. Not hostessing a party for my lecherous friends, or whatever other nonsense your solicitor implied I would be demanding. I have no intention of parading you about as my paramour."

She set her jaw. "What do you intend?"

He took a huge breath, like a boy about to plunge into a cold lake. "There is a play I would not mind seeing. Tonight. We have a box—my father does—at the theater. It is as private as anything can be in a public theater. My parents are not in town. The box will otherwise be empty."

"You wish me to go to the theater with you?"

"We can stay in the box during the intervals." He could not make the rounds with her on his arm. "And let others come to us." He had a few friends who almost certainly would. No ladies, of course. It would be horribly improper for a lady to acknowledge his mistress. Even so. There must be someone who would befriend Vanessa privately, if he asked it of them. "But, of course, I understand, if it is too much…"

She shook her head. She looked grim. But to his surprise, she said, "I will do it."

"You will?"

"I can either live my life afraid of censure, or I can accept it as I have chosen it." She fixed a look on him. "Yes, I would like to attend the theater with you."

The third thing he knew, the most important thing: Vanessa was brave.

# Chapter Seven

Vanessa was not natural mistress material. It took effort, and she had yet to master the basics even though it had already been two months.

She understood the main requirement was to accommodate Jasper in the bedchamber, though to her…surprise? enlightenment? … said chamber was not actually that often required. On the whole, his inventiveness was playful and certainly not vexing; even so, after enduring rather primitive conditions with poor Henry, she sometimes wished Jasper better appreciated the benefits of a reliably soft bed. And pillows thereupon. She quailed to imagine his intentions for the pianoforte. Hopefully, he understood the delicate instrument was not designed to bear weight.

Still. She believed he was satisfied, more than satisfied, with their bed sport. It was in other areas she feared she fell short.

Mistresses were supposed to be amusing. They soothed the brows of their harried lovers and provided them with light, untaxing conversation. Poor beleaguered Jasper had taken up the burden of initiating conversation himself. Also, although he evidently wished his mistress to be frivolous and require pampering, Vanessa could not be that woman. And now, Jasper seemed to feel it was *his* responsibility to entertain *her*.

Could she be a more troublesome mistress?

He wished to attend the theater. She could do that. She would show him that she could.

"Magnificent!" he exclaimed, beaming at her proudly.

"It will take me a few hours to prepare."

"Of course." He pulled her close and gave her a resounding smack of a kiss on her lips. "Show me what you will wear."

That took the wind from her sails. He thought she would not know how to dress for Society, even though he'd provided her with more than adequate clothes.

Two days after they signed the contract, a modiste had appeared at the door, having been instructed to create, from scratch, an entire seasonal wardrobe. Vanessa cringed, cast back to a time when her father would bestow similar gifts upon her. If given his way, she would have worn hideous things, clothes that shouted: *Look how much money my father has. Look what you may possess in exchange for your title.*

Of course, this was different. Jasper's chosen modiste had taste. They agreed upon nearly everything: a variety of day and evening dresses, lovely, delicate underthings, and even a few night rails she thought Jasper would appreciate. But she ordered fewer dresses than the modiste suggested, knowing she wouldn't wear even half of those.

Vanessa knew how to dress well. But let her lord master supervise her first public appearance if it would set his mind at ease.

"My gowns are in the dressing room. Would you like to choose?"

He made a sour face. "No, I would not like to choose. I simply want to see it."

"Why?"

"If I say, you will not be surprised."

"I don't like surprises."

"You will refuse."

"In that case, I emphatically do not wish to be surprised."

"Vanessa, you cannot go to the theater without jewels. And,

except for that very lovely piece you've stopped wearing, I have never seen you in jewelry."

Her necklace. A very thin chain of gold with the tiniest sapphire pendant. Henry had given it to her. It was kind of Jasper to call it lovely. She knew it was, but most wealthy men would scoff.

And, of course, Jasper was correct. She could not go to the theater naked of jewelry. She'd be embarrassed to do so. And it would reflect very poorly on him.

She sighed. "I won't refuse. Just a moment."

Her shift was on the cold tile floor. She reached and snagged it, then pulled it on over her head. Jasper could prance about unselfconsciously without clothing, but she had not mastered that art.

She went to the spare room, studied her evening dresses, and chose a blue-black gown, sparsely decorated with tiny, deep red scrolls. The neckline was squared off, but the cut of the bodice nevertheless accentuated her bosom—which, frankly, needed accentuation. The short, puffed sleeves would draw attention to her glove-encased arms. She liked her arms.

She returned with the dress slung over her shoulder, then shook it out and held it before her.

"This one."

Jasper regarded it a moment, then nodded, satisfied, and said, "Rubies, if I can find a set on time. Otherwise, it may have to be garnets. Unless you have a different preference."

"I am willing to be surprised."

He started, then smiled.

Jasper was profligate with his smiles, using them skillfully in myriad, differing situations. He was better with them even than most women. Vanessa was learning which ones to discount. But there were some that she stored away in her heart, banked like an ember, for some future date when she might need the warmth.

⇉⇉⇉⟩⟨⇇⇇⇇

JASPER SHIELDED HER. They arrived unfashionably early so that he would have no one to greet in the crowd outside. He steered her up a back stairway and ensconced her in the shadows of his semi-darkened box. He behaved as if she were a duchess he was escorting, sitting beside her without closing the space between them. Not for Jasper the carelessly sprawled thigh or artlessly draped hand. But of course, she'd known he would not crassly proclaim his ownership of her. It was more subtly done.

Most people did not attend theater to watch the play, but rather to observe the audience. She was aware of the craned necks and the opera glasses tilted in her direction, but she kept her own eyes upon the stage, partly because she was afraid of who she might see. Yet, she reassured herself, even if she were recognized, it would not be by anyone who would approach an earl's box.

It helped that the play was delightful. A well-acted comedy. It pleased her to discover that she and Jasper were laughing at the same lines and that when he leaned to whisper a comment in her ear, he echoed the thoughts in her head. However, the evening reinforced her impression of him as a man who thrived in public places. As the newness of their arrangement faded, he would certainly wish, more and more, to draw her out. To accommodate him, she would find herself on display.

He was going to learn things about her; perhaps more than he bargained for.

Midway through the play, the curtain came down and some houselights were lit, allowing Society to see and be seen. Vanessa tensed. Jasper had said they would let people come to them. She suspected she was such an object of curiosity that they would.

"The lad that plays the coachman is better than the lead, don't you agree?" Jasper said.

"Yes, he's very good. But he is too slight of build to carry off the role of the highwayman."

"They could pad him up with layers."

"I suppose they might. They obviously have done so with

Lady Agatha."

The flighty heroine was impossibly buxom.

Jasper cut a look at her and grinned. "How disillusioning."

"Have I spoiled the play for you?"

A reverberating clamor sounded at the door to the box, and then two gentlemen tumbled in. The air grew redolent with gin fumes.

Jasper grimaced, then stood, offering a hand to her. She touched it as she rose.

"Mrs. Wardrip," he said, "may I present to you Lord Carleton and Mr. Stevenson."

She nodded. "Good evening. I trust you are enjoying the play."

The Stevenson fellow merely goggled, but Lord Carleton stumbled forward, snatched her hand from Jasper's, and planted a slobbery kiss upon the back of it.

"Delighted," he said, though the word was garbled. "Why has Jasper kept you hidden?"

She retrieved her hand and iced her voice. "Has he?"

Jasper waved his hand before his nose. "God, Carleton. Did you leave any for the other patrons? Step back, if you would. You are making our eyes water."

Carleton took an obliging step backward, nearly tumbling, while Stevenson guffawed.

"What lovely friends you have, my lord," she murmured.

His face darkened. "They are not representative of the lot."

"Oh, come now!" Carleton protested. "We've seen you slide under the table at Lionsmead—"

"That wasn't because he was foxed," Stevenson said, shaking his head. "He had an assignation."

The two laughed uproariously. Vanessa felt a strong wave of longing for Lydia, who would clap the men's heads together and shove them out the door. Oh, but so-called gentlemen were not to be shoved.

The door clicked open, and a third man entered. He appeared

to be a few years older, though perhaps that was simply because he was sober. He was better dressed as well, with an elaborate twist in his neckcloth and a very high shine to his boots. He raised a quizzing glass to his eye and studied the two drunkards, then lowered it and sighed.

"I do beg your pardon, Lord Taverston. It was my turn to tend them tonight, but I turned my back and they escaped."

He managed to sound very bored and very droll.

"Mrs. Wardrip," Jasper said, and Vanessa was certain she did not imagine the relief in his voice, "this is Viscount Haslet."

"I answer only to 'Hazard,'" the man said. "Though I assure you there is no significance to the name."

She nodded. "Good evening, my lord."

He pulled a handkerchief from his pocket, wrapped it across his hand, and then took Carleton by the arm, his nose wrinkling with distaste.

"I am afraid if I squeeze too hard, the gin will ooze from his pores," he explained. "Carleton, if you recall, you promised to stand the next round."

"Yes, I will, but—"

"I do not hear 'buts.'" He tutted. "Lead the way."

It seemed to her Hazard was pushing more than being led, but the two made their way back to the door without incident. Hazard beckoned to Stevenson to follow. He opened the door and ushered them through. Then said after them, "I will meet you downstairs." He shut the door.

"Honestly, Jasper." He crumpled the handkerchief and dropped it on the floor. "If I were your mother, I would have barred those two from the house from the moment they sprouted their first chin hairs."

"They may well find themselves barred." Jasper lowered his eyes. Then raised them. "Thank you."

"That was my undeniable pleasure. However, this next is not." Hazard crossed his arms over his chest. "I take it you are not acquainted with the Marquess of Hilyer."

Vanessa felt as if the floor dropped away. She braced her feet and tried to keep a neutral look on her face, but she felt she might rather die than live through what would come next.

"I know the name only." The name alone was enough to bring out Jasper's scowl. "Why?"

"You are more fortunate than I. He was a friend of my father's. Or so he claims. My father had many faults, but I would like to think that was not one of them. Still, on the basis of that claim, Hilyer often accosts me when he is in London."

"You have my sympathy." Jasper cocked his head. "I presume you did not come here merely to solicit it."

"No. He is here tonight. He asked for an introduction. Well, for me to bring you to him to be introduced. He is enamored of his own consequence. I said no, of course."

"Why on earth does he want to know me?"

Vanessa took quick shallow breaths.

Hazard shrugged. "I shudder to imagine. But that was not the end of it. He claimed a prior acquaintance with Miss Cul—" He caught himself. She could tell by the way his eye twitched that the slip had not been intentional. "With Mrs. Wardrip. He said she would introduce him if I would not, so it was no matter. To shorten this unpleasant account, he, too, is awaiting me downstairs, because I told him that, in that case, I would come to find you so we could meet him there. I expect he will shortly realize I lied."

"Are you suggesting we leave?" Jasper gave a disbelieving huff of laughter.

"No. I am *insisting* that you leave." He turned to her. "The highwayman is, in fact, Lord Thistlerood. And that pretty coachman is his sister in disguise."

"Hazard!" Jasper complained. "You've spoiled the play!"

"Obviously, that was my intention, so you have no reason to stay. Hilyer gave me a preview of the conversation he wishes to have. As I have no desire to serve as your second—I've seen you shoot—I ask you to withdraw."

Jasper turned from him to Vanessa, then back again. His face was tight, as if angry. But his anger did not appear directed at her, despite the revelation that Hilyer claimed to know her, or at Hazard, whose serious tone did not match his joking words. Jasper's voice dropped to a frightening calm. "What did Hilyer say?"

"Nothing that is any of my business. And nothing I will repeat." Hazard redirected his appeal. "Mrs. Wardrip, will you add your entreaties to mine?"

"My lord," she said to Jasper, unable to control the quaver in her voice, "Viscount Haslet's concerns may have some validity. The marquess is...an unpleasant man." She was only stating what they already knew, but Jasper would want to know how *she* knew. How could this soldier's widow possibly be acquainted with a marquess? She'd have no choice but to explain. But she could not let Hilyer confront Jasper. Not here, publicly. Not ever. "Please, my lord, we should go."

Jasper's expression darkened further. He didn't speak, but he lifted her wrap from the back of her chair and draped it over her shoulders. He took her elbow, his grip unnecessarily strong, and guided her to the door. Then he gritted his teeth and turned back to his friend.

"I am again in your debt."

"Oh, probably," Hazard drawled. "But don't thank me yet."

# Chapter Eight

Jasper was not a coward, but neither was he a fool. Any confrontation involving Vanessa would sink her.

He called for his carriage, and they waited in silence. Although her fingertips were light upon his arm, he felt her trembling. When his carriage drew up before them, one of the footmen opened the door and Jasper handed her up. Then he mounted the block and directed the driver.

"The Bleeker Street house. The long way. Through the park."

He climbed in and settled on the bench across from her. The carriage rolled away from the theater. He waited for her to speak first.

Finally, she said, "You deserve an explanation."

"Vanessa, no. This is not about me. Except to say that my support is fully yours."

She sighed, a hitch catching in her throat. "I am acquainted with the Marquess of Hilyer. We were—at least in my father's eyes and Hilyer's—betrothed."

Jasper ground his teeth to keep his jaw shut.

"My father being," Vanessa continued a little breathlessly, "Frederick Culpepper."

"Culpepper!" He nearly choked on the name. He had guessed Vanessa's family had money, but not to that degree. Not Culpepper wealth. The man owned half the cotton mills in the

North. He had a reputation, among the worst of his class, for abusing his employees. Of bribery. Corruption. And boorishness. The sod could not understand why his money could not buy him, at the very least, a baronetcy. A man's own greed did not make him a worthy servant to the Crown!

The devil. The bloody devil. Jasper could draw a straight line. Culpepper had sacrificed his daughter to his futile ambition. He'd promised her to that disgusting lecher.

Jasper had not thought to close the curtains. Enough lamplight shone inward for him to see Vanessa was crying, making no sound. He moved to the bench beside her and pulled her against his shoulder.

"You don't have to say anymore." Jasper had never before wished to ruin a man. Now he wished to destroy two.

She wept. Not loudly or long, but she wept, and his heart wept along with her. When she sat back, he handed her his handkerchief. She wiped her eyes, then drew another deep breath.

"I'd like to explain about Henry. I did not…we were legally wed. I did not run off with a soldier."

Jasper's mind had not yet drifted to that conclusion, but admittedly, it might have. "Of course not."

She said, "But we were wed in Gretna Green. It was not the most respectable marriage, but it was a marriage. Henry was the most honorable man I have ever known."

That included him. Or excluded him, as it were. But he could not resent Henry Wardrip. He could do nothing but admire him.

"I told you I had few friends when I was young. Henry was one." She paused and blew her nose, then made a sound of dismay. "I beg your pardon."

"Vanessa, all ladies' noses drip when they weep. Tell me about Henry. I wish I'd been privileged to know him."

"I had no female friends because my father feared I would be polluted by them. Instead, I had more governesses, tutors, instructors, stylists—oh, anyone he could think to hire. My days were full. And I had *things*, Jasper. So many things. So many useless, hideous *things*. I used to lie awake at night on the Peninsula, oppressed not by the lack of them but by the memory of the appalling weight of them."

The story bothered him because he understood, deep in the dark recess of his soul, that he owed Frederick Culpepper a debt of gratitude. Had the father not molded Vanessa into the form of a lady, Jasper would not have taken to her so immediately. Perhaps not at all. Had Crispin sent some costermonger into his care, he would have given her money and sent her on her way.

"He did not banish Henry?" *Or Will Collingsworth?* "What idiot father banishes female friends but allows young men?"

"Not at first. Henry was—oh, I was not allowed to associate with the sons of my father's business acquaintances. God forbid. Can you imagine the designs upon, not my person, but my father's mills?"

"You're an only child?"

She shook her head. "I have a brother. We were close once, but I suspect Freddie has become a copy of my father." She grimaced. "My father insisted upon it."

He took her hand and squeezed it. He could not envision being so at odds with one's brothers. Well, he could not envision any of this, truthfully.

"I did not stand to inherit any of the business, of course. But the connection would have been enough. That and the dowry my father advertised to anyone who would listen."

"Don't tell me." How disgustingly crass. "But Hilyer is flush. Why…oh, God. Never mind. I know why." Young, virginal, pretty, without significant connections or a father who cared. Hilyer would be slavering.

"I didn't associate with men of my father's ilk. But I wasn't locked away in a hidden room. I knew some of my father's more elevated associates. His attorney for example. And Will often accompanied his father. We had occasion to speak from time to time. Not often. But enough to grow an affection between us."

"An affection?"

"A casual friendship. Jasper, please don't—" She reached to touch his arm.

"I won't. I'm sorry. Of course, I won't."

He clamped down hard upon the teeth of jealousy that had begun to gnaw. He would not sully her friendships with coarse suspicion of men's motives.

"And there was Henry. His father was Dr. Wardrip, my mother's physician. My mother considered herself an invalid. I don't know what her malady was. It seemed to be constantly changing. But the point is, Dr. Wardrip was a frequent visitor to our house. Henry accompanied him from the time we were children. Little children. I've known him longer than I've known Freddy."

"I see. But he was not banished when he became old enough to be viewed as a suitor?"

"Well, no. Because he did not need banishing. He went away to school at St. Thomas's. I hadn't seen him for three years, and then he returned as his father's assistant." She pulled her hand away, fluttering. She was not a flutterer. "The story grows so sordid from here, I…"

"Nothing you have done is sordid." He turned her chin until she looked him in the eye. "Vanessa, *nothing*."

She blinked. Nodded. "I don't know when it dawned on me that Henry was falling in love with me. I didn't love him. I recognized that much. But I didn't go out of my way to discourage him because I *liked* him. I considered him a good match and assumed my parents would think so as well."

"You were unaware of your father's intentions?"

"I was aware, but I thought them to be ridiculous. He had money, but not the connections. I could see that, even if he did not."

The carriage hit a rut, jostling them against one another. Jasper used the opportunity to slide an arm across her shoulders, to reassure her—seeing what was coming—that he was on her side.

"But then he managed, somehow, to gain an introduction to the marquess. Hilyer declined an invitation to supper, but Frederick Culpepper never takes no for an answer. He made me dress up like a ladybird. It was not the first time. He liked to parade me about. I hated it, Jasper, hated it so much. I didn't know he meant to waylay the marquess in the street. He even managed to work a mention of my dowry into the conversation. The marquess looked at me as though…"

She flushed deeply. Jasper blanched. He could not find words contemptuous enough.

"Within a week, my father had his offer. It didn't matter that I refused." Her voice thinned. "Contracts were drawn."

"My God."

"I resorted to the airs of a gothic heroine. I threatened to kill myself. I refused to eat. My father scoffed at first, but eventually, it alarmed him. I suppose he recognized he could not deliver a corpse to the marquess."

"Vanessa," he murmured. He kissed the top of her head. He didn't know what to say. Only that men were brutes, and he was ashamed to be one. Look at Carleton and Stevenson. Look at Crispin. Look at himself.

"Father called in Dr. Wardrip. He was appalled by me. He warned me that I must eat. He told my father that if I had taken nothing in three more days, he would return, and force feed me. He described the process to me in detail. Henry was in the room, but he would not look at me. Jasper, that night I prayed for hours that I would die before the doctor returned."

More tears rolled down her cheeks. This time, she brushed them angrily away.

"The next morning, Henry appeared without his father. He carried a sugared loaf and explained that Dr. Wardrip had sent him to try to tempt me to eat. My mother followed him up to my bedroom. She watched him tear off a large piece. He pressed it into my hand. Then he took a smaller one and said, 'Open your mouth, Miss Culpepper.' I don't know why, but I did. He put a piece of bread into it along with something else. I pretended to swallow. He said, 'Promise me you will eat the rest.' I could only nod. He suggested to my mother that they leave me alone, and she was so impressed with him that they did."

"What did he put in your mouth?"

"A note. It said he would be outside my window at midnight. He said if I was willing, he would take me to Gretna Green and marry me. He said I must know that he loved me and that he only hoped that one day I would feel the same. That night, we eloped."

"Thank God for Henry Wardrip."

"Yes." Then she burst into heaving tears. "I killed him, Jasper. I killed him."

---

THEY RODE TWICE through the park, stopping once when Vanessa needed air. Well, frankly, she needed to cast up her accounts, and then, she needed air.

She hadn't killed Henry, of course. That was done by Boney's soldiers. And Jasper laid the blame for that squarely at Frederick Culpepper's door.

Crispin wrote that she was the widow of a fine British soldier. Jasper had no doubt that was true. But the boy was a bacon-brain.

From what she'd said, they had been two eighteen-year-old children. Children, because they knew nothing. Even Jasper, at eighteen, had understood more of the world. They had scarcely a few pounds between them. Vanessa had not thought, before lowering herself from her bedroom window, to stuff a few necklaces into a reticule to pawn. Despite her father's vast wealth, or more likely because of it, she had no concept of money. Not then.

Henry may have been less naïve, but not much less. His father earned a good living by doctoring. Henry apparently believed they would return home blissfully wed and all families involved would simply adapt.

The stupidity of it all galled Jasper. Because of course, the families did not adapt. Accusations flew. Either Henry was a serial seducer, introduced by Dr. Wardrip into the homes of his wealthy patients to snare an heiress by means most foul, or Vanessa was a harlot who ruined young Henry's budding career. Both families cut them off. The marriage had been consummated. It could not be undone. Not unless Vanessa accused Henry of forcible abduction. He would be arrested. A divorce could then be arranged. Hilyer was still willing to have her.

It was at that point in the tale when Jasper had to stop the carriage. He had not thought to bring brandy. Why would he have? He could do nothing but kneel beside her and rub her shoulders while she retched. As they remounted the carriage, one of the footmen passed him a flask. The man could be fired for drinking on duty. He could be fired for even acknowledging he'd overheard anything being said. But when Vanessa gratefully took a few sips, Jasper vowed to himself he would raise the man's wages.

She managed to continue.

Henry had enlisted. There had been no other option. He thought he might serve as a surgeon, but they needed cannon fodder. The only blessing in the whole horrible narrative was that she had been one of the few wives chosen to accompany the new recruits. And so, she'd followed the drum.

After the story's conclusion, they finished the ride in near silence.

Upon their return to the townhouse, Jasper ordered a bath for her. He waited for her to reappear. He had undressed but kept on his shirt, with his banyan on top for good measure. She came to him, finally, still damp, a little pink about the eyes, wearing a clean shift but nothing else. He knew she was drained. He was.

He tucked her into bed.

He said, "Vanessa, they can no longer touch you. I won't let them cause you any more pain. You must know that."

"I am already ruined, Jasper. They will hurt *you*."

"You cannot believe that."

"But—"

He brushed a few damp, stray curls from her forehead. "Trust me."

She sighed. He continued stroking her hair until the tension eased from her and she started to drift to sleep. Just before she fell, she murmured, "I do."

# Part 3
## Time to Let Go
### July 1813
### London

# Chapter Nine

Despite posing as a recluse while his heartwound refused to knit, there was one invitation Jasper could not refuse: tea with the Duke and Duchess of Hovington. These were Lady Georgiana's parents. Or, he should say, Mrs. Taverston's parents. She had lost status by marrying Reginald. And the lady might have been a countess!

It was funny, he supposed. Thankfully, the so-called wits at his club had moved on to more current sources of amusement. The only part that still rubbed was picturing the arse he'd made of himself in front of his brothers. He didn't blame Reg—the poor fellow had clearly been suffering pangs of conscience along with his love pains. But Crispin had played the sham for all it was worth.

Reg and Georgiana returned to London last night in preparation for next week's ball honoring Georgiana's cousin's debut. Very late in the Season, but poor Alice Fogbotham was low in the pecking order. Jasper accepted that invitation as well. He supposed it was time to stop hiding from Society.

He walked the approach to Watershorn, the stately ducal home, climbed the steps, and pounded the knocker. The butler admitted him into a high-ceilinged, well-illuminated, landscape-decorated entrance hall that managed to simultaneously welcome and impress.

Reg and Georgiana waited there. Georgiana, red-blonde, statuesque, always beautiful, somehow looked more so. And Reg? His shorter, darker, bookish brother? Jasper had never seen him looking so...so *comfortable*.

Jasper chose a paternally fond smile to greet them when nothing more natural sprang to his face.

"Jasp," Reg said, drawing him into a two-armed embrace.

Were they now a family that hugged? Well, so. He hugged back. Next, he turned to Georgiana. He started to bow, then stopped, shrugged, and held his arms open. In for a penny, in for a pound.

"Sister?"

She stepped into his arms, and he hugged her as well.

"How was Binnings?" he asked. It was an old family property, now in Crispin's hands. Crispin had suggested the newlyweds honeymoon there. Jasper meant, of course, what was the condition of the property; no one had been there in quite some time, but the faint reddening of his brother's face made him realize the alternative interpretation of the question.

Georgiana answered smoothly, "Absolutely lovely."

"The grounds need tending," Reginald said, apparently realizing what Jasper was actually asking. "I wrote Crispin about replacing the gardener."

Now they were assuredly all talking about the same thing.

"Crispin may prefer it overgrown," Jasper said. One never knew with Crispin. "And how are you finding Cambridge?"

"The house is perfect for our needs." Reg turned and smiled at his wife. "But Georgiana is overhauling it anyway. I am given to understand it is something brides do."

Jasper wondered fleetingly if there was a nursery involved. How galling it would be if Reg sired a son before he did.

Georgiana said, "I'm so glad you'll be coming to Alice's ball."

"How could I not? I'm looking forward to it." He glanced about. "Is she here?"

"No, she went for a carriage ride with Hazard."

"Hazard?" Jasper blinked. He understood their friend had done his part to raise Alice's prestige and divert attention from the Jasper-Georgiana-Reginald morass, but he hadn't realized that the two were still playing a role.

Georgiana nodded, a rather bemused look on her face. She said, "Oh, don't ask me. I haven't the faintest idea. Come in." She swept her hand toward the parlor. "There is no reason to stand out in the hall." She led the way, and Reginald fell into step alongside Jasper.

"How are *you* doing?" Reg asked in a lower tone.

Jasper's heart warmed a shade, grateful to be asked. Father's last weeks had taken a toll on them all.

"As well as can be expected." He paused. "No, better, I suppose. Parliament is taking most of my attention."

Sitting in Parliament was, in fact, eye-opening. For the last several years, joining in the small gatherings of peers discussing politics in Father's home, Jasper had said little and nodded much, his opinions forming, as it were, at the old earl's knee. He had thought Father's stance would be easy to emulate.

"And that is a good thing?" Reg pressed, his skepticism showing.

Father had said Jasper's guiding principle should be "Church and King." And, when in doubt, listen to Liverpool. Unfortunately, that was proving overly simplistic. He voted Tory, of course, but had made the mistake of listening, truly listening, to the speeches on both sides. He was disturbed to find his conscience sometimes leaned Whig.

"I'm learning quite a bit."

Reg grinned. "That *is* a good thing."

Jasper laughed. For his brother, learning was not simply a good thing, it was the only thing.

They entered the parlor. There was a small, unnecessary fire in the hearth. Some people could not abide the appearance of a cold hearth even in summertime. The windows were open for the little breeze they might afford. The duchess was seated on a plush, pale blue Grecian couch. The duke rose from his straight-backed chair to greet them.

"Iversley, welcome."

"Your Grace." Jasper made a small bow. He bowed also to the duchess. The deuce—the last time he'd seen her had been at the wedding, where his role as best man and jilted quasi-fiancé provided elements of farce. "It is good to see you again."

"Come in. Join us, please," the duchess said. "Reginald says your mother and Lady Olivia are doing well?"

"They are, thank you."

He paused a moment, considering where best to sit. He supposed he should be paying compliments to his hostess. He knew he should. He stepped toward her.

The duke crossed his path.

"Iversley, I noted with great satisfaction your applause at the end of Hazard's speech yesterday. I daresay it was not merely a measure of your regard for our friend."

"No. Not at all. The speech was laudable."

It was the one Hazard had asked him to read for glaring errors. It covered the Whig's opinion on the Leather Tax, about to be increased by a pittance.

Jasper had sided, with very little thought, with his father's party. Yes, shoemakers would find their costs increased. And yes, they would pass the cost on to their customers. But how much? A few shillings? That would hardly send Englishmen scurrying to foreigners for what were bound to be inferior shoes. The tax increase was needed to bolster the Treasury. For the war effort. And wasn't that the most crucial issue before them? Supporting Wellington and the troops? Supporting Crispin, with every fiber of their being?

Before the debates, the text of the speech, delivered in Jasper's head in his friend's usual flippant, disinterested voice, had raised interesting points but had not been persuasive. Jasper had read it mainly for the barbs, directed at certain personages, that he had known would be there. He'd been amused.

But when Hazard spoke on the floor, it was in a different voice entirely. Measured, statesmanlike oratory replaced his usual affability. Some of the jocular wording was changed: his barbs were sharp. The people affected by the tax were those who could not afford a few extra pennies. Farmers. Laborers. Their children. Saddlers and shoemakers would suffer the loss of business. And soldiers themselves would be provided inferior boots by war profiteers—a gamble of a statement given there were likely profiteers in the room.

When the Whigs applauded Hazard, Jasper did too. Those beside him on the bench, his good Tory allies, chuckled at his greenness. Perhaps they found it refreshing to see a young lad cheer a friend as if it were a cricket match. Of course, they rapped his knuckles that night at White's: no more of that, young fellow. It would be an insult to his father's memory not to carry on the strong Tory legacy of the Earls of Iversley.

"He's a fine speaker," Hovington agreed. "A strong command of the issues. A shame we cannot use him more often."

*We.* Hovington was one of the more conservative Whigs, but a Whig, nevertheless. It was fortunate that his new Tory-by-birth son-in-law had no interest in things political. Though Jasper did wonder what they all discussed around the supper table.

But why couldn't they use Hazard more? He seemed to enjoy the task.

"Why can't you?" he asked. He was just curious. Not digging for weaknesses in their strategies.

Hovington tutted. "He is too clever by half at times. And he cannot afford enemies."

"I suppose not." Jasper tried to sound noncommittal. "Enemies do no one any good."

People liked Hazard too much to make open accusations. But that could change.

"Quite right." The duke clapped him on the back. "Dare I ask if you were persuaded to cross the aisle? On this bill at least?"

He heard his father's voice in his ear: *Church and King.*

He shook his head and tried to answer the way he imagined the old earl would have, but cringed inwardly, because the words, in his own voice, sounded heartless rather than sensible. "I want children in shoes, naturally. But there are charities for such things. We need to defeat Napoleon first. Then we can bring taxes down."

His argument was simplistic, but the Leather Tax was hardly significant enough to risk alienating the men his father had worked with year after year. Fortunately, this session of Parliament would close in a week, and he would be granted a few months to better formulate his own opinions on other matters. A daunting task. An absorbing one. And one that would help keep his mind from returning to Vanessa. Though here it was again, turning to Vanessa, and that knife twist of pain in his heart.

"Enough of politics, Hovington," his wife chastised, then shared a smile with Georgiana. This must be a common complaint. "This is a tea. You are not in session."

Georgiana rang for tea to emphasize the point. They took their seats: the duke back in his solid rosewood chair, Reg and Georgiana on a two-seated couch, where they were at liberty to be close. Discreetly close: Reg was still Reg. Jasper sat opposite the tea table from the duchess.

Servants arrived with tea and cakes. Conversation ebbed until the servants retreated. Then the duchess turned her attention fully upon Jasper.

"I suppose you have guessed why you're here."

The bite of cake dried in his mouth. He swallowed with difficulty. "Have I?"

Georgiana groaned. "Mama!"

"Darling child, soon you may be as unconventional as you wish, and you, too, Reginald, dear—"

Reg's startled expression informed Jasper that his brother had not expected to be drawn into whatever this was. Or, more likely, had thought it nothing but a tea party.

"—but until Alice is safely wed, the order of the day is propriety."

Jasper wanted to defend Reg and Georgiana, who had done nothing at all improper—though he was willing to grant the duchess "unconventional"—but he feared he was being accused as well.

"Propriety?" He managed to lift an eyebrow at her but doubted he used it quellingly. Crispin was the effective eyebrow lifter. Jasper considered his own weapon the disarming smile. He should have led with that. It would not work after deploying the eyebrow.

"Alice and Hazard have been spending far too much time in each other's company. I understand the initial rationale, and truth be told, I encouraged them. But he's hardly about to ask for her. And even if he did, we would not allow her to accept." The duchess seemed on the verge of losing her composure and finished with a huff. "They may well enjoy each other's company, but enough is enough."

It felt odd to admit to himself that he agreed with every word she said. "And so?" he prompted.

"Well." She drew a deep breath. "You may be disinclined, and I certainly have no reason to expect—"

"Mary—" Hovington tried to interrupt, and at the same time Georgiana said, "Mama!"

"I merely wish to ask Iversley to claim Alice for the first dance."

Jasper smiled his relief. "I would be delighted."

"And then dance the next with Georgiana. We'll ensure it is not a waltz."

His smile faltered. Granted, a country dance was not as intimate as a waltz, but still, how *awkward*.

"You see," the duchess went on, "we must squelch any lingering rumors. This ball will be the first opportunity for the ton to assess how we feel about…" she swirled her hand, "everything that passed. Our friends, of course, know that we are all excessively pleased with matters." She squeezed a smile at Reg. "But *people* will say—"

"That I am small consolation," Reg finished.

Jasper was appalled. Were people actually suggesting such a thing? But Reg laughed. He didn't seem to care. "And what am I to do, Lieutenant?" He lifted his hands in a shrug.

The duchess laughed as well, turning a little pink at the throat. Evidently, Reg had found his own way to deal with his mother-in-law. "I don't expect Alice will ever be left unpartnered. Not at her own ball. But if you see such a disaster may be imminent, do not allow it."

"I would not," Reginald said with a brisk nod.

"And then I would like both of you Taverstons to keep Hazard at bay. I don't want to seem ungrateful, but he really must withdraw. Or else agree to ask her in full expectation of being refused."

Georgiana protested. "You can't mean Hazard is scaring away Alice's suitors. I thought she was succeeding wonderfully."

"At first, yes. She had several admirers. Four were, I thought, very likely candidates. But she shows such a marked preference for Hazard's company, I fear Mr. Gamby has begun looking elsewhere and Sir Mikton has stopped sending flowers."

Georgiana's expression grew worried. "Should I speak with her?"

"I have." The duchess bit her lip. "But yes, a word from you might do more good. She merely tells me they are 'only friends.'" Her voice dropped to an impolite mutter. "As if the ton permits such a thing between a bachelor and an unmarried lady."

Jasper came back to the point. Which was evidently a battle plan. "So I am to dance charmingly with Alice. Then pleasantly with Georgiana. Then head Hazard off if he appears to be approaching Alice. It sounds simple enough."

The duchess nodded. "But you mustn't show a *preference* for Alice."

Reg said, "And you certainly must not show a preference for Georgiana."

His wife slapped his arm.

The duchess continued, "And you and Reginald must display warmth toward one another."

"More of a challenge," Jasper said dryly.

"And, of course, you must also dance with some of the other ladies."

Jasper felt a wave of exasperation. He knew to do his duty at a ball. He would not leave wallflowers tapping their toes and holding back tears.

"Have you prepared a list?" He regretted the edge in his voice.

"Nonsense. You are not my project." She hesitated, the expression on her face hovering between offense and guilt. She opened her mouth and then closed it. Then she said, "However, if you wish a suggestion, you might show favor to Miss Felicity Brewer."

He knew her. A pretty chit. A little colorless. But then, compared to Vanessa, every woman lacked color. Miss Brewer had nothing particular to recommend her. Was her mother friendly with the duchess?

Courting intrigues wearied him. He asked outright, "May I inquire why?"

The duchess pouted defensively. "I suspect Sir Mikton's bouquets have been diverted to her sitting room."

Jasper's jaw dropped. Matchmakers were cutthroats!

And then, two things happened at once.

Georgiana cried, "That is too much, Mama! It isn't fair to raise Felicity's expectations and ruin her chances with Sir Mikton. Moreover, if Alice had wished to hold his attention, I'm certain she could have done so."

While she argued, Hovington stood and marched across the room. A flask appeared from some hidden pocket. He'd unscrewed the cap before reaching Jasper's chair. Then he splashed a bit of something into Jasper's tea.

"And this is why we don't allow them in politics."

Jasper smiled weakly and raised his cup in solidarity.

But then Reginald spoke.

"On the contrary, Your Grace. Were we to allow them charge of weightier manners, we should not find ourselves floundering in half so many quandaries."

Jasper would have laughed, but he was ninety percent certain his brother was not joking. He raised his estimate to one hundred percent when he caught a glimpse of Georgiana's expression. Love and awe. The beauty there made his eyes sting.

Or maybe it was something else: the realization that a fortunate man might be granted one opportunity in a lifetime to be loved in such a way. And he had squandered his chance.

*Ah, God, Vanessa.* How sorry he was.

# Chapter Ten

Vanessa knew she had to take this day by day. She must trust herself to make decisions as they came. Any mistakes would have to be lived with or corrected. This was all simple: she should not make it hard.

Her money was low. Not her assets, her coin.

She scrutinized the contents of her jewelry case, now spread across her narrow bed. And discovered she was not the coolly detached assessor of gemstones that she claimed to be. She remembered each gift. Each occasion. Each non-occasion. Jasper had not thrown presents at her as an easy way to buy affection or evade apology. He'd chosen special things for special moments. Oh!—her pearl necklace. Her eyes moistened. She couldn't part with any of this.

What a fool she was being! She could not afford sentiment. *She had to let go.*

She should have sold it all before leaving London, and given the money to Will to invest in some sort of trust. It surprised her that he hadn't thought to suggest it, but she could not blame Will. Not when she'd made such a point to him of her independence.

She picked up a bracelet studded with sapphires. Everything was real. Jasper did not believe in paste. One could not sell jewelry, not this type of jewelry, in Cartmel. Either it would brand her at once as a retired courtesan, or people would suspect she had been a lady's maid who absconded with the family jewels.

This was not an unsolvable problem. She needed only to write to Will and he would come fetch whatever she needed to sell. Yet she hated to inconvenience him so dreadfully. Perhaps she might write to Mr. Taverston. Crispin said Reginald could be counted upon. But what an embarrassing request to make. And what would Lady Georgiana think?

Vanessa had never met the woman, this erstwhile rival for Jasper's affection, but Crispin admired her. What a futile thing, to wish for the good opinion of a lady whom she had never met and would never meet.

Besides, contacting Reginald would be tantamount to contacting Jasper.

She didn't have time for this, she thought impatiently. Charlotte Gowe would be here any moment.

Vanessa and her neighbor had developed a Monday morning ritual. Charlotte would send her two little boys to the fields with her husband, tuck her baby girl into a basket, and bring her down the road. She also brought two cups, drizzled at the bottom with honey from the hives her husband kept. Vanessa supplied the boiled water and the tea. It was her near-empty tea caddy, in fact, that had alerted her to the dwindling of her funds.

Imagine, the Earl of Iversley's mistress unable to afford tea. But she wasn't that, anymore. She was a woman with finite resources. If she wanted funds, she would have to do without some of her jewels.

Vanessa took another glance out the window to see Charlotte walking toward the house. Her cotton frock had all the color washed out of it, but her round face was pink with the heat. She swung the basket to and fro gently. Sweet Kate would be sleeping by the time she arrived. That's what they called her. Sweet Kate. Never Katie or Kitty or Kate. Always Sweet Kate, as if she had been christened so.

Vanessa dug her nails into her palms. Another emotion she

would not allow herself to feel, not even to name. Of course, she and Jasper never had any children. And she and Henry…had no children either. No living children.

Charlotte came up the walk, careful not to bump the basket against her legs. Vanessa shut the door to her bedroom, then opened the front door before her friend knocked.

"Come in! The water's boiling."

Charlotte handed her two copper cups. "I can't stay long. Petey's got the trots. Dan took him but says if he's not better, he'll send him home. I figure I've time for just a quick cup."

"Oh, poor Petey! Does he hurt?"

"That boy never hurts. We wouldn't have known he was sick except—" She made a sniffing sound and wrinkled her nose. "You know."

Little Dan was six. Petey five. Sweet Kate would be a year old come August. Vanessa clenched her hands around the cups. Then she set them on the table. "I'll fetch the pot."

The teapot was a chipped old clay thing that had come with the house. Vanessa suspected the previous occupant had brewed up some earthy concoction from local herbs rather than actual tea by the lingering odor of it. The first few times she'd used it, she yearned for the delicate Wedgewood teapot left behind in Bleeker Street, then resigned herself with the thought that at least it wasn't the gaudy, gilded pot that her mother had used.

But then once, watching Charlotte sigh over the honey-sweetened tea, with a wistful smile on her face and the words—"Aren't we just like the Queen, now?"—Vanessa decided the pot wasn't the important thing. In fact, she wondered if the Wedgewood wasn't gaudy too, just in a different way.

Vanessa returned to the table, poured, and then sat in the chair she would drag in from the parlor whenever Charlotte came to call. She could picture the look on Jasper's face were he to see her like this. A mixture of consternation and amusement.

Oh, good Lord. Enough of Jasper. Looking at his gifts had put her in a mood.

"No alphabets today?" she asked Charlotte.

Charlotte had asked Vanessa to teach her to read. The woman had applied herself to the task with vigor at first, but it was slow going. Her enthusiasm had faded. Vanessa hesitated to push her. Was it condescending to wish her neighbor was literate?

"No time." She sipped. "Maybe you should teach Petey and Little Dan instead." She added a mirthless laugh.

"You all three could learn."

"No, I don't mean to bother you more. Besides, I'd have to convince Dan." Charlotte rolled her eyes.

Vanessa hadn't figured out yet whose word held sway in that household. Charlotte acted as though she bowed to Dan's will, but Vanessa had yet to see the evidence.

"Oh, but since we're talking about reading! I almost forgot," Charlotte said. "Sherwood has a letter for you over at the tavern."

Here in Cartmel, the tavern was the post. The letter had to be from Will. No one else knew she was here.

"I hope it hasn't to do with the house." Vanessa bit her lip. "I thought I signed everything I had to sign. I suppose I better walk over there later."

Charlotte giggled. "I'm sure Sherwood would be happy to bring it by. I could have Dan drop a word."

"No, thank you. I could do with a stroll."

Sherwood considered himself quite the Corinthian. Amusingly enough, many of the ladies of the town seemed to think he was too.

"Have you talked to Lydia recently?" Charlotte asked.

"Just quickly. At church."

Charlotte flushed. Vanessa noticed she missed church fairly often. She once mumbled an excuse, something about Sunday being Dan's day to "sleep late," which sounded rather scandalous for Cartmel, so Vanessa never referred to it again. She refilled Charlotte's cup.

Charlotte swirled her tea, mixing the last little bit of honey at the bottom. "She didn't say anything about Herve's cousin?"

"Who?" Vanessa knew nothing about Herve, let alone a cousin.

"Herve's a tanner over in Barrow. His cousin lost both his legs. Both of them. Herve asked Jon if there might be a place for him at the boot mill."

Jon Compton called his cottage a mill. Vanessa understood that people for miles around ordered his semi-customized boots for men of theirs in the army, knowing that the government procurers could not keep the constantly marching soldiers well shod. The Comptons tried to price their wares low—not to undercut their competitors but because their customers were not well off. They turned out several pairs a week. Quality boots. Vanessa admired them. But a tiny part of her scoffed at the notion that an output like that qualified their endeavor as a mill.

"Lydia didn't mention it. But I'm sure they'll find something he can do."

Charlotte nodded, but not as though she were convinced. "He wasn't a soldier though. The cousin. He was drinking and fell down a hill."

"And lost both his legs?"

"It was a big hill."

Vanessa caught back a laugh. It wasn't funny. But she had an image of a foxed fellow tumbling down a hillside and leaving his legs at the top.

"He isn't a drunkard though. Just had one too many."

"You know him?"

Charlotte nodded. "I was born in Barrow."

"Well, talk to Lydia. I'm sure if you vouch for him…"

Sweet Kate startled awake with a cry. Then a grunt. Then a foul odor filled the air.

"Oh, no," Charlotte groaned. "Sweet Kate's got what Petey's got. I better get her home and wash her off." She scooped up the basket and cast a sorrowful glance at the cups. "I'll come back for them or send Little Dan." She hurried out the door.

Vanessa watched her go, but her thoughts were elsewhere.

With the Comptons and their boots and the two desperate old soldiers they employed. They could grow it. Their "mill." They could grow it. Mr. Brunel's building in Portsmouth, with at least two dozen men, churned out a hundred shoes a day.

But Mr. Brunel was an engineer. With machinery. Complicated, precision machinery. That took money. More money than four years of accumulated jewels were worth.

Vanessa sighed. What had gotten into her? She didn't think about mills. She didn't *want* to be thinking about mills. Certainly not thinking about investing in mills. *Ever.*

※

VANESSA TIDIED HER cottage, worked in her garden, let down a hem then tacked it up. She made herself a meal of bread and chopped boiled eggs. Then tidied again. Anything to avoid sorting jewelry into piles.

It made sense to retrieve the letter first, she decided. Then send a brooch along with her response to Will. She'd only send one piece and pray it arrived unpilfered. Afterward, she could tell her tale: she'd borrowed something from a friend in London who needed it back.

She tied on her bonnet and walked to the tavern. Better to do so early in the day before men started to gather. It was a short walk. Just two dusty roads. She passed two ladies from church who were picking flowers by the roadside. Vanessa exchanged greetings with them, but since they seemed deep in conversation, she did not stop.

The tavern was a two-room affair. A large one for drinking and a small one for everything else. Sherwood was sweeping out the large room in preparation for the evening's onslaught.

"Mrs. Wardrip!" Sherwood beamed at her. He had a gap between his two front teeth she could drive a barouche through. "Come for an ale?" He tried out a wink. Most men shouldn't and he was no exception.

"Just my letter, thank you. Mrs. Gowe said you had one for me."

"Indeed, I do. Just a minute." He swept his motes into the corner, propped his broom, and left her, saying, "May take a few to find it."

She waited. Sweeping wasn't enough. The floor needed a scrubbing. The walls, too. She shifted from foot to foot. What could Will be writing to her about? It couldn't be about the house. He'd handled the transaction, and he was scrupulous.

Worry pressed down like a weight.

It wasn't just Will's letter. She was worried about all of it. Money. Boredom. She liked Charlotte very much, but she had to admit, their conversation didn't flow. She liked Lydia, too. But she remembered Lydia differently. She'd been a general to them. Now she was just Lydia.

Vanessa didn't need a general. She needed friends. She missed Effie and Rose back in London. The two women along the roadside—she didn't even remember their names—had made no effort to draw her in. Why would they? She had nothing in common with anyone here. She couldn't even pretend to be flattered by Sherwood's attention. It was indiscriminate and the man had no charm.

It was all so much effort. Trying to make a new life. Hiding her old one. She knew she was being crotchety and probably snobbish. But she feared she would never belong here. Or anywhere. Ever again.

She had no one. She was beginning to wonder if even Jasper had forgotten her. If he'd found his countess yet.

"Here it is." Sherwood emerged from the back room waving a letter like a banner. "A man's handwriting. I guess I have a rival."

Subtle as a hammer.

She took it from him, glad at least that it didn't occur to him to keep waggling it playfully out of reach, and stuffed it quickly into her reticule.

"Thank you, Sherwood."

"Stay a while. I'm not too busy for a chat."

"I'm afraid I am." What excuse could she make? "Washing to do."

He nodded sagely. She made her escape. She walked a half mile to the crossroad where an ash tree shaded the path. It was a pretty day. There was no one near, and her dress was lightly blotched anyway from her earlier gardening, so she sat on the ground and took out her letter.

The handwriting was not Will's. She wasn't sure whose. It bore a simple wax seal with no mark. The paper was beset with creases and dull with grime. It had come a long way. She broke the seal.

> *My dear Mrs. Wardrip*—*No doubt you will have heard by the time this finds you, but I am filled with an uncharacteristic enthusiasm for putting pen to paper and could not put head to pillow until I wrote to you, too. We have won. Won. Shout with me: Vitoria! The rest is sweeping spent ashes into the hearth. Do not let anyone tell you*—*not that anyone would*—*that Wellington is less than a god. (I do not say God, lest I find myself stricken down in the moment of celebration.) There is much to mourn. And I will begin to do so tomorrow. But for tonight, I am merely joyous to have been here, to have added my small piece. Vanessa*—*Henry and his brethren*—*all those brave, brave men*—*did not sacrifice in vain. That is what I wanted to say. Not to crow our victory. But to tell you your husband's death had meaning: if not to you, if it still does not seem so to you, then know it has meaning for hundreds of thousands. Napoleon's defeat is nigh.*—*By the Grace of God, Your servant*—*Lt. Crispin Taverston*

*Oh, Crispin.* Tears ran down her face. She murmured, prayer-like: "Thank you for remembering Henry. And all of them." Those dead in battles already forgotten. Lesser battles. Lost battles. Crispin did not forget them. He had not forgotten her.

# Chapter Eleven

Despite the heaviness of heart he could not seem to shake, Jasper was glad for the excuse to end his self-imposed prohibition against attending balls; after all, he had always enjoyed dancing. It would help pass an evening. Moreover, who could miss the first ball to be held in the wake of Wellington's success at Vitoria? Spirits were so high—not his, but everyone else's—it was a wonder London wasn't airborne.

The Hovingtons' ballroom was one of the largest in London and probably the most exquisite: marble floor, crystal chandeliers, floor-to-ceiling windows, with silk-damask coverings on the walls to mute the sounds. If her cousin Alice's debut was this fine, Georgiana's must have been splendid. Poor Reg would have been out of his depth. It was funny, really, how things worked themselves out.

Well, not funny for him, of course. He escorted Alice onto the floor. He reminded himself he needed to make conversation with the young lady. "How pretty you look, Miss Fogbotham. I trust you've been enjoying your Season."

"Very much so, *Iversley*. Especially with Georgiana and Reginald back in London. I only wish Crispin and Olivia could be here."

He recalled how she, how they all, had teased him at Chaumbers for clinging to formal address while they—

unbeknownst to him—had progressed to using given names. Lud. Quite a bit had been going on unbeknownst to him. It would be too scandalous for her, here, to call him Jasper. Especially as he was now the Earl. But of course, she knew that. He winked at her, so that she would know he was teasing too.

He led her to the top of the reel. The music began and they danced. She had nimble feet and a quick smile. But after a few admittedly banal compliments, he realized she was not paying attention to him. The pattern of the dance took them away from each other and then back again.

"Am I so dull?" he asked. In his head, the words were teasing, but they emerged from his mouth like blocks of wood.

She blinked, startled, then said, "Oh, good Heavens, no. Please! I am indebted to you for favoring me like this—"

"Well, that's nonsense."

"The truth is, I am distracted by something. It's terrible form for me to ask about it. Yet I can't think of anything else. Especially talking to you."

And then they were obliged to whirl away from one another. It occurred to him he hadn't devoted much time to Alice when they were at Chaumbers. Was she sincere or was this some new way girls were trying to flirt?

They faced each other again. The little furrow between her brows suggested sincerity. He suppressed a sigh. Did it matter? So long as they presented a picture of amusing one another.

"You've piqued my interest. It would be rude, now, not to ask."

She took his permission and ran with it. "How was Hazard's speech received? I asked him, but you know how it is when he wishes to deflect attention."

"His speech was magnificent."

"Was it?" She beamed. "I knew it would be. So, he kept serious then?"

"Remarkably so." Then he thought about her words. "How did you know?"

"How did I know that he was making a speech?"

"That he would be serious. Hazard is never serious."

"Yes, but it is a serious topic."

"Good Lord, Alice!"

She shushed him. Then she slipped off on Mikton's arm while he twirled with Miss Felicity Brewer. He absentmindedly flashed a smile at her that he had not used since he was Reginald's age. He hadn't meant to. The duchess would be thrilled with him. He gladly relinquished the startled, blushing girl to Mikton and hurried back to Alice so quickly that he missed a step and nearly crushed her foot.

"Jasper," she hissed. "Ouch! Georgiana said you danced well!"

"I do." He sorted himself, annoyed. Now the duchess would be wringing her hands. The point was to convince people there was nothing here to gossip about. Instead, they would be saying Iversley was falling all over Miss Fogbotham and flirting outrageously with all the debutantes. He *must* be carrying a torch for his brother's wife.

For a moment, he danced with more decorum, a bland smile on his face that Alice copied. Then he imagined the triviality of what the gossips could say about this. And how little it mattered. Then he remembered what had set him off.

"Is Hazard discussing politics with you?"

The little furrow deepened to a brow-wrinkling frown.

"Don't do that," he warned, through smiling teeth. "We are enjoying ourselves."

She pasted back her smile. "He mentioned he was giving a speech."

"He mentioned the Coal Tax?"

"Leath—" She bit off the word. "All right. Yes. He wished to practice it, so I listened."

He recalled how much sharper the arguments were in the speech Hazard had given versus the one he had written. And how very serious Hazard had been. *Laying the groundwork*. Ha! He certainly was. But not for this bill, which hadn't a chance of failing.

The music drew to an end. They could not continue this conversation, but he was heartily intrigued.

"Thank you, Miss Fogbotham." He bowed. "I see Mr. Gamby approaching. And I am off to claim Mrs. Taverston."

"That should be fun for everyone. Don't mash her toes."

He bowed again, leaving her to her inconstant suitor. It *would* be amusing, dancing with Georgiana. But he was more looking forward to locating Hazard. The man was not courting Alice. Or pretending to court her. The clever chit was launching his political career.

---

WHEN THE MUSICIANS began playing what must be the final set, Jasper thought he might finally, without incurring the duchess's censure, make his goodbyes. He had danced with enough young ladies to have done his duty and had even danced with Georgiana twice. He may have had one too many glasses of champagne. It was time to depart.

One thing he had not had to do was bar Hazard access to his strategist. Hazard was not monopolizing Alice—he had not even bothered to attend the ball. It wasn't unusual for Hazard to skip ton events. He'd had his fill of them over the years. But this was different. The duke and duchess were friends of his. Moreover, Jasper had wanted to talk to him. To twit him, yes, but also to find out what was truly going on.

He wasn't the first to leave. The duke and duchess were standing together, near the doorway, not encouraging people to go but not discouraging them either.

"Hovington. Your Grace." He bowed over the duchess's hand. "An exceptional ball. Your niece is a diamond." Alice was a resounding success.

The duchess smiled. She looked a bit misty eyed. "It went

well, did it not? Thank you."

"Me? For what?"

"For your graciousness. About everything."

He chuckled. Graciously. "All's well that ends well."

He left Watershorn. His house was not far, a little over a mile. He hadn't come in a carriage, so he would walk home, late though it was. It was not the cleverest thing to do, but he had never yet been accosted by a footpad.

He marched along briskly. He should be keeping his eyes open for trouble, but he had one of the waltzes stuck in his head. He couldn't hum it out because he couldn't hum on key. The imaginary music took his mind back to dancing.

He should have danced more with Vanessa. She loved waltzing. She was featherlight on her feet. It wasn't as though they never were able to dance together. After the first few difficult months, with a little strong-arming on his part, they were invited as a couple to some small, very small, private parties. He and Vanessa even hosted a few parties themselves. There was generally dancing. He'd taken her to Vauxhall several times. Once, they went to a large, masked ball, but that had been a mistake. The masks never provided the degree of anonymity that the ton liked to pretend that they did.

Reginald had danced thrice tonight with Georgiana. It was considered bad ton to dance with one's own wife at a ball. Another rule with no rhyme or reason. And Reg broke it without a qualm.

Jasper wished he'd danced with Vanessa more…married her and then danced with her more.

God. His head ached. He should not have had that last glass of champagne.

He turned from the road to the walk to his house. In the moonlight, there were strange shadows amongst the shrubbery. One flickered. Moved. Jasper gave a startled shout.

"It's me." The voice was unrecognizable, but Hazard emerged, practically fell, from a narrow space between two shrubs. He took two steps, and then he did fall. Jasper caught him.

"Good God! What happened?"

The side of the man's face was coated with blood. Mostly dried. Some not.

"If it isn't too much to ask, can we have this conversation inside?"

"The devil."

Jasper wrenched one of Hazard's arms across his shoulder and practically carried the man to his door. He banged on it with his foot. Finley opened it.

"My Lord? My Lord!"

"Brandy. The study. And…and…"

"Towels? Hot water?" Hazard suggested. His voice was not at all steady and his grin was distorted by a fattening lip. But he went on, "You are alarmingly bad at this. I'm beginning to think I should have chosen a different shrub."

"Why did you pick mine?"

"It was closest."

"Bring it all," Jasper ordered. "Quickly."

"Quickly is a nice touch."

Jasper was very much not in the mood for Hazard's flippancy. Stupidly, he hauled his friend up to the study—he should have used a room downstairs—and sat him in a chair.

"What the hell, Haz? Do you need a doctor? Let me send for—"

"No! If I had needed one, I believe it would now be too late. And there is nothing worse for one's constitution than an unnecessary physician." His strained breathlessness gave lie to his amusement.

"What happened?"

"Footpads. Obviously."

"You were set upon by the world's most incompetent thieves?"

"Incompetent?"

Jasper tapped Hazard's gold watch fob, then flicked the chain of his purse, which had not been cut.

"Yes, well, I beat them off."

Jasper shook his head. It wasn't theft. "Them? How many?"

"Enough? Or too many. It was dark. I can't say for sure."

Finley entered along with two maids. They brought towels and bandages, water basins, soap, brandy, and glasses. The maids arranged it all on the reading table, and then Finley ushered them out.

"Will there be anything else, my lord?"

Jasper looked at Hazard, who said, "Thank you. This should do."

When they left, Jasper poured Hazard a large glass, which he took and finished in four gulps. His hands were shaking. And his knuckles looked mashed.

"Here," Jasper said, bringing a water basin closer. "Put your hands in here."

Hazard did. The water turned pink. Then brown. Jasper leaned to the table to take a towel to dip into the clean water bowl. Then he started dabbing at the blood on his friend's face. Hazard sat stoically. Quietly. From time to time, something Jasper did made him wince. After a while, he pulled his hands from the water and took the towel from Jasper.

"Have you a mirror?"

Jasper fetched the one hidden on the side of the bookshelf and brought it close. He held it in front of Hazard. Hazard's breath caught, which made him groan and press his upper arm against the side of his chest.

"Ribs, too?" Jasper asked.

"Just bruised, I hope. I need a favor."

"God, Haz. Anything."

"Can I stay here? A few days. Until my face looks like mine again."

"Yes. Of course, you can. But who are you hiding from?"

"Ah." He laughed a little. "My mother, actually."

"Haz."

"No, I am serious. Eyes like a hawk." The jesting tone fell away. "I've caused the poor woman enough heartache."

"Who jumped you?"

"I don't know. That is the truth. Three men. Strangers all."

"Who stole nothing." When Hazard didn't answer, Jasper tried another tack. "Was my house really closest? How far did you have to walk to make it here?" Hazard still didn't answer. Jasper said, "Were you on your way to Alice's ball?"

"Damn it. No. No, I was not. I'm not selfish enough to ruin her prospects."

Jasper felt the ache behind his eyes start to throb. It wasn't his business. And he probably didn't want to know.

But Hazard mumbled, "Vere Street. I had to walk, practically crawl, all the way from Vere Street."

Not just a male brothel, the most notorious of them. Jasper couldn't believe all the things said about it could be true. He couldn't picture Hazard there. He didn't want to.

"I left the Flying Horse, and three bastards caught me and dragged me into the alley."

"Why did you—"

"Why did I? Why did I?" Hazard's voice rose. "God so help me, Jasper, if you dare ask me why I did this to myself, why I *do* this to myself—" He choked. Then tried to stand. "I'm going. I shouldn't have come here."

Jasper pushed him back down. "Stop. You're staying. I insist that you stay. And I apologize. I didn't mean...anything. Hazard, you're the best man that I know. The very best man."

"Crispin? Reginald?"

"You are the third best man that I know."

Hazard laughed, not well-amused, but he laughed. "I need another drink. When will you learn to stock the place with gin?"

"I hate gin." He poured more brandy.

This time, Hazard merely rolled it around in his mouth, then spat into the basin. Great gobs of bloody spit and brandy. Hazard swirled the basin.

"No teeth. I am giddy with joy. I sincerely believed I was to be prematurely toothless."

"Can I ask you one more question?"

Hazard hesitated, then said warily, "Go on. Just one. Then I'm going to bed."

"Is Alice your mentor?"

A slow, grotesque smile spread on his face. Jasper could only tell it was a smile by the way Hazard's eyes crinkled.

"You may keep your Liverpool. That girl has the sharpest mind since Walpole."

# Chapter Twelve

Vanessa did not share the glad tidings about the battle at Vitoria. Not even with Lydia. How could she? Lydia would be incredulous. After all this time? *Lieutenant Taverston?* She'd want to know why the lieutenant would have written to her.

Never mind the *how*. It was foolish to imagine Crispin would have had any trouble uncovering her tracks. But *why* was a reasonable question. He said he wrote to her too. *Too.* Who else? All the Taverstons? Did he include her as one of them still? *In every way that mattered*?

If so, she mattered only to him.

After the initial rush of warmth from his letter receded, Vanessa was left feeling lonelier than before. He remembered her, yes. But he also reminded her of everything that she'd lost.

Regardless, within a few days, word of the battle seeped into Cartmel. Corporal Compton insisted upon a celebration. Sherwood offered the tavern. Everyone attended. Even Vanessa. Even though she didn't want to dampen the festivities with her mood.

They gathered at dusk to eat, drink, and twirl about. Vanessa didn't think she had ever been to a party that started at dusk. In London, parties started well after dark and ran into the early hours of the morning. Sometimes until dawn. But the ton never rose before noon. Here they woke at cock's crow. As if in the army or following the drum.

Although the battle at Vitoria was the excuse, there was very little discussion of the war. Little more than, "Well, certainly, our boys will kick Boney back to France. Just wish they'd get on with it instead of dragging their feet!"

Sherwood preened as he poured out the pints, implying he would have wrapped things up there by now.

To Vanessa's annoyance, she saw too many nods. Not Lydia's. Not Corporal Compton's. Anyone who had been there had not seen foot dragging, but rather courage and dogged persistence.

How dare these people! This party was not honoring Wellington's victory, or recalling to memory the fallen. Whose deaths, Crispin had waxed lyrically, had meaning—except, apparently not to these men. It was an excuse to drink, that was all.

"The nobs, you know," Dan Gowe said, wiping spilled froth from his beer onto his smock. "They don't want it to end. Too much profit in it."

She thought of Crispin's unleashed exhilaration. Tempered only by his kindness. And dismissed the words of these men who knew nothing.

Cartmel's folks didn't talk of the war, of the victory, but of their crops and the weather, the boot mill, and the damnable Leather Tax. And the nobs, of course. It was the nobs always wanting taxes they did not have to pay. Vanessa heard the man Herve's name. And the cousin, whose name was Bitter or Blither. Words twisted on the men's tongues as they grew louder and laughed harder. Bitter had not *lost* his legs. They remained attached, but useless. Something in his back had snapped when he fell. There had been a contest, Vanessa made out, that Bitter had won by putting away a vast quantity of beer. The men admired him, pitied him, and swilled as if imitating him.

Such false courage they had: easy when death was too busy to come looking for them.

She edged her thigh away from Tam's, beside her on the bench, a lank-haired farmer who stank of beer and sweat and goat. A sprawler, not a lecher, but still. Oh, she did not wish to be here, seeing this. Feeling this revulsion for her neighbors and their coarseness.

She was not better than them. She knew that. If she hated the rigidity that made her lesser than, she must equally reject notions of her own superiority. And Henry's.

After all, she'd seen Henry drunk, too. Worse than this. Every soldier received a rum ration. They drank more rum than water. They drank rum *in* their water. The first few months, he had shared his ration out, trading it for food for them both. Or sometimes he simply gave it away. But that didn't last. It couldn't. The things he saw. The things he did...poor, dear Henry who had wanted to be a *doctor*. She didn't fault him for the degrading condition she sometimes found him in. He never grabbed her lustfully when he was rum soaked. He'd never raised a hand to her either. She had never, like so many of her friends, needed to hide a blackened eye, split lip, or reddened fingermarks around her neck. Henry had drunk from desperation. She'd understood that. She didn't understand how these men drank so carelessly.

Jasper could also drink in quantity, carelessly. Why hadn't that bothered her? Because it was fine cognac or champagne instead of grog? Because he'd never fallen down or threw up? Because when liquor made him amorous, he'd still managed to retain his charm? He'd never seemed drunk. Merely foxed or a trifle disguised or a little bit bosky. All their little euphemisms for lapses without consequence. Jasper would never tumble down a hill, or accidentally discharge his weapon into his own gullet as Henry's friend Dixon had.

"Dance with me, Mrs. Wardrip," Jon said, holding out his hand. "You are too pretty for such a long face. This is a party."

"Oh, no, but—"

"Go along with you," Lydia urged. "Let Jon try out his new boots."

Lydia settled her hand on Vanessa's shoulder, that sustaining hand that had not permitted her to lie down and surrender after the fight she had lost, but rather made her leave a blood-soaked bundle under a bush and march on to Corunna.

"Lovey, Henry is smiling tonight. Our lads are all smiling. Let Henry watch you dance one more time."

Here again was Lydia the general. Vanessa stood. Yes, she would march on. What else was there? If Cartmel was a mistake, she must learn to live with it. She felt, or imagined she felt, a whisper-breath on her ear. *Dance, Vanessa.* It was not Henry's memory whispering. She had never danced with Henry.

*What do you know about this stranger, this Jon?*

If she was truly tired of living amongst strangers, there was a remedy. A modification of Jasper's game.

*Learn one thing about each of them. One good thing.*

Jon? She knew he was a generous man.

"I don't know the steps. You'll have to show me."

---

A WEEK LATER, Vanessa walked to the Compton's cottage. Their mill. She was on a mission. The front door was ajar, so she let herself in.

"Good morning, Bitter, you idiot," she said.

His name was Peter, not Bitter. Everyone called him Bitter because his wife of twenty years, whom he had married at fifteen, was deaf and could say only a few intelligible words. "Bitter" was how *she* said, "Peter." He would answer to nothing else.

Except now. Now he answered only to, "Bitter, you idiot." Apparently, that was how he coped with what he had done. Generous Jon had hired him at first meeting, giving him light work he could do from a chair.

He beamed at her. "Mrs. Wardrip, isn't it? What can we do for you?"

"I need a pair of boots."

"I thought as much. For who?"

"Myself."

His head tilted to the side. "We can do small ones, I suppose. But they'll be plain."

"That's just what I want. To walk about the fields; they don't have to be pretty."

She'd seen women wearing boots to match their husbands'. Maybe they *were* their husbands'.

Bitter glanced down at her feet. "Seems a shame to give up those."

She was wearing her only remaining decent pair of shoes. Silk slippers. They would not last. They would not have lasted long in London either, not in London's mucky, uneven streets, had she walked them. But in London, she had hardly ever gone about on foot. That was what the carriage was for. She had done enough walking for a lifetime, sometimes twenty miles in a day—and in ill-fitting boots salvaged from dead men. She'd sworn she would never wear awful, ugly shoes again. She didn't know what she'd imagined, coming to Cartmel. That it would all be pillowy meadows of grass paved with wildflowers?

"Too frivolous, I'm afraid. I shouldn't have bought something so fine. I need shoes that will last."

"Ah." He chuckled. "So Nan's right. She says bonnets for finery. High up on the head. Says I'm daft for wanting to make pretty shoes to scuff about in the dust."

Nan could not have said all that. Nevertheless, she believed Bitter had heard it.

"Perhaps I'll buy a bonnet next."

"Climb up onto the box. Let me measure the foot."

She imagined Jon would have squatted down to measure. But for Bitter, customers stepped up. She stood on the box beside his chair and let him chalk around her feet.

"It's ten shillings, 2 pence, Mrs. Wardrip." Then he frowned. "Seems a lot for such tiny feet. Maybe..."

"The work's the same, isn't it?"

"Less materials, though."

"Well." She wasn't going to argue to pay the full cost. No one would. But she made no effort to bargain him down.

Will had sold the brooch she sent him and returned to her a staggering sum. She'd gone straight to the market in Paxton Downs, a two-hour walk, and filled her tea caddy. She stocked her larder. Then she went back three days later and asked Mr. Filbert, whose shop seemed the most likely, if he could place an order for her for a few books. She had an idea of how to reignite Charlotte's enthusiasm. The purchases made no visible dent in the mound of coins stashed in a box under her bed. So it seemed petty to argue over a few pence's worth of leather.

Bitter pulled at his lip. "I'll ask Jon what he thinks."

"I appreciate it. But I need these boots. I'm willing to pay full price."

"Ha! Promise me you won't ever go alone to a horse trader."

She stepped down from the box.

"Two weeks?" he said. Then hemmed and said, "Maybe three. For you, pay on delivery."

"Why, thank you." It still surprised her that people were ever expected to pay in advance. She was certain Jasper would think she was inventing such a tale. He paid his people on time, meaning no more than three months late. That was how it was *done*.

"Wish they were all like you, Mrs. Wardrip. Make my life easier."

She wished there was a way to make it easier. No matter his good humor, it had to be hard. She stepped to the door.

"Have a good day, Bitter."

"What?"

"Bitter, you idiot."

He laughed. "Good day to you, too."

She had no further business at anyone's cottage but her own. A cold pot of soup awaited her. It wouldn't take long to heat it for supper. If she had her new boots, she might wander off into the countryside, pick mushrooms, or gather flowers, but her feet already hurt.

She slowed her steps and let her thoughts drift.

Little Dan had somehow set fire to the Gowes' chicken coop Sunday morning while Charlotte and Dan were not paying attention. Charlotte had rescued all the birds but one. That, she plucked and cooked—"finished cooking" she explained, relating the story while sipping tea.

Charlotte Gowe was unflappable.

Jasper's voice: *So were the wings on that bird. I have one for you—Dan Gowe is the rare man who looks forward to Sunday morning.*

*One word, Jasper. That's the challenge. To distill to the essence.*

*Hmm. What about this Bitter?*

Bitter was sweet. Kind. Good-looking, too. She would say the poor man was cursed, but he wouldn't agree. He insisted he was blessed. Hadn't God kept him around to look after Nan?

*Jasper: That is diluted, not distilled.*

*But I can't think of one word to encompass it all.*

*Jasper: Admirable?*

*No. Not quite.*

*Admired, then.*

Yes. Bitter, the idiot, was admired. And what did Jasper think of Sherwood?

*Jasper: Laughable? Annoying? Pathetic?*

*That is three.*

*Insignificant.*

*No, that's too cruel.*

Jasper had called Hilyer that once, to his face, so Hazard had said.

*Jasper: Coxcomb*

*Oh, perfect.*

She reached her cottage. Tam had repaired the cobbled walk to her door for her. She'd tried to pay him with a plate of biscuits, but he wouldn't take them. There was nothing wrong with them, she told Jasper in her head. She made very good biscuits. It was simply that he'd had a spare two hours and the men in the church took seriously the command to look after widows. Apparently, God wouldn't count it if Tam took something in return.

She opened the door and stepped inside, still musing. She didn't have a word for Tam. Not dutiful. Or pious. Not even good-hearted. Unfortunately, the word *lumbering* kept coming to mind. She shut the door. The latch fell into place with a thud.

*Lonely is mine*. Or alone. Not fearful, but still waiting, always, to hear footsteps.

*Crispin, piping in: Resilient.*

*Thank you, but you were not invited to play.*

*Jasper, searchingly: And what one word have you for the Earl of Iversley?*

Could she distill what she knew of Jasper to one word?

*Impossible.*

And now, the game was not amusing anymore.

# Chapter Thirteen

Jasper was a terrible moper. Meaning, he did it badly. He was not constitutionally suited to mope. His body would not sit still for it.

Instead, he went about his usual activities. And then, once an hour at least, with no warning, no trigger, he would be seized with an almost unbearable sadness. It spread over him like a wave of nausea. He would have to pause to let it work its way through. Vanessa was gone. Gone. And then it would pass. The feeling would harden away, shrink into a stone that would sink, sink inside him. He was cobbling his innards.

Maybe that was what hardened men. These types of stones. Then they were inured to any future love pains.

Jasper hadn't the fortitude. He could not lie about and mope. Nor had he yet turned into stone. So, he'd spent the afternoon at Tattersalls. Buying carriage horses for Reg.

One had to love Reg, the silly arse. So determined to support himself and his wife on that—what did he call it? A stipend? Reg had been obligated to resign his Cambridge fellowship when he married—University regulations—but the don he worked with wanted him nevertheless and paid the salary out of his own pocket. Reg had Georgiana's dowry, but it seemed he was reluctant to make use of it. Jasper told him he was welcome to keep his allowance, but Reg firmly said no. He was not Jasper's dependent. Which was admirable, in its way.

But for pity's sake. Reg was a Taverston. And his wife was a duke's daughter. When Georgiana said she loved traipsing up and down the streets of Cambridge and didn't mind riding the mail coach to London, Reg *believed* her. Jasper shook his head. He was not accusing Georgiana of lying, or feminine wiles, or not knowing her own head...well, lying maybe. She meant well. But the devil. He'd known Reg longer. His brilliance and obliviousness. Enough was enough.

There was a landau going to rust in the carriage house. Jasper insisted Reg take it. And to come spend the afternoon with him at Tattersalls. He used a wistful, lightly embarrassed smile that even Reg could not mistake for anything but a plea for company. Poor lonely Jasper.

And then, damned if he hadn't enjoyed the experience. He knew horses. The one thing in the world he knew better than Reginald was horses.

He enjoyed it right up until the moment he had to pause, stop chattering, and let himself feel his loss all over again. Reg, bless him, rather aimlessly lifted and examined hooves, felt legs, inspected teeth, and said nothing until Jasper picked up the thread of the conversation where he'd dropped it.

A splendid day, given it all. He was arriving home with enough time to have a bite and change his clothes for the evening. When he would drag Hazard to White's.

Hazard had spent five days letting bruises fade and swellings go down before returning to his own house. He had missed the closing day of Parliament, despite Jasper's urging him to attend. One could not tell he had been beaten unless one looked hard, and men did not look at each other's faces that closely. Usually. Hazard would not go. Hovington, in passing, grumbled that the Viscount was unreliable. Alice must be heartbroken if Hovington repeated that at home.

It was all in a piece with the new timidity Jasper was noticing in his friend. He'd caught him startling at sudden noises. Worse, his wit was off.

There was nothing for it but to cast Hazard into the ring and let him slug his way out. A horrible metaphor under the circumstances. But Jasper had no doubt that, when surrounded by lesser wits at White's, who spouted their conservative opinions accompanied by brandy-scented spittle, Hazard would rally. He just needed a shove.

Jasper entered his home—Lud, his sepulchral castle—feeling just a tad full of himself. Vanessa would poke him in the arm and say a long *"pssshhhhh,"* to let the gas out.

Finley hurried to him, reaching for his walking stick.

"My lord. There is a Mr. Carroll waiting in the study." His nose twitched. "I asked to take his card, but he said he would wait. Should I send him away?"

"Benjamin is here?" His spirits lifted higher.

"He said you sent for him, but—"

"I did. Months ago." He'd offered his old friend the job of steward at Chaumbers. The ship Benjamin had said he would be on, from Canada, had put into harbor two weeks ago, but he wasn't on it. No further word had come, and Jasper had gone from peeved to worried. "I'll go straight up. Did you offer him anything?"

"No, my lord. He—" Whatever Finley had been about to say, he thought better of it. "Shall I bring brandy?"

"Yes." No. He had White's to get through. He couldn't start drinking yet. "No. Coffee will do. Well, no, wait until I send for something." God. He was practically giddy. How absurd of him. This was a man he was *hiring*. Nevertheless, he bounded up the stairs.

He flung open the door. Benjamin sat on one of the least comfortable chairs: uncushioned mahogany with a low back and no arms—they should burn that chair. He rose when Jasper entered the room. He bowed.

"My lord."

Jasper stopped in his tracks. "Mr. Carroll. Thank you for

coming."

"Old Oxford chums" only carried men so far. Jasper could not stop his eyes from picking out details. Benjamin's jacket needed pressing and there was a sheen of wear at the elbows. His boots appeared never to have seen a lick of polish. And there was an odor, a musty odor of sea and fish, that he must have carried from whatever ship he'd been on.

"Thank you for the offer of employment. I hope I am not too late."

"No. Not at all." Then something cracked inside him, and he said, "I simply assumed you were paying me back for all the times I failed to be punctual."

In earlier days, he had left Benjamin waiting. A lot. Jasper did not grin often anymore, but he hadn't forgotten how. Benjamin chewed his lip, then acknowledged the memory with a grin of his own. Jasper waved him into a chair.

"For God's sake, not that one. Sit over there." He took his own chair. He was a good deal taller than Benjamin and didn't want to have this conversation standing. "I admit I was worried. Did you miss *The Prince George*?"

"In a manner of speaking. I took the next ship I could find."

Jasper nodded. "Well, the job is yours. I cannot think of anyone better. And yours was the first name on my brothers' lips as well."

Benjamin looked amused. "Well, maybe that partly explains…" He leaned forward in his chair. "I stopped at the post to see if they were holding anything there for me. There was nothing from you, but there was a package in brown paper, with two pristine-appearing ledgers filled with the tidiest figures I'd ever seen. Two years' worth. And a note from Reg—" He caught himself—"Mr. Taverston, saying they were up to date through June. That if I had any questions…" He chuckled. "He gave me his direction in *Cambridge*."

Jasper laughed. "Yes, well, Reg has not changed. I asked him to put things in order for you and he never does things halfway.

Cambridge is another tale."

He felt the sadness threaten and pushed it, pushed it away.

"I suppose we should do this properly. I'll have Wilkerson draw up a contract for you to look over. Have you a salary in mind?"

"Just pay me what I am worth."

"Very shrewd. All right, I will. You can bring your things here, of course. I'll have a suite opened in the west wing until you go to Chaumbers."

"If it's all the same to you—" Benjamin's eyes grew hooded— "I have let rooms for myself down near the Thames. I would like to acclimate myself back to London." The words sounded rehearsed. But then, the whole thing was awkward. Benjamin used to be invited to 8 Grosvenor Square and to Chaumbers as a guest. Jasper supposed there was some acclimating, on both their parts, to be done.

"Yes, of course."

"So, tell me about the Taverstons!" A clunky transition clumsily delivered.

"I don't know where to start."

"It sounds as though we could spend the day unraveling Mr. Taverston." That was carefully done. *Mr. Taverston.* Jasper pushed back.

"Reg settled in Cambridge after a little private rebellion against the Church of England. He has gone back to the ancient gods," he joked.

Benjamin's eyes widened.

"That, of course, was after marrying my intended fiancée."

Benjamin exploded with laughter. Then he tried to stand. "I'm going back to Canada. In my absence, England has gone mad."

"Not all of it. Crispin is still Crispin. Only now he is Lieutenant Taverston of the King's Army."

"He had just purchased his commission when I left." That sobered his mirth. Jasper's too. "I assume he is doing well?"

"I think so. He doesn't say much about his duties."

Benjamin sobered further. He glanced away. "His health?"

Jasper shrugged. Benjamin had nursed Crispin through a short bout of illness at school, sworn to secrecy until Crispin recovered. Jasper would have lugged him back home again if he'd known. "He does not speak of that either. But he looked well when I last saw him."

At that, Benjamin's expression softened. "I'm sorry about the earl. I—he was always very good to me."

Father was civil. He made a point of it.

"Thank you. It was difficult. Seeing his decline."

"And your mother? Is she well?"

"She's coping." He sighed. "I think sons never truly understand how much of a mother's life is simply coping."

Benjamin eyed him strangely, and Jasper thought perhaps he was sharing too much. But he hadn't said anything, really. Then Benjamin looked at his hands. "And your sister? I imagine her coming out was a triumph. Who did she wed?"

"Ah, Olivia. No, I'm afraid she has had the worst of it. My father's illness was lengthy. She did not debut when she should have. And then, this year, too, she could not. She is in mourning. But next year…" He tried to chuckle. "I believe all the swains are holding their breaths waiting, and I will have to walk around with pistols."

He waited for the jest. His pistols would frighten no one. But Benjamin did not look entertained. He looked stiff.

"Oh, God, Benjamin!" Was that why he would not take apartments in Jasper's home? "She's not carrying a torch for you."

"No. Of course not." The man's face turned crimson.

"It has been years! She was a child. I know she embarrassed you, but—"

"Not embarrassed. It was flattering…in an embarrassing way. She is a force of nature, your sister. And I liked her. Who wouldn't? I hated to hurt her."

"Well, that is very noble. But she was a child. You needn't

punish yourself for a hurt she has long forgotten."

Benjamin nodded. "All right then. Good. I know it's foolish of me, but I am relieved."

"Not foolish. Kind-hearted." Jasper shook his head. Of all the idiotic... "We've covered the Taverstons. I want to hear all about your adventures."

"Except for you," Benjamin said. "I suppose the fact that your brother married your fiancé explains the lack of a countess?"

"In part." He saw Benjamin's curiosity. "That tale would require a full night to recount and a bottle of brandy a piece."

"Not brandy." The man snickered. "I smuggled back some whiskey from the American colonies."

"We may not call them the colonies, I don't think." There was a war there too. Colonies they may be again. Though when he'd asked Crispin, he merely shook his head *no*. "Is it any good?"

"It will burn a hole down through your boots."

But would it melt stone?

"Another night then. We'll catch up on each other's lives. If I had known of such a delightful prospect, I would not have made plans for this evening." He could not invite Benjamin along to White's. Unfortunately.

"No, tonight will not do."

Jasper started to rise but saw something in his old friend's face. A hesitation. He lowered himself back down. "I am horribly rude. I was taken aback by seeing you. I meant to send for coffee. And sandwiches. I have no idea how long you were waiting but I'm starving. I imagine you—"

"No, I cannot stay." He cleared his throat rather decisively. "Iversley, I must make a clean breast of this before...well, before." He looked strangled and pushed out the words. "I became rather embroiled...what I mean to say is there is a child. Not mine!" he added hurriedly, reddening. "But, well, yes mine. Lud. I practiced this, and now I'm muddling it."

"Take your time." He knew his tone had become icy, but what the devil was "mine but not mine" supposed to mean?

Benjamin's voice shook. "I had a business partner. My judgment is usually sounder, but, well, that's unimportant. We went to the interior. It seemed like an adventure, I suppose. He was accompanied by his wife and daughter. I will summarize: the couple died. It was tragic. For all I wished him to the devil by that point…well." He drew a breath. "We were in the middle of no place I could pinpoint on a map."

"We?"

"Myself and the child." He swallowed hard. Jasper did too. Benjamin raised his eyes. "It was terrifying."

Jasper nodded, terrified for him.

"The child…she became rather attached to me."

What did one say to something like this?

"I would think so."

"I managed to get back to Halifax. Her grandparents were there. I located them."

He glossed over details in a way that Jasper, who thought he had done a good job glossing, could only marvel at. They would have to break out that whiskey one day soon.

"They wanted nothing to do with her. Their own grandchild. And I would be damned if I would force the girl on them."

"You did the right thing. Unless, of course, you think they will come to regret—"

"Damn them if they do!" He made a visible effort to control himself. "I think it very unlikely." He shrugged. "And they will never be able to find her."

Jasper let out a long breath of his own. "Tell me what you need."

"Employment. You cannot know… you can't know. Your letter was like a gift from God."

"If so, you cannot thank me. I needed a steward. What else?"

Benjamin ground his teeth. Then said, stiff with wounded dignity, "If you could provide me an advance."

Jasper remembered his old friend's pride had always been prickly. Benjamin was too aware of the fact that he was a commoner, mixing with gentlemen. He seemed to believe he was more tolerated than welcomed, when nothing was farther from the truth. How like the man to take in a waif—likely saving her life in the process—and yet be embarrassed to ask for help. It embarrassed *Jasper* to think how much it cost Benjamin to ask, when granting the request was of so little consequence.

Jasper rose, went to his desk, and pulled out a slip of paper. He scribbled a draft, saying, "Take this to Coutts."

"Do I speak to anyone in particular?"

Jasper waved away the question. "No. There is no need. Anyone there will see to it." Arrogant but true. "What else?"

"If I could have two days to settle in before I begin?"

"Two is enough?"

Benjamin nodded. Jasper did not press the issue. He knew this was hard. They used to be drinking friends. This was hard on Jasper too. He was bewildered on how to proceed.

"Her name is Hannah. She is but two." Benjamin sounded bemused. And tender. "She has curls."

Jasper nodded. "Thank you for telling me. I didn't know how much I was permitted to ask. Where is she now?"

Benjamin stood "With my landlady." He looked weary, but at the same time, unburdened. Lesser burdened. He waved the draft and then put it in his pocket. "Thank you, Iversley. The woman has been grand, considering, but it will relieve her, I suspect, to see me return with the ready." He smiled weakly. "I don't think she believed me when I said I had a job waiting with an earl."

"Ha!" Jasper scratched his nose. There must be more he could do. "I'd like to meet Hannah. Will you bring her?"

"At some point. But I am not going to take advantage of your generosity. I know you'll make it too easy to do so. She likes attention. I cannot work while dandling her on my knee. I'll hire a nanny."

"Have you someone in mind?"

He shook his head. "I disembarked this morning. But I imagine there is an agency."

"Wait." Jasper went back to his desk for another slip of paper. He wrote a direction. "Mrs. Lockwood." He walked the slip to Benjamin. "Tell her I sent you. She'll have a few names."

Benjamin's lips twitched. "And you know where to locate nannies because…?"

He sighed. "Because elderly ladies at tea parties like to corner me and chatter my ear off. Because I always listen as though I am interested. Because I am polite."

"Yes, I recall that about you," Benjamin said, suppressing a smile. "You are very polite." Then the smile broke through. "This Mrs. Lockwood will be thrilled you thought of her. I will have half a dozen perfect candidates at the door before supper. My only difficulty will be choosing amongst them." He gave Jasper's arm a light punch. "*You* are as annoying as ever."

Jasper made his face stern. "Two days, Carroll. Two days and your arse better be parked behind a desk sorting my accounts." Then, for good measure, he opened the door and said, "George, have Finley see Mr. Carroll out." He added sotto voce, "Bring the whiskey when you come."

When the door shut, he regrouped. Hazard next.

But first, he had to sit down. Duty…friends…they were not distraction enough. The ache was still there.

# Part 4
## There Are Obstacles
### March 1809
### London

# Chapter Fourteen

Vanessa Wardrip trusted Lord Jasper Taverston. She did.

So, when she awoke the morning after the dreadful night at the play—where she had been humiliated in front of his friends, *by* his friends, and then been chased from the theater by her ghosts—to find the bed beside her cold and empty, she did not doubt Lord Taverston. She would not allow herself to doubt him.

When long minutes turned to long hours, she had to tamp down dread. That *I-am-left-alone* dread. Jasper's friend, that wonderful man Lord Haslet, would not permit Jasper to call Hilyer out over a confrontation that had not even taken place. *Dear God, don't let that confrontation ever take place.*

She'd made herself rise, dress, send for breakfast, eat a few bites of dry toast. Then she'd given in to her fears and crawled back into bed. He found her there. Not sleeping. Just waiting. He made love to her so gently, so tenderly—in the bed with the pillows arranged just so—that after juddering through tension to release, she lashed out. She didn't want his pity.

"Pity!" He stared at her, confused. "Vanessa, I can assure you this is not pity."

"What then?" He had never treated her with such kid gloves before.

He blinked at her, then shook his head. "Not pity."

He rose and went to his washstand to splash water on his head, then took up a wet cloth to rub over himself. Her eyes followed, hypnotized by the beauty of him. The long taut line from ankle to hip. The muscled thighs. The graceful curve of his buttock with the symmetrical hollows on either side. She liked to rest her hands there, to feel the working of him as he moved inside her. She'd learned to sense the moment when his control deserted him. When he gave over to his need. In those last few moments, she liked to imagine *she* was anchoring *him*.

He threw the cloth into the basin and came back to her, brows knotted.

"I think, protectiveness."

It startled her. He'd been pondering all the while she had been ogling.

"Vanessa, I want to be your knight. I know that sounds patronizing, but I recognize it as a fault of mine rather than any perceived deficiency in you."

"What on earth are you talking about?"

"I want to take care of you. I want to do battle for you." He winced. "That must sound practically blasphemous."

"It sounds terrifying."

"Well, you needn't be frightened. I'm not a violent man. I suppose I could be if there were a need, but I would not lower myself to violence against a decrepit stinking pot of flesh like Hilyer."

She breathed a little more easily. She believed him.

"I'm more calculating," he went on, sitting on the edge of the bed, absently pulling a blanket over his lap. "He will rue the day, Vanessa, but…"

"But what?"

"This won't be easy for you. I don't see any way through this but to proceed. And I know you can do it. I've seen you."

"Jasper, you've lost me." She shook her head. "What is it that I am supposed to do?"

"You can't let them shame you. Firstly, we have to be seen in company together. I'm not parading you or flaunting you. I would never. But we cannot appear ashamed. You see that, don't you?"

She nodded slowly. "It's difficult. Much more so for me than for you."

"Differently difficult. It hurts me to see you hurt." He waited for her to grant him her understanding. Then he said, "But I was so proud of you last night. When those two idiots burst in on us, you cut Carleton the way a countess would have done."

"I cannot imagine a countess ever having the need. One would think she would simply ignore."

"Maybe." He stood up again and picked up his shirt from where he had dropped it, to pull it on over his head. He cast about for his drawers, found them, and stepped into them. Pantaloons next. He was buttoning his fall by the time he had reasoned out his answer. "It would depend upon the slight. But ignoring Carleton when he was drooling on you would not have been as effective. You disregarded him. It was superb. It defused some of my fury. Even saying this now makes me understand I can't truly go into battle for you. I have to go into battle *with* you."

"Jasper, I'm willing." She shook her head. "But I don't know that I am able."

"I'll help you. Trust me. We will start with Carleton. You have no reason to believe this, but he's not a terrible person. He can't hold his drink. I've told him so before, but once he starts, he has no voice in his head telling him that it's time to stop."

"Do you?"

"Yes, of course." He flushed. "I haven't always listened to it, but I do know when I've had enough. I will give oath that Carleton has only a vague idea that he was insulting last night. And he has spent the day praying he was not *too* insulting."

"Will you tell him that he crossed the line?"

"No. I will give him the cut direct. At White's. He will be as mortified as he made you."

"So you will break with him? But you say he's not a terrible person. Jasper, I don't want for you to break with all your friends."

"I won't." He smirked. Then he crossed the room to her dressing table for one of the fresh neckcloths kept in the drawer. He draped it around his neck and came back to her. "Carleton might try to apologize a second time. I will cut him again. He'll be frantic. Hazard will take him aside. He'll make him see that the apology must be to you."

"Oh." She felt chilled. Jasper might be giving this too much thought. "And am I to accept or refuse?"

"Accept, if you will. But with that same magnificent frostiness. Tell him it was no account. You understand that he was 'not himself.'"

She smiled a little. "I am to pronounce the man unable to hold his liquor." Then she laughed. "You don't think that is too cruel?"

"You'll be doing him a favor. Drink will ruin him if he lets it."

It all sounded so clever. Too clever for her. She shook her head. "I cannot carry it off. I'll be too aware of myself playing a role."

"Ah, but I will stage it. I'll allow Carleton to pay a call. Only you, I, and Hazard will be here. Even if you don't pull it off perfectly, when Hazard repeats the tale, he'll present it as though you did."

She considered it. She didn't know why Viscount Haslet would be so kind to her. Perhaps he enjoyed the chance to be malicious and kind in one turn.

"Is it worth all the effort simply to win Carleton back into the fold?"

"Unfortunately, Carleton matters. His brother is the Duke of Dorchester. Moreover, he will be an example. I wish I could say that was the first and last slight you will endure, but there will be others. Still, I daresay it won't take too long to put a stop to it."

But it would not put a stop to it.

"Jasper, Hilyer will not come crawling to apologize. And he is a marquess. And there were marriage contracts."

He took her hands and rubbed them between his palms. "I went to see Wilkerson this morning. My solicitor, if you recall."

"Yes. Will said he was tough."

"And Wilkerson said he hoped to never cross pens with young Collingswood again. Vanessa, there was a marriage contract, but no marriage. No banns were read. You never stood up with Hilyer in front of witnesses. If he intended to take legal action, he would have had to take it against your father. It's likely too late to do so now. At any rate, he can't touch you. You wed someone else. And he can hardly sue Henry." He grimaced. "I'm sorry. That was not meant to be flippant."

"He can't sue you?"

"What grounds could he possibly have?"

"I don't know. But you must understand, I feel like a piece of property. First my father's. Now yours. Hilyer must feel…" ausea swept over her. "Entitled to his share."

Jasper flushed. "Hilyer has no claim, none, on my mistress. No matter what prior claim he may think he had on a wife."

"Well, that's fine, Jasper. But it addresses only the legality. Hilyer can still humiliate me. Us. And he has powerful friends who could make trouble."

"Hilyer has not a single friend in all of Society. He has a few hangers-on, but they are not worthy men. And they would desert him without a moment's hesitation if faced with—well, this is blatantly arrogant, but they won't wish to incur the displeasure of the lords of Iversley. My father has far more influence than Hilyer. Reginald inspires a kind of amused awe wherever he goes. And Crispin is not a person men care to cross."

"And you?"

Jasper shrugged. "I have vastly more friends." Then he rolled his neckcloth and tied it in a simple knot, done perfectly. "When I am done with him, he will be cut off from Society altogether. He won't show his face in London again."

※※※

Jasper snubbed Carleton at White's. It did not take doing twice. The next morning there was an enormous bouquet of lilies delivered to her door, with a card, humbly begging an audience.

She passed Jasper the card. He glanced at it, then nodded.

Vanessa laughed. "Oh, don't look so smug. What next?"

"We will permit him to call next week. That is generous; it should be two weeks. But I believe he is honestly contrite. Tonight, if the weather holds clear, I will take you for a carriage ride in the park."

She gritted her teeth and nodded. "I'll wear my brown dress and the yellow bonnet."

The point, after all, was to show her face.

Jasper disappeared during the days, attending to his usual cares or to his new schemes. He wouldn't say. But he did have plans for their evenings.

The first, he drove her down one of the less popular paths in Hyde Park where they would be seen but he could still let his horses clip along. At that pace, it was less obvious that no one greeted them. He was unperturbed, greeting none of them either. Instead, he focused on his ribbons and on her. And it was a lovely evening for a ride.

Jasper said, "Lilies are not your favorite flower. That would be bluebells. And hollyhocks make you sneeze."

"You carry two handkerchiefs in your breast pocket. One large and one small. I have yet to discover why."

"A gentleman always carries a dainty handkerchief to offer a lady if a need should arise. But that little wisp of cloth does not suffice for my nasal needs."

"Ah. A man of mystery no more."

They were no longer strangers. Yet he did not know all of her secrets. And despite his evident openness, she suspected he must have some as well.

He said, "You butter your toast out to the very edges. And lick your fingers when you think I am not looking."

She slid a glance at him. "I lick my fingers when I know you *are* looking."

He laughed. Not to show the world the delightful time they were having, but because he was having a delightful time, she was sure of it. After all, so was she.

The second night, she thought she noted a hint of impatience. When they returned home the third night, cold and drenched from the sleeting rain they had ridden in, he was exasperated. There were so few people in the park, that it was painfully obvious they were being ignored by those there.

"Jasper, it isn't important."

"It is. But I know what went wrong." He huffed. Then confessed, "There were a few lines in today's *Morning Post*. There will not be again."

She wanted to swear like a soldier. Instead, she said, "What did they say?"

"Nothing that bears repeating. It was vulgar."

"Of course it was vulgar. It was the *Post*. But it will hardly shock me."

His gaze slid past her, and she noticed he was reddening.

He recited, "It has come to our attention that the daughter of a notably moneyed cit prefers a handsome bed to a purchased title."

She felt faint and hoped she hadn't gone pale. She'd said it wouldn't shock her. "At least it is accurate."

"It was heavy-handed. I can't imagine Hilyer is pleased with it." He tossed his head. "The people who write these things are generally cleverer. He likely didn't pay them enough."

Jasper was peeved at being called a *handsome bed*. How…revealing.

"Well," he went on, "we have taken the carriage rides as far as they can go. Tomorrow afternoon, we stroll."

"Walking? Past people who turn up their noses and avert

their eyes?" She didn't know if she could do it.

"They will acknowledge us. I'm bringing the heavy guns."

>>><<<

THE EARL OF Iversley descended from his gleaming black coach. Old-fashioned and boxy, it was substantial enough to require six horses to draw. Vanessa and Jasper had been awaiting him at the entrance to Kensington Park, but he hadn't kept them long. Crowds were milling about. They stopped milling to observe.

The earl held himself erect, though he gripped his walking stick tightly. It was more than decoration. His hair was a faded blond version of Jasper's. He had the same color eyes, a vivid blue, but his were more piercing. More like Lieutenant Taverston's. And if Jasper's demeanor hinted at friendly arrogance, this man's oozed it.

"Jasper."

"Father. May I introduce to you Mrs. Henry Wardrip?"

He turned to her. She curtsied and he waited, then said, "Mrs. Wardrip. My condolences on your loss. Jasper tells me your husband served on the Peninsula."

"He did, my lord."

He glanced down the long grassy path. "The gauntlet, eh?" Then, to her surprise, he offered his arm. Of course, she took it, and he began to walk. And to talk.

"I don't suppose you've met General Wellesley, no? Strange chap. Strange. I don't deny his military brilliance."

"Crispin wouldn't let you," Jasper said, falling in alongside.

"Ha. No. But when I was in Ireland..." He paused and bowed to the couple who were walking towards them, unavoidably. "Whetherby. Lady Wetherby. Lovely day to be about, isn't it? My son and his friend, Mrs. Wardrip, invited me for a stroll." He chuckled. "He says I don't walk enough. I think my physician pays *him*."

They laughed politely. Then they were obligated to include Vanessa in their goodbyes as they moved along.

And so it went, with a succession of aristocrats out for a stroll, all yielding to the Earl of Iversley. It was not arrogance, she decided. Or only partly arrogance. It was power. And she could see where Jasper had gotten his charm.

He didn't require much from her. A word or two here and there. He pointed out a few brown stubs of plants lining the way and she obligingly sniffed them. Although there were no flowers, the dormant twigs had a fresh scent of their own. Jasper added his part, but he was deferential. It was nice to see him deferential for a change. And Vanessa was acknowledged. Not warmly. Certainly not with a lovely-to-meet-you-you-must-come-to-tea. But she was acknowledged.

They reached the end of the path. They paused. The earl looked over his shoulder.

"And down again?" He sounded faintly winded.

Jasper said, "I don't think that's necessary. I had my carriage sent around to meet us here. We can drop you back at yours." He touched his father's arm and smiled. "And thank you."

The earl nodded. "Well, it was…fun. Haven't done anything like that in a while."

"Thank you, my lord," Vanessa said.

She saw Jasper's carriage pulling towards them. The earl relinquished her, and she took Jasper's arm.

"Ah, wait." Jasper gestured with his chin to a young lady hurrying in their direction. Hurrying. Hand on her hat, skirts billowing behind her. It was possible that she was running in public.

"Oh," she said, patting her heart as she reached them. "I'm glad I caught you."

She was a curious woman, perhaps Jasper's age, with pale eyes and a square jaw that made her interesting rather than pretty. Vanessa's first reaction was petty: that the lady was hoping to catch Jasper. But she turned her pale eyes on Vanessa.

"You are Mrs. Wardrip? You followed the drum?"

Vanessa nodded, perhaps gaping a little. This was not how introductions were done.

"Rose Posonby," the lady said.

Vanessa could not have been more surprised if the woman had stuck out a hand to shake.

Jasper said, "Lady Posonby, permit me to introduce Mrs. Henry Wardrip."

"Slow out the gate, Lord Taverston. As usual." Then she smiled at Vanessa. "Please call on me. Or permit me to call on you. I have so many questions, I could burst."

⇉⇇

They arrived home. Jasper could not stop smiling. Vanessa found herself smiling too.

"Your father is…exactly what I would expect your father to be."

"I'm very fortunate. I knew he would agree to help, but in truth, I thought I would have to apply more pressure than it took. My mother, a wonderful woman in her own right, don't misunderstand, will not be pleased."

"No. Of course not."

"I don't expect you will ever meet her." He sounded apologetic.

"Of course not." He didn't mention his sister, Olivia. Meeting her was so far beyond the realm of possibility, he did not bother. Vanessa refused to let that hurt.

He tossed his hat on the rack and rested his walking stick against the wall. Then he spotted something on the correspondence table and frowned. A few letters meant for him found their way here instead of his parents' home. She didn't know why he looked so alarmed.

He picked it up and tore it open.

"God."
"What?"

He handed it over to her without speaking. There was only one word on the page. He must have recognized the handwriting.

EXPLAIN

She looked at him, questioning.
He said, "Crispin."

# Chapter Fifteen

Jasper felt the rebuke as if Crispin had appeared in the flesh to slap sense into him. He stared at the letter and repeated, muttering, "Crispin."

Here he had been congratulating himself on his success. Vanessa's success. He didn't think she understood just how much of a triumph the day had been. Especially after those lines had appeared in the *Post,* designed to make a mockery of everyone involved.

And Father! Jasper had never loved him so much. When he'd presented the dilemma, Father sighed and said, "Hilyer is a dog." He agreed to publicly acknowledge his son's paramour—no small favor to ask—all while sparing Jasper the moralizing that was a father's prerogative.

And Lady Posonby. What a stroke. How had he not thought to approach her first? The woman was an unabashed bluestocking, but her birth was impeccable. She made it her life's work to defy societal conventions. And she led a small, tough cadre of like-minded daughters of the ton. Vanessa would have friends. She would probably have to spend time reading poetry or Wollstonecraft, but if she could face down Napoleon's finest, she could hold her own with Rose.

If that little peep in the *Post* was Hilyer's worst, they had already won. But Jasper had one more card to play. The following night, Hazard would be hosting a private party at Brooks's. His club. He invented something to celebrate. Hazard was choosier about his friends than Jasper was. As a consequence, men clambered to be included in his set. Hazard invited many of them, even the few peers who still regarded the marquess as worth knowing. He did not invite the marquess, who would arrive at Brooks's to find the gaming room essentially empty and the doors of the party swing back, closed to him. Jasper, not even a member of Brooks's, would be there. The Prince Regent as well. A decided coup to obtain that commitment. Jasper could not imagine how Hazard had finagled it—unless he had lent Prinny more money than he admitted.

If Hilyer blustered—and he would—he would find himself tossed out of his own club on his ear.

The devil. Jasper had been so busy congratulating himself on the way he was "protecting" Vanessa, that he'd lost sight of the reason she needed protection. Crispin reminded him. He had taken a grieving widow and made her his paramour.

Vanessa looked white about the mouth.

"Why does he feel he deserves an explanation? Is he your confessor? Is he mine?"

"I don't think being angry with Crispin serves any purpose," Jasper said wearily. "He sees through defensiveness. He exploits it."

"Defensiveness? Jasper, aren't you the one who keeps saying we must not be ashamed?"

"Yes. Yes, and we should not. You, especially, should not." He heaved an enormous sigh and confided in her. "It is important to me to have my brothers' respect."

"That's only natural, but—"

"No." He laughed a little. "I think it is unnaturally important to me. They are—" She waited for him to find the words. "Talented," he finished. "It is as though God asked, at my conception, which talents I would most wish to have, and then he allotted them to my brothers. Which is actually a wonderful God gift." His jaw ached from clenching. "It is so very humbling."

"You cannot tell me you have not been gifted with enough."

"Reginald is brilliant. Eye-wateringly, stare-at-the-sun brilliant. He is six years younger than me, and I swear, by the time I was twelve, I knew not to challenge him on anything factual. Or for that matter, mythological. But I don't particularly envy him that peculiarity." He sniffed. "No, I am jealous of his aim."

"His what?"

"His aim. Gentlemen are supposed to be able to shoot. Vanessa, I cannot keep my eyes open when I pull a trigger. I have a terrible tendency to jerk my arm at the last moment. God alone knows where the bullets end up. Even Olivia laughs at me."

"Jasper, that's ridiculous."

"Yes, and I know it." He didn't want her to think he was merely whining. "I could see the fun in it. But Reg, who is nearsighted to boot, can put a bullet through the center of a target at fifty paces. Probably farther. And he never trained himself. He plucked up my father's pistol the first day he was permitted to shoot with us and boom."

"For Heaven's sake." Her lips twitched as if she was picturing his dismay when it occurred.

"And then there is Crispin. He should have been Father's heir."

"You can't say that. You are the very image of the earl."

"He has authority."

"*You* have authority. You just wield it more nicely."

"And he plays the piano. By ear. He will look at sheet music, out of habit, I suppose, but he doesn't need it. And he plays with an emotion that brings my mother to tears."

"That's hard to picture."

"I know. Which is also annoying. He does not give the impression of being a musician. Meanwhile, I cannot even sing. My family will not even tolerate my humming."

At that, Vanessa laughed. "Yes, well, I have heard you."

He gave her a weak smile. "These are but small examples. I

look at them, with their many talents, and I look at myself…sometimes I wonder why they don't scorn me."

"Jasper!"

"That is self-pity, I know. Or you may accuse me of false modesty if you wish. I know I have gifts." His lip curled deprecatingly. "I am handsomer." Then he shook himself. "The devil, Vanessa. You must want to slap me. I'm thrown off balance because Crispin just did slap me. I don't owe him an explanation. Of course, I don't. Nevertheless, I'll hie off to the drawing room and try to compose some sort of response."

<hr />

A PILE OF crumpled foolscap in the bin beside the leather-topped rosewood writing table testified to Jasper's inability, over the course of the next three hours, to find an answer to Crispin's single word. Moreover, the brandy bottle was drained. There had only been two glassfuls in it, and he was sensible enough not to call for another. But damn. Why was this so hard?

He didn't owe Crispin an explanation. But he owed one to himself. And he could not come up with one except that he had been captivated by Vanessa. Which was not enough.

When he heard the knocker on the front door below, he was relieved before he even knew what distraction it might bring. Then he heard Hazard's voice and felt downright elated. Vanessa brought him to the drawing room.

"Hazard wishes to speak with you, Jasper."

"He's always welcome. Come in, Haz. I'm sorry but I've finished off the brandy."

"Ah. That answers my question then."

Jasper wrinkled his brow. "Which is?"

Hazard glanced at Vanessa.

"She may hear anything you have to say," Jasper said.

Vanessa said, "Thank you, but I think I would prefer to leave you two alone." She backed out and closed the door.

"She has been holding up very well," Hazard noted.

"She has. Better than I am, at the moment."

"What did Crispin say to inspire you to empty the brandy bottle?"

"Ha! Not much. What did he say to you?"

Hazard pulled a letter from his jacket. "Only requested that I give this to you, but not until I had ascertained that you had read his previous note."

"He must have written them sequentially and the order mattered."

Shaking his head, Hazard handed over the missive. "One of these days, one of your brother's blunderbusses will blow up in his face. I don't wish to be there to see it."

"I doubt it will be this one. Not when Crispin is so thoroughly right."

"I'm surely not the first to say your brother is an impressive man. But if I may, I'll be the first to say his moral outrage is wearisome. Don't take it so much to heart."

Jasper ignored that and started to break the seal.

"Jasper, a moment." Hazard looked pensive. He held his hands low, in front of him, fingers entwined. "You know, I suspect he is here. Crispin. In London. Your letter was wrapped in mine, delivered by hand, not by post. He was here last night or early this morning. I can't imagine why he would be sneaking around like this."

It irritated Jasper to think Crispin might be in London. He could have done his scolding in person, without all this drama.

"Anyone could have delivered it."

"Yes, but letters back and forth to the Peninsula do not move this fast."

Jasper tried counting weeks in his head. Surely there had been time enough for Crispin to hear that Lord Taverston had taken a mistress, a pretty war widow. And for Crispin to fire off a one-word response to him and a letter to Hazard. Hadn't there been?

"Maybe he is here. He carries dispatches sometimes." Jasper swore under his breath. "If he's here on Wellesley's behalf, he's busy. He won't be thrilled to have to deal with me as well."

Hazard made a sound through his nose. "He doesn't *have* to deal with you." He sauntered to the door, then muttered, "Makes me glad I'm an only child."

⁂

*J.—Never mind. What's done is done. I understand you have marshaled your considerable forces and will soon erase H. from your world. Bravo. However. Your world is tiny and your weapons paltry. You don't simply wound a dangerous creature. You must go in for the kill. (Metaphorically speaking.) You must destroy this letter. It is damning and you should not have it in your possession. Now—the army cannot function without rum. One hundred barrels, recently opened, were found to contain faintly rum-scented water. I suspect there will be more. You may guess how W. took the news. In short, there is a chain leading back to our friend. Use this. Frighten the blood from his veins. Mention his concerns in Ireland. Lest you shun blackmail, etc., don't be an arse. We are dealing with treason. My dispatches are on their way higher up. Meantime—H. is nervous. Make him more so. He has gold and a cache of military secrets (ha!) that he will, should he be forced to leave England, take to France. If we try to arrest him here, there are those who will shield him. H. is too stupid to have concocted this alone. We need to catch him with both feet offshore. Make him run. Make him run and we will catch him.*

*—Yours very humbly, etc.,—C.*

*P.S. I do apologize for the* Morning Post. *It is piquing to see idols fall.*

The devil. The very devil. Jasper dropped his head into his hands. What was Crispin digging himself into? Then he rubbed his face hard. If Crispin got himself shot...playing at espionage...

He rose and walked to the table, stuck the letter into the globe of the lamp, and watched it burn.

Make Hilyer run? What the hell, Crispin? Was this a game? Some sort of test? What if he failed? Crispin's instructions were not very explicit.

And his irony. *Bravo. Idols fall. Very humbly yours.* Damn him! At least Jasper knew he was not, thank God, as arrogant as Crispin.

He sat a moment. Stewing. But then he could not help snickering, picturing his brother—face scrunched and tip of the tongue between his teeth, as when he used to attempt his abysmal poetry—in the midst of whatever all he was embroiled in, taking time out to compose an *on dit* for the *Post*. Jasper should have recognized the handiwork. Crispin was not good at everything.

But damn him. Damn him for dragging them all into this. They had all better hope he was good at whatever he was playing at now.

# Chapter Sixteen

I N THE MUSIC room down the hall from where Jasper and Hazard were meeting, Vanessa played a mournful sonata much too loudly.

*What a strange day. What a very strange day.*

"Ouch! What did that pianoforte ever do to you?"

She looked over her shoulder to find Hazard slouched in the doorway.

"I am attempting not to eavesdrop." She let the music soften appropriately.

After a moment, he said, "That's very pretty."

"Thank you." She kept an eye on him, glancing back and forth. It was not a difficult piece and it felt rude to turn away completely.

"Jasper did say you were welcome to stay," he pointed out.

"Jasper may permit me into his confidences, but whatever you came to say might have been yours. He put you in an awkward position."

A smile brightened his face and he straightened from his slouch. "How remarkable! My dear, we do not do *discretion* here in the ton."

She brought Pleyel's *Adagio* to a premature close and turned.

"Is he all right?"

Hazard shrugged. *"He* is. How well do you know Crispin?"

"Lieutenant Taverston? Not well at all."

"Yet from the little I have pieced together, he saved you at Corunna."

"Yes, and I used to wonder why. What made me special. But I have started to suspect that I am not. I think rather in those final desperate days, Lieutenant Taverston ran around saving everyone that he could. It is simply that my story is the only one that I know."

"A fascinating theory. And very likely correct. And now you may be irked that having saved you, he feels he is entitled to a say in how your salvation turns out."

"That is also a fascinating theory. And possibly correct. I'm finding it difficult to be irked and grateful at the same time."

"And that, I would wager, answers your question: How is Jasper? Irked and grateful. Maybe toss in guilty too."

Guilt came too close to shame. Which they were not permitted to feel.

"So may I assume you brought Jasper more word from Lieutenant Taverston?"

She gestured to a chair, so as not to leave him standing in the doorway, but he shook his head.

"Do you suppose you might call him Crispin? Every time you say Lieutenant Taverston, I have to pause a moment and think who you mean."

Vanessa stifled her laugh. "I hear his name so often I fear if he were to appear I would call him Crispin to his face."

"Are you afraid of committing a *faux pas*?"

"Yes, very."

"Well, you are doing very well. The earl was impressed. As am I. And I am much harder to impress."

"Why you are so nice to me?"

"I don't know." He reached into his waistcoat for a snuffbox. "I suppose there are some people it is impossible to be mean to." He sniffed. Then sneezed. Then he dabbed beneath his nose with a handkerchief. "Or maybe I am fascinated by the saga of the

Taverstons and your recent entry into the tale has me agog."

"So back to the tale. You did bring more word from Crispin."

"Yes. But I don't know what the word is. It was a letter that I left with Jasper."

She sighed. Frustrated. She supposed Jasper would show her the letter, but she was wearying of their brotherly chest-thumping. "Explain" in all capital letters. Good Lord.

"I hope that doesn't mean he'll take another three hours agonizing over his response."

"Vain hope. It must, of course, be composed just so."

"I think," she said grumpily, "he should simply not respond."

"The cut direct? Via correspondence?" He chuckled. "You *are* worthy of a spot at the Taverston gaming table. You must, of course, meet Reginald next. He's the sanest of the lot."

"Sanest? Jasper portrays him as some sort of maniacal genius."

"He is. But still. The sanest of the lot." Hazard paused as though considering whether to go on. "He is off at school now. Which is fortunate for him. When those two truly go at it, Reg steps into the breach as peacemaker and often catches the brunt."

She regarded him a moment. In all of Jasper's wide acquaintance, there was an inner circle, and Hazard was clearly in it. But how did he fit? Was he an impartial observer or something more?

"How long have you known them? The Taverstons?"

"Oh, for years and years. I am like the *older* older brother they never had." He drummed his fingers against the doorframe. "He adores you, you know." He looked away. "Well, I am off. People to see."

⇉⇇

VANESSA CREPT INTO the drawing room to see if she could help.

"Can I bring you anything, Jasper? Something to eat or—" She sniffed. "What is burning?"

"Nothing," he said. Too quickly. And the look on his face—

like she'd caught him pinching a maid.

She narrowed her eyes. "Hazard stopped to say his goodbyes. He told me he'd brought you another missive from Crispin."

"Did he?" He snapped the words.

"I meant to say Lieutenant Taverston," she said, flustered by his ill grace. "Hazard complained it baffled him when I called him that. But I will not—"

"Don't be silly." He laughed. Or tried to. "I don't care what you call him."

She'd never seen Jasper so nervous. He shouldn't let his brother rattle him so.

"What does he say now?" She held out her hand for the letter, though, curiously, she didn't see one in his possession.

"Just more of the same." His eyes skittered away from hers.

Jasper was—oh! He was lying to her! And she definitely smelled something burning.

"Did you...Jasper, how childish!"

He started.

"You burned Crispin's letter!" She could hear her own voice rising with disbelief as she cast about for the source of the odor. The bin was overflowing with crumpled paper. The hearth was cold. She spotted the lamp. The grimed globe. An appalled laugh burst from her mouth. "In the lamp, Jasper? Really? In the lamp?"

"Well," he said, pulling at his earlobe, "I-I was angry. He can be irritating."

"You two are ridiculous. What did he say—that made you angry enough to *burn* his letter?"

His jaw was working. He didn't want to tell her. Oh, this was too much.

"Then don't tell me, Jasper. I won't command you to *explain*."

"He sent the notice into the *Post*," Jasper blurted. "It was him."

She stared. "Crispin did?" That was hurtful. It was a *hurtful* thing to do.

"Yes, well, but then he regretted it. He apologized. Of course, I was furious, apology or no. And, yes, it was childish to burn the letter, but…" He ran out of excuses.

"But you didn't want me to see it." Now he was even trying to shield her from Crispin. Or maybe protect Crispin. Maybe he didn't want her to see how malicious his brother could be.

He gave a small, tight nod. "You shouldn't be caught in the middle of our squabbles."

"You're squabbling about me. That is somewhat more than being caught in the middle."

"But we have stopped. That is, I'm pretty sure we've stopped. We were both angry. We are both contrite. That's how these things usually end."

Wouldn't that be lovely.

"I hope so. Because I'm tired. It is so much effort, Jasper. And now to see the two of you at each other's throats. I can't bear it." She saw concern flash across his face. "I'm not saying I regret it. I'm not saying that I wish anything different. Except…except this constantly being made to feel in the wrong."

He stood and came to her, then put his arms around her. She breathed in starch and soap, a hint of brandy, the wool of his jacket. Comfort. Security. Even when she was angry with him, he made her feel safe.

"The wrong was done to you, not by you." He kissed her temple. "It will get better, Vanessa. I promise it will."

⸻

TO HER RELIEF, Jasper had no gauntlet planned for that evening. Instead, he listened to her play the pianoforte, then they supped at home. After, he challenged her to play cards. Piquet. After losing twice, she offered to teach him Commerce.

"What is that?"

"A betting game. The soldiers played it. Henry taught it to

me."

"What did you wager?"

"Pebbles. Don't scoff. It passed time."

"Show me."

She explained the rules and they played a few hands. He caught on so quickly, she guessed he had played it before.

"I take it gentlemen play this as well," she said, a little sourly. She had wanted to share something with him. Something new to him.

He chuckled. "I suppose I cannot sharp you." He picked up the deck and shuffled. "But let's try something different. The wagering. Let us bet articles of clothing."

"Clothing?"

"That we are wearing."

Her eyes widened as she caught his meaning. "Certainly not."

He laughed. "Kisses then. On the hands are worth one, lips five, and then…"

"Oh, for Heaven's sake." Oh, but she lived for that look in his eyes. A little shiver ran down her neck. "Deal the cards."

※

They might as well have played for clothing. The outcome was the same. She slept heavily that night and missed his leaving in the morning. But he was back just after her luncheon.

"You're back early," she said, as he joined her at the small tea table in the drawing room. "Would you like something to eat?"

He plucked the end of her sandwich from her plate and popped it into his mouth. "No. I ran into Evershard, and we went to a pub."

"That's a new name."

"Is it?" He shrugged. "He's a good fellow. Quiet though. Haven't seen him much since he got leg shackled. I hadn't meant to be gone this long. I just needed to walk about. Restless, I suppose."

"Yes, well, tonight is the big night. Hilyer's comeuppance."

Jasper's face tightened. Then relaxed. He reached across the table and squeezed her hand. "I have something for you." She waited. He produced a slender box from his jacket pocket. *Wilson and Clark*. His preferred jewelers. "I am eager to see you in this."

She opened the box. An exquisite and very long string of pearls. "Oh, Jasper. You really shouldn't."

"You know," he said, his voice dropping low, "the glimpses that you allow me are tantalizing. And it is arousing, shifting bits of cloth out of the way. But the image I have in my head of you wearing these…just these…"

"Jasper!" Her face heated.

"Well, it hardly seems fair," he exclaimed, laughing. "I let you look as much as you want."

"Oh, my word." She turned her head. Mortified. But she laughed too. Of course, he had noticed her staring.

"Vanessa."

"No, don't talk to me."

"Look at me."

"No." She laughed, putting her hands over her eyes. "I don't think I will ever look at you again."

"Ha!" He shifted his chair to draw closer. "Just a peek. I'll loosen my neckcloth."

"Jasper!"

He pulled her hands away. He was smiling, but gently, and his eyes were more worried than playful. "I need to talk to you. Seriously. About tonight."

"You want me to wear the pearls," she guessed. "To celebrate." But she knew, even as she teased him, that it was not that.

"I want you to do something difficult. Hear me out. Before you say no."

Her own laughter faded. More difficult than what they had been doing? "Go on."

He leaned his elbows on the table. His forehead creased. "I

may have underestimated Hilyer. His wrath. I've been wracking my brains for where to hide you."

"Hide me! Jasper, how ridiculous. You can't think he will come here."

"I don't know." He settled back. "He will be...insulted. I've never purposely insulted anyone before. He may react badly."

"*May* react badly?" She scoffed. "I thought that was the point." She'd thought it foolish. Now he was realizing it when it was probably too late to turn back. "He isn't going to come here. What are you picturing? That he will snatch me out of your home and carry me off to his lair? Or maybe tie me up and hold a pistol to my head until you return so he can taunt you?"

"Of course not." He said it sheepishly, as though he had been considering things equally outlandish.

"That doesn't happen in real life, Jasper. You aren't pirates or highwaymen. He's an old goat and you are a snob. All you are going to do is snub him. Grandly, yes. Theatrically. You will humiliate him so badly he will run off to the country, tail between his legs. But that is all."

Jasper had a very strange look on his face. As though he were listening to her but thinking of something else.

"My fear," she said, "if there is anything to fear, it is that he will call you out."

"He is too cowardly."

"Maybe he has heard how you shoot." She meant to say it lightly. But did not.

Jasper scowled. "You needn't concern yourself—"

"I needn't? But you may? You're the one who wants to hide me somewhere."

"If it will set your mind at ease, I've already considered the possibility that he will call me out." His face fell into something resembling a pout. "If he challenges me, I will have the choice of weapons. You may rest assured I will not choose guns." He attempted a wry smile. And almost pulled it off. "I thought swords."

"Are you skilled?"

"I was when I was twelve." Then his smile became real. "But surely I can prance about and jab better than Hilyer."

He saw, too, the absurdity of it all. The only thing that made this plan credible was that Hilyer was roundly despised. While the Taverstons were universally admired. Hilyer would be as much an outcast as…as she was. And that had to be enough for her. For Henry. Dead in a gully in Spain. For the baby, too tiny to live, born dead—left in a shallow grave under a bush.

A storm of anger shook her. Mocking the marquess at a party was *not* enough. And her father. Where was Frederick Culpepper's comeuppance?

"Vanessa," he said, all humor falling away. "I want you to spend the night at Grosvenor Square."

His parents' house? Absolutely not. They would turn her away at the door. She would be more humiliated than Hilyer.

He saw her face. Her refusal. Her confusion.

"Please." He said it forcefully. Not like a request. "Do it. For me."

※

HE DID NOT permit her to veil herself or steal into the house through the servants' entrance. He took her up the wide walk to the massive front door. A very stiff butler opened it.

"Peters," Jasper said, hand on her elbow, steering her inside. "Will you ask the earl if he can see me? I'll wait in the small parlor. Please tell him Mrs. Wardrip is with me."

"Yes, my lord."

Vanessa had never seen a face so blank of expression. Her father's butlers, a succession of them, tended to sneer.

The earl's house was grand. Grandeur did not awe her. Old money was still money. Things were just things. But there was, she had to admit, an atmosphere here. Rarified air. As if all loudness, all unpleasantness, must be muffled.

She and Jasper were very quiet. They had used up all their words.

They entered what Jasper called the small parlor. Decorated in forest green damasks, with mahogany furnishings, it was, of course, not small. There was no fire in the grate. Jasper lit a lamp. He indicated one of the chairs. Floral cushioned. She was comforted, against all reason, to see the seat cushion was indented from frequent use. Jasper had taken her into one of the family rooms.

Nevertheless, the earl could not walk in to find her seated as if she belonged. What was Jasper thinking! They stood there. Listening to the wall clock tick.

The earl arrived. He did not look as affable as he had at their parting in the gardens. He looked coiled with controlled fury.

"Jasper, what is the meaning of this?"

"Good evening, Father. Perhaps you didn't see Mrs. Wardrip standing right here?" He gripped her elbow, pulling her a hair closer. She realized she had tried to hide in his shadow.

The earl closed his eyes and breathed...mightily. He opened them.

"Good evening, Mrs. Wardrip. I did not mean to be rude."

"My lord." She dipped a curtsy. And thought better of saying anything more.

"I apologize, Father, for this intrusion. I would not impose like this, but I'm concerned for Mrs. Wardrip's safety."

The earl pursed his lips. "Because tonight is Hazard's gamblers' rout?"

"You know—

"Yes, I know about it. Hazard invited me. I told him he was absurd."

Jasper looked a little hurt. "I know it is rather melodramatic, but..."

"It's clever enough." He sniffed. "But Hazard knows I won't step foot in Brooks's. Bunch of foxed Whigs! But that's neither here nor there." He looked from one to the other. "Has Hilyer made threats?"

"No," Jasper said. "Not threats."

"You cannot have been intimidated by that pea-brained insult in the scandal sheet."

Jasper groaned. A muffled but definite groan. He was not pleased his father was aware he'd been deemed a handsome bed.

"It's an overabundance of caution, but I don't want to leave Mrs. Wardrip alone."

Was *that* it? Her heart melted, just a little. He meant well. But he didn't understand. She would still be alone. Still listening for his footsteps.

"I don't know, Jasper. This is beyond—"

The door sprang open and another Taverston skidded into the room.

"Crispin!" Vanessa and Jasper both cried out at once.

Crispin halted. He turned to her with a brilliant smile—different from Jasper's, asymmetrical, thinner lipped—yet sparkling with evident delight. He clipped his heels together and bowed at the waist.

"Mrs. Wardrip. Such a pleasure." He straightened and turned. "Father, Mother is—oh, hello, Jasp—Mother is coming. Fair warning."

The earl clapped a hand to his temple. "Jasper, you have gone beyond the pale."

"What are you doing here?" Jasper demanded.

Crispin's eyes widened. "I live here."

"Crispin is home on a few days' leave. *Very* few."

"It isn't my fault, Father. Wellesley stuck his letters in my hand and ordered me to be back the day before I left."

Vanessa heard a gasp and turned to the doorway. The countess stood there, staring, white as chalk. Jasper evidently got his height from both parents. Her hair had gone gray but was styled elegantly and her face, classically beautiful, was only beginning to show fine lines. This was what a lady should be. Before her,

Vanessa felt like a tramp.

"Mother." There was a slight tremor in Jasper's voice, and she hated him for it. "Permit me to introduce—"

"No." His mother turned her back. "Take her out of this house. Good God, Jasper. What if Olivia were here!"

Vanessa felt faint. Jasper took her elbow in a pincer grip.

"If I leave with her now, Mother, I will not be back."

The earl spoke next. "Jasper, don't be foolish. Beatrice, you needn't receive her. I agree, it is too much. But I have given permission for her to use the Rose Room for tonight."

"In this house?" The disgust in her tone made the air around them seem to pulse.

"Jasper will not be here. He will be out with friends."

"Doing God knows what," she said. "A rake. That is what he is becoming. Ever since that woman put her cat claws—"

"Mrs. Wardrip," Crispin cut in, "you do not know, by any chance, your husband's recipe for his cordial, do you?" He stepped to her side, opposite Jasper, the two of them, buttresses, then addressed the earl. "Dr. Wardrip was under my command. He found me one morning...inconvenienced. His intervention was timely. I could not have marched." He faced her again. "Most usually, cordials are not effective. He didn't tell you any of this?"

She shook her head. She had no idea what he was talking about. And Jasper looked as though *he* might faint.

"Then I am even more indebted." His voice lowered on a sigh. "Even if the recipe is buried with him."

"Oh, Crispin," the countess said, without turning about. "That's enough." Was she angry or anguished? "Mrs. Wardrip may use the Rose Room tonight. But I want her gone in the morning." She stormed away.

# Chapter Seventeen

The Rose Room scarcely belonged to the rest of the house. It was tucked away in the south wing. Far away. It was where they stashed great aunts who came visiting, the ones who complained of the noise of London and the hullabaloo in the Taverstons' home. The difference, Jasper thought bitterly, was the great aunts asked for the isolation. They weren't shunted from the family's view.

Vanessa made no comment about the chamber, its fussy, outdated décor, its persistent and faint odor of lavender water, merely murmuring, "This will do comfortably," as though speaking to an invisible maid.

"Vanessa, I'm sorry. If I had known Mother would behave so badly, I never would have brought you here." He had never seen his mother treat anyone with such a lack of courtesy. It wasn't like her.

"It is no matter."

The hurt in her eyes haunted him. The resignation.

"It matters to me," he said. "*You* matter to me. She will have to learn to accept that." Vanessa made a dismissive noise, but Jasper was bothered by something else. "And Crispin! That was even more uncharacteristic than Mother's rudeness. He never refers to his ailment. Never. And bites off the head of anyone else who dares do so."

"He has an ailment?"

"Well, yes." This made him uncomfortable. Crispin guarded his privacy so jealously. But then, Crispin had brought it up first. "Since childhood. A recurring...internal complaint. That's why he needed the cordial your husband gave him."

"A cordial? How preposterous. I can't imagine why he said that. Where on earth would Henry obtain such a thing? Or ingredients to make one? From salt pork and stale bread? I have no idea what Crispin was talking about."

He stared. Unable to fathom...not that Crispin would lie; he was not averse to lying, but that he had broken his own taboo to distract, possibly even to shame, their mother. In order to shield Vanessa. And now Jasper was *very* uncomfortable.

Could Crispin care for Vanessa? She had been adamant there was nothing between them, but what if she wasn't aware of how he felt?

He felt a sinking in the pit of his gut. He would never have pursued her if he'd known. Yet should he have known? *Had* some part of him known?

He'd told Crispin not to disappear while he showed Vanessa to the Rose Room. To wait because he needed to talk to him. It seemed they had more to discuss than he'd thought. The devil. There wasn't time for this. Not today.

Crispin had answered flippantly: *Hurry up then*. Flippantly because Father was still standing there. But Jasper was not supposed to take it lightly. He knew that much.

"Vanessa, I have to go. I have to talk to Crispin before Hazard's party tonight."

"He's going too?"

"I assume so."

He saw Vanessa let out a little breath. It eased her concern to hear that Crispin was also involved. That stung. As though she didn't even trust Jasper to carry off a snub without his brother's help. Well, but of course she trusted Crispin more. He'd rescued her from the French horde.

He gave her a brief kiss on the temple. Anything more would feel like a sacrilege in this house. Then he left her. And practically kicked himself the whole way down the stairs. He shouldn't have brought her here.

Crispin and Father were still in the small parlor. If he heard right, they were discussing horses. Crispin should have used the time to change his clothes. A lieutenant's uniform would have been acceptable, but he was not in uniform. His simple dark jacket and fawn pantaloons might have passed muster for a typical night on the town, but not for a party where the Prince Regent was expected. And the black greatcoat he had slung over his shoulders was dirty.

"No, it's selfish, perhaps, but I'm leaving Mercury safe here," Crispin said. "But I do appreciate—"

"Nonsense. You need more than one decent mount if you are riding all over creation. Take Jasper with you."

"I intended—"

"Where are you taking me?" he asked, entering the room. "I hope not Spain."

"Tattersalls," Father said. "Crispin had Firebrand shot out from beneath him. He needs a new mount."

"Oh, Crispin. I'm sorry." Jasper turned to his brother. He'd had that horse for five years. It was a damn fine animal.

Crispin shrugged. "It was a horse. Are you ready? Kissed the lady goodbye and all?"

He put his hand on Crispin's shoulder and shoved. "Let's just go."

They left the earl and walked without speaking until they were outside. Then Crispin said, "I doubt I'll have time to look, but if you would find me something in the general way of Firebrand, and have him shipped over on the next transport, I would appreciate it. Father said he'd foot the bill."

"The army doesn't provide horses?"

"Nags, Jasper. And few enough of those." He shook his head with disgust. "The poor creatures die in droves." Then he set off, his long legs making quick work of the muddy cobbles. They were heading toward Brooks's and would be too early at this pace. Jasper looked his brother up and down. He really wished Crispin had changed his clothes. Well, that was not worth the argument when they had others.

"Apparently," he ventured, matching his brother stride for stride, "the army doesn't supply its surgeons with the means to make cordials, either."

Crispin scowled. "I could not stand there and listen to that. Mother was awful!"

"She was. She truly was. I never would have brought Vanessa to the house if I imagined—"

"You were right to bring her." Crispin was emphatic. "I was relieved to see you thought to do so."

"But you can't really think there's any danger. To Vanessa? She was angry, you should know, that I insisted she—"

"You didn't." Crispin stopped dead. "Tell me you didn't say anything to her."

"Of course not. What do you take me for? She only knows about Hazard's soiree. That I intend to make a fool of Hilyer."

"Good." He breathed out sharply. "Good."

"She mocked me for the grand gesture." He didn't know why he was telling his brother this. Maybe to see his reaction. Maybe to see how Crispin spoke of her.

Crispin's head tilted. "Mocked you?"

"Yes, well." He plunged ahead. "Essentially, she said I was no hero. Snobbery is not as impressive a weapon as I think it to be."

Crispin stared a moment. Then he put a hand on Jasper's shoulder, his face softening into something approaching brotherly commiseration. He could not carry it off. Crispin broke, doubling over with laughter, clutching his knees and howling.

Jasper took a step back and glanced around nervously. They were on the street in front of their house, for pity's sake.

"Crispin," he hissed. "People will think you are ape-drunk. Stand up!"

After a few moments, Crispin straightened, still shaking. "She is a gem, Jasp. I really don't think you deserve her."

Did Crispin mean that?

"Did I step on your toes?"

"Did you what?" he asked, pressing a hand into his side as his laughter subsided.

"Step. On. Your. Toes."

Crispin's breath hitched as understanding dawned. Then he scowled. "Christ. What do you take me for? Her husband was not two days dead when I packed her onto that transport."

*Oh.*

"I didn't know. Not the timing. She doesn't…she doesn't talk about those last days. How Henry died."

"Have you asked? Or do you expect her to just blurt it out?"

"I'm not insensitive, Crispin. She loved him. I don't pry. I just don't understand how you involved yourself. You must have sought her out. That could not have been part of your remit."

"Walk, Jasper. This way." Crispin took off again. Down a cross street. "Yes, I sought her out. Do you know what we had been doing? Our grand army? We weren't simply retreating. It was a goddamned rout. Sir Moore, God rest him, was in command because the idiots at home recalled Wellesley to chew him out over what was not his fault. So Boney came himself to press the advantage. We damn near lost the war right there."

Jasper gulped. The public version was that it had been a tight spot, but they had prevailed.

Crispin said, "The retreat was a headlong flight. We lost far too many soldiers. My regiment, fortunately, kept its discipline." His voice dropped and he murmured, "God, they are good men, Jasper."

Jasper imagined if they kept their discipline, it had more to do with Crispin than with them.

"We had to get across difficult terrain. We were close to Corunna when we met with an ambush." Crispin kept stomping ahead. Jasper, a little more careful of his own attire, threaded more cautiously alongside. "We fought our way out. But I lost—" He sucked in a breath. His words came out clipped. "Six men. Five fast. But Wardrip died slowly. At my feet. I could do nothing for him. Bayoneted. His guts were splayed over my boots. His last words were, *Lieutenant, take care of her.*"

Crispin halted. He spat something into the mud.

Then he gave Jasper a cold look. "You did not step…on…my…toes."

No. He'd done worse. He couldn't think what to say. But finally managed, "I will take care of her."

"You had better."

Crispin started walking again and Jasper ploughed on to keep up. Then Crispin turned left again, doubling back, heading away from Brooks's, paralleling Grosvenor.

"Don't say anything to her," Crispin said quietly. "I told her he died instantaneously. She doesn't need to know…"

"Of course not. Crispin, where are we going?"

"I am eventually going in the general direction of the Thames. You should go to Brooks's. You said you needed to talk to me? Make it quick."

"I-I will press him tonight. If you are ready for—"

"Unless you keep delaying me."

"Don't be such an arse, Crispin. *You* may be adept at spying—"

"I'm not a spy," he said derisively. "Must you always be so melodramatic?"

"What do you call it?"

"I'm a field officer." He gave an off-handed shrug. "Sometimes one or the other of my superiors has a question. Usually, it's something they could find out for themselves if they tried. But I answered one too many questions for them and now they dump them all on me."

"But you're not a spy? I don't need to worry you'll be executed without trial?"

"I'm not putting on false mustaches and slipping behind enemy lines." Crispin smiled sourly. "No. I will not be shot except in the usual way."

With that fear out of the way, Jasper confessed. "I'm concerned I will err and your plans for Hilyer will go awry. Your instructions were not at all detailed."

"Because flexibility may be required. You can adapt."

"Crispin! I don't know what I'm doing."

"I cannot give you details. You aren't supposed to know any of this."

"I don't need to know details. I need to know…how you think."

Crispin glanced across his shoulder. His smirk was telling.

"Mock me another day, Crispin. I cannot convincingly imply knowledge I do not have if I cannot fathom how I might have obtained it."

Crispin frowned. "That actually makes sense."

"Can you at least tell me how you think where to look?"

They walked in silence. Jasper watched Crispin's mind churn. Then his brother tapped his arm and they stopped again, by a garden wall. Crispin hauled himself up a few inches to look over it, then lowered his feet back to the ground. He leaned against the wall.

"Bare bones, Jasper."

"All right."

"Rum comes from sugar cane. Men with property in the West Indies might be suspect. But how would that work? Poor quality sugar yields watery rum? Unlikely. So let's look at the distilleries. Most are in the Americas. We aren't importing much from them currently. That leaves Australia. But Australia is too far away. I could hardly go there and snoop in their barrels."

"God, Crispin." Haphazard guesswork and expediency? Maybe he didn't want to know how Crispin's mind worked.

"Ah, but barrels!" Crispin lifted a finger in the air. "I had barrels. Barrels full of water. And barrels are marked with a distinctive cooperage signature."

"Are they?"

Crispin nodded. "They are."

"Aren't they also stamped with the name of the distillers?"

"Don't make this too easy, Jasper. Of course, they are."

"Well, then?"

"I didn't think the distillers would be stupid enough to sell water for rum directly to the king's procurer. The barrels would be switched somewhere between the distillery and the Peninsula."

"Oh." Jasper tried on his own. "But coopers are not contracted to sell liquor."

"No. It gets complicated. Suffice it to say, the rum is purchased. It's shipped here. Offloaded. Stored in a warehouse. Reloaded. Then shipped out. The way I think, Jasp, is to say *wouldn't it make the most sense to switch barrels in the warehouse?* And then figure out how it might be done."

"And by whom?"

Crispin nodded.

Jasper said, "You wrote I should hint at Hilyer's Irish concerns."

"There is a cooperage in Dublin. Gentlemen do not engage in commercial enterprise, but we all know investments come in through backdoors." Crispin folded his hands. "Hilyer owns a large share of that cooperage. Barrels are not only sold to distillers. And distillers' stamps are not difficult to forge."

"Crispin, your evidence sounds shaky."

"It is no evidence at all," he conceded, undisturbed. "Nevertheless, I know I am correct. Too many pieces fit. But he is a peer. And pieces aren't enough. So we will catch him another way."

"Running to France with supposed military secrets?"

"Yes." Then Crispin grinned. "So in a way, this all depends on you. Sad that you cannot boast of your heroics to Vanessa."

While Jasper glared, Crispin pulled his watch from his vest and glanced at it. Then his grin fell away.

"Damn." He shoved the watch back. "Give my regards to Haz."

Then he took off at a run.

# Part 5
## Time to Adjust. Or Not.
### August 1813
### Cartmel

# CHAPTER EIGHTEEN

VANESSA WARDRIP WAS reaccumulating things. It had started with books. First a few, then a few more. It was silly since she was not even much of a reader. A variety of tutors had soured her on the activity when she was young. Nevertheless, the adventure novels she purchased to reignite Charlotte's enthusiasm for learning thrilled her as well. They read them together over tea. Then Charlotte recounted the stories at night to her boys. Vanessa looked forward to the day when she might lend Charlotte the books to read to them. But for now...

She tried to wiggle her latest purchases onto the shelf Tam had built.

In addition to books, she bought herself a tea set. It wasn't an extravagance; she'd dropped her clay pot and it cracked. The replacement she bought over in Paxton Downs, which included four matching teacups, was not Wedgewood but rather an inexpensive imitation that was just as pretty. She christened the set by inviting the two women from church who were always together. They were sisters, she learned, wedded to brothers who were fishermen. They both had sons who were now old enough to go out with their fathers. And Mary and Myrtle had wanted to make her acquaintance for oh-so-long, but were shy.

Vanessa had also bought herself a straw bonnet to keep the sun from her face. Little by little, she was beginning to feel settled. Things were not important, but perhaps what one did with them was.

And now, she must go claim her boots. When she'd tried two days earlier, they were not yet ready, and Bitter had been so apologetic he seemed almost fretful. He'd promised they would be done today. She worried if she didn't go claim them, he would search for a way to bring them to her.

She tied on her bonnet and set out. Down the street, she saw Charlotte spreading laundry in her yard to dry in the sun. Mostly Sweet Kate's nappies. Vanessa waved, but kept on, reminded that she had her own laundry to wash when she returned. Mostly underthings. She would not spread them outside. They were lacy and delicate and would not belong to the woman she pretended to be.

The day was hot which made the walk seem longer, which returned her thoughts to where they had been. Her slowly accumulating things. She let word slip out that she'd received a small inheritance from a great uncle in case anyone noticed.

Another purchase she'd recently made was writing paper. She wrote letters to Effie Andini and Rose Posonby, short notes, just to say she was settled into a comfortable cottage near a friend of hers from the Peninsula. She could not tell them where, but if they were so inclined, they might write to her care of Mr. Will Collingswood.

She didn't post the letters. Will had told her he would not serve as her go-between. He'd meant, of course, between her and Jasper, but he might think she was writing to her friends seeking information about him. She was not. Not really. She missed her London life. But she'd decided she must ask Will first if he would mind being a conduit. Unfortunately, she was finding that letter too difficult to compose.

She wrote also to Crispin. She thanked him for his kindness in thinking of her and sharing his news. She told him, too, that she was settling in, making friends, and that Lydia and Corporal Compton were also well. She didn't bother asking him how he had located her. He wouldn't explain. But she tore up that letter rather than send it. It would take weeks to find him if it found him at all. He might or might not reply. And she didn't want to spend the next few months…waiting. Nor did she think she should strike up a correspondence with Jasper's brother.

She also composed letter after letter to her one-time lover. Telling him little details about her life here. Asking about his. Sometimes telling him how desperately she missed him—his conversation, his smiles, his touch. Oh, his touch.

She wrote those letters only in her head. Never committing words to paper.

Her forehead was damp with perspiration and her clothes felt heavier and dustier, but there, ahead, finally, was the Comptons' cottage. Tidily constructed, it was smaller than her own. The front door stood open inviting a breeze and, of course, customers. Six bootmakers were working there now, including Lydia, her husband, Jon, Bitter, and two other injured soldiers. All Vanessa could think was that it must be unbearably cramped.

As she understood it, Lydia and the corporal slept in the loft. Brother Jon slept downstairs in the corner of the workshop. Another corner now housed Bitter and Nan. The lack of privacy made Vanessa cringe. Of course, on the Peninsula, it had been worse. She and Henry had never been truly alone. But life with Jasper had spoiled her. Or returned her to the expectations of the comfort of her coddled youth. Expectations of unlimited resources. What a skewed vision of life she had had.

She approached the door and heard voices. Raised voices.

"If we increase the price to cover the tax, we will lose the few customers we have."

That was Jon speaking. Although it was wrong of her, Vanessa paused outside the door.

"But if you don't, you'll lose money on every pair you sell," said the corporal. "It's not as if we can compete on price with the likes of Brunel and his factory."

"Even Brunel may have trouble selling boots once the war

ends."

"The difficulty is your labor," Bitter put in. Vanessa barely recognized the voice as his. It held none of Bitter's usual sunniness. "You cannot keep us all. It was good of you, Jon, to take me on, but I understand…"

"No talk of that," Jon said gruffly.

Just then, Lydia tapped Vanessa on the arm, and she jumped. Lydia carried a basket draped with a large napkin. She'd been to Cartmel's market. Or perhaps to one of the neighbors to barter. She frowned. Vanessa expected to be scolded for listening to what was none of her business. Instead, Lydia said, "Are they arguing again? Come in." She took Vanessa by the elbow and dragged her inside.

"A customer come for her boots," she announced.

The small front room was dimly sunlit and felt blessedly cool. The Compton brothers stood along the back wall, beside the door leading into their workshop-living space. Vanessa could not help looking at Bitter, seated behind a narrow table with a battered ledger in front of him. He hadn't had time to mask his anguish.

"Ah, Mrs. Wardrip," Jon said. "Your boots are ready. I'm sorry. I can't imagine what took so long. They're in the back. I'll fetch them."

"Oh, it's no matter." They all looked so dejected, she could not bear it. If the boot mill closed, what would they do? She glanced again at Bitter, who looked the most agitated. Of course, he had Nan to worry about. And that went both ways. From the times she'd spoken with Nan, Vanessa thought her a more than capable woman despite her impediments, yet Nan must have her hands full caring for Bitter.

Jon returned with a canvas satchel.

"Try them on," he urged, handing it to her. "If they don't fit, we'll make it right."

"If she doesn't like them," Bitter said, shooting an anxious look not at her, but at Jon, "I'll make it right."

It made her self-conscious, all those eyes upon her. She sat on an empty stool and slipped the first boot from the satchel. Her jaw dropped.

The leather had been tooled, and decorated with roses on a trellis. The workmanship was superb. She shook the other boot from its bag. It was a mirror image of its mate.

"What is that now?" Jon said, stepping closer.

"Oh, but they're beautiful!"

She heard Bitter's little sigh of relief. She kicked off her worn slippers and pulled on the left boot. It was tight, but not uncomfortably so and she knew the leather would give.

"Perfect! I'll try the other."

She had never seen boots this sturdy look so lovely. Nevertheless, she was aware of the eyes in the room. Lydia looked stunned. Bitter, pleased. The corporal, confused. And Jon looked wary and annoyed.

"Did Bitter have your permission to attempt this?"

*Nan says I'm daft for wanting to make pretty shoes to scuff about in the dust.*

"He certainly would have, but I would have offered to pay more. I should pay more. Jon, anyone would." The words soured in her mouth. Not anyone. They made boots for men who could barely afford the ten shillings and two pence.

Jon sniffed. "You pay what you agreed upon, Mrs. Wardrip. We should refund your payment, seeing as they weren't what you ordered."

"Refund?"

"I didn't take her money," Bitter said weakly. "I thought…"

"I brought payment with me," Vanessa said, fishing the coins from her reticule. She thought again of offering more, but feared that would add fuel to the fire. The Comptons' boots were not meant for ladies who could have the bills sent to moneyed protectors or indulgent husbands. But they could be.

She stood, marveling again at the snugness of the boots after her thin, worn slippers. She put the coin in Jon's hand. "These are perfect, Jon, truly, I couldn't be happier. They would fetch thrice the price in London." Thrice? Five times. She mused aloud. "If they were placed in the right shops, it would be ten times."

Jon blew a raspberry through his lips. "Ladies don't want boots like these. They want flimsy things."

Vanessa thought of Lady Posonby. She would buy them. And the six young ladies, her disciples, would copy her. But a small cadre of bluestockings wearing decorative Hessians would not set a fashion.

The corporal was more disparaging. "Even with Lieutenant Taverston's good word, we couldn't sell boots to the army. London ladies' shops will not be knocking down our door."

Vanessa blushed, as much from hearing the Taverston name as from fear of giving away her own secrets.

"Well," she said, a little ashamed of her own mercantile instincts, "not London shops but perhaps you could place a sample in Brideley's in Paxton Downs." It was the nondescript little shop where she'd purchased her bonnet. Then she had another thought. "Or there are shops over in Binnings."

She'd been planning to hire a conveyance in Paxton Downs to take her to Binnings. She had never been there but heard it was a quaint village with shops frequented by a wealthier clientele than Paxton Downs. Some Society people—no one she knew—owned properties there. There were no large country estates, just small playgrounds and hunting copses for aristocrats. Her father, who would have hated the isolation but loved the cachet, had once attempted to purchase a Binnings cottage, but no one had anything they were willing to sell.

She hadn't been intending to buy much in the shops, only to walk through them and imagine a connection to a life she no longer lived. Moreover, she'd thought she might find a place where she could sell a piece of jewelry when it came to that so that she wouldn't have to involve Will again. Now she had an urge to visit their shoe shops.

"Shops won't take a risk on something so outlandish," Jon said. "They suit you, Mrs. Wardrip, but you know the value of strongly made shoes. And I daresay Lydia wouldn't mind a pair so pretty. But most women—"

"Most women don't have a choice," Lydia said. "They wear what men make for them to wear. And I'd wager most men like their girls a bit hobbled."

"Be that as it may," Jon said, "we're fortunate Mrs. Wardrip likes her boots. Bitter, you idiot, you should have asked first."

"Yes," Lydia said. "She might have preferred bluebells."

Oh, she would love bluebells. But she couldn't order a second pair of boots. Rather she could, but she mustn't. Not yet.

※

VANESSA TRAVELED WITH company: Mary and Myrtle. She hired a coach and driver and rented a small room for two nights, a room over a tea shop in Binnings proper. She convinced the sisters to accompany her by saying she could not go alone. They understood her timidity or thought they did. In truth, the only thing that frightened Vanessa was *talk*. Traveling with the sisters lent her respectability.

She enjoyed the women's company, to a point. However, they told so many stories about their sons, who were now nearly men, that Vanessa was pleased when, after two hours of aimless shopping and a half hour of fortifying tea drinking, Mary begged a chance to retire to their rented room upstairs to rest. Myrtle added her plea.

"Of course!" Vanessa said. "I didn't mean to run you ragged." It must be fatiguing to look at pretty things one could never afford. "There are a couple more shops I would like to visit, but I'm comfortable going alone. We can meet for dinner."

So it was agreed. Vanessa took herself to a dressmaker. She was tired of turning hems and attempting to discreetly mend tears, and a little annoyed she'd sold so many of her clothes before leaving home. Before leaving *London*, she amended. It would not hurt to order two simple day dresses to be sent to her in Cartmel. They would not be finished here, of course, because she could not return for multiple fittings. But she could do the finishing herself.

She stepped into the shop and a small bell tinkled. A good-looking, dark-haired young man, who was sitting patiently with a large book in his lap, glanced up. Vanessa gasped.

The man jumped to his feet. "Van—Mrs. Wardrip. Good Lord!" He came toward her. She had nowhere to run.

She nodded. "Mr. Taverston. This is a surprise."

To her horror, a very beautiful woman—strawberry-golden hair, flawless skin, a dainty nose, no wonder Jasper had courted her—stepped out from behind the rolls of fabrics. She had a question on her face. "Reginald?" She turned a smile upon Vanessa.

"Georgiana, this is Mrs. Wardrip. She was Jasper's—" He froze, and his face contorted as he realized what he was about to say. In a choked tone, he finished, "Friend."

"Well, how delightful!" The woman moved forward, graceful as a goddess. "You must, then, be our friend as well. Will you have tea with us? Reginald has been complaining he is parched."

"I think..." Vanessa risked a glance at Reginald, who looked as though he wished he could drop through the floor. What a disastrous encounter. Vanessa decided honesty would put the quickest end to it. "I fear that would be unfitting. Iversley and I are no longer 'friends,' as Mr. Taverston so generously puts it." She raised one eyebrow archly. A defense. "We severed our friendship when he began to court you."

Lady Georgiana looked confused for a moment, but no more than a moment. Her eyes went wide, then she said, "Oh. Oh, I see." Then she turned to her husband. "And you were all acquainted?" It sounded more like curiosity than accusation.

Mr. Taverston's eyes closed, and his throat worked. Then he opened them and said, "Yes. But not well acquainted?" He offered the apology like the weak excuse he knew it to be. Vanessa felt a pang. These two were such innocents. She didn't wish to be the source of any discord.

The next moment, Georgiana laughed. "This is awkward. I'm so sorry, Mrs. Wardrip."

"You are?" Vanessa felt bewildered. She'd expected a cut. She'd invited it. "For-for what?"

Georgiana laughed again, then turned up her palms. "I don't know. For my naivete, perhaps." She elbowed her husband. "And Reginald's. I suppose he should not have approached you. But now that he has, and the air is cleared, would you have tea with us?"

She'd just had tea. And she could not imagine what they would talk about. But she was struck by a sudden, overwhelming desire to spend time with Jasper's people. With ton people. Lord, she was as bad as her father, wanting in where she didn't belong.

She nodded. "I would like that."

"Let's go to Mundy's," Georgiana suggested. A different tea shop, thank goodness, but several blocks away. "All day, I've been craving their cardamon cakes." She laid her hand on her abdomen in an absent way that spoke volumes. Vanessa felt an almost unbearable pang, amplified when Reginald placed a fond, protective hand on the small of his wife's back.

"Mundy's it is."

They left the shop and walked down the street. Reginald kept his hand on his wife's elbow, but there was room to walk three abreast, so Vanessa did not feel too much like a third wheel.

"So," Reginald said, "you've been in Binnings all along?"

"No."

He looked embarrassed again. "I beg your pardon." He shook his head. "I won't say anything to Jasper."

"Won't you?"

"No. Crispin wrote that you might contact me should a need arise." Reginald grinned. She could see, then, the family resemblance. Although Reginald did not possess the fair aristocratic features of his brothers, he had Jasper's mouth and humor-filled blue eyes. "He threatened me with some unspecified retribution if I revealed your whereabouts."

"Then I suppose I must trust your word."

Georgiana smiled wryly. "Reginald is not afraid of Crispin. But he is a man of his word."

Vanessa said, "I'm not living in Binnings. I live a fair distance away. I wouldn't have come if I thought I'd run into anyone who might know me." And now, she would never come back. "You have property here?"

"We don't," Reginald said. "Crispin has a cottage that he has let us use. We returned to check on some work being done."

Good Lord. She couldn't believe Crispin, of all people, had a hideaway in Binnings.

"We came to steal away for a second honeymoon," Georgiana corrected him. "Even though it is rather too soon after our first."

Vanessa almost rolled her eyes at the deep blush that stole over Reginald's face.

Georgiana went on. "We have a house in Cambridge. Reginald is working for Frederick Bastion on a translation of several Greek manuscripts." She beamed proudly and Vanessa understood the work must be impressive, even if she didn't understand why. But Jasper had always spoken so highly of his youngest brother's intelligence, that it made sense he'd be involved with something scholarly.

They reached the curb in front of Mundy's. Vanessa raised her skirts a couple of inches and stepped as best she could around a large puddle. Georgiana attempted to follow her, but Reginald put his hands on her waist and swooped her over it. He possessed the Taverston strength, despite being a few inches shorter than his elder brothers.

They entered the tea shop and chose a table. Reginald asked a server to bring tea and cardamon cakes. Just as they were about to sit, Georgiana touched Vanessa's arm.

"May I see your shoes?"

"My-my shoes?"

When Georgiana nodded, Vanessa raised her hem again.

"Oh! How splendid! How lovely! Reginald, look!" Georgiana raised her eyes to Vanessa's. "They are boots like Hessians, are they not? Are they comfortable?"

"Yes, very."

"I do a lot of walking, you see. Around Cambridge. The streets are just as bad as London's. Oh, and boots like that would be perfect for traipsing about Crispin's cottage. Did you buy them here?"

Vanessa could not have envisioned it could be so easy. "Not here. But if you are truly interested…" She waited for Georgiana's enthusiastic head bob. "I can take a tracing of your foot and a string to measure around your calf and have the boots sent to you. It may take a month or so."

"Would you?" She reached over and clasped Reginald's arm, turning to look at him. "Do you think I might?"

His expression was melting. "Of course, you may have shoes." He laughed a little, reddening, then explained. "We have been playing at budgeting and failing miserably. Jasper gave us a landau and two horses, for pity's sake."

She flushed also. Hadn't she been playing at budgeting while sitting on a small fortune gifted to her by the same man?

"Well," she said, thinking of Bitter and Nan and inflating the price as high as she dared, "these will cost three guineas."

Reginald waved his hand in the same way Jasper would have done. However, Georgiana leveled a shrewder glance at her.

"That is steep. Considerably more than my riding boots."

Vanessa nodded. And took another leap. "The craftsmen are injured British soldiers."

"I see." The suspicion fell from Georgiana's face. "A fair price."

"In advance."

It was Reginald's turn to look leery, but Georgiana said, "Yes, of course."

A server brought their tea and a plate of cakes. The cakes sat on a small square of brown baker's paper. Reginald glanced at the plate and then said, "Could you bring us a piece of that paper?" He indicated a size by squaring his hands. "About so big?"

"Paper?" The server looked at him as though he were daft.

"Yes, the paper. And a length of string." He smiled. "I have my own pen."

The server scuttled off.

"How is..." Vanessa squeezed her hands into fists and asked, "Crispin?"

"He was near to giddy in July," Reginald said. "His latest letter was more somber. He says we will win. Boney overplayed his hand in Russia. But we have not yet won. We'd hoped he might be back in London for the recent celebrations, but of course, it's too soon for him to return."

Vanessa looked quickly at Georgiana, trying to gauge how well she knew Crispin. Then she asked Reginald, as if off-handedly, "His health is good?"

Reginald bit the inside of his cheek, then said, "As far as anyone knows." He added, "It was quite good a few months ago when he was home."

Georgiana dipped her eyes to the table, as though recognizing they were having a veiled conversation they were not supposed to have. Then she asked, "You know Crispin very well then?"—the same question Vanessa had wanted to ask of her. Georgiana sounded hurt. Well, Jasper had been courting her and they had all kept Vanessa's existence a secret. Vanessa felt a bit hurt as well. She stepped back—they were family, and she was not.

"Lieutenant Taverston was my husband's commanding officer. Mr. Wardrip died during the retreat to Corunna. Lieutenant Taverston arranged for my passage back to London."

She thought that was explanation enough. But something twisted across Georgiana's face, and Vanessa realized she was not as naïve as she seemed.

Georgiana said, "Crispin introduced you to Jasper?" Vanessa

heard the words "procured you for him" and her whole body tensed. Georgiana looked disbelieving, yet horrified.

"It was not like that. You can't possibly think such a thing of Crispin." Then she thought of how desperately Jasper needed his brothers' respect, and suspected that extended to his sister-in-law too. "Or of Jasper. You may believe whatever you wish of me; it doesn't matter."

Reginald cleared his throat and said, thin voiced, "Jasper is well also."

Georgiana had the good grace to look mortified for her suspicions.

"You see him often?" Vanessa murmured, wanting whatever Reginald might give her.

"Not since July. Just before Parliament closed. He has been devoting himself to politics, if you can believe it. I think, in a few weeks, he will retire to Chaumbers. Is there…is there anything you would like us to tell him?"

"No. No, nothing. Please don't mention that you've seen me."

"All right." Reginald sighed. He sounded frustrated and perhaps sad. "Though I think it would do him good."

The server appeared with a large square of baker's paper, a piece of string, and a questioning look. "Is this what you wanted, sir?"

"Yes, thank you." He dropped it on the floor by Georgiana's feet. Then he pulled an implement and a tiny capped inkwell from inside his jacket and knelt beside her chair. Rather tenderly, he traced around her shoes, then wrapped the string about her calf and made two knots to indicate the circumference. He rolled up the paper before handing it to Vanessa. Then he opened his purse and took out a few coins to put in her hand. "Our direction is Crumbley House in Cambridge."

Vanessa looked to Georgiana, who appeared to have recovered from her embarrassment. "Do you want roses also?"

"Do you mean I have a choice? Oh, how splendid! Do you

think lilies?"

Vanessa smiled. "I suspect he can do lilies." At that point, she stood. "Thank you both for treating me so kindly. I can't tell you how much it means to me." She squared her shoulders. "But I must take my leave. Should our paths cross again in the next day or so, it would be best to pretend we are not acquainted."

Reginald started to sputter a protest, but Georgiana put her hand on his and dipped her chin, acknowledging what Vanessa had said.

"We won't unmask you," the lady promised. "But if a time comes when you would like to have our friendship, we would not hesitate to welcome yours."

# Chapter Nineteen

The earl's coach was two hours outside of London before Jasper stirred. He opened his eyes, testing his aching head, then closed them quickly, but not before taking note of Hazard, slumped in the opposite corner. Hazard looked wrinkled. And mottled.

"Unbearable," Hazard moaned. "What were we thinking not to postpone this horror until tomorrow?"

"To do all our suffering at once?"

It was what they had agreed upon late last night. Or early this morning. Now with his mouth feeling stuffed with cotton, Jasper knew the decision had been the wrong one. Even though they were expected at Chaumbers tonight, they should not have embarked on this journey. The coach was hot. The motion nauseating.

"God," he muttered. "We are too old for this."

"I will never," Hazard said, "*never* drink with Carroll again. The man is hollow-legged."

Jasper's lips tried to twitch into a smile but failed.

"And no fluid of any sort from that ungodly hemisphere will ever touch my now befurred tongue again," Hazard continued.

"Well, that promise is easy to keep. I'm fairly certain we finished it off." American whiskey had an unpleasant taste that somehow improved the more one drank. Jasper could still smell it. The stink would never come out of his clothes. His stomach rolled threateningly.

"Clever of Carroll to refuse your invitation. Seven hours baking in a carriage…"

Jasper made no reply to this. He had invited Benjamin to Chaumbers and had been refused. Too much work yet in London. And the child to think of. Jasper hadn't pressed, even though he thought Chaumbers a healthier environment for a two-year-old than London in late summer. But he had a regrettable memory of importuning Benjamin again, rather aggressively, last night. God. He even said—if only this were a false memory—that Olivia would be sorely disappointed if he did not come.

He hadn't been so foxed, no, so despicably *drunk*, in years.

A snicker sounded from Hazard's corner. "Was Reg really kissing Georgiana behind your back while you were courting her?"

Now it was Jasper's turn to moan. Had he recounted all of that? Surely not all.

"So he claimed." At least he could trust Hazard and Benjamin to keep their mouths closed. "I have no reason to doubt such a tale."

"It is just that it is so hard to picture."

Jasper snorted. It was an image he tried to keep out of his head. "I suspect Crispin caught them at it."

Hazard guffawed. Then he clutched his head and groaned.

They lapsed into silence. Jasper dozed in the gut-sick way of the recently inebriated. When he awoke again, they had stopped to change horses. They eased themselves from the coach, then rocked on their heels and stomped their feet to bring back the blood. The air was sultry. The grass, for as far afield as Jasper could see, was dry and brown.

"Do you think tea?" Hazard said, gazing skeptically at the posting station.

Jasper put a hand to his middle as if that were a fair gauge. "I can attempt it."

They wandered inside and ordered a pot from the proprietress, then sat at a corner table, away from a common-looking couple who were bickering none too quietly about their biscuits.

"Carroll said surprisingly little," Hazard mused. "All I gathered, really, was that his so-called business partner was a charlatan. And his heart is hopelessly lost to the little imp."

Benjamin had said almost nothing, growing stiffer and stiffer the more that he drank.

"I think he is trying to behave professionally."

Hazard sniffed. "Ridiculous. Didn't the two of you whore together at Oxford?"

Jasper scowled. He didn't like to be reminded of his youthful indiscretions. "Not at all. We drank a good deal, yes, but..." He finished acidly, "The only person I went whoring with was Crispin. And that sparingly." Crispin ran rings around him.

The proprietress arrived with their tea. Jasper flushed, hoping they had not been overheard. When she stepped away, he said, "Change the subject."

Hazard looked amused. "I had hoped Crispin might return to London for the celebrations. Am I correct that he didn't?"

Jasper shook his head. The main reason he'd stayed so long in London was for the Vitoria celebrations: parties, a parade, an evening of fireworks, and the Prince Regent's gala at Carlton House—all the while hoping to see Crispin. And no, he had not come home.

The whole thing had been arduous. Any grace period the matchmakers of the ton had granted him had evidently expired. Everyone knew his first attempt to woo a countess had failed. And that he'd put aside his mistress. He was now fair game. He made the mistake of taking Rose Posonby for a carriage ride and found their names linked in a gossip notice the very next day. The only reason he'd asked her, and the only reason she'd accepted, was that they were both hoping the other had had word from Vanessa.

"Crispin sent a letter," he said. "Vitoria may have turned

things around, but it is not the end of it."

Hazard nodded morosely. They both drank their tea. When they'd emptied the pot, Hazard patted his chest and said, "That sat pretty well, considering. I should be recovered well enough to go riding tomorrow."

"With Olivia."

"Oh, right." He bit his lip. "The day after tomorrow then."

Jasper laughed. Keeping up with his younger sister on horseback was a challenge. Hazard had agreed to spend two weeks at Chaumbers helping him entertain her. Poor Olivia had twice been denied a Season in London. She took that in stride; she was a rock. But she must be bored to distraction. The least Jasper could do was try to ease her loneliness, although, of course, it would feel wrong to bring any bachelor friends around just yet. Hazard being the exception.

Jasper was looking forward to rusticating a bit and thought Hazard was too. They would ride, hunt, play cards and billiards, perhaps talk some politics. Although Hazard was physically recovered from the incident on Vere Street, he remained withdrawn and...jumpy. Jasper was doing his best to draw him out. He'd even asked Olivia to invite Alice to visit these two weeks, but Alice had gone to the country with her father after Mr. Gamby had not come up to scratch. Well, he'd stir Hazard up without her.

Jasper stood, stretching his legs. The tea had been reviving. He pulled his watch from his pocket. "We'd best be on the road. It will be a late supper." He grimaced. "I believe I will adopt Crispin's 'no liquor' policy this fortnight."

Hazard chuckled. "Thank God."

---

HAZARD WAS A very smart man. Although he liked to play the lazy aristocrat, Jasper knew he took very good care of his tenants and his fields yielded well. So when they toured the Iversley estate and its environs—all Jasper's responsibility now—he tried sounding him out.

"Do you think sheep?" he asked. A good number of peers were trying this.

Hazard shook his head with an air of impatience. "Farmers are not shepherds. You have good soil here. Sheep will just tear up the ground."

"Yes, but, a lot of the young lads are leaving the farms. Hieing off to the city."

"The better of them will come back."

Jasper doubted it. But didn't argue.

"Besides," Hazard said, "they won't stay to follow sheep around either. You're better off investing in machinery and encouraging them to use it."

Jasper sighed. He imagined Benjamin would have a head for this, but it would mean coming out to Chaumbers to look around, which Benjamin seemed reluctant to do.

"Your people are doing well," Hazard said. "That's evident just from looking. You don't need to change much of what your father was doing. Just stay alert. Head off small problems before they become large ones."

"For example?"

Hazard laughed. "The most obvious is ensuring your line."

"God." Jasper huffed, peeved even though he knew Hazard was teasing. "I thought I'd have two weeks without harassment."

"I was joking." Hazard gave him a long look that Jasper found difficult to duck. "Jasper, don't let anyone rush you. You may be able to put Vanessa firmly in your past, but it will be a mistake to try to force a relationship with someone else until you do."

"And what makes you so wise?" he scoffed.

Hazard looked off into the distance. "Experience, my friend. Experience."

Jasper decided to let that topic lie.

THE DAYS GREW increasingly hot. Jasper, Hazard, and Olivia rode out to the lake. Hazard pulled the skiff from the boathouse and took Olivia for a row, while Jasper sat, sweating, in the limited shade. He'd brought Georgiana here, he remembered, but could not recall what they'd discussed.

And that, he supposed, demonstrated the effort he had put into wooing her.

Irritated, he stripped down to his drawers and dove into the water. It was bracingly cold. He swam with brisk, strong strokes until his body warmed and his muscles started to ache. Then he returned to shore and dropped to the grass to dry off.

He heard far-off laughter, Olivia and Hazard's. He peered across the lake to see Olivia rowing and Hazard lounging. It made him smile.

He lay back in the grass and closed his eyes. He drifted a bit, not fully asleep but dreaming. The itch of water evaporating from his skin pulled him back in time to the bath he had given Vanessa. For such a beautiful woman, she was shy about her body. It drove him mad. He'd convinced her, once, to wear nothing but a long string of pearls. She was a sight to behold. But she hadn't been able to relax, and he suspected it had not been very good for her. The bath though, that she had enjoyed.

A smile curved on his lips. He'd washed her hair first. Massaged her scalp. And then used that bit of silk to tickle every part of her. He'd been desperately aroused. He was aroused now, remembering.

Her enjoyment had been...loud. And she'd thrashed enough to empty half the tub onto the floor. His shirtsleeves and trousers ended up soaked.

*Ah, Vanessa.*

He heard the boat scrape against the dock. He opened his eyes to see Hazard handing Olivia out. Hazard saw him. Then he spun Olivia around.

"Did you see that fish jump? Look! My God. It looked like a whale!"

"Where?" Olivia laughed and slapped at Hazard's arm, while he held her firmly. "You're imagining things. Again."

Jasper grabbed his trousers and yanked himself into them. Then pulled his shirt over his head. Hazard cast a look over his shoulder before releasing Olivia. Hazard's expression was strange. Annoyed, yes. Half amused. But mostly embarrassed. Jasper was horrified.

He pulled on his stockings, then his boots, slowly. Hazard walked Olivia in a rather wide circle past him. Then he helped her mount her horse.

"Why don't you fly on back to the house?" Hazard said. "Your brother and I will lag behind. He looks sun stricken."

Olivia cast a glance his way, then laughed. "No, he always looks that way."

Hazard slapped the horse's rump and Olivia started homeward. Hazard did not move from his spot.

Jasper got to his feet ungracefully, staggering a little if truth be told.

Hazard cut a look at him. "You should probably spend an hour with a woman."

"Shut up."

"Have you not? Since…" He counted back. "Since *November*?"

"That isn't any of your business."

Hazard shook his head. "Not since November. Tell me: Have you even been tempted?"

"Shut up."

Hazard walked around, cinching the saddles on their mounts. Giving Jasper time to shake off his torpor and his embarrassment. Then he mounted his horse and looked to Jasper with an expression that said: *Are you ready?*

Jasper put his foot in his stirrup and swung a leg over his saddle. They started for the house in silence. And Jasper realized how odd it was, how unlike Hazard, to shut up.

---

Politics was the safest topic, though it should not be, given they had diametrically opposite views.

Dusk had deepened and footmen had lighted a few lamps on the small terrace. Chaumbers was beautiful in the late evenings. Ha! Much more beautiful than it was during the day. Daylight accentuated its architectural flaws.

There was a cool breeze on the terrace and a few stars had begun to peep out. In only three days, Jasper was due back in London and wished now that he had arranged to stay longer. He and Hazard were sipping lemonade and arguing. No, not arguing. Discussing.

Jasper said, "I fall back, again, on Liverpool. 'Every class of religious persons deserves the support, the toleration, and the protection of a rational state.' But that is civil liberty. Liberty. It does not mean Catholics and Dissenters should have access to political power."

"And how much liberty do they have without such power? Good God, man. They cannot sit in Parliament. They cannot hold military office. They cannot even legally marry in their own churches and have those marriages recognized as valid."

"They can have their little ceremonies and then have legal ones. It amounts to the same."

Hazard gave him a hard look. "I will give you a hypothetical. Suppose a Dissenter, or let us say more simply a man with unorthodox views, wishes to teach at Oxford. His brilliance is undeniable. His loyalty to England is unquestionable. But his innate honesty makes him pause over professing to subscribe to the Thirty-Nine Articles."

"If he cannot swear to the tenets of faith of the Church of England, he has no business at Oxford."

"And if that man is Reg?"

Jasper faltered. Then he said, "Reg's quarrel with the church is intellectual, not spiritual."

Hazard laughed. "I suspect he would say they are one and the same."

Jasper gathered back the threads of his argument. "If Reg cannot in good conscience subscribe to the Thirty-Nine, then he cannot teach young Englishman. I make no allowances for family. And will give no preference to friends. The law is the law."

"I agree with you. Which is why I say some laws must be changed. Jasper, do you not think that with a measure of reasonableness, we might have held onto the American Colonies? Do you not see the danger with Ireland—"

"Two different situations entirely."

"Yes. The Irish are far more volatile."

"Their allegiance is to the Pope. Not to the king. You would have us grant political power to hordes who will not accept the authority of the state."

"Church and King," sighed Hazard, shaking his head. "You are the echo of your father."

"There are worse men to echo."

Hazard raised his glass in tribute. "Indeed." He took a drink, then smacked his lips. "A shame Hovington's niece is not here. Alice would have you voting for Catholic Emancipation before sunrise."

"We invited her, but she could not come."

Hazard looked askance at him. "You invited her? I hope not for my sake."

"I'm not matchmaking." Jasper sniffed at the very idea. "She's Olivia's friend."

"Not matchmaking, no. But you are trying to draw me back into the arena."

"You have strong opinions. You should voice them."

Hazard let out a long sigh. "My voice, if I were to raise it too loudly, will only harm a cause so worthy."

"That is not—"

"Moreover, and perhaps more significantly, I have grown too staid and too cowardly to draw unnecessary attention to myself."

Words died on Jasper's lips. Uncomfortable with the direction of the discussion, he resettled in his chair and leaned his head back to count the stars. More were emerging against the blackening sky. Hazard was right, of course. Unfair though it may be, it was wiser for him to fade into the background. And it was an unfair world that would force Reg to swear against his own conscience in order to hold a position he was more than qualified to hold. Qualified, except that he was too highborn to be a don, so he would likely make all his contributions from the fringes. And Alice could write persuasive speeches but never deliver them. And he could not marry Vanessa.

"We live in a cruel world," he murmured.

"We have made it so."

Jasper drained his glass. Then slapped a biting bug on his arm.

"Let's go inside. The billiard table is calling."

## Chapter Twenty

Vanessa read aloud to Charlotte and Sweet Kate, pleased that Charlotte was peering over her shoulder, picking out words. A knock on her front door interrupted them.

"One moment," she called, rising. She handed the book to Charlotte. "Save the page."

She exited the kitchen and went through the parlor to open her door. Lydia stood there, framed against the gray sky and dirt road, an odd expression on her face. She wore a crumpled bonnet, a dusty yellow dress, and her usual weathered boots. But the boots now sported tooled butterflies on the toes.

"Lydia!" She wasn't expecting a visit. Lydia was generally too busy to walk all this way. "Come in. Have tea with us. Charlotte is here." She waved her inside and closed the door. Vanessa felt a little embarrassed by the spaciousness, the spare cleanliness of her parlor. She hardly ever used it. It seemed an extravagance when compared to the clutter and crowding of the Compton home and workshop. "What brings you?"

"Charlotte is here?" Lydia frowned and lowered her voice. "I-I have news."

Vanessa paused, made wary by Lydia's caution. "News?"

"Mmm-hmmm. About the boots Jon sent to that couple you met in Binnings."

Bitter had shown her the boots, artfully engraved with lilies.

Lady Georgiana was sure to love them.

"What about them?"

"This morning, Sherwood brought over a letter."

"A letter?" Vanessa's heart sank. She had thought it safe to allow Jon to send the boots to 'Lady Georgiana' at Crumbley House in Cambridge. Georgiana and Reginald would learn only that the bootmakers were in Cartmel, but wouldn't necessarily conclude that she lived here as well. If they did, she supposed she had to trust that Reginald would say nothing to Jasper. But she certainly never thought Georgiana would write back to the Comptons. "What did it say?"

"Only that the lady was well pleased with her boots." Lydia's smile was strange. Strained. "And that her friends were agog. They sent six pounds and two tracings with a request for two more pairs. One customer asked for kingcup. The other could not make up her mind and said any flower would do. Vanessa, six pounds for two pairs of boots!"

Vanessa's heart swelled. She wished she could embrace Georgiana. She wished she *had* embraced her.

"Can Bitter make them?" It seemed to her it must be a tremendous amount of work.

"Oh, the others will make them. Bitter will do the decoration—and quicker now he's not hiding his efforts. Jon is...well, you can imagine. Thank you. Even if this is the most that comes of it, the work could not have come at a better time. It's only...I'm not sure they should be too hopeful."

Vanessa nodded. "Yes, I understand. There is no guarantee there will be more."

She would write to Rose and Effie. Today. But she wouldn't say anything yet to Lydia. She didn't want to raise hopes and then dash them. If only Lady Georgiana would parade the boots around London.

She took Lydia's arm. "Come in. We'll celebrate. Charlotte brought over a couple of buns, drizzled with honey. Dan's hives are doing well."

Lydia resisted. "I won't interrupt."

"Nonsense." Vanessa's smile faded at the expression on Lydia's face. Questioning. Concerned. Perhaps even a little irritated.

"Vanessa." Lydia spoke quietly but there was an underlying hardness to her tone. "The letter was from a Mr. Reginald Taverston."

Vanessa froze.

Lydia waited, then pressed, "Any relation?"

Vanessa was caught. Caught. "A brother." She hurried to try to explain. "The meeting was coincidental. But I suppose their kindness was not."

Oh! How foolish. So anxious to do a good deed, it had made her careless.

"I see." Lydia's expression was doubtful. "But you said nothing. I agreed when Jon said if it was happenstance, it was odd you made no mention it. And the corporal said he does not believe in coincidence where Lieutenant Taverston is concerned."

It could not be any worse.

"You all discussed this?"

"Only to scratch our heads. If Lieutenant Taverston is involved, it seems wisest not to ask too many questions."

"It is nothing secretive. Good Heavens. How ridiculous." Vanessa scrambled. "It's only that the corporal tried to get a small contract from the army and Lieutenant Taverston was unable to help. He wrote to his brother, suggesting that he buy boots and encourage his fellows to do so. But when Mrs. Taverston saw my boots…"

Was she making any sense at all?

Lydia narrowed her eyes. "So you *have* been in touch with the Lieutenant?"

"No. Well, yes. But only once in a while. I saw him a couple of times in London. And he wrote to me once here. After Vitoria." Vanessa swallowed hard. Tallying her lies and half-truths. "It must appear strange, I suppose."

"Not so very." Lydia smiled smugly. "He was always politer

to you than to most—well, most of us weren't always so polite to him, if you take my meaning."

Women in camp flirted outrageously. They meant nothing by it. It was a means of coping. But she had never been able to talk salty or swish her skirts. On campaign, she had only rarely spoken with Crispin. When they did speak, he'd always treated her with respect. As if she were a lady.

"Lieutenant Taverston was *not* interested in me." How often must she say that?

"Yet he found you in London. And wrote to you here? Lovey—"

"I-it's because of Henry." Vanessa remembered something strange that might serve as an excuse. "Henry was a physician. That is, his father was, and Henry had been apprenticed to him. Lieutenant Taverston was not feeling well one day, and Henry advised him. I think Lieutenant Taverston felt he owed Henry something."

Lydia's expression softened. "Your Henry was always helping like that. He was a good one."

Vanessa started to relax, but Lydia put a hand on her arm.

"Why didn't you ever say anything?"

"I don't know." She couldn't think of any reasonable excuse, so she just piled on. "I suppose I didn't want you or anyone thinking Lieutenant Taverston favored me."

"Well, if that isn't the silliest thing. Lovey, it isn't anything to be ashamed of. You've been a widow for four years! That's more than long enough. Lordy, the corporal said it was past time for Lieutenant Taverston to stop fiddling around. He's ready to write him to come claim you before Sherwood makes a bigger fool of himself than he already has."

"No!" Vanessa shuddered. "Good God, no. Don't let him write to Cr—Lieutenant Taverston. He isn't going to come claim me. I cannot imagine anything more ridiculous." Or humiliating. Crispin would be appalled. Or laugh himself sick. "Lydia, he was a friend to me. That is all. Please do not embarrass me. Please!"

"Calm down. I won't embarrass you. I wouldn't have said anything at all, since you seemed so determined not to. It's only that Bitter is so convinced there is a market for his boots. And even Jon is hopeful. But if this is just Lieutenant Taverston's charity…"

"No. It isn't." What had she said? About Crispin and the boots? Oh! She could not keep her stories straight. "It wasn't charity. It might have been if Mr. Taverston bought three pairs of plain boots. But Mrs. Taverston was truly charmed by mine. And I didn't ask her to show them to her friends. She just did. I can't promise there is a market beyond this, but there may be."

Good Lord. Now even she had doubts. It was a coincidence. It had to be. Reginald said Crispin had property in Binnings, but he couldn't have known she was going there. Not even Crispin could read her mind from Spain.

"I-I thought I could write to a few friends in London who might be interested. I think Jon has reason to be hopeful. If more ladies wear the boots, more ladies will see them."

"You have such wealthy friends in London?"

Oh! She should keep her mouth closed. "Acquaintances, only. Of course, nothing may come of it." She wrung her hands and tried to smile.

"Well, we'll keep our fingers crossed." Lydia gave Vanessa a long look and seemed poised to say more. But she tossed her head and said only, "I suppose I should get back. I've a pot bubbling on the stove and the corporal never remembers to stir. I don't mean to intrude on your visit but tell Charlotte I say hello."

Vanessa let her go, not wanting to continue the conversation. How stupid she had been. She should have recognized the risk that the Comptons would find out the boots had gone to a Mrs. Taverston and make the connection to Crispin. But perhaps it wasn't so bad. Of course, they gossiped about her. Speculated. But no one *knew*.

With a heavy sigh, she returned to the back room. Charlotte looked up abruptly. Her eyes were wide and her jaw slack. The book fell to the floor.

Charlotte's head dipped. "I-I didn't. Vanessa, I didn't mean—I just peeked ahead."

"And lost the page?" Vanessa asked. Why on earth was Charlotte so pale? "No harm done, Charlotte. I read a bit ahead myself the other night when—" When she'd cut the pages. Oh, God. Oh, God, no.

Vanessa dashed around Charlotte's chair and knelt on the floor. She lifted the book hesitantly. There, beneath it, lay the slip of paper she'd used to mark her place. Intending to read a bit more in the morning. But she had not. In fact, she'd forgotten all about it. Because she had not been as engrossed in the novel as she'd been in her own daydreams. Running her fingers over the bit of foolscap again and again. Tracing the words on the bit of paper she should have burned, but never did. She snatched it up.

Charlotte could not read much. Oh, but the words were simple. *I love you. Always.—J.T.*

Vanessa crumpled the paper in her hand. Charlotte blinked several times and fixed her gaze on the ground.

In a small, determined voice, Charlotte asked, "What is this Lieutenant Taverston's Christian name? Who you say does not favor you?"

Vanessa bit her lip. She'd thought they had been talking quietly, but Charlotte must have heard every word.

"Crispin." It did not begin with a *J.*

Charlotte's face fell. "And the other?"

"The other?"

"The gentleman you met in Binnings. With his wife."

What was Charlotte accusing her of? She snapped, "Reginald. It begins with an *R.*"

Charlotte scooped Sweet Kate, who had begun to fuss, onto her shoulder and patted her back.

"But Taverston does begin with a *T.*" She rocked Sweet Kate back and forth. "It isn't my business who. I know it isn't. It's just—" She searched a minute for the words. "It has been more than four years since Henry's death. And this man *loves* you."

"It doesn't matter."

"And you're holding onto his letter. You must care—"

"It doesn't matter."

"Well, for pity's sake, Vanessa. Why not?"

Why not?

"Because," she said, sitting down heavily. She was so weary of this. "Because he is a gentleman. And gentlemen do not marry for love."

All Charlotte answered was, "Oh."

Vanessa kept quiet a moment, waiting for questions, waiting for sympathy, then she spoke.

"I don't want to be teased or pitied, Charlotte. Can I ask you to keep this to yourself?"

Charlotte scowled. "I'm not going to spill your secrets. It's just that it makes me angry. He says he loves you, but what kind of love is that?"

"He has obligations."

"Oh, now, don't go defending him. He had no business falling in love with you if he was going to cry off."

"It's not that simple."

"No? Well, it should be." Charlotte tossed her head and gave Sweet Kate another bounce. "Put him out of your head. There are plenty of men, good men, who'd marry you in a minute. You don't want to be alone, do you? No children? A cold bed?"

No, she didn't.

"Sherwood is a little too full of himself," Charlotte went on. "And Jon is probably too old. But Tam is good-hearted. Just too shy to ever say much. And over in Barrow—"

"Charlotte, don't." The last thing she wanted was a matchmaker. "I'm not ready."

Charlotte harumphed, then sat back down and loosened her neckline so Sweet Kate could nurse. Vanessa took a sip of cold tea.

"Should I read a bit more?"

Charlotte nodded. "I suppose. But Vanessa, if you just look around, you'll find someone right quick, and this J.T. will fly out of your head."

Vanessa was not about to argue. But Jasper would never "fly out of her head." Or her heart. She loved him. Always. She always would.

# Chapter Twenty-One

Back from Chaumbers, at home in London, Jasper sat in the library of all places, reading a collection of Walpole's papers. Hazard's hero. Parliament would open again in a couple months and, this time, Jasper wanted to understand the opposition better. He wanted to not simply vote Tory because it was what Taverstons had always done, but because he believed in the positions he would be espousing. The problem was, that it was hard to argue against some of what Walpole said.

Some, but not all. Even Hazard disagreed with Walpole's vehement anti-papism. Of all the Tory's steadfast dictums, Jasper was now finding that refusing to grant basic rights to Catholics stuck most in his craw. Reg would certainly agree with Hazard that religious discrimination against Catholic Englishmen, even against Irishmen, was blatantly wrong. And Jasper trusted no man's opinions more than those of his brilliant brother.

Good God. Imagine if his maiden speech before Parliament was a cry *for* Catholic Emancipation. The stir that would cause. Father would roll over in his grave.

Could he do it? Break from the Earl of Iversley mold? If the cruel world they inhabited was one of their own making, should he not work to change it?

He closed the book in his lap, thinking, and grew aware of a pulsing in the room. Like the air was gathering momentum for a storm. In fact, the house, the dull tomb of a house, had developed a chatter. A noise. Which was absurd. His mental energy was insufficient to create a thunderclap. Yet he was not imagining it. There was noise.

Before he had a chance to rise and investigate, the library door clicked open, and Crispin strolled in. As if returning from an evening promenade in the park.

"Hallo, Jasp. The library? Really?"

The deuce.

Jasper vaulted from his chair and crashed across the room to wring his brother in an embrace. For a moment longer than Jasper expected, Crispin held on.

Then Crispin stepped back. "Do we *hug* now?"

"Don't blame me. Reg started it."

Crispin's eyes widened. "Good God!"

While Jasper laughed, Crispin paced a few steps and then sat in Jasper's chair. He picked up the book Jasper had dropped, scanned the title, dropped it, and rose.

"I'm in the wrong house. That explains."

"Sit down. Tell me everything. When did you get back?"

"Ship got in yesterday." He plopped back down.

"And you had better things to do last night than be hugged by me?"

"Yes." He crossed his legs at the ankles and lounged. "Long boat ride. Men have needs."

Jasper snorted. Very likely Crispin had reveled the night away in Southwark. Equally likely, he'd been in meetings at the War Office from debarkation until dawn. He was still in uniform, red cutaway jacket with gold buttons, white pantaloons, and waistcoat—the crisp cleanliness suggested duty rather than pleasure, but with Crispin, it could go either way.

Wellington's success at Vitoria was evidently as impressive as the dispatches for public consumption made them out to be, though perhaps it could have been more complete. But there was more to it. There was always more. The army was pushing on into France. And Crispin would be as tight lipped as ever. Still, he might have something burdensome to talk around.

"So, Lieutenant Taverston, Vitoria? I will grant you five minutes to boast of your deeds."

"That is Captain Taverston to you."

"Captain?"

Crispin shrugged. "I may have been mentioned in the dispatches."

"Crispin!" He took a proud step closer. "That is wonderful! Congratulations!"

Crispin cringed. "You aren't going to hug me again?"

"No. But tell me! What you can of it. I want to know. More than what came in that letter of yours. I could have sworn you'd been drinking by the—"

"I had. Paid for it dearly. But just in the common way. So there is that."

It was unlike Crispin to refer to the uncommon way of it. For a moment, Jasper was nonplussed.

"I don't want to talk of war, Jasp. My throat is raw from it. I feel I've been grilled over a firepit."

"Bathurst? Liverpool? I hope not Canning."

"Let us speak of love, instead. Yours."

"Ha." He grumbled and turned his back. "There is nothing to say."

"I was hoping to hear a word from Vanessa. But she is stubborn. She has a right to be, I suppose."

"Enough, Crispin. I was wrong. Don't rub salt in it. I should've married her, not taken her as a mistress." He walked farther away, to the window to look out, so as not to look at his brother. But Crispin's gaze was inescapable. It seared holes through his back. He repeated his *mea culpa*. "I should have married her."

"I have a quibble with that, but we will come to it."

"Leave it, Crispin."

"Who says you should have married her?"

"Everyone thinks it."

"Surely not."

"Crispin." He turned to confront him. Anger building slowly. He didn't want to be angry. Not with Crispin and not with himself. "Don't play your games with me."

"I understand why you did not. Honestly. I do. She's a commoner. And while that occasionally does not prove a barrier to men of our ilk—money, beauty, even that strange intangible called 'love' have been used as excuses—you don't make excuses. Not when it comes to duty. You just do it. And earls marry blood; it is their duty to carry forth the line."

"You think I'm cold."

"I admire you. I won't repeat that ever, but it is true."

Again, Jasper was nonplussed.

Crispin, of course, had more words. "Yet I have never known an aristocrat who did not possess a quirk. It's a duty, too, I think, to do one thing wrong. You're allotted one mistake. It's courteous to use it; perfection is obnoxious."

Jasper groaned. "You will play your games regardless."

"Granted, you were due a blushing virgin on your wedding night."

"Stop." His tone threatened.

"But she was a pretty young widow. Widows are acceptable enough. Even for you."

"Stop." He used his earl's voice.

"You could have married her."

Damn, it. Nothing stopped Crispin once he began. So Jasper surrendered.

"I know that. Do you think I do not thrash myself every day? I was a different man, then. A blind one."

"Not so different," Crispin murmured. "Say it again. What you should have done."

"I should have married her! Now go to hell."

"That, your verb tense, is my quibble. Though I'm not thrilled with the imperative, either." The damn eyebrow arched.

"So you say that you thrash yourself with this daily? Do you envision these your dying words?"

"The mistake is made. I can't go back and undo it."

"My God." Crispin laughed his disbelief. "Your head is thick. Move forward. Not back."

"If you have something worthwhile to say—"

"Marry her. Is that plain enough?"

Jasper stared. "You're a lunatic. I can't marry her. Not…God, Crispin. You aren't naïve. Don't pretend to be." He cut off any rebuttal. "It's my fault. I accept that."

"Exactly what do you accept? Say it aloud."

Jasper's anger was now well and truly stoked. No one could needle him as thoroughly as Crispin could.

"That I *ruined* her. *I* did. Is that what you want to hear? She was my mistress. Everyone knows—"

"Here is that 'everyone' again." Crispin sighed, rolling back his shoulders.

Then he rose, striding to a cabinet where Father kept liquor stashed. The old earl was not a secret tippler, but he liked a nip before bed and didn't always want to be after the servants. Jasper kept his nips in the study rather than the library. But Crispin? Jasper watched him with concern. Crispin did not drink spirits. It made him ill. Yet he'd gone straight for the cabinet?

Crispin took out a bottle and poured a hefty glass. He set the bottle back and brought the glass to Jasper.

"Ha! That look on your face. Did you think I meant to swill it?"

Jasper said, "Or throw it at me." He took the glass. "Why does this feel you wish me to brace myself, rather than console myself."

"You don't deserve to be consoled." Crispin stepped away. "Tell me more about this 'everyone,'" he said, moving to the bookshelves. "This 'everyone' who says Vanessa is 'ruined.' Tainted. Dare I say a—"

"Don't!" Jasper slammed the glass down on the windowsill,

shattering it. Shards of glass littered the carpet. Brandy dripped down the wall.

"The Prince Regent? Wellington? Are they everyone?"

Both were flagrant adulterers. And Wellington's older brother had married his longtime mistress. It could be done. But society shunned the woman. That argument held no water.

"Or are you more concerned with the good opinion of everyone close to you?" Crispin wrinkled his brow as though he were considering the question. "Your friends? Surely you don't fear *Hazard* will take you to task for impropriety?"

"Leave Hazard out of this."

Something in his tone alerted Crispin that Hazard was out of bounds. He acknowledged that with a nearly imperceptible nod.

"It is Carleton then. Or Penworthy. Men whose respect you cannot bear to lose."

"Crispin, shut up. You've made your point. We are all base creatures."

"That isn't my point. Who is *everyone*, Jasper? Your family? Will Reginald judge you harshly? Will I?"

"You always do."

"Not always." Crispin rubbed a hand over his eyes. A momentary illusion of weariness. Or maybe not an illusion. "Mother and Olivia?"

Jasper nodded slowly. "Mother would be disappointed. And I could not—expose Olivia to—"

"Oh, bollocks. You prig! You unworthy prig!" Crispin shouted. Then lowered his voice. "Mother adapts. That is what she does. And Olivia will be her own person no matter what you *expose* her to. Good God. This is Vanessa we are talking about. Not some disease."

"I know it's Vanessa, damn it."

"Then who is everyone, Jasper?" He leaned forward. Earnest. Almost menacing. "Tell me. Who is this *everyone* who believes Vanessa is unacceptable? A ruined woman. Who? In whose eyes does it matter?"

Jasper ground his jaw. Crispin stood glaring. Waiting for him to speak. If he did not, Crispin would answer his own question. And Jasper could not bear it. He couldn't bear to be so accused. Because he had no defense. He was guilty and knew it.

"Mine. You want me to say it matters in my eyes."

"Is she acceptable to *you*? To you, Jasper? Or is she not?"

Jasper crumbled. Leaning against the window, turning his head, he felt hot tears in his eyes and shook his head hard to dash them away. What had he *done*? His shoulders heaved. He caught his breath. Desperate not to break down in front of Crispin. Not to break down at all.

"Have I pulverized you sufficiently?" Crispin sounded bored. "Are you mush? God, Jasper. Buck up. I didn't even use the thumb screws."

Jasper whirled on him. Snarling. But there was something in his brother's eyes that stopped him cold. Something deadened. And behind that, something…dying. What had this war done to him?

"I suppose," he said, his own myriad emotions flushed away in a wave of compassion, "that Britain is fortunate to have you."

"Huh." Crispin backed away. "But my brothers, not so very." Then he coughed. He sank into the nearest chair, a spindly lady's chair that made Crispin, with his height and his skin-and-bones frame, appear macabre. "Sometimes…sometimes I get carried away." Then he gave the weakest smile Jasper had ever seen him attempt. "I was joking about the thumbscrews."

"I will choose to believe that."

They were quiet for a long moment.

Jasper surprised himself by breaking the silence. "I don't know what to do. I don't know where she is. No one knows. Except Collingswood." He practically spat the name.

"Well." Crispin turned up his hands. "If you found her, what would you do?"

"I don't know."

"That isn't the right answer."

"Apologize abjectly. Propose. On my knees. Beg if I must." The ton be damned. He would bully Vanessa's entrée into it or be done with it. Abandon London for Chaumbers and never look back.

"And if she says no? And means it? If she won't have you?"

"If she truly does not want me back, then I-I will have to let her go. I can't make her life a misery. I mean, I have. But I won't again."

Crispin put his hands on his knees and pushed himself up. Unfolded himself. He nodded. Like a soldier accepting his orders.

"Give me a few days. There may be something I can do." He started for the door.

"Crispin! Wait, Crispin. Do you know where she is? Damn it. You've known all along?"

"I knew where she was. That doesn't mean I know where she is. I said, 'Give me a couple of days.'"

He walked out the door.

Jasper stared after him. He should not, still, be astonished by Crispin. But he was. Every time. A few days to sort out his brother's mess over four years in the making? Crispin had made no promises, yet Jasper felt light with hope. If only he could prove to Vanessa that *he* believed her to be a perfectly acceptable countess...

And then it came to him. How he might convince Vanessa. He'd have to hurry if he had only a couple of days before Crispin...what? Brought Vanessa back to London? Arranged a meeting elsewhere? What did he mean by he might be able to do something? Crispin, damn it!

All at once, his frustration ebbed, then turned inward. *Crispin.* He should have asked after Crispin's health. Not that he would have answered. And it would have annoyed him to be asked. But he appeared thinner, did he not, than he had a few months ago at Chaumbers? Jasper should have looked closer. *Was* he thinner?

The devil. Jasper was the elder, the head of the family. How could he have allowed Crispin, once again, to take charge and then disappear?

# Part 6

## This is Love

**March 1809**
**London**

# Chapter Twenty-Two

The Rose Room smelled of lavender, a trivial incongruity that should not trouble Vanessa as much as it did. Perhaps it was because she had nothing to do except breathe it in. Or, perhaps it was because every thought in her head was troublesome.

Jasper's mother hated her. Well, fine. She'd expected as much. But the countess accused her of turning Jasper into some sort of libertine. Which was nonsense. Yet how long until his mother's disapproval influenced the way Jasper saw her?

She was afraid of what might happen tonight. It was silly to be fearful—as silly as Jasper wishing to hide her from God knew what. He was investing a good deal of time and effort into merely embarrassing Hilyer. Vanessa was pleased to envision the marquess's humiliation, yet she worried that it would prove both too much and not enough. Hilyer would slink away from London. But what prevented him from just slinking back?

What were they attempting to accomplish? Jasper wanted her to be comfortable in his world. Perhaps, in some small way, she could be. He had friends who were kind enough to make her welcome in limited settings. Yet if Hilyer chose to make trouble for her, she would find herself shunned even by them. So Jasper meant to strike first.

He understood the ton. He knew what he was doing. She accepted this. She wanted Hilyer gone. But she was frightened.

What if he did call Jasper out? Or worse. What if Jasper lost his temper and challenged Hilyer? The marquess would choose pistols.

Oh, dear God, don't let her be the cause of Jasper's death too. Surely Hazard would not let that happen. Or Crispin.

And that was another thing bothering her. Why on earth was Crispin here? She couldn't decide if the man's presence reassured her or frightened her. It seemed too odd, too serendipitous, for him to be home. Jasper hadn't known he was coming. That much was clear. Jasper had been shocked to see him. And yet, here he was. Now.

She was surely making too much of this. But.

She would never say anything to Jasper, but there had been whispers amongst those in their regiment about the lieutenant. She'd paid the rumors little mind. If men admired their superior officer, they tended to inflate his importance, and by extension inflate their own. Henry had been very, very drunk one night and boasted that their lieutenant gathered intelligence for the War Office. He said it with such slurring admiration that Vanessa gave it as much credence as silly Marybelle claiming the lieutenant was a pirate.

But now she'd heard from Crispin's own mouth that General Wellesley had put letters into his hands.

Yet how ridiculous to read anything into that. How long had Crispin been in the army? A year? A little over a year? His father was an earl. That was why he was carting letters to and from London. It was a posh assignment for a well-connected young lord. That was all.

His presence in London had nothing to do with Jasper's ploy to publicly embarrass Hilyer. How could it? She was only on edge because Jasper was. She wished he'd simply left her at home.

Vanessa ceased her pacing and lay down on the bed. It was comfortably soft. It, too, smelled of lavender. The ceiling, she noted, was decorated around the edges with painted tea roses. Pink and white. Quite lovely.

Everything she'd seen in this house had been lovely. Such a contrast with her father's mansion. He might as well have plastered the walls with banknotes. Mother never once stood up to him. Never. And Freddy…Freddy was timid. She'd tried to take his part when Father rampaged, but that made things worse. So Freddy, her sweet little brother, had come to resent her for stirring up Father more.

Seeing Jasper and Crispin together hurt her somewhere deep in her heart's core. They might bicker, but no one else had better dare cross them. They were a force. Together, a force.

She supposed she needn't worry about Hilyer.

She jumped up from the bed and strode to the window. She pulled back the curtain and looked out—out upon a rose garden of course. The bushes were all trimmed back neatly. It would be gorgeous if it were not midwinter.

It would not be difficult to escape. There was a trellis against the wall with a few trailing vines. She could climb out the window and down. There must be a back gate from the garden to the street. She could escape the countess's wrath and go home.

Or she could escape and make her way to Brooks's. They would not let her in, but she could wait outside for Jasper.

And do what?

She could see Lydia shaking her head. *Don't go looking for trouble. There's enough of it looking for you.* Women were just as prone to foolish heroics as men. Lydia had prevented untold disasters by reining in desperately frightened—or just desperate—wives. If she were here now, she would order Vanessa to lie down in that comfortable bed and quit fussing over nothing.

She let the curtain close.

Then heard a knock on the door.

"Come in."

A maid entered, followed by a second. The first carried a bowl of water and had clean towels draped over her arm. The second brought a covered tray.

"Supper, miss. If you please." The maid bobbed a curtsy and

put the tray on the table.

The first said, "If you'll be needing help with your dress or your hair, I'm to attend to you."

Vanessa blinked at them, wondering who had sent them. Jasper? Before leaving? Or the earl? Surely not the countess.

"Thank you. But I won't need anything else."

She would be a fine soldier's wife if she could not get in and out of her own clothing.

The maids dipped their heads and went out. Vanessa lifted the lid from the tray. A veritable feast. Chicken or perhaps duck. Gravy and peas. Bread thick with butter. Cherries. And a small cup of wine.

She sat to eat. The food was piping hot. Except for the chilled cherries and wine.

The meal was not resentfully provided. It was not bread crusts and water.

She tasted it all, though she was not hungry. She wouldn't send it back to the kitchen untouched in case the fact might be reported to someone. She wouldn't add rudeness or ingratitude to her faults. Then she rose, went to the door, and put her ear against it, listening for house sounds. Just wind and creaking. No voices. No footsteps.

Oh, for Heaven's sake. She was being foolish. It was only a snub. Jasper had marshaled a small army for a snub. If this were all it took to ruin a man, the ton's pretensions to superiority were ludicrous. When her father had ruined rivals, the men were left destitute.

It was too early to try to sleep. The evening would be endless.

Something spattered against the window. Like hail, but rapid fire, then quiet, then spattering again.

She stepped to the window and looked out once more. A tall, slender, blond man stood in the garden, draped in a dark greatcoat. Crispin. She pushed open the window, and he began ascending the trellis. She watched, gaping, as he rose.

Something was wrong. Very wrong. Something that he had

to hide from the earl and countess.

"Ouch! Damn it!" He swore as his head crested the sill.

"Is Jasper all right? What happened?"

"Jasper?" He laughed shortly. "He's fine. *I* am bleeding." He held up his finger to show her the prick. "I forgot the vines had thorns." He stuck the finger in his mouth.

"What are you doing?" She could hear her blood pounding in her ears. Jasper was fine. Crispin said he was fine.

"There is a…complication. I need to know, quickly, about your brother. His character."

"My *brother*? Crispin, what on earth?" She shivered, not only from the cold evening air. How could Freddy be involved in anything that would interest Crispin?

"How would you describe his character? Please."

She thought a moment, perplexed, frightened, then answered as best she could.

"Weak."

"Ah." He looked past her, chewing his lip. Then he said quietly, "Vanessa, if someone were to harm either of my brothers, or my sister, even inadvertently, and I were to find out, I would never forgive them. Ever. So…"

"Someone wants to hurt Freddy?"

His face softened. *"Freddy*? Not Frederick?"

"Oh, not to me. He's a boy, Crispin. He's sixteen."

"Hell." Pity and frustration washed over his features. "So his character is malleable."

He started to lower himself back down, but she grabbed his wrist and held tight.

"What is happening? Crispin, tell me."

Crispin emitted an annoyed sigh. "Your father's son is in a place he shouldn't be. I needed to know if it was worth the effort of extricating him. It seems it is."

"He's in danger?" Vanessa's heart clenched and clenched again when Crispin nodded. "What can I do?"

"Nothing. Except let go of me."

She let go. "I want to help."

He started to shake his head, but then paused and peered at her. "What motivates him? What would be the best way to lure him from one place to another?"

"From where to where?"

"It's best I don't say."

"For Heaven's sake." She glared at him. "Do you know how absurd you sound?"

"Yes. Sorry." He rubbed his injured finger against his coat. "Would money lure him? Or a girl?"

"He has money enough. I don't know about girls. Surely he's too young." Freddy's motivation? "He wants to please my father."

Crispin gave her a pitying look. "I suspect that's why he is where he is now."

"You need only to make him leave a place?" How curious. And that shouldn't be so hard. "Nothing more?"

"He needs to leave quietly and stay away for a few hours."

A few hours. "Maybe…" Oh, it was unlikely, but Crispin was looking at her expectantly, so she continued. "Maybe if I were to send him a note. Asking him to meet me somewhere."

Crispin shook his head. "You can't meet him."

"All right." She wasn't sure that she actually wanted to see Freddy. "But I could ask him to meet me all the same." She considered the possibilities. "If I were to tell him I was in trouble and needed to flee…I could tell him I'm afraid Hilyer will claim me after all and make me suffer for insulting him by running away."

"Go on."

"I could tell him to please bring me ten pounds, enough to flee to the countryside. To a friend's house."

"Would he go, do you think, to Trafalgar Square? To the bronze Charles? That is a good distance and should keep him busy for a while. If you were to ask him to meet you after midnight, perhaps one o'clock, would he go? And wander and wait, looking for you?"

"I think he would." She shrugged, saddened to think of it. He hadn't tried to help her when she needed help, but what could he have done? Perhaps he regretted his inaction. Or perhaps he resented her for the trouble she'd caused. "Either he will bring me the ten pounds, or he will come with one of my father's bully boys to see me delivered to Hilyer himself."

"Christ." Disgust contorted Crispin's face. "If that's even a possibility, I should leave him where he is."

"I don't want him harmed."

"No, of course you don't." Crispin shifted his weight and the trellis creaked beneath him. The wind blew hard, and Vanessa wrapped her arms across her chest, but Crispin didn't seem to notice the cold. "There is paper in the top right desk drawer. Foolscap. And there should be pens and ink too. Will Freddy recognize your handwriting? He will believe it's from you?"

"Yes. How will you deliver it?"

He flashed a grin at her. "I ask the questions, Vanessa." The smile fell away. "Don't say too much. Just what you said. You need help. Ten pounds. Trafalgar Square. Close to one o'clock."

She moved to the dresser and found the writing materials. She scribbled out the words and signed it: *Devotedly, Nessa*. Then she folded it and took it back to the window to put it into Crispin's hands. He glanced at it and nodded.

"Vanessa, I make no promises. But you should know I tried, and you did your best. And Jasper knows nothing about any of this."

Jasper's ignorance relieved her more than she could say.

"All right."

"And, Vanessa, if your brother should come to you in the next few days, or write to you, you have to deny any knowledge of this. Deny all of it. You did not write this. You have no idea who forged your signature or why."

"But I signed it *Nessa*."

"Is that a secret between you two?"

"No. Not a secret. Just not well known outside of the family."

"That's all right. He *is* your father's heir. It should make sense to him that your father arranged his rescue. Vanessa, if my name is mentioned at all, Jasper will be dragged into something he should not be dragged into."

That sounded like a warning.

"Frankly, Crispin, I am frightened enough of you without explicit threats. If you tell me to lie to my brother, I will."

He smiled delightedly. "Smart girl." He tucked the letter into his shirt. "I have to go." He lowered himself a foot, then looked up. "Oh. Lie to Jasper, too, if you can."

"I'm not sure I can."

"No matter. I can."

Then he climbed down another few feet, jumped to the ground, and disappeared through the garden.

# Chapter Twenty-Three

To pass the time before Hazard's gambling party, Jasper walked. This was what he did when his mind was unsettled, or his body was restless, or he was bored. He found London's streets endlessly soothing and fascinatingly varied. Of course, as a general rule, he stayed away from the stews. When he was in the mood to be sociable, he walked to places where he was likely to come across friends. Tonight, he avoided those, saving up his sociability for later. Most of the time, he preferred quiet, settled areas where common folk lived crowded together in neat little houses. Sometimes he peered at the pale light of the windows and wondered at the occupants. What did they discuss? What did they *do*?

It was too soon to make his appearance at Brooks's. He had taken Vanessa to Grosvenor Square far too early, intending to show her about the family home. His callowness galled him. His father had treated Vanessa so kindly the other day that he'd mistakenly envisioned a better reception. But this was the Taverston family home. He was wrong to bring his mistress to it. His heart ached to think Vanessa would never be welcome there. Or at Chaumbers.

He wondered if the commoners had similar woes.

At last, as dusk deepened to night, Jasper turned his feet toward St. James Street. He made sure to reach more traveled, safer roads before footpads started to make their rounds. Many of his peers walked with burly footmen at night. Or only went out in carriages. But Jasper liked to walk and to walk alone. He tipped his hat to men he knew who were going elsewhere, and fell in alongside Lord Mountjoy who was also on his way to Brooks's.

Lord Mountjoy patted his purse. "I won four hundred pounds last week. Shame to see it all go."

"You plan to lose?" Jasper asked.

"Prinny is coming, is he not? We'll all lose."

Jasper laughed. That was true enough. It was considered the height of bad manners to win money from the Prince Regent. They were all expected to graciously lose.

They reached the yellow-brick and Portland Stone clubhouse and entered, handing over their coats, hats, and walking sticks. Hazard came out to greet them, rubbing his hands together.

"New knot?" Jasper asked, examining Hazard's neckcloth. The folds were intricate. He'd never seen the style before.

"Yes, Philip finally attempted it. Did a fine job, too, if I do say so." Hazard ran a hand over his temple as though brushing back a stray lock. Jasper wondered if he was nervous. Hazard turned to Lord Mountjoy, "How is Lady Mountjoy's dandie?"

Lord Mountjoy grimaced. "Damn dog chewed up my best Hessians. All Bess said was I shouldn't have left them lying around."

Hazard laughed. "Console yourself at the bar. I need to borrow Lord Taverston for a few minutes. To show him the set-up in the card room. He's not familiar with Brooks's, you know."

"Ha! Damn Tory." He gave Jasper's arm a shake and moved on.

"Come," Hazard said. He gestured about as he led Jasper through the high-ceilinged Great Subscription Room where the gambling was well underway. Gaming tables cobbled the floor and soft-footed servants circulated with drinks and fresh decks of cards. "We have a bit of a crowd already, as you can see."

This was more than the usual collection of Brooks's clubmen.

Jasper recognized quite a number of faces from White's and several lesser-knowns from Boodle's.

Hazard opened a side door, and they entered a smaller room that was also designed for card playing. Several four-to-six-person tables were surrounded by round-backed mahogany chairs. Plush curtains muffled the street noise. Along the back wall, a long table held platters of food, glasses, and a scandalous amount of champagne.

"And we are ostensibly celebrating what?"

"My mother's birthday."

Jasper made a face. "Seriously?"

"Why not?"

Shaking his head, Jasper said, "And the bottle I sent over earlier?"

"Here." Hazard walked to the window and reached behind the hem of the blue velvet curtain, puddling on the floor. He retrieved a bottle of cognac, a very fine tinted-glass bottle that was sealed with wax. "I haven't sampled it, as you can see. But I am curious. Is it to celebrate afterward?"

"No. Put it back. I don't want it accidentally served."

Hazard looked at him questioningly, then returned the bottle behind the curtain.

"A private jest," Jasper offered. "Aimed at Hilyer. Simply to add insult to injury."

Hazard shrugged. "I suppose you know what you're doing. Now here is what is planned so far. Most of the guests will move in here shortly and continue gaming. But a few men will stay in the Subscription Room. I think you should as well. Once Hilyer arrives, the rest of my guests will dribble back here in twos and threes. You should come back quickly after he shows up so nothing will start prematurely. Caro will be among the last."

"Caro?" Jasper was unacquainted with anyone by that name.

"A new fellow. You'll find him amusing." He hesitated, then said, "Crispin brought him around earlier and asked me to keep him for a few days. Entertain him. Crispin *is* in London you know."

"Yes, I saw him earlier at home."

"Oh? Good. He acted offended that I thought you two may have fallen out and said he'd make it a point to talk to you before he sails away." Hazard shrugged. "At any rate, he thought Caro would be bored at 8 Grosvenor Square." A smile crept out. "I invited Crispin to this, but he said he had business at Madame LaFontaine's to take care of."

"Typical."

Hazard dropped his voice to a confidential volume. "He looked well. Army life agrees with him, it seems."

Jasper nodded. Oddly enough, it did. It occurred to him then, rather abruptly, that this "Caro" was likely Crispin's fallback. It didn't annoy him—much—that Crispin had so little faith in his elder brother's abilities. Crispin probably had a backup for the fallback.

"Prinny will be late," Hazard said. "He always is. But as soon as he does arrive, we'll direct him back here. Everyone else will follow fairly quickly. Caro will remain in the Subscription Room to keep an eye on Hilyer. I suspect it won't be long before Hilyer tries to join the party. If he does not try on his own, Caro will goad him into it."

"What if he tries before the Prince Regent arrives?"

"Then we proceed without Prinny. He isn't necessary to the scheme. He's the icing on the cake. There are enough peers here to witness the cut."

"Fine." He was less concerned now about the insult than the aftermath. He had to time things well if he was to push Hilyer to run.

"Come," Hazard said. "I'll introduce you to Caro."

They returned to the Great Subscription Room. Hazard gestured to the far corner where a fop sat reading a newspaper. He was dressed splashily in white knee britches and a bright yellow jacket. He had jet-black hair that fell in lush waves, covering half his left eye. Jasper approached warily.

Hazard smiled. "Caro, this is the man of the hour, my friend Lord Taverston."

Caro rose slowly, setting down his newspaper. He looked Jasper up and down, then licked his upper lip like a cat and said, "Well, hello."

Jasper tensed and said a wooden, "Hello."

"Ah, that went well," Hazard said, then laughed. "Caro hails from Italy. An exile. Not fond of Bonaparte, you see."

"He's in good company."

"I am an artist," Caro said, glancing at his fingernails before sliding a hooded gaze back to Jasper. His accent was slightly foreign. "I would like to draw you."

Jasper tried not to frown. "Well, perhaps. I may be due for a portrait—"

"No," Hazard said. He tapped Caro's arm and said sternly, "No." He turned to Jasper. "I've seen some of Caro's art. It should be reserved for select tastes."

Jasper felt his face redden.

"Join me," Caro suggested, gesturing to the table holding his newspaper. "I think we have some things to say to one another."

Jasper looked to Hazard, whose face was blank, then back to Caro. He nodded, then lowered himself into a chair. Caro sat also. Hazard slid away. Caro pulled a sketchbook from underneath the newspaper and began making stray marks.

"I understand there is to be a…a dustup."

"A small one. Yes."

Caro smiled. It was not a pleasant smile. "Viscount Haslet says there is to be no duel. He will ensure that." Caro's smile disappeared. "If he fails, you are to name me as your second."

"Oh?" Jasper didn't know what to make of that. "Why?"

"There will be no duel."

"May I ask—"

"There will be no duel. Only I will make sure this Hilyer creature will be permanently disgraced, and your name will not be mentioned."

Jasper swallowed something sour. "You sound like Crispin. I can believe you two are friends."

"No." His eyes went black. "Lieutenant Taverston and I are not friends. He is far too...fastidious? Is that the word?" He waved his hand. "But he's young."

Young? Jasper supposed he was. Crispin would have recently turned twenty-three. There was a time when they did not think he would survive childhood. He wondered if Crispin felt old.

Caro flipped a page in his sketchbook and showed Jasper a picture.

"Chuckle," he said.

Jasper did, understanding they were role-playing a more trivial conversation. The drawing was more intriguing than amusing: Hazard's head and shoulders. A very good likeness. A very handsome one. Though the shoulders were naked and more muscular than Jasper thought they would be in life.

Caro leaned forward. "Tell me what you will do. And how I may assist."

He was certainly more direct than Crispin. Jasper wondered if this was clumsy or efficient.

"After we cut Hilyer, I will step back out here to console him. Crudely if need be. I'll offer a conciliatory drink of very good cognac. It will be water. Then I will tell him I've made the authorities aware, and he will be arrested in the morning."

"In the morning. Good. He will think you very stupid."

"I don't care what he thinks."

Caro nodded. He flipped another page to display a grotesque faintly resembling Napoleon.

"These are not my best," he said with a shrug. "Viscount Haslet would not let me bring my better work."

"I think you should not have that sketch of the Viscount here either."

"No?" His eyebrows flickered. Then, with a twist of the wrist, he tore out the front page and extended it to Jasper, evidently amused. "You may keep it safe."

Appalled, Jasper took the paper, folded it twice, and shoved it into a pocket inside his waistcoat.

"The lady is worth it, the viscount says," Caro said, leaning back in his chair. "I find that difficult to believe, but unimportant. As far as the viscount knows, it is all about the lady. Do you understand?"

"Yes." Jasper was relieved to know Hazard was no more involved in this than he needed to be. He hoped he hadn't said too much. He didn't think he did.

"Perhaps we should play cards. Are you skilled?"

"Not particularly."

Caro smiled "Good."

⇛⇚

CARO WAGERED CONSERVATIVELY, which was a good thing since he won nearly every hand. If he cheated, Jasper could not see how. The man also pattered about Italy, waxing poetic, and occasionally cursing Bonaparte. It passed the time until Hilyer arrived.

The marquess glanced around the by-now half-empty Subscription Room. He started, visibly, upon seeing Jasper, but acknowledged him with no more than a sneer. If he noticed noise coming from the card room in the back, he ignored it. He took a seat at a table across the room, greeting two fellows who rather grudgingly returned the greeting and allowed him into their game.

Caro said under his breath, "Go. I will join the marquess so that the others can excuse themselves after another hand or two."

Jasper nodded. He rose and strode to the card room door without looking toward Hilyer. He knocked lightly and was admitted. Hazard came to him at once.

"He's here?"

"Yes." Then Jasper remembered the sketch. "Here. Take

this." He pulled it from his waistcoat and gave it to Hazard. Who unfolded it, glanced at it, and laughed.

"A fair likeness." He stuffed it into his own waistcoat.

"I doubt your shoulders are that broad."

Hazard sniffed at him. "Have a glass of champagne before you choose a table. Just don't get too bosky."

Jasper went to the back and claimed a glass and a small mutton pastie. Then he sat down beside Mountjoy and Sir Penworthy.

"Winning or losing?"

Mountjoy sighed. "At this rate, I won't have anything left to lose to His Royal Highness."

"My luck has also been poor. Let's see whose is worse."

Penworthy said, "With that to recommend you, I will happily deal you in."

They gambled desultorily, trading hands. About half an hour later, the two men who had allowed Hilyer to join them wandered in. Jasper could not hear what they said to Hazard, but they appeared amused. Jasper hoped Caro was cleaning Hilyer out.

Another half hour passed before a commotion was heard from the Subscription Room followed by a loud knock. Prinny tumbled in, two footmen in tow.

"Have I missed it?"

"Of course not. We waited for you," Hazard said, smoothly handing him a glass of champagne which the man quaffed in a gulp.

Then things happened quickly. Hilyer thrust open the door. Hazard stepped around the Prince Regent and blocked Hilyer from entering.

"This is a private party."

"Private?" Hilyer scoffed. "Half the damn ton is in here."

"Half? Three-quarters, at least, I would say," Hazard protested, as Hilyer tried to jostle his way in. "But exclusive nonetheless."

Jasper rose and went to Hazard's side. He was significantly taller and broader, and it gave him satisfaction to bar Hilyer as Hazard made room.

"Problem, Haz?" he said, letting his eyes droop and slurring his words.

Hilyer said, "Get out of my way. You don't even belong here."

Rather than argue, Jasper looked away from him and said, "Hazard, would you like me to summon the porter? I'm sure you don't want to sully the evening arguing with this insignificant codger."

"Go home to your whore," Hilyer sneered.

Jasper knew how he should have reacted. He knew how he'd planned to react to such expected provocation. Instead, he hauled back and threw a punch into the old man's jaw. Hilyer reeled. He was caught by Caro, who was just entering. Caro propped him, heavy though he was, with no evident effort.

"Fisticuffs!" Prinny shouted gleefully.

Hilyer said, "You will pay for that." He spat on Jasper's chest. Jasper clenched his fists but did not retaliate.

Hazard said, "Well, Hilyer! That is something we'd all like to see." He smiled at Prinny. "Your Royal Highness, I promised you a match, did I not? Shall we clear a space?"

"I will not engage in—"

"Oh, fie, Hilyer!" The Prince Regent laughed. "Don't be such an old man. Put up those fists."

"Indeed not. We will meet like men. Not scuffling dogs."

"Coward," muttered Caro, loud enough to be heard.

"No good," the Prince Regent complained. "Lord Haslet, you promised better."

"I didn't know the marquess would be so…reluctant."

"Hilyer, get out." Prinny sounded miffed. Worse than miffed. Annoyed. "You were not invited, and you are not welcome. Certainly not in our presence."

Cut by the Prince Regent himself! Jasper marveled. How in

God's name had Hazard inveigled Prinny's cooperation to this degree?

Hilyer stared, slack jawed, with a regrettable strawberry blooming on that jaw. Or maybe not so regrettable. Hazard had evidently promised Prinny a fistfight. Hazard must have anticipated that Hilyer would insult Vanessa, as well as Jasper's violent response. He wished he'd laid him flat. He could permissibly beat the man bloody with the Prince Regent urging him on.

At just the right moment, a very large porter appeared in the doorway.

"Pardon, Lord Haslet. Mr. Albert sent me to see if there was a disturbance."

"Yes, thank you. Please escort that man out." He gestured dismissively to Hilyer.

"Don't touch me!" Hilyer said, shaking off the porter's hand. "I've been a member here since before you were born. I'll lodge a complaint and you'll be out on your arse."

Jasper said quickly, "I suppose he might remain in the Subscription Room where he won't bother Lord Haslet's guests."

Hazard shot him a look. The plan had been to remove Hilyer bodily. He nodded slowly. "I don't care. So long as he ceases to *impose*."

Hilyer tried to gather his shredded dignity and turned, to find Caro in his way.

Loudly, with a thicker accent than he'd used earlier, and with a fine display of drunken ill humor, Caro said, "Good. Give me a chance to even the score. Back to the table, *vecchio sporco*."

The door closed behind them. Jasper hurried to the window and dug out the bottle. He straightened to find himself nearly flush against Hazard.

"Do not challenge him, Jasper. *Do not*. I don't care what he called Mrs. Wardrip. It isn't worth you ending up dead or a murderer."

"I'm not calling him out."

"Then what?"

"I'm just going to rub salt in the wound."

"Jasper—"

"Don't draw attention, Haz. Let me go."

Hazard stepped back. He looked angry and worried, but Jasper brushed past. He wove his way to the door and reentered the Great Subscription Room. Hilyer and Caro were alone in the vast gaming hall. Caro was slapping down cards and muttering drunkenly.

Jasper swiped three glasses from the bar and approached. Hilyer looked up and glared.

"I don't know what you think you and that—"

"Here." Jasper set a glass in front of him, then one in front of Caro. He pulled up a chair but didn't sit down. He might as well use his body to intimidate. "I thought I would give you an opportunity to retract your words. I understand your pique. After all, she preferred to sleep on the wet Portuguese ground and be shot at by frogs than be your marchioness."

"Used goods. You're welcome to them."

Jasper refused to take the bait. Instead, he broke the wax seal and uncorked the bottle. He sloshed fluid into all three glasses.

"Go on," he said. "Drink with me. I think it will be better for all if we put this behind us."

Caro put a hand on his glass, but rather than lift it, he let his head drop onto his arm, face smashed against the table, and let out a tremendous snore.

Hilyer sneered at him, then picked up the glass and squinted. Jasper had tried soaking a bit of charred wood in the water jug overnight, but it hadn't imparted much color to the liquid. Hilyer sniffed, then sipped. Then set down the glass with a thud.

"Disappointed?" Jasper asked. "Imagine how our men on the Peninsula felt when they got water instead of grog. Crushing soldiers' morale is aiding and abetting the enemy."

Hilyer's head shot up, startled. Then he narrowed his eyes. "I don't know what you are talking about."

"Don't you? Let me help. The barrels came from Ireland."

Hilyer pushed back his chair. "You're drunk. You're talking nonsense."

"I was not drunk when I wrote Bathurst. The letter will be delivered first thing in the morning."

Another table-shaking snore came from Caro's lips.

"Nonsense."

Jasper shrugged. "If you say so. But last I checked, treason was still a hanging offense."

He set down his glass and walked away.

# Chapter Twenty-Four

THE NEXT MORNING, Jasper woke to sunlight warming his face. He opened his eyes and then shut them quickly. His head ached so badly he could not turn it without his eyeballs cracking. Where the devil was he?

He was tangled in a sheet that stank of curdled sweat and stale champagne breath. He wore only his shirt and drawers, but his clothes must be around somewhere.

He sifted through a befogged, disjointed cluster of memories. He'd been in the card room. Hazard would not let him leave, even sat him down at the Prince Regent's table so that no excuse would serve. The very devil. Prinny could *drink*. And every man in Brooks's had wanted to shake Jasper's hand and slap a glass into it.

He felt he'd been run over by a carriage.

But it was a triumph. He'd collected invitations—invitations that included Mrs. Wardrip—more than he could count. Of course, the majority of those would be rescinded or forgotten once wives and mothers caught wind. But not the one to Carlton House. Prinny wanted to meet the brave lady. He'd called her that. Brave lady.

God. He'd left her worrying at 8 Grosvenor Square. Damn Hazard. That's where he was. At Hazard's. Another memory crashed back. Hazard and *Prinny* hauling him from Brooks's and tossing him into a carriage. The Prince Regent had found it all hysterically funny. It must have been near dawn. And now it must be noon, at the earliest. He'd left her alone. He hadn't sent word. God.

He opened his eyes a slit and tried sliding to the edge of the bed. His stomach roiled. He lowered his feet to the floor and raised himself slowly, closing his eyes as the room spun. Then he opened them rapidly, dropped to the floor on his knees, and vomited into the chamber pot. For a long moment, he rested his forehead against the cool marble flooring.

Eventually, he managed to crawl back into bed and roll his face out of the sunlight. He couldn't go home. Not yet. He moaned himself back to sleep.

⇢⇢⇢⇠⇠⇠

IT WAS NEAR to two o'clock in the afternoon when Hazard shook him awake and dropped a clean shirt and newly pressed evening clothes onto the bed.

"Wake up. That's enough."

Jasper groaned, but opening his eyes, he discovered that his headache had dulled to a quiet throb and his stomach no longer threatened revolt.

"What did you do to me?"

Hazard laughed. "You did it to yourself. I merely provided the means."

"Vanessa—"

"Will be fine. But you've worn out your welcome. Time to go."

Jasper sat up.

"You should have let me go home last night. Damn. How much did I lose?"

"Not enough to worry about. A few hundred pounds." Hazard scratched his chin. "I stopped you from wagering Mercury.

Prinny may never forgive me, but that is not your mount to bet."

"God." Then he scowled. Remembering more. "Why on earth did you pin me to that chair? The party broke up hours before—"

"Blame Crispin."

"What? Why?"

"He said to keep you in my sight until well past daybreak. And, if possible, to keep you in the sight of other reliable witnesses as well. I think the Prince Regent qualifies."

"What the hell? Reliable witnesses?"

"Crispin was concerned for your welfare. Firstly, that Hilyer would exact some sort of revenge if you went stumbling towards Grosvenor Square in the wee hours of the morning. But also, he said that if anything happened to Hilyer, it should not happen after the two of you publicly squabbled."

"What did he imagine would happen to Hilyer?" What—that he would confide to Hazard?

"I don't know." Hazard ruffled his hair, then scratched his earlobe. "Footpads most like. Or there is apoplexy. A heart seizure. The man is not a healthy specimen, and he was choleric. Moreover, you're not the only one with a grudge against him. Yours was only the most recent and most visible grudge."

"I never knew Crispin for such a nervous old maid."

"Well, he managed to frighten me as well. I don't know what he will do when he finds out I've misplaced Caro."

"You've *what*?"

"You left him snoring in the Subscription Room, but apparently, he woke and slunk out. Haven't seen him since. If Crispin complains, tell him I'm not a nanny." Hazard stood, appearing well-pleased with himself. "You may borrow that shirt. I have some calls to pay. I assume you can find your way out."

⇉⇉⇉⇇⇇⇇

VANESSA DID NOT sleep. She lay in bed. She closed her eyes. But sleep eluded her the entire night. When dawn broke, she rose and dressed. And waited.

It was midmorning before a maid knocked at the door with a tray. When the girl left, Vanessa lifted the cover to find tea and fresh buns. She sat to eat, hungry despite her anxiousness. When she lifted the teapot, she found a folded note under it.

*They are both fine.*

She let out a long, shaky breath, then started to cry, the ferocity of her relief making her aware of how truly frightened she had been.

<hr>

JASPER ENTERED 8 Grosvenor Square fully intending to go straight to the Rose Room. But Peters met him at the door and said staidly, "Lord and Lady Iversley wish you to attend them in the small parlor."

He decided it wasn't worth antagonizing them further. And Vanessa had waited this long, a few more minutes would not matter.

He trod into the small parlor with a scowl on his face. His mother sat by the fire embroidering. His father, in his usual chair near the brightest lamp, read the afternoon newspaper. Crispin sprawled on the davenport, smirking over a copy of the *Morning Post*.

"Have a seat, Jasper," his father said without looking up.

"Have you eaten?" his mother asked.

Jasper nodded, though he had not.

Crispin chuckled.

"What?" Jasper said.

It irritated him to see Crispin so relaxed in loose trousers, a crisp shirt, and an unbuttoned waistcoat. A light gray jacket was draped over the arm of the davenport. His riding boots had small scuffs at the heels. He looked every bit like a soldier on a well-deserved leave. One who had slept. Slept well.

Crispin rolled up the *Post* and tossed it to him. "The cartoon."

Jasper unfurled it. A large-headed, small-bodied caricature of Hilyer stood alone in a cavernous room with empty card tables, banging his fist against a closed door. A scribbled sign on the door said *gentlemen only*. On the other side of the door, hordes of men, well-dressed but with indistinguishable faces, played cards at tables laden with champagne glasses. Near the window, a very large Prince Regent smiled broadly. Above his head, a bubble read: *You promised fisticuffs!*

"Caro was busy last night." He rolled the paper and lobbed it back at Crispin, who caught it one-handed.

"Busier than you can possibly know."

"Hazard was worried he'd lost him."

Crispin snorted.

"You are being rude," the countess said, setting aside her embroidery.

Crispin stood up and brought the *Post* to her. "I'm sorry, Mother. Let me explain." He opened it. "This is the Marquess of Hilyer. You know. The old goat who tried to purchase a young girl with his title."

She pushed it away. "Don't be vulgar."

The earl started. "Good God."

They all turned to him. He looked up from the news.

"A ship caught fire in the Pool last night."

"Is that so unusual?" Crispin asked.

"The whole thing burned and sank." Father rubbed his brow. "Fortunately, it slipped its mooring and floated away from the rest or the whole lot of them could have burned."

"I'm surprised it doesn't happen more often." Crispin shook his head. "The Pool is far too congested."

"What kind of boat?" Jasper asked, a disturbing thought creeping into his brain.

"A merchant ship of some kind. One of Culpepper's." The earl snorted. "He can afford to lose a few."

Jasper glanced at Crispin, who did not return the look.

"Two charred crewmen floated up this morning," the earl continued. "Unrecognizable."

Mother cleared her throat and said, "Iversley."

"Well, Beatrice, I'm only reporting what happened. The boys are old enough. I'm sure Crispin has seen similar horrors."

"Unrecognizable?" Jasper asked.

"A shame," Crispin said. "But I suppose it could have been worse." Then he returned to the davenport, dropped the *Post* onto it, and began buttoning his waistcoat. "Jasp, can you go change into something less…*less*? More appropriate for Tattersalls?" He picked up his jacket. "I'll fetch Vanessa."

"Crispin!" Mother slammed the embroidery into her lap.

Crispin rolled his eyes. Then he whispered loudly and made broad hand gestures. "While you change your clothes, I will, you know, remove the person from the Rose Room."

Father squelched a laugh. Jasper didn't think Crispin's tack was particularly helpful. Nevertheless, he stage-whispered back. "I'll meet you at the front door."

※※※

IT WAS CRISPIN who came to her in the Rose Room.

"Jasper will meet us out front."

"Is he avoiding me?" she asked sourly, lifting her wrap from a chair near the door.

"Should he be?"

"What happened?"

"Nothing untoward. Freddy went quite alone to Trafalgar. I imagine he had the blunt in his purse. He wandered about for a good two hours before giving up."

Vanessa's eyes watered. "Oh, Freddy." Then she tilted her head to study Crispin. "How do you know?"

"I had someone keep watch on him. It isn't the safest place

for a wealthy boy on his own at that time of night."

She swallowed hard. "Thank you. Where did he go afterward?"

Crispin did not look at her. "Back to where he'd come from. But he'd been gone long enough. I imagine he went home from there." Then he did look at her. His expression was stern except for a small quiver on one side of his lips. "He wasn't followed after that. My resources are not unlimited."

"I appreciate all that you did. I'm not sure why you did it, but thank you."

"Say nothing to Jasper. In fact, say nothing more at all. You may hear things. You may draw conclusions. I will ask you not to ask questions and not to speculate aloud."

As she nodded, he took her wrap from her and draped it around her shoulders. Then he took her elbow and murmured, "We'd better get to the receiving hall before my mother has a fit. It is quite improper for me to be here with you."

"Oh, for pity's sake."

He walked her down the hallway, pointing out features of the wing, what was behind some of the doors, and the provenance of the large landscape painting on the wall. It was not even a full day since Jasper had brought her along the same hallway, silently, roiled by fury he was struggling to control. And she had been shaking with shame and fear. It felt like forever ago.

As they reached the main part of the house, Vanessa slowed.

"Is Hilyer going to leave London?"

Crispin said, "You'll have to ask Jasper. I wasn't at Brooks's last night. Although I did see a cartoon in the *Post* that suggests he was successful."

"Ah. The *Morning Post*. A favorite of yours."

Crispin halted. He faced her stricken. "Vanessa, I'm sorry. Truly. I was peeved at Jasper, but I didn't mean to hurt you."

"Crispin." She stiffened her spine. "I've listened to you. Now you must listen to me. You have no right to be peeved at Jasper. None. You are not his keeper, and you are certainly not mine."

She held up a hand to silence him. "I am grateful to you for seeing me safely out of Corunna. However, I was unaware that your help was conditional."

"It wasn't."

"Apparently, it was. You seem to think I owe you more than my gratitude."

"That's ridiculous."

"It is. My life, and my choices, are my own. I chose…I choose…to be with Jasper. We decided on the terms. That decision is no one else's concern. So it is unclear to me why you think you had cause to be peeved with your brother."

Crispin was quiet. She could see his brow cloud. Then he said, "You're right."

"I think you are less peeved with him than you are disappointed in me."

"But I'm not disappointed in you." He sounded genuinely confused by the accusation.

"With the idea of me. I think you are. I was quite the soldier's-wife-heroine, was I not? Until I succumbed to Jasper's wiles and became no more than a common courtesan."

"All right. Enough. Let me think." He stood a moment, staring at the wall. He tapped his fingers together. Then he said, "You may have a point. But I think, too, that I sometimes feel a responsibility for my men that extends beyond my remit. I felt responsible for you. I should have realized that Jasper was not…was not taking advantage of someone helpless. That had you not wanted to be with him, you would not be."

Now it was her turn to ponder his words. It seemed they had reached an understanding. Of sorts.

"So now?" she asked.

"Now?"

"You will agree I am not your responsibility."

He shrugged. "Now you are Jasper's." Then he grinned. "And he is yours."

She pursed her lips. "That must be a great weight off your

shoulders."

"Ha!" He tapped her elbow and led her the rest of the way, more quickly, back to the entrance, where Jasper paced back and forth. When he saw them, he rushed forward and caught her in his arms. Crispin stepped back.

"Vanessa, I'm so sorry. I should have come for you last night. I should have sent word."

"Is Hilyer leaving London?"

"He—I believe he's already gone."

"But will he come back?"

She saw Jasper raise his eyes, looking to Crispin, then he lowered his gaze to her and said, "No."

"Good."

"Vanessa, I promised you I wouldn't leave you alone, waiting—"

"And I said I would eventually outgrow such neediness. Do you think, Jasper," she pulled his arm, turned a little aside, and said, "that we could have this conversation at home?"

He flushed, glanced at his brother again, then back at her. "Yes, of course."

Crispin laughed. "I'll be at Tattersalls. If you join me there, fine. If not, I think I can manage to choose my own horse."

⊱⊰

As Vanessa and Jasper approached their townhouse, she noticed a young man lurking at the gate.

"Wait here a moment," she said, putting her hands on Jasper's chest. "Please." Then she hurried to her brother.

"Freddy?" She drew closer. "Freddy! It is you. What on earth?"

"Nessa!" He raced to her and threw his arms around her.

"Vanessa!" Jasper shouted.

"It's all right, Jasper. I know him. Wait a moment. Please."

To his credit, Jasper remained where he was.

"If you want to run," Freddy said in a low voice, "I have my pistol. I will keep him…"

"Oh, Freddy, hush." Her brother looked disheveled. Wild-eyed and disheveled. He had not returned home. He must have spent the last several hours tracking her down. "I have no wish to run from Lord Taverston. Don't be foolish."

"But he—"

"But nothing. I am a widow. I'm of age. I'll do as I please."

"But you wrote you were afraid."

"Not—" She bit her tongue. She almost said she was afraid of Hilyer, not Jasper. "I didn't write." She laughed a little falsely. "What on earth could I be afraid of in London?"

"I-I brought your ten pounds," he stammered, confused.

"Ten pounds?" She made her face curious. "What ten pounds?"

"You said you needed to hide out in the country."

"Freddy, what in the world are you talking about?"

He pulled a crumpled letter from his pocket. "This."

She looked at it. Widened her eyes. Then said in a frightened tone, "I didn't write this, Freddy. Who did? Who knew about…" she dropped her voice and whispered, "the marquess?"

"Oh, everyone knew." He practically whined the words. "Nessa, what do you mean you didn't write to me? Last night? He said it was from you."

"Who said?"

"A beefy fellow. Foreigner, I think."

Vanessa shuddered. "Why would someone do this?" Crispin had said not to speculate aloud. She needed to end this conversation. Quickly. But Freddy paled.

"Never mind," he said. "I suppose I know. Father—" His voice caught as if he might gag. "The marquess won't bother you again. Not anymore. I don't know—" Freddy looked increasingly terrified. "I don't understand. But Father must have wanted…" He shuddered.

"Freddy? What is it? What's wrong?"

"Nothing."

"What did Father want?"

"Nothing."

He tore up the letter and dropped the pieces into the muck of the road.

"I'm sorry, Nessa. I'm sorry. I wanted to make it up to you somehow. Show you…" He clenched his fists. "Well, now he knows. I'll deal with that."

"With *what*?"

"Father. Don't worry. Here." He pulled a ring from his finger. "Send this. If you ever do need to write to me, send this. So I won't be fooled again."

"Freddy—"

He hugged her hard again, suddenly, before she was ready to return the embrace. Then he turned away and fled.

As she stared after him, her heart hurting, Jasper drew up beside her. "Your brother?"

She nodded. Jasper let out a long sigh.

"Is this something we need to worry about?"

"No." She looked up at Jasper. She pretended to smile. "No, I think we are done with worrying about brothers for a while."

# Chapter Twenty-Five

Jasper wanted to take Vanessa to bed. No. He wanted *to want* to take her to bed. But he'd eaten nothing all day and his stomach was still sour. He felt unwell.

After seeing her settled into the drawing room, he gave her an apologetic smile and said, "Would it be terrible of me to go meet Crispin at Tattersalls? I suspect he's sailing out soon and I don't know when I'll see him again."

"Go. Of course, go." She exhaled a long, tired breath. "Jasper, I didn't sleep last night. What I want most is a nap."

"Oh." How deflating. "All right, then."

He fussed about for a few more minutes, then took his leave. He'd bring her something. Maybe not jewelry. Flowers, perhaps. Or gloves.

Despite his penchant for walking, he had the groom bring the carriage around to take him to Tattersalls. The horse market was vast—with labyrinthine covered alleys and expansive stables—yet he found Crispin fairly easily. His brother had apparently bypassed several prime horses and was examining one that was long in the tooth.

"Crispin?"

"Jasp." He frowned at the nag. "I don't know."

"Well, not that one."

"I don't need speed. I don't do all that much darting about. I need a horse that can plod all day long."

"Still. Not that one." And Crispin knew better. "Come. Let's look for something bred for stamina."

Crispin patted the horse's flank and followed Jasper, scuffing his feet in the straw, but he glanced over his shoulder for another look.

"Why?" Jasper said. "You said you wanted a mount like Firebrand."

"I don't want to kill another horse." He sounded angry. Or not angry—rather, aggrieved.

"What?"

"I've been looking at these fine animals and it sickens me to have to choose one. The bill of sale will be its execution warrant."

Jasper sighed. "Nevertheless, you need a decent horse." Then he peered at Crispin more closely. He had his hand splayed over his midsection. Like his gut hurt. The image brought to mind a frail schoolboy, paler than milk, insisting he was fine. "What's wrong?"

Crispin didn't reply, but left the stall behind and walked towards the carriage horses. Jasper followed. Abruptly, Crispin turned.

"I wasn't there. At the boat. I don't want you to think I was there."

"I'm not sure I take your meaning."

"My role was merely to find out who and then make sure he tried to leave England."

Jasper smiled wryly. "I thought the latter was my role."

"Ha. You and...," he tapped three fingers against this thumb sequentially, as though counting, "...three others. With methods increasingly crude and desperate. I am impressed by the elegance of your plan. And am pleased that it worked as well as it did. But..."

Jasper knew about Caro. He was not surprised there were more.

"...but I was worried it might not and worried that one of the others might also go wrong, horribly wrong. And I was worried that Hilyer could end up dead in the street if we could not get him to the boat."

"So you had Hazard sit on me all night."

Crispin nodded. "Jasper, I'm a drudge. I was not privy to the plans of the higher-ups. I don't know if what ultimately happened was intentional or a foul-up. I keep thinking it can't have been authorized, and yet..." The look he shot Jasper was anguished. "I'm glad he's dead. You don't know what it's like for our men. How they contend with wormy flour, wet powder, and boots that fall apart after a day on the march. Hilyer was not the only profiteer, only the most egregious. Tampering with the rum was the last straw." He ground one fist into the other. "But I thought he'd be arrested. Tried. Honest to God, Jasper."

Jasper was unsure how to respond. If Hilyer had been caught trying to smuggle military secrets to France, he was a spy subject to execution. But if the documents were faked, as Crispin's letter had implied... Finally, he said, "He might have avoided punishment if he'd gone to court."

"Yes, I know. As I said, I'm glad he's dead. They must have executed them both on the spot—Hilyer and whoever the unfortunate lackey with him was. Then they burned the corpses, loosened the moorings, and set the whole ship afire. That had to have been planned. Don't you think?" His voice dropped. "I could not have plotted something like that."

"No, of course not."

Crispin rubbed his sleeve over his eyes. "But what a hypocrite that makes me. I can deliver a man to slaughter. I can wish him dead. But if it came down to it..."

"You're a soldier, not a cold-blooded killer. That doesn't make you a hypocrite." He shook Crispin's shoulder. "I'm glad he's dead, too. I'm glad *someone* killed him. I'm also glad it was not you."

"I didn't want you to think it was."

Jasper nodded. He didn't. He'd put his money on Caro.

"Come on." He grabbed his brother's arm and pulled him roughly along. "I'll pick your horse. I don't care if it comes back in one piece. So long as you do."

※※※

Jasper was glad to find Vanessa awake. He wanted to be with her. He wanted to bathe in her honesty and innocence. He was tired of scandal and intrigues and plots. She sat before a fire in the parlor. The flicker of the flames brought out the chestnut in her hair, falling loose about her shoulders. He didn't know why he'd ever imagined her chin too severe. She was the most beautiful woman he'd ever known.

The parlor was one of the smaller rooms in the house. She seemed to prefer it. Perhaps because it was warm and bright. Perhaps it was the muted browns and beiges of the furnishings. One could sink into its comfort with nothing to distract except an oversized leafy potted plant by the window. She was embroidering a design on a pair of gloves, white floss on white gloves. It was all so peaceful.

He felt like he should tiptoe into the room.

"How was Tattersalls?" she asked, glancing up at his approach.

"Loud and odiferous. But successful. Crispin has reluctantly fallen in love with another horse."

She nodded. He walked over and sat in the armchair next to hers.

"How did it go at Brooks's?" she asked, her voice measured, falsely calm.

"Everything went as planned. The only surprise was how thoroughly Prinny threw himself into the project. I can't tell whether he despises Hilyer as much as we do, or if he simply found playacting to be fun."

Vanessa tossed her head. "I know he'll be our king soon, but the man is a buffoon."

"Shh. We are not supposed to say that out loud."

She sniffed. Then she picked out the stitch she had just done. Focusing on her handiwork, she asked, "And so, what happens now?"

"What do you mean?"

"Hilyer is no longer going to bother us, but what of the rest? Going out into Society. Bringing me into your world."

"What would you like to do?"

"I don't know. Nothing for a good long while. But it doesn't make sense to back away and lose ground." She set down the gloves and pushed back her hair, running her fingers through it as she did so, seemingly without paying attention to it. Though he did. "I suppose I might pay a call on Lady Posonby."

"She would like that. And I think you'll like her." He offered the next piece of news with some hesitation. "The Prince Regent wants to receive you at Carlton House."

Her eyes went wide. "Jasper!" Then she shook her head. "Good God."

"You don't have to go if you don't wish to."

"Yes, I do. That is not an invitation one can refuse."

He said nothing because she was right. Even if the man was a buffoon.

"Jasper, please don't get your hopes up too high. Notoriety may bring me into fashion for a moment, but I will only ever stand at the fringes of your world."

"Society is at the fringes. *You* are central to my world."

She flushed. "And Grosvenor Square? Where I am an embarrassment to you?"

"My mother was the embarrassment. Not you." But he was casting blame where it did not belong. "No." He sighed. "It was wrong of me to spring you on her like that, with no preparation. I-I'll talk to her."

"I don't want to cause friction in your family." She stood up, frowning. "That's the last thing I want. Let it lie for now. Be kind to her. I'm not a threat. Don't make her see me as one."

"All right." It was cowardly, probably, to give in so readily but he had no idea how he might speak to his mother about any of this. And he didn't want to argue with Vanessa either. "Come, sit with me."

She gave him a wry look. "You mean sit *on* you."

"I do."

She came to him. Sat on his lap. He pulled her close and tucked her head beneath his chin to breathe in the tree-bark scent of her hair.

"I remember the first time I kissed you."

She relaxed into his embrace. "So do I. You came three nights in a row to 'see if everything was all right.'"

"I couldn't stay away." He held her tighter. "You kept surprising me."

"Yes, apparently, you'd never seen a woman build a fire before." He heard the teasing in her voice. She was flirting with him. And he, with her.

"Not one I'd paid any attention to." He laughed a little. "Yet there you were. Kneeling at the hearth. Hands coated with smut."

"You scolded me for not having Madeline do it. And then again when I told you I'd given her the night off."

"I'm sorry about that. It was kind of you when her mother was sick."

"Well, about that." Vanessa ducked her head against his chest. "Her mother was not."

"She wasn't?" He moved her shoulders so that he could stare down at her. "You wanted to make me feel awful for telling you how to treat your maid!" It made him chuckle.

"I gave her the evening off because I thought you might come by again and I wanted to be with you alone. You arrived earlier than I expected."

That silenced him for a moment. Stirred him. And reassured him. She'd wanted this too. From the beginning. She'd wanted this too.

Then she laughed, shaking as she fell back against him. "The look on your face, Jasper." She mimicked his voice. "'*Then I'll do it. Move aside.*' So I did. And you knelt down and picked up a log and stared at the cold hearth as though you'd never seen one before."

"I'd seen them. I just had no idea what to do with one. I'd only ever thrown wood onto a burning fire. You didn't have to laugh so hard."

"Yes, I did. You looked so ridiculous I couldn't help it. But then, you laughed too. Oh, Jasper. I adore that about you. I've never known a man who can laugh so readily at himself."

"I've had a lot of practice," he said dryly.

"And then, you kissed me."

"*I* couldn't help it." Or any of what came next. It was all, still, beyond his control. "But that was not the first time I kissed you."

"Of course it was!"

He shook his head, then tilted her chin so that she would look at him.

"The evening before, I came to the house twice. The first time, you never saw me. I came inside and heard your laughter. It drew me upstairs, curious. Especially when I heard tears, too. Madeline's, I discovered."

"Oh my God." She buried her face in her hands. "The dress! You saw me in that dress?"

"It was a horrifying sight. I've never seen, or hope to see again, anything in that color. Was it supposed to be green? That shade, with your hair?" He laughed along with her.

"It had all those pink bows!"

"And best of all, it showed a good three inches of ankle. Yet you were going on and on about adding a ruffle and it would be fine."

"Oh, poor Madeline. She was devastated."

Jasper sobered. "But you were so kind." His heart melted all over again. "I knew at once what must have happened. I hadn't given her enough money—"

"You provided more than enough for a few dresses at a second-hand store. Don't blame yourself, for pity's sake. What do you know of working-class women's clothing? Madeline walked into a shop and saw the dress and thought it the most beautiful thing in the world."

"And you were doing your best to convince her it was. You were so full of grace, Vanessa. I could only wonder at you. A soldier's wife. A widow. So much hardship and yet you were not hardened. I think it was then that I lost my heart to you. Right then. I wanted to take you into my arms."

Vanessa's eyes glistened.

"But," Jasper said, "I could not walk in, of course. It would have turned farce into tragedy. So I blew you a kiss." He showed her. Putting his first two fingertips on his lips, kissing, then tossing the kiss forward. "It was silly and romantic, and I felt like an idiot tiptoeing back down the stairs…I was very glad there was no one there to see."

"I wish I had seen it." She kissed him on the nose. "I adore silly and romantic."

"Do you?"

She started to untie his neckcloth. "Um-hmm. I'm not *always* pragmatic and serious."

"No?" He helped her, then tossed the cloth to the floor. Urgently. She undid the top buttons of his shirt and began kissing and nipping his neck.

"You still have *so* much to learn about me, Jasper Taverston," she murmured against his ear.

"Fortunately," his voice hitched, "I have a lifetime to devote to the task."

"Sometimes I am frivolous and adventuresome. And sometimes…"

He groaned when her hands moved to the buttons of his fall. "Show me."

# Part 7
## Holding Onto Love
### September 1813
### Cartmel

# Chapter Twenty-Six

Vanessa stepped into Sherwood's Tavern bearing three letters. To Will, she wrote little except to explain that she was aiding a bootmaker in an effort to expand his business and so had directed Lady Andini and Lady Posonby to post letters to her through her attorney. To them, she rewrote the letters she had previously given up on sending and added requests that they support a small bootmaker who employed wounded soldiers. She assured them they would not be disappointed.

Yes, she was relying on their charity. But they would be pleased with the results, and she was hopeful they would wear the boots around London and spread the word.

"Mrs. Wardrip!" Sherwood emerged from the backroom, displaying his gap teeth in all their glory, a dirty rag in his hand. "How good to see you!"

"I have letters to post." Then she realized how rude she was being, so she smiled. "It's good to see you as well."

She dug them from her reticule and gave them to him. He scanned the directions and then looked up.

"You're writing to nobs?"

In London, she would have frosted him. But in Cartmel, blatant nosiness was simple friendliness.

"Acquaintances. If they remember me, I hope they might be persuaded to buy a pair of boots from Jon."

He nodded with enthusiasm. "That would be great. Hold on. I have a one for you. Came yesterday. I was going to bring it to you—"

"Oh, no, you mustn't put yourself out. I'm always coming into town for one thing or another."

He looked disappointed. "Just a minute then."

He went into the back, taking her letters with him, and returned quickly. She recognized Will's handwriting.

"Thank you, Sherwood. Good day."

She stepped out into the sunlight and opened Will's letter. She scanned the polite greetings to find the nub. Then her heart skipped a few beats.

Mrs. Wardrip, Henry's mother, had passed. This, after Dr. Wardrip had died sometime last year. The estate, which was not much but included a house that was to be sold, had been placed in trust for Kathryn Wardrip, Henry's sister.

Absently, Vanessa fingered the only jewelry she now wore, the thin gold chain, the one Henry had given her with its small sapphire pendant. For sentiment's sake, she'd also strung onto it the ring her brother Freddy had pressed into her hand. Memories bore down hard.

Vanessa remembered Kitty as a baby whom she had seen once, perhaps twice. Henry adored her. But Dr. Wardrip never brought her around to the Culpepper house. She must be thirteen or fourteen. Poor child.

Will said he would be remiss if he did not recommend contesting the will to achieve for her Henry's portion. *Please advise how you would like me to proceed.*

She turned around and went back into the tavern.

"Sherwood, I need to see my letters again. I have to add something. Pen and ink, too, if you please."

He fetched them for her. She found Will's letter, dipped the pen in the inkpot, and wrote on the outside near the wax seal: *Received your letter re: Kitty. ABSOLUTELY NOT.*

"Thank you, Sherwood. Good day."

She wandered out, feeling maudlin. What did Will take her for? Someone who would rob an orphan? She could not send condolences to Kitty. The girl would know her only as the harlot who had stolen away her brother and sent him to his death. She headed toward her cottage; all pleasure drained from the day. The prettiness of the fields she passed failed to cheer her. She was nearly halfway home when she saw Charlotte coming up the road. Rather quickly. She picked up her own pace. Pray nothing was wrong with the children or Dan.

"Charlotte?"

"Vanessa! You're heading home?" She pressed a hand to her chest and panted a moment. "You have a visitor. A man."

Vanessa balked. Who? Who could have come? "What do you mean?"

"He passed by, and I was outside and he tipped his hat and asked if that was your cottage and I said yes." Charlotte drew a breath. "I don't think he would've said his name, but I introduced myself."

"Charlotte!" Introducing herself to strange men?

"Mr. Frederick Bastion, he said. Just like that. Proper. Like you."

"Bastion?" Why did that name sound familiar?

"He said he fought with Henry in Portugal and came to pay his respects. He has some memories and a couple of Henry's things." Charlotte looked at her hopefully, as if this were the man she must be waiting for, who would whisk her away.

"I-I'm trying to remember him." How would a fellow soldier know where to find her?

"Hard to believe he was an infantryman though." Charlotte tugged at the tight waist of her dress. "I've never seen such a horse."

*Ah.*

"Was he very tall and blond? Thin?"

Charlotte giggled. "Like a fence post."

Crispin. She hoped nothing was wrong.

"I remember him." She started walking again. Faster. Charlotte trotted alongside.

"Handsome fellow."

"Yes. Yes, he was." She changed the subject. "I wrote to the ladies I knew back in London. I think they will buy boots."

She babbled on until she could think of nothing more to babble about. Charlotte dove back in.

"Is Mr. Bastion married?"

"Yes." Thank goodness. An easy out. "I recall his wife. Lovely girl. There were two children, too, if I remember rightly."

Charlotte's face fell. Vanessa walked even faster so that they both grew breathless and could not continue conversing until they reached Charlotte's house. Ahead, Vanessa could see a horse grazing in front of her own cottage. She could see what Charlotte meant. That had to be the fabled Mercury.

"Should I come with you?" Charlotte asked.

She probably should. But Vanessa decided going into her cottage alone with a man could not scandalize Charlotte any more than the conversation she and Crispin would have. And she was tired of stepping so carefully all the time to protect a reputation for propriety that she did not deserve.

"Oh, no. It's fine. He's not dangerous." Ha! "And I want to hear what he has to say about Henry."

She left Charlotte staring after her and tried to walk more sedately the last many yards. Closer, she saw him. Lolling at her gate.

"Mr. Bastion?" she said coming up to him, heart in her throat.

He turned and grinned, then bowed. "Mrs. Wardrip." His manner of greeting told her nothing was wrong. She almost floated with relief.

"Why do I know that name?"

"Do you? He's Reginald's mentor. Or perhaps a colleague. I hadn't an alias planned, and it was the first name that popped out on my tongue. How would you know—"

"It's a long story. Come inside, will you? I'm so pleased to see you, I'm about to hug you and Charlotte is still watching."

"I would say that is the nicest welcome I've ever had, but Jasper hugged me so hard when I got back to London I think he dislodged something."

Vanessa laughed from pure happiness. She opened the door and ushered him inside. Three days ride, yet he smelled of soap. Soap and horse. She did hug him. Hard. But she pulled away startled.

"Crispin, you're skin and bones! What's wrong?"

His face tightened. "Nothing is wrong." He stepped back and shook his head as though shaking off annoyance. "I had a touch of cholera. It went through the regiment. Three men died. While I got two months' leave."

"I'm so sorry." Looking closer, she recognized he did look peaked.

"Well." He shook his head again. "I'm not here to discuss my health."

"I don't suppose you are. Come in back. Would you like tea?"

"I would actually."

He followed her and sprawled in one of the chairs while she went to the hearth and stirred the embers.

"It will be a bit before it's ready. I'm sorry. I don't leave the fire going when I'm out."

She laid on a bit of fluff, blew on it, then fed in the kindling, mindful of Crispin's eyes on her back. When the fire was burning well, she set the kettle over it and turned.

"You are a marvel, Vanessa."

"Because I can start a fire?" She felt an ache, starting in her chest, that spread all the way to her toes.

"Among other things." He patted the table. "Sit with me."

"Would you like a bit of toast?"

"No. Sit with me."

She pulled two teacups from her countertop and came to the table.

"All right, Crispin. Why have you come?"

"Do you miss him?"

"Of course, I miss him. But it doesn't matter."

"Vanessa, he is dying."

She dropped the cups, fumbling one onto the table but the other fell to the floor and shattered.

"Dying inside, I should say," he continued. "Outwardly, he's hale enough."

She sat heavily into her chair. "That was cruel. Cruel. Don't try to manipulate me. I will not stand for it."

"You still love him."

"Crispin, this is unnecessary. Nothing has changed." She rubbed the damp from her palms onto her skirt.

"Except that Jasper has finally come to his senses."

"You told me once that you would not plead his case."

"I told you once that he was your responsibility now."

The words stabbed at her.

"That was a jest. Even if it was not, Jasper is a grown man. I am not responsible for his actions or his care."

He chewed his lip. She could practically see him choosing tacks and then discarding them.

"Just say what you want from me, Crispin."

"I will. In a moment." He drummed his fingers on the table. The kettle began to boil. "Tea?"

She rose to prepare it. Then brought the pot, another cup, and a small bowl of sugar to the table.

"It needs to steep," she said, sitting back down.

"Just talk to him. Once."

"No."

"It cannot make things worse."

It could. She wanted far too desperately to say yes. To see Jasper again? To talk to him? She would not have the strength to leave him twice. And fundamentally, nothing had changed.

She poured out weak tea and passed the sugar bowl to him.

"Charlotte would have offered honey. I prefer it now. But I only have sugar."

He dropped a lump into his cup and swirled it.

"Take another for Mercury. You'll wear that poor creature out."

He smiled at her, took a handkerchief from inside his jacket, wrapped two lumps into it, then slipped it back. She waited for him to speak again, but he was waiting for her. She broke first.

"No, Crispin. I cannot." *I must not.*

"Then I will play my last card." He took her hand and squeezed it gently, somehow drawing her eyes to his. "Do it for me."

She pulled her hand away.

"Crispin, don't. I know how indebted I am to you—"

"No." His eyes darkened. "Friends do not tally debts. I ask you, as a *favor*, to speak one last time to Jasper."

She shook her head, tears filling her eyes.

"Vanessa." He whispered her name, so gently her tears started to spill. "Vanessa, you know what my brothers mean to me. I cannot bear to see him hurting like this. Please."

"Oh, God," she said, half crying and half laughing. She told him he could not manipulate her, but he could. "I can't win this." She would talk to Jasper. It was, after all, what she wanted also.

He leaned back and rubbed the back of his hand across his eyes.

"Thank you, Vanessa. Thank you."

"He can't come here," she said, clearing her throat. She stood again and found a napkin to wipe her eyes and blow her nose.

"London?"

"There are too many memories there."

"All right." He closed his eyes, then opened them. "Do you know where Binnings is? It's not too very far."

He surprised a gasp of laughter from her. Maybe he *had* planned this all since Corunna. "Now you will tell me you have a cottage there."

He started. *Good.*

"I-I do." He gave her a quizzical look, but she decided she

would not say anything. Let him wonder for a change. "In fact, I sent Mercury to Binnings for stabling. I was planning to come see you regardless."

"Mercury was at Binnings? How did you get here from London?"

"By post chaise to Binnings. How did you think? Vanessa, it's well over two hundred miles to London!" He shook his head at her, grinning in a mocking way. "Mercury is a horse, not a Pegasus."

"Very well," she said, embarrassed by the foolish image in her head of Crispin traveling day and night on a miraculous steed to come find her for Jasper. "I'll come to Binnings. When?"

He counted fingers. "A week from Saturday. That will give a letter time to reach Jasper and Jasper time to reach Binnings."

"Not much time."

"He will sprout wings if he must. I'll send a carriage for you on Friday."

"No." By this evening, Charlotte would have described Vanessa's visitor in detail to Lydia, who would know it had been Lieutenant Taverston. If he were to sweep her off in a coach, they would all congratulate themselves. "I will go by stage on Saturday."

"You won't get there until late. It will be better if you are there—"

"So you can orchestrate the grand reunion? I think not. Crispin, I'm not staying alone with you overnight in your cottage."

He blinked. "Is that a serious concern?" Before she could reply, he said, "If so, I will hire someone. A chaperone of some sort. I do know the rector's wife rather well. But that won't allow you and Jasper much privacy."

"Perhaps that's a good thing." But perhaps not.

"I'd like you there before Jasper so that you won't walk into a space he will already control."

"You make it sound like a battlefield."

"I hope it will not become one. But if it does, I'm offering you the high ground."

"And where will you be?"

"On the property somewhere. But not orchestrating."

"And servants?"

"A caretaker and his wife, who can cook if I ask. Reginald has brought a few gardeners in to spruce it up for me, but they're not there all the time."

That surprised her. "It's quite small then? Your cottage?"

"Oh, no. It's vast. A family retreat at one point. But it was sold, then repurchased so that I would have something to inherit. Reg says it's in a bit of disrepair, but I haven't been out to see it yet; I stayed overnight in town. I suppose I'll have to hire staff and do something with the place." He made a face. "Or deed it over to Reg when he has a brood."

She refrained from saying that might be sooner than he anticipated.

"Fine." If she was yielding to Crispin, she might as well surrender unconditionally. "I'll be there Friday."

"Chaperone?"

"No, I suppose not."

"May I send a carriage?"

She thought a moment. It would be so much more comfortable than the stage.

"Send it to Paxton Downs. To the inn there."

He nodded. "Good. This will be good. I'll get a letter off to Jasper right away."

"Send it from Binnings. Not here."

"Certainly."

He drank his tea then poured himself a second cup and dropped in a bit of sugar. Then he leaned back in his chair and smiled, drumming his hands on his knees.

"I'm dying to know how you guessed I had a cottage in Binnings."

"It wasn't a guess."

His eyebrows flickered. He whispered, "Who are your

sources?"

She laughed. She poured another cup for herself. And told him everything he had missed.

# Chapter Twenty-Seven

*B*E PREPARED. How was one to prepare for something like this? Vanessa decided to confess to Charlotte and Lydia that the caller who had come to pay respects and reminisce about Henry had, in fact, been Lieutenant Taverston. He gave a false name to Charlotte so that Lydia and the corporal would not draw false conclusions but when she'd told him that they already had, he merely laughed.

She told them all, too, that she was going back to Binnings to parade her boots around and wander the shops. Now that she had seen it, it seemed a safe enough place that she didn't feel the necessity of dragging Mary and Myrtle along.

Once she swept up the mess Crispin's visit might have created, she concentrated on the next steps.

She decided what to wear: her two best dresses—one from the dress shop in Binnings and one from London. Neither was particularly fine. She removed the cuffs and collars from the old dress and added new lace. She didn't want Jasper thinking she was living in poverty, but not extravagantly either. She would pack only a single valise that she could carry by herself to Paxton Downs. It seemed pragmatic and commonsensical once she made up her mind, but she was embarrassed to admit how much time she'd spent on the decision—even whether to bring two dresses or three.

She spent the next few days cleaning, tending her garden, and choosing a bracelet to sell in Binnings so that she would not have to bother Will when the time came.

Friday was slow to arrive. Then she rose early, walked to Paxton Downs, and waited at a tea shop for Crispin's hired carriage.

She encountered no difficulties en route to Binnings. After a few hours, she found herself peering out the window as the carriage entered a long, winding drive. The first several hundred feet were overgrown with brambles but then the way cleared. The road was rutted and lined on either side by trees that had been recently cut back and wildflowers doing their best to flourish.

The carriage pulled up to a two-story stone cottage with large windows and an impressive double-doored front entrance. The roof was newly thatched. The windows appeared clean though the glass was yellowed. The lawn was weedy. And one large tree at the side of the house was dying or dead and should really have been removed.

The carriage halted and a groom opened the door and let down the step so she could descend. He grabbed her valise from the roof and carried it up the walk, then set it at the door. Some of the bricks in the walkway were cracked and grass grew through the crevices.

It was not difficult to see the charm of the place beneath its disrepair, but the time and effort that would be required to bring it back must be discouraging.

She put a coin in the groom's hand. "Thank you. Good day."

He gave the house a skeptical look, then nodded and headed back to the carriage.

How very curious this all made her. She had so many questions. Questions to which she would never know the answers. Why had this house been sold and then repurchased? Why purchased for Crispin's inheritance if it had been a family retreat? Did it break his heart to see it like this? Or did he see it as a burden he would happily transfer to Reginald?

She reached for the door knocker. A simple black iron ring. The door needed a new coat of paint.

"Vanessa! Good. You're here. I heard the carriage."

Crispin emerged from around the side of the house. But for his voice, she might not have recognized him. He wore loose trousers tucked into dirty boots and a smock rather than a shirt. No jacket. No neckcloth. No gloves. His hair had the tumbled wild appearance men strove for with layers of pomade and a skilled valet, but she was certain his was merely unwashed and badly combed. The smock was smeared with mud and his trouser legs showed blotchy green stains.

He came up to her and bowed. Then he grinned, gesturing to himself. "Sorry. We were clearing things out a bit down by the lake. I intended to change clothes before you arrived, but mistimed."

"We? Are you working with the gardeners?"

"Don't tell Jasper." Crispin put his hand to the door and opened it. "He'll write a draft for some ungodly sum and tell me to hire more people."

Yes. Jasper would.

Crispin looked…happy and had a healthy glow that he had certainly not possessed a few days before.

They stepped into a cool, dark entryway and a woman skuttled around the corner.

"Captain! Oh! The lady is here?" She shook her head, tut-tutting. The woman was plump and gray haired and red cheeked and looked very, very peeved. "You were supposed to—"

"I know! I know!" Crispin laughed, cringing theatrically. "Mrs. Wardrip, this is Mrs. Badge. Mrs. Badge, Mrs. Wardrip."

"How do you do?" Vanessa said.

The housekeeper flushed. "Well enough, thank you."

Crispin said, "I'll show Mrs. Wardrip to her room." He took Vanessa's valise out of her hand.

Mrs. Badge looked scandalized. "I'll take her. You go clean

up."

"It's on the way. We'll be wanting supper in an hour."

He grabbed Vanessa by the elbow and hurried her away, through a dark corridor toward a sturdy set of stone stairs.

"She has a great deal of trouble with steps. Reg tried to warn me, but I didn't realize…" He shook his head. "I'm going to have to hire more help."

She had far too many questions so only asked the first. "Captain?"

"Ah." He nodded, looking a little abashed. "Didn't I tell you?"

"No." She hesitated before asking. Men, even of Crispin's undeniable caliber, were not promoted until a position opened above them. Then there would be jockeying and shifting.

He said, "Colonel Harrington. Damn it. Not dead, thank God. His horse fell on him and crushed both hips."

"Oh, Crispin. I'm sorry." Harrington was admired, though not particularly well-liked. He was arrogant. Well, so was Crispin. But differently.

They started up the steps and Crispin wiggled her valise. "Not much in here."

She said, "Travel light."

He smiled at her. "Good for you." They reached the landing.

"You'll be in the countess's room." He laughed as she started to protest. "Don't make too much out of that. It's where Reg and Georgiana stay and it's clean. I don't want to cause more trouble for the Badges than I have to."

She stopped arguing and merely followed him down a hallway. Doors were closed. The hall was dark and a little dank. Crispin halted and turned to her.

"I should explain." He chewed his lip a moment, then said, "This property was deeded to me years ago. I sold it to buy my commission since my father refused to pay for it. He didn't want me in the army. An excess of love, I suppose." He shrugged. "Unfortunately, I was very young and stupid and a bit angry, so I sold it to…well, some half-crazed poet who really hadn't the means to afford such a place. He let all the staff go. Drank and scribbled for a year, then sold it back to my father."

"But the earl didn't rehire the staff?"

"He didn't realize they had been released. There were only five permanent people here. Others traveled with us from Chaumbers. Our steward at the time was an elderly man whose faculties were not what they once were. He simply paid no attention to the fact that those few salaries were no longer being paid. When he realized the error, he hired a caretaker to keep watch on the place, but that was about all the man did. Watched it fall to ruin." Crispin laughed a bit ashamedly. "I offered the cottage to Reg and Georgiana for their honeymoon sight unseen. I shudder to think what they found."

Vanessa did too.

"However, I suspect they made do." Crispin snickered.

Vanessa gave him a small shove, thinking of that generous, warm, but very proper young couple.

"Actually, they were wonderful," Crispin continued. "Reg fired the caretaker, found the Badges, and brought them back—as a kindness, I suspect—but it's too much for them as it is now. He hired some workmen to clear up the drive, at least, until I had a chance to look at it and see what I wanted done. Georgiana saw to ensuring a couple of the rooms were livable. And bless them both, they didn't tell Jasper."

"Why?"

"Because it's my responsibility and unfair to expect Jasper to take it on." He sounded wearily exasperated, but then he frowned. "And because Reg treads more lightly than Jasper."

"You can't mean that." Jasper was not a pushy man.

"No?" He lifted his eyebrow. "Jasper is well-intentioned, I grant. But he'd look at this mess and sigh and set it to right. He'd hire someone to hire someone to oversee all the necessary workers to restore it to the idyllic retreat of our youth. I'd return, eventually, to find it exactly as it was."

"Which is not what you want?"

"Not now. Because it would look the same but not *be* the same." He paused at the end of the hallway and put his hand to a door. "Countess's room." He pushed the door open. "No, Reg let me see what time has wrought. Through neglect that was partly my fault. And now it has to be reshaped. Re-formed. I suspect there is something even more beautiful here than what I remember." He went on into her room and dropped her valise onto the bed. He gave her an ironic smile. "There is a metaphor in there somewhere."

She stood in the doorway, feeling awkward. Everything about this was inappropriate.

Crispin glanced about then seemed to realize she had not followed him into the bedroom. Which was clean and airy with delicate furnishings, brushed and polished. The carpet, curtains, and bedding appeared new. He returned to the door.

"Excuse me." He slid past her and smirked. "You can go in now."

"Crispin, you said you had just two months' leave. How do you intend to reshape this place in two months?"

"Another week is all I can spare. At most." He laughed at her expression. "Yes. So it's idiotic of me to have spent the day clearing a few feet of brush from the lakeshore." He swiped at the dirt on his smock. "I'll go change. Then we can have supper. Then, if you are interested, I'll walk you down to the lake."

⟫⟫⟫⟪⟪⟪

THE TREK DOWN to the lake was arduous. But worth it. They emerged from the trampled path into a small clearing surrounding a large rock that jutted into the water. Crispin helped her onto it, and then they sat, regarding the moon beginning to show itself above the trees. A sliver of moonlight shone on the rippling lake. She understood why, if Crispin had only a week, he prioritized this.

They sat in silence. Crispin had likely talked himself out at dinner when he'd told her about Vitoria. Not the triumph of it, but the bitter conclusion. Rather than pursuing the French and destroying the western division of Napoleon's army, the British soldiers descended on the town they had just liberated to engage in an orgy of looting. Crispin said the war would now drag on another year. Or maybe longer.

At supper, he also had asked if she'd ever been contacted by her brother. She told him about the one time, long ago after Crispin had saved him.

"It was just as you said. Freddy believed the letter was forged. He gave me this." She'd looped her finger under her necklace and retrieved the ring and pendant from her bodice. "This ring. He said if I ever did need him, to send this, so that he wouldn't be fooled again."

"It would seem his character was not so weak, after all."

"No." She didn't mention the fact that the Marquess of Hilyer had not only disappeared from London that night but disappeared altogether. It was something she and Jasper never talked about, and she suspected Crispin would not want to speak of it either. "I heard from an old friend that Freddy is taking a larger role in running the Culpepper mills."

"Because your father is declining."

"I don't know. Will did not say—"

"No. *I* am saying. He's declining. Some of his more recent decisions have been erratic."

Vanessa had only scowled in response. Her father was none of Crispin's business.

"Have you ever considered a reconciliation with your family?"

"Not with him."

Crispin's expression had been unreadable, but he nodded his understanding, and she didn't feel judged. They spent the rest of the meal talking about lighter things. Cartmel, mostly.

Now it felt peaceful and comfortable to simply sit there by

the lake in quiet contemplation. She was grateful to Crispin for saying nothing more about Jasper. For not pressing his brother's case. She couldn't go backward. She would not.

They were there for nearly an hour, lost in their own thoughts, when Crispin rose and extended his hand.

"We should get back before it gets any darker." As he helped her to rise, he took a half-step back to anchor himself. "Would you like—" But the rock was slick and uneven. He slipped, reflexively clenching her hand and yanking her with him as he gasped with alarm. Too late, he let go of her.

For a moment, Vanessa saw trees and sky whirling to a blur as she fell, pulse bounding, shrieking, toward the edge of the rock. Somehow, Crispin rebalanced himself and caught her, one hand in her armpit and the other on her shoulder. His hands clamped vise-like as he hauled her against his torso, pinching her neck and bruising her arm.

He righted her and, after a moment, stepped away. His wide-eyed fear gave way to a flush of mortification.

"Vanessa, I am so, so sorry. That was the clumsiest thing I've ever done. Are you all right?"

Breathless with terror, she tried to laugh. "Thank you. I can't–I can't swim."

"To swim, we dive off the other side. If we'd fallen here, we would've had our brains dashed out. My God. I'm so sorry."

"I'm all right," she said shakily. "Are you?"

"Fine. Let's get down from this rock."

He clambered down, no worse for the wear except for his embarrassment, and helped her to follow. She moved slowly; her legs had all the stability of wet bread. At the bottom, on solid—if muddy—ground, Crispin glanced about, then cleared his throat.

"I wanted to ask if you would like to meet Jasper out here. Rather than in the house."

Ah. He was orchestrating after all.

"Is that the reason you spent all day clearing this spot?"

Moonlight splashed across his face, illuminating his grin. It was a little weak with chagrin, from being caught out or perhaps still embarrassed over his stumble.

"One reason. But not everything I do is for Jasper."

"No," she said, her composure regained. "I imagine you do things for Reginald as well."

"Hmph." He pointed to her feet. "Splendid boots."

"Thank you. The Comptons make them."

"They make boots that are too expensive for the army, unfortunately."

"They are trying a different avenue."

"So Georgiana told me. I am not the only do-gooder here."

She laughed. "The only thing you're defensive about is your kindness. Why is that?"

"Brothers, I suppose." He tugged out a piece of leaf that had somehow threaded its way into his hair. "Competitiveness. Jasper is innately kind. It's his default behavior. And Reg could not be unkind if he tried. I'm terrible at kindness."

"Oh, what a fudge."

"I have to work at it. It is much easier for me to be resentful and mean-spirited."

She stared at him. He meant what he was saying. Or believed he did.

"Well, if you are faking it, you do a very good job."

"Thank you." He started up the path, gesturing for her to follow. "But I don't actually have time for this. If Jasper and you botch all my efforts tomorrow, you will see my true self."

<hr>

CRISPIN'S THREAT STILL rang in her ears the next morning when she came downstairs for breakfast. He could not bully her into returning to Jasper. Could he? Well, he wouldn't. He had been joking. Sometimes with Crispin, it was hard to tell.

She'd slept poorly, tossing and turning and worrying about

seeing Jasper again. She'd wanted to look her best and knew she didn't, and was annoyed with herself that she cared.

She examined the offerings on the buffet. Tea. Milk. Sugar. Also, a bit of honey in a pot. *Oh, Crispin*. He remembered her offhand comment about preferring it. There was not an overabundance of food, just a small selection of cakes that she recognized as being purchased from Mundy's. She wasn't hungry, but picked a cardamon cake and found it two-day-old stale. She envisioned Crispin making the trip into Binnings before her arrival, sparing Mrs. Badge the effort—supper last night had proved the woman was a barely competent cook—and yet he claimed he was not kind.

She poured herself tea, added a drizzle of honey, and then sat down, distracted and fidgeting from nerves. A few moments later, Crispin entered. He was dressed appropriately for a gentleman. He took only tea and drank it standing.

"I don't know when he'll arrive," he said, without preliminaries. He sounded like a major, strategizing. "It will depend on where he timed his stops along the way. But I expect it will be earlier rather than later. I have a few letters to write, then I'll take them to the post." He sipped. "I'm stabling Mercury in town. I'll take him out for some exercise. And it's a long walk into town and back." He set the cup down, studied the cakes a moment, and then picked his cup back up without choosing one. "I won't be back until late."

"I thought you said you would be on the property."

"I changed my mind."

"What if I asked you to stay?"

"Why?" He gave her a narrow look. "Jasper is an honorable man. You don't need my protection. And I refuse to loom about as some sort of deterrent to your falling into bed."

"My God!" Her face heated. "Could you be any blunter?"

"No. I think I stated my mind fairly accurately." He leaned against the buffet and glanced over his shoulder at the cakes again.

"They are fine, Crispin. Delicious, really."

"I'm sure they are. I ate earlier though." He cocked his head. "What is it?"

"Damn it. A carriage. Well." He looked amused. "He must have risen before daybreak."

She heard it too. She set down her fork and wrung her hands together.

Crispin said, "I suppose your choices are now limited to meet him at the door or greet him here."

"Here." Her voice was weak and choked. Her legs trembled too much for her to stand.

She heard the front door creak open, then a shuffling of footsteps that must belong to poor Badge, hurrying to welcome the new earl. She had no idea where Mrs. Badge was.

"What the devil?" Jasper said loudly. Angrily. Vanessa heard, or swore she heard, a female voice. Then she was sure of it when Jasper said, "No, wait here. Badge, where is Captain Taverston?"

She could not hear poor Badge's response. Crispin sighed, set his cup down, and started for the door. He filled it just as Jasper's shadow fell across the threshold.

"Crispin, what the hell? Why didn't Reg say something? This place is a ruin!"

"Jasper—"

"Damn it. How am I supposed to woo Vanessa in a hellhole? Are you trying to sabotage me?"

"No, I think you are capable of fouling things up without my help."

Crispin stepped aside as Vanessa stood up, her legs no longer wobbly. Jasper saw her. She watched his fury leak away. He stared at her. Stared.

"Hello, Jasper."

"My God." He stepped into the room. "I-I, my God. I wanted to do this right."

His voice was shaking, and it made her heart quiver. Her mouth was too dry to speak.

"What is it?" A girl's excited shout echoed down the hall, coming closer. "Is that Crispin?" Then she stepped into the doorway Jasper had just vacated. Tall, slender, pretty—a young woman, not a girl—she had the Taverston blue eyes, framed by extraordinary lashes for a blonde.

Crispin murmured, "Good show, Jasp."

Jasper looked pained. "Mrs. Wardrip, this is Lady Olivia."

The lady barreled into the room. She socked Crispin's arm on the way past and came right up to Vanessa.

"You're here! I'm Olivia. I hope I may call you Vanessa. I've heard so much about you." She rolled her eyes. "All with my ears pressed against closed doors."

"Only ever good things," Crispin added.

"Oh, yes." Olivia beamed at her. "I hope we will be friends. I'm great friends with Georgiana, even though she doesn't like to ride. Oh." She bit her lip. "I hope you do."

"I…" She cast Jasper a helpless look. This was his *sister*.

"Vanessa prefers to ride in carriages," he said. Then, "I'm sorry, Vanessa. If Olivia were a racehorse she would be disqualified for false starts. And I stumbled out the gate. May we please go outside and come in again?"

"I have a better idea," Crispin said. "I will take Olivia down to see the lake." He put his arm around his sister and steered her toward the door.

Olivia cast a glance over her shoulder. "Please say you will still be here when we come back."

Crispin said, "No fair, Olivia." Then he drew her out and kicked closed the door.

# Chapter Twenty-Eight

Jasper could not pull his eyes from Vanessa. After ten months without a glimpse of her, months when he feared he would never see her again, he could scarcely bear to blink and miss another moment.

She gestured absently toward the table as though to offer him breakfast, but her hand shook, and she didn't speak.

"Vanessa, I wanted to do this perfectly."

He'd meant to charm her. Woo her. Had he thought it would be easy? A fairy tale ending in a quaint country setting? Instead, he'd stormed in screeching like a banshee, as if it mattered that Crispin's cottage was falling down about their heads.

"Do what, exactly?" Vanessa asked. He recognized that tone, that struggle to keep her voice calm. "What did you mean by bringing your sister?"

He groaned. He hadn't meant to lead with Olivia.

"She was supposed to swoop in when needed to convince you of my sincerity."

"I've never accused you of insincerity." She frowned, baffled.

Could a proposal of marriage be so far from her mind? Surely, she couldn't be expecting him to once again offer her *carte blanche*. The thought knifed him.

He stepped toward her, but she stiffened as though fearing he would try to gather her into his arms. So he halted. The room was cozy enough with a fire in the hearth and the scent of freshly brewed tea. There was no perfect place or perfect moment that would ensure her answer. She would take him back, or she would not.

He reached into his pocket and then went down on one knee. He held up a ring.

"Please, marry me, Vanessa. Please."

"Marry you!" She took a step back. Away. She might just as well have stabbed him. He would never have imagined her to be frightened by him. Or *repelled*.

"Please tell me it isn't too late."

"Of course, it's too late! And not just too late. It was never possible. Jasper, what are you thinking? You are an earl! Reginald says you're involving yourself in politics. You can't—"

"*Reginald* says?" He jumped up, involuntarily looking right and left as if his brother would emerge from the shadows. "*Reginald* says! Good God!" When had she talked to Reg? "Did you tell everyone how to find you except me?"

"Our paths crossed by accident."

"By accident." He wanted to hit something. Throw something. This was his brother! Both of his brothers. They'd known where to find Vanessa. They'd spoken to her. About him. They'd seen his misery and yet said *nothing* to him? "I expect as much from Crispin," he spat, "but not Reg."

"Expect what?"

"Disloyalty!" Or God knew what. What a prig he sounded. "If not their loyalty, I deserve their pity, at least. My God, Vanessa. You can't know how this has been for me."

"Can I not?"

"God." He pulled out a chair, sank into it, and put his face in his hands. He was showing her his worst self. "I am ruining this. Ruining it."

"Jasper—"

"Do you see what a destroyed man I am?" He laughed bitterly, more of a mutter than a laugh. "I can't even…"

"Be inoffensively charming?"

She sat down beside him. He opened his eyes and faced her. She wasn't mocking him. She looked sad. Understanding and sad.

"Yes," he said, mocking himself. "I can't even be inoffensively charming. The one thing I held over my brothers. Crispin cannot be inoffensive, and Reg cannot charm."

"Stop it, Jasper. Just stop. Talk to me rationally. How on earth do you imagine we could marry? I've been your mistress."

"That does not make it illegal."

"It makes it wrong."

"Wrong how?"

She shrugged, scowling with annoyance. "Wrong as in scandalous."

"I think it should correct the scandal I should never have caused. I should have asked you to marry me then." He put his hand tentatively on her arm, but she brushed it off.

"When? When we were strangers to one another? If you recall, we were in bed before I was even comfortable using your Christian name."

"Then what, Vanessa?" Exasperated, Jasper rested his hands on his knees, making an effort not to reach for her again. "How could we have made this right? We belong together. You know we do. Everyone knows. How do we make this right?"

"I don't think we can. Marrying now would not change what we were."

"No. But it will change what we are. And what we can be. I can't live without you."

"That is a cliché. You can. You will. You'll find—"

"Please don't say I will find someone else."

"You need an heir."

"Crispin is my heir."

"*Crispin?*" She might have laughed but his seriousness evidently unsettled her. She shook her head and murmured, expressionless, "He won't stand for that."

"There are some things Crispin cannot control."

Vanessa rose and began pacing, as if too agitated to sit still.

"Marrying me will frustrate your political aspirations."

This gave him hope. She was discussing it. Arguing, but not saying no. His pulse beat fast in his ears.

"I have none. None beyond voting my conscience. I'm not a leader."

"You could be. Don't you see? That is your gift. Your talent. People like and admire you. You have a responsibility."

That was essentially the same argument he had thrown at Hazard. And Hazard rejected it. So could he. Britain would not miss one more blowhard Tory.

"Vanessa, I have a responsibility to you."

"I am not your responsibility."

"To myself then. I'm not willing to lose you." He remembered what he had promised Crispin. "Unless you refuse me. If you don't want me—"

"I want you, Jasper. Of course, I want you." She spoke with a matter-of-factness that was somehow more dismissive than if she told him she did not. She retook her seat. "But I recognize that I can't have everything that I want. And, earl or not, you can't either."

"But if we both want the same?"

She shook her head and then stared, glassy-eyed, down at the table. "Tell me what would happen if I said yes. Tell me what you foresee. If you've thought it through."

She was giving him a chance. He took her hand.

"We'll marry. I-I'll get a license. Have the banns read. We'll have a small service in Iversley. Like Reg and Georgiana."

She curled her lip. "Oh, exactly like them. Young and innocent. Then what? Where will we live?"

"Chaumbers. And Grosvenor Square while Parliament is in session."

"Am I to come to London with you?"

"Of course." He squeezed her hand. She slipped it away.

"Am I to play hostess to your friends in Society? Do you

imagine their wives will attend my soirees? Will they invite me to their balls?"

"Some will."

"No. They won't."

"Vanessa, you had friends in Society before. Why do you think they will not welcome you again? Don't falter now—"

"Where will your mother be?"

"The dower house at Chaumbers. She will be welcome, of course, at Grosvenor Square when she comes to London."

"*I* am to welcome her?"

"Would you not?"

"Would she come?"

Jasper scraped back his chair to lean forward, elbows on knees. "This is when I would have brought in Olivia. Vanessa, do you think I abducted her? My mother knows she's here. Meeting you."

"She knows you intended to propose marriage to me?" Vanessa looked stunned.

He nodded. Waited.

"And what was her reaction?" He heard the skepticism in her voice.

"She said that I should do the right thing."

He hesitated to use his mother's pain to his advantage. Yet it was something he felt Vanessa should know. He sat up straight again.

"Just before my father died, I learned something...terrible. I had always believed my family to be close. To be blessed beyond measure."

"It is."

"My parents seemed to me to be loving. They certainly created a loving home for us. They were always courteous to one another." His voice caught and he cleared his throat. "But my father had a mistress before he married my mother and kept her throughout most of their years together. I have a half-brother Reg's age."

Vanessa's eyes went wide, and she put her hand on his leg. "I'm so sorry. What a difficult thing to discover. And at such a troubled time." She frowned, turning away, and removing her hand. "I can hardly believe it. He was so upright. So…"

"So false? So hypocritical? So cruel to my mother?"

"She knew?"

He nodded. "I don't know when or how she found out. Maybe she knew all along. She doesn't discuss it, naturally."

"No wonder she doesn't like me."

"It isn't personal. She doesn't want pity. She said she did not. She was a countess and that was important to her. She cared for my father, and he was good to her—her words. In the eyes of the ton, he was better than most. And she says she would not have traded the family we have for anything in the world."

"But he didn't love her."

Jasper shrugged. He could not, even now, believe his father had been cold to his mother. But he said, "Not enough. And not in the way that I love you. I can't…I can't emulate him. I admire him in so many other ways, but I won't marry another woman when I feel this way about you. I was a fool to think I could. Thank God Reg and Georgiana found one another. I would have made her miserable."

They sat for a long moment in silence. Vanessa coughed, then took a drink of her cold tea. She rubbed her palms on her skirt, still staring ahead. She was not saying no. He held onto that. He was afraid to ask her again, to push her, so he waited. She cleared her throat again.

"Will your coach take me to Cartmel?"

"To Cartmel? Why?"

"It's where I live. I need to go home."

He stared at her. Heart sinking. "Why?"

"I'm not hiding from you anymore, Jasper. But I have a life there. You haven't asked me about it."

"I would have. I want to know everything, Vanessa. You can't think I am not desperately curious about what you've been doing. Tell me now." He stroked her arm. "Talk to me."

"Stop." She jumped to her feet and stepped behind her chair. "Jasper, I need to think. Away from you. You make it all sound...possible."

"Why isn't it?"

"For you—for you it is. Because you're a man. And an earl. But think of me. There will never be a time when the majority of your society, the people we must associate with, will not look upon me with scorn. Perhaps they won't cut me openly. But I'll know. I'll feel their contempt."

"Then we'll stay in Chaumbers. I'll vote by proxy. We'll only associate with—"

"No! That is being ashamed. I won't live in shame."

He swallowed his pain. He could not make her life a misery.

"You are refusing me?"

"No. I mean...I don't know." She wrung her hands. "I can't reason with myself when I'm here with you. I want to say yes. You can't know how much. But we jumped into something once far too quickly. I don't regret it. I don't. But I'm older and wiser now. I hope I am. I can't say yes without considering what I will lose as well as what I will gain."

"How long do you need?"

"I don't know."

"The horses cannot...I'm not making excuses, but the horses need to be rested before they can undertake the trip to Cartmel. If you can wait until morning..."

"I think we both know that is unwise."

"Ah." He could control himself. Probably. He tried to jest. "We could have Crispin stand guard at your door."

"No. He refuses to do that."

"What!"

Vanessa hummed an embarrassed half-laugh. "Well, he did. You know how he can be."

He stood. He would rather kiss her until she yielded, but he would do anything, anything, to convince her of his good faith.

"I'll take a room tonight at the inn in Binnings. Tomorrow, my coach will take you to Cartmel. But, Vanessa," he tried not to sound pleading, "when will you send word that I can come to you for my answer?"

"Will you be here? Or in London? Or at Chaumbers?"

"Wherever you want me to be." Then he added, "But here is closest." Soonest.

"Three days. Come to me in three days unless you hear otherwise."

"Otherwise?" He felt as though a nail had been driven through his chest. "Do you mean this may be the last time I will ever see you?"

"Maybe," she groaned. "I don't know."

*No.* No. No. No.

"May I, Vanessa, will you kiss me before I go?"

"I can't. Jasper, don't ask that. I can't."

He didn't trust himself to speak. He turned and walked to the door. Stiffly. Afraid of breaking. Afraid he would never see her again. Never hear her voice. Never touch her. Never raise a family with her. He couldn't bear it. It took all his strength not to turn back, run to her, and crush her in his arms. Convince her. But that might drive her further away.

As he started to open the door, she said, "Jasper?"

He turned.

She put two fingertips to her lips and blew him a kiss.

# Chapter Twenty-Nine

Vanessa had not forgotten the advantages of security and comfort afforded her as Lord Taverston's mistress. She had to admit she missed them. She didn't need them, but she missed them. And those advantages paled in comparison to what awaited his countess. The carriage they had used in London, sometimes together, sometimes apart, had been fine enough, but riding in the Earl of Iversley's coach, marked with the family crest, pulled along by six horses, accompanied by liveried footmen and four outriders, felt like some bizarre dream.

Unfortunately, it was her father's dream, not hers.

She could not swoop into Cartmel in this. She told the driver to take her to Paxton Downs.

The long ride gave her time to reflect.

Crispin had given her "the high ground." Surely, he hadn't planned Jasper's little tantrum, but seeing him thrown off-kilter rather than suavely rehearsed had only made her love him more. Even at his worst, Jasper had a beautiful soul.

He left the cottage at once. The remainder of the day, she had made herself useful helping Mrs. Badge in the kitchen so they would not have to suffer through another meal like the one served the night before—Crispin hadn't even tried to be polite but pushed most of it to one side of his plate.

Mrs. Badge hadn't seemed interested in prying. Rather, she

lived a bit in the past and she was a talker, so Vanessa heard interesting tales. For one, the older boys bloodied each other's noses regularly. Not, Mrs. Badge assured her, ever over grudges. It was because scuffling like street urchins was forbidden at Chaumbers, while the earl and the countess relaxed their rules here.

They were not allowed to hit the little one, naturally, until he caught up some. So they contented themselves with tormenting him. But oh! That child was a clever one. He must've been no more than eight when he sneaked into the boathouse and punched holes in the boys' skiff. The next time they rowed out to fish, the boat sank, and they took a dunking.

"The countess, Lordy, she was angry! She told that boy he might've drowned his brothers dead. But dang if the little one didn't tell her, serious as can be, 'No, Mother. I made the holes so it would sink at two rods from shore. They can both swim that far.'"

Mrs. Badge erupted with laughter and Vanessa had to laugh with her though she thought the story far-fetched. Reginald had evidently been her favorite.

"The baby was always the pet. And hasn't she grown up lovely?"

Vanessa had agreed. Olivia was lovely. And the most open-hearted lady she had ever met.

The coach rolled along so smoothly one might be floating. Vanessa pulled back the curtain to look at the countryside. They had come away from the trees and now the road was surrounded by yellow meadows covered with dwarf furze. Here and there, in the distance, she could pick out cottages and cleared fields.

She wondered what the countryside around Iversley was like. What Chaumbers was like. Beautiful, probably. She would certainly love Jasper's home. She already loved his family.

Crispin had kept Olivia away until suppertime. He was startled—she should say peeved—to learn his brother was already gone. His face had hardened a moment, then he shook himself and made himself thank her, if woodenly, for consenting to speak with Jasper.

Olivia burst out, "You can't have said no!"

"I didn't. I said 'maybe.'"

And then it had seemed they were all friends once more. Apparently, the Taverston siblings believed maybe meant yes. Who, after all, could refuse Jasper?

Over supper, Olivia had taken it upon herself to explain how one must deal with her brothers.

"There is no point arguing with Taverston males. You must ignore them. You'll only waste your time disagreeing with Reginald because he's always right. You can't argue with Crispin because he will bully you into submission."

"I do not bully!"

Olivia arched an eyebrow in his direction, and it was as though she had learned the technique from him. He closed his mouth and returned to his beans.

"And you can't argue with Jasper because he is far too agreeable. You will think he is concurring with you and then you discover you somehow ended up in agreement by agreeing with him."

While Vanessa had laughed quietly at the truth in that, Crispin roared. She wondered what specific memories it had evoked, but he didn't share, so she didn't ask.

She couldn't help quizzing Olivia. "Who wins when they argue with each other?"

Olivia rolled her eyes. "They each think they do." Then she considered it a moment and said, "Reg, of course, but they would never admit it."

Crispin had given her a tender, admiring glance and said, "Livvy-pet, when did you become so wise?"

*Oh!* She could marry Jasper just to be part of his family.

But was it fair of her to do that to them? They would befriend her and defend her. She had no doubt. But could she burden them with that?

She shut the curtain, closed her eyes, and tried not to think about the dilemma for the rest of the journey. She wanted to think away from all this.

But also, there was this: She should have told Jasper about the baby. Not this morning. Not as a confession or deterrent or a plea for his pity. It was something she should have shared with him long before now. Would he wonder why she'd kept it from him? It wasn't that she meant to hide it. There had simply never been the right time to bring up so private a hurt. But now that children were something to be desired rather than avoided at all costs, it seemed critical that she tell him. She didn't consider herself at great risk for barrenness. Lydia had assured her she was not. But what if she never did bear Jasper a child, and he learned, somehow, of her miscarriage. What might he think?

After Jasper's coach let her off, the walk from Paxton Downs felt particularly lengthy. Although footsore and tired, she went first to the Comptons. Oliva had requested boots like Georgiana's, so she brought the tracing and payment to their workshop. The moment she walked through the door Jon embraced her.

"We got two more orders from Cambridge and two from Oxford Village. It seems your friend threw a dinner party, and all the ladies want boots."

"Oh, Jon! How wonderful! And here's another." She opened her valise and took out Olivia's tracing. "Lady Olivia Taverston asked if she might have apple blossoms."

He beamed. "Bitter will say yes. Mrs. Wardrip, this has been such a blessing." His smile shrank. "But tell me, honestly, do you think there will be more? Or will your connections run out?"

"I can't say for certain." She wished she could give a better answer. "I think there will be more, but you are right not to rely on my circle. The boots have to prove their appeal more widely."

Jon's expression fell into more contemplative lines. "I've had a letter from the vicar over in Chilton. There's a cavalryman back from the Peninsula, burned real bad, the vicar says—"

"Who needs a position."

"I want to say yes. He can live over the stable with Tom and Liam. If there's work enough…"

*If* she were a countess, moving about in Society, she could flood them with work. Although, no. What was she thinking? A countess was not permitted to peddle her wares. She'd be better situated to help them as Jasper's mistress than as his wife.

"I wish I could be more certain."

He bobbed his head. "I know I can't ask for more than that. I'm sorry. It just—"

"You aren't asking for yourself. You're a generous man, Jon. I'll do what I can. Is Lydia around?"

"She's over at Myrtle and Mary's. I'll tell her you paid a call." He waved the scrolled tracing like a magician's wand. "This will bolster my argument."

Vanessa left the Comptons' and continued her walk home. Each step put her in mind of other walks back and forth, but the most forceful memory was of Charlotte bringing word of a visitor, and her first sight of Crispin in nearly a year. She'd been so shaken.

She saw a figure coming up the road, but it was not Charlotte. A few yards more, and she realized it was Sherwood. There was nothing down the rest of this road but the Gowes' little farm and her cottage.

"Mrs. Wardrip!" He shouted and waved. She returned the wave, but not the shout. He began to hurry. There was no point slowing her step to avoid him; they would reach one another regardless.

He stopped in her path.

"Charlotte said you went to Binnings. I can take that." He reached for her valise. "I'll walk you home."

She dodged him. "That isn't necessary, Sherwood, but thank you."

"Mrs. Wardrip!" He huffed, exasperated. "I'm trying to court you!"

And Jasper thought *he* had been clumsy.

"That's kind of you, Sherwood, but—"

"You shouldn't live alone. A pretty lass like you. And a widow…"

She wasn't sure what being a widow had to do with it, but she didn't like his insinuating tone.

"I am not interested in your opinion," she said, freezing him. "Now let me pass."

His face slackened. "Well, wait just a moment."

"Sherwood—"

"No, wait. I have a letter for you. It's why I came out all this way." He searched the pockets inside his jacket. Then he pulled out a thick bundle wrapped in paper and tied with a string. "From that London fellow, I bet."

There was nothing to indicate the sender but the masculine handwriting. She took the bundle from him.

"Thank you. Good day."

She walked on. Sherwood was annoying but harmless. And he had a point; she didn't want to be alone. But just as Jasper said he would not marry anyone but her, she would never care for anyone the way she loved him.

But if she loved Jasper, how could she wed him? She had no idea how to carry out the duties of a countess. Moreover, Jasper needed a wide social circle to be the man that he was. No doubt he would still be able to command attention during political debates. He would still be welcome at White's. But he would find himself invited to fewer balls, teas, and musicales. And then what?

The Gowes' place came into view. It was not Charlotte spreading laundry out to dry, but rather Nan. Vanessa waved and called a hello, which brought Charlotte around from the back of the house. Her apron was folded up into a pocket. She must have been tossing feed to the chickens. Vanessa headed over to relate that her journey had been uneventful and the shops pleasant. But a closer look at Charlotte—the way she walked with a sway and the tight fit of her dress—revealed that she must be increasing again. It brought a sharp lump to Vanessa's throat. She wanted children. Jasper's children.

"Good afternoon, Charlotte!" She walked up to the fence and waved again. "Nan. I stopped at the Comptons. They have more orders for boots."

"Isn't it wonderful!" Charlotte said.

Vanessa lowered her voice. "And I think you have some wonderful news as well."

Charlotte nodded, blushing. "Can you already tell? Dan says he wants another boy, since I got my girl. But I said Sweet Kate needs a sister. We've been bickering and now I'm getting big so fast I think God will show us what's what and send twins."

"I'm so pleased for you. Will you come over for tea? You and Nan? I brought some new in Binnings."

"I can't. I'd love to but I can't." Charlotte wiped her brow. "There's too much to do. We have some vegetables to pull and put up. You should pull your turnips."

Vanessa nodded. She knew which were the turnips because she had stolen bunches of them, and other things, raiding gardens in Portugal. Lydia had shown her how. It hurt, still, to think she may have caused innocent families to go hungry. She remembered Colonel Harrington scolding the wives for pillaging their allies, "creating a hostile environment." Crispin had been there, standing at attention, wearing a furious expression more daunting than the Colonel's scold. But she didn't think he was angry with the wives. Around the same time, Henry had tended to one of his fellows, a man he disliked intensely, who had been flogged so severely he couldn't walk for three days. It was generally known that Lieutenant Taverston had done the flogging. Henry would not name the offense and when Vanessa asked Lydia if she knew, Lydia just scowled and said, "What do you think?"

Not stealing vegetables.

Some things, Vanessa had tried to forget.

Charlotte was saying something about slaughtering a pig.

"Nan is going to help with the boys and Sweet Kate for a

while." Charlotte scratched her flank. "Dan asked her to come."

"Are you well?"

"Only tired. But Vanessa, I don't know that I can keep visiting for tea. Not every Monday. When the harvests start coming in, there is so much to do. And then the babe will come…"

"It's a busy time. I understand." Vanessa felt uncomfortable. Had she imposed too much on Charlotte's friendship?

"How was Binnings? Did you see the Taverstons?"

"It was very nice. Yes, yes, I did," Vanessa answered truthfully but untruthfully. "I didn't buy much though. Just the tea." She set down her valise, stretched her aching fingers, then picked it back up. "I should get home. I'll tell you all about it later."

Charlotte nodded. "I'll get back to my hens."

Vanessa waved again to Nan, then walked the last steps to her home, counting the friends she would have to abandon if she were to leave Cartmel. They were good, decent people who had made her so welcome.

And she had been lying, for months, to them all.

※※※

THE PACKAGE WAS from Will and included letters from Effie, with orders for two pairs of boots, and one from Rose, who ordered one pair for herself as well as three pairs for others. Vanessa held the tracings in her hands, marveling at the goodness of her friends, and wondering if this enterprise could be the saving of the Comptons' mill. Were they all just being kind? Or would the popularity of the boots grow?

If it did, how many orders could they fill? Could Bitter keep up or would they have to hire another artist? And even more bootmakers?

Vanessa forced thoughts of the boot mill from her head by reading the letters, which were full of news of London and gentle questions about her life. They both avoided mentioning the Earl of Iversley, and Vanessa found herself hungry for their impressions of him. How had he spent the last few months? Had he seemed to them as miserable as he'd made himself out to be?

She went to bed and then tossed all night, weighing her options and coming to no conclusion. She wanted to be Jasper's wife. But she was afraid.

She spent the following morning pulling turnips and weeding her garden yet again; then she visited Charlotte. She traded tea for a half dozen eggs.

She read a portion of one of the adventure novels, but it didn't hold her interest. She went out to the edge of the woods and gathered kindling. She hemmed the second of her new dresses from Binnings.

What she did not do was make up her mind. Thinking rationally, away from Jasper, did not help. For every reason to marry him, there was one against it. For every reason to stay in Cartmel, she thought of a reason to leave.

Finally, she hauled water from the well, heated it, washed her hair then bathed—the standing-up type of bathing that she loathed.

Scrubbing her neck, she realized her gold chain—Henry's necklace—was gone.

Frantically, she searched the floor, the washtub, her bed, and her nightstand. Her habit was to take it off at night and don it again in the morning. She couldn't remember doing so that morning or taking it off the previous night. The last time she could recall, definitely recall, seeing the necklace was when she had shown it to Crispin at supper the first night in Binnings. It could be anywhere.

That night, she went to bed melancholy. She shouldn't have worn it. She should have kept it tucked away safe. The necklace had been her last tangible connection to Henry and she'd been careless with it. What was *wrong* with her?

Freddy's ring was gone, too, of course. That hurt as well but in a different way.

The next day, she baked biscuits before walking back into town to deliver the new orders to Jon. He decided then and there to offer a position to the cavalryman. Jon's pleasure, Lydia's satisfaction, and Bitter's delight took the edge off her agitation.

Later that afternoon, she sat in her parlor feeling a mixture of gratification and restlessness. She stared at the bare white walls. In the nine months that she had been in this cottage, she had never really spent any time in this room. She claimed to love it. Yet she never used it.

What she should do was invite Nan and Bitter to live with her. They could have her bedroom and she could move into her dressing room. Bitter could work from here and Nan would be closer to the Gowes. Vanessa could travel to shops in other towns to try to convince them to display Bitter's boots and take orders for them. The possibilities excited her and gave her purpose. Even so, it bothered her that she was thinking like a Culpepper.

The room was beginning to darken as the sun started its descent. Vanessa felt confused and dejected. And lonely. What did she want? For *herself*? What did she want?

She wanted Jasper.

And if she wanted to be Jasper's wife, how could fear stop her? Fear of what? Nasty gossip? She'd marched alongside General Wellington's army!

Little by little, she grew aware of the sound of hoofbeats coming up the road. She went to her door. No doubt Charlotte was peering out her own window, bursting with curiosity.

The approaching horse was not much to look at, nothing like Mercury, but the rider was unmistakably a lord of distinction. His traveling clothes were simple enough: dull brown breeches and a dark green frock coat. But Jasper could have ridden a goat and dressed in rags, and he still would carry himself like an earl. She watched as he reached her cottage and dismounted. Her heart beat faster. She walked quickly to her gate to greet him.

"What are you doing here?"

He started, then directed his gaze away, his expression hurt.

"You said I might come in three days."

She meant three full days. But he sounded so unsure of himself that she ached for him.

"We count to three differently." She spoke gently but not gently enough.

"I'm too early?" His face fell and he swore under his breath.

*Oh, Jasper.* It was just as well. She'd made her decision. No, it wasn't a decision. It was a choice. She once had said she could live her life afraid of censure or accept it as she had chosen it.

"Come inside, so we can talk."

# Chapter Thirty

The cottage was small. It was terribly small. Jasper's chest constricted as he imagined Vanessa, the woman he loved, reduced to this.

At least, it appeared in good repair. The paint was relatively new, and the thatch was not rotting. A diminutive garden on the side of the house, one that appeared utilitarian rather than decorative, was not overgrown with weeds. Vanessa must be able to afford a decent groundskeeper. Still. God. Still.

He had to duck beneath the lintel to follow her into her home.

There was no entry hall. One stepped directly into what must be the parlor. It was empty of anything except a single worn chair, a cold hearth, a lamp, one small table, and a bookshelf—one shelf with fewer than a dozen books—on the otherwise barren walls. It was a devastating sight.

"Vanessa—"

"Come into the back. I'll make some tea."

If she noticed his perturbation, she called no attention to it. He followed her into the back room, a small kitchen of sorts. Here he had more of a sense of her presence. The windows were open, and a floral breeze wafted through. Vanessa gestured to a chair next to a table covered with a prettily embroidered square of linen. There was a bowl of wildflowers in the center. He sat and watched her stir the embers of a stove, then set a kettle on top.

She was perfectly at home here. And that made him feel hopeless. If this was what she wanted, he had nothing to offer. Vanessa could not be swayed by his wealth or his title—of course, he'd always known this. He could give her nothing but himself.

He was asking her to give up her way of life for him when he had never truly considered giving up his for her. Yes, he'd claimed he would abandon his newfound interest in politics, but in truth, he needn't. There were many lords in Parliament who had been involved in scandals far worse than falling in love with a mistress. The sacrifices would *all* be on her part.

She sat on the second chair and murmured, "It will be a few moments."

Her answer must be no, or she would have put him out of his misery at once with a yes. He did not want to hear no. Not yet.

He reached into his waistcoat pocket and retrieved a tissue-wrapped gold chain with a tiny sapphire. He'd recognized it the minute Crispin put it in his hands.

"Crispin found this. By the lake."

She unwrapped it carefully, then tears stood in her eyes as she said, "Oh, thank God. I thought I'd lost it forever."

"The clasp is broken. I would have had it fixed for you but…" But it wasn't his place. She had been wearing Henry's gift, not one of his.

"Thank you, Jasper." She wrapped it back into the tissue paper and put it into an empty teacup on her countertop. She regarded it quietly for a long moment. Then she faced him again, smiling wryly. "Safe for now. I'll put it up later."

"Tell me about your life here, Vanessa."

"You mean, how have I gotten through the days?"

He nodded, a sharp ache in his throat. Had she gone through the motions as he had, only to be struck, over and over, by waves of sorrow?

"The daily activities of life take up more time than you might think when one has no servants. And I've made friends here."

"Lydia?" His voice rasped with the effort to speak naturally. No servants? Was she trying to relive the experience of the Peninsula? Why? Was that the key to understanding her? Had he pushed too much of himself, his life, his friends, and his wants, upon her? "Crispin said there was a woman here that you knew. That's why you chose Cartmel."

She nodded. Then she said, "Jasper, I do want to marry you."

"You do?" His heart jolted. He'd been prepared for a no. Now he waited for the *but*.

She answered with a whisper. "Yes. I do."

"Vanessa!"

He leaped from the chair and dropped to one knee beside her, reaching, fumbling in his pocket for the ring he'd dared to bring. She let him slip it onto her finger. Then her words, her actual words, registered.

"You want to. But will you?" he asked.

"Yes. Jasper. Unconditionally yes."

He kissed her hands, so, so very grateful, then the tender inside of her wrists. He stood up, pulling her into his arms and kissing her as he'd dreamed of doing, as he'd been yearning to do. Vanessa returned his embraces just as hungrily, making the mewling noises in the back of her throat that always drove him mad with desire. He kissed her neck, just beneath her ear, knowing what would arouse her, and when she clutched his shoulders and moaned his name, he lost all control.

Lifting her up, he backed her against the wall, hoisting her skirts so that she could wrap her legs around his hips. It was not new or even particularly unusual for them to make love standing, but it felt clumsy. She wore oddly heavy footwear and if he didn't lay her down it would become awkward. He considered, briefly, carrying her to her bedroom—there must be one—it couldn't be more than ten steps away—but ten steps were too far. Swinging her about, he laid her down on the table, knocking the wildflowers to the floor. He bent over her, reaching beneath her skirts.

There was no sweeter sound than Vanessa, murmuring *Jasper,* no sensation more pleasurable than her fingers twining through his hair. They should talk things through, somewhere deep in his brain he knew they should talk first, but she had said yes, and he was on fire.

"I need you," he begged. He needed her desperately.

"Yes, Jasper. Please."

He tugged at his trousers and let them fall around his ankles, then yanked her shirts above her waist. He tried to be considerate of the discomfort of her position, at least to slow down, but she responded to his haste with an urgency of her own. They didn't speak, didn't tease one another, didn't play with one another to savor the experience. He lost himself in a whirlwind of lust too long denied, giving over to it with an incoherent shout of release. Too late, he realized he'd spent his seed inside her.

Vanessa gasped, then laughed a little. She shifted position, her eyes dewy and her cheeks reddened. She gestured toward the stove, making him aware that the kettle was boiling. It probably had been for some time.

"Do you still want tea?"

"I'm sorry," he said, embarrassed. "That was selfish of me." He continued stroking her thighs, but when she pushed down her skirts and wriggled up to be seated, he fixed his own clothing also.

She laughed again, less awkwardly. "I'm sure you'll make it up to me."

"Again and again." But it was not only taking his pleasure without ensuring hers that had been selfish. His haste, his careless haste, may have robbed her of the opportunity to decide differently. Apparently, he'd given her two days, not the three she'd requested. And now, they must marry soon.

She went to fetch the kettle. He watched every movement, memorizing her all over again, replaying in his mind her acceptance of him. Of *them.*

*Unconditionally, yes.* An odd way to respond to a marriage proposal.

He waited for her to bring him his cup.

"You accepted me using the language of surrender. I don't want to...to win if it makes you feel that you've lost."

"Jasper, the one thing I can't bear to lose is you." She sat beside him.

"But you're giving up things that are important to you." He touched her chin, trying to get her to meet his gaze, but she would not look up.

"I merely meant I don't want our solicitors negotiating another contract. I don't want to argue over conditions."

"Not conditions, Vanessa. Not negotiations. We won't argue. But tell me your concerns."

She hunched over her teacup. She seemed to want to say something. He gave her time, but she didn't speak, so he pressed.

"You have concerns."

"We've discussed them before. They're irresolvable. I'm concerned that the ton will never truly accept me. I don't care so much for myself. I don't belong in that world, not fully, but you do. And I don't want you to be hurt when we're excluded from it."

"I won't be hurt. Anyone who would exclude us is no one I care to remain friends with."

"Jasper." She laughed as though groaning. "You're being too agreeable again."

"Too agreeable?" Olivia had accused him of something similar once. As though amiability was a fatal flaw.

"You think you are addressing my concerns. You even make me believe you're addressing them. But you're really only dismissing them."

He stared. He tried to sort through what she was saying. He didn't know what she wanted, but tried again.

"I don't mean to be dismissive. Perhaps I'm being naïve. I might be unpleasantly surprised by people I consider my friends. Then, likely, I *will* be hurt. And angry. But if you're concerned that will lead to regret, it won't." He frowned, hearing his own words. "Is that still dismissive?"

Her lips curled.

"Skip that one," he said, frustrated with himself. At least he was amusing her. "What other concerns do you have?"

"I don't know how to be a countess. And your household must be huge."

"That's valid." Damn it. He was trying to be disagreeable by agreeing with her. He forged on. "There is a ridiculous amount of protocol for you to learn."

"Ridiculous but critical."

"Georgiana and Olivia will help you. Vanessa, my mother will help if you let her. I don't think you'll find it as onerous as you fear. And as for running the household, I'm certain you'll manage. I have an excellent staff besides." Good God. He was doing it again. She lived in four tiny rooms with no servants. Her friends were commoners. "It will be an adjustment…" He trailed off before saying "but" and assuring her he believed her up to the challenge.

"I don't want to abandon the mill."

*What the devil?* "The mill?"

"The Comptons. Their boot mill. Didn't Olivia tell you? Or Crispin?"

He shook his head. The two of them had rather infuriatingly refused to tell him anything of their dinner with Vanessa, though he'd tried begging and bribery.

"Tell me."

"My friend, Lydia, and her husband and brother-in-law are bootmakers. They made these."

She twisted sideways in her chair and lifted her hem to display a pair of tooled leather Hessians. They were unconventional in appearance and, as he'd just learned, packed rather a kick when one was in too much of a hurry to remove them. There was something absurd about them, yet ladies' shoes had always seemed absurd to him, so why should combining prettiness with practicality not make sense?

"We've just begun to sell them—"

"We?" He heard the beginnings of enthusiasm in her voice and tempered his own confused disapproval with a tentative smile. "You're not simply a customer?"

She shook her head. "I've been spreading the word."

He nodded warily. "And?"

"Georgiana, Rose, Effie, and I suspect Olivia will also model Bitter's boots."

"Bitter?"

"He's the engraver. He can't walk. And the other bootmakers are wounded soldiers." She spoke quickly, earnestly, with a furrowed brow. "But they can't sell the boots if no one ever sees the product. They need ladies with means to parade their wares. They need samples in shops. In London shops. And they have to be ready to expand production if orders come in as quickly as I think they will."

If he understood correctly, she meant to market these boots. To utilize her connections, *his* connections, to sell footwear. He did not like this idea. Not at all. It would draw more attention to Vanessa, more unwanted attention.

Of course, he couldn't stop Georgiana and Olivia from doing what ladies did, passing along word of new fancies. But Vanessa's role was evidently more mercantile. Samples in shops? Expanding production? Good God.

"You want me to allow you to become a boot peddler?"

Vanessa bit her lip. Then nodded.

He shook his head. That was simply not possible.

"It...it would be crass. It's *trade*. I know I sound toplofty, but allowing my wife to engage in trade would be thumbing my nose at the ton."

"Thumbing your...for pity's sake. You are marrying your mistress!"

The ton would consider boot peddling a step *below* courtesan.

"Vanessa, we shouldn't make this *harder* on ourselves."

She stood to snatch up their teacups and carted them to the

basin. Her back to him, she said, "So I am to sacrifice my friends for our convenience?"

Her voice had taken on a peeved tone, so he made his own even more reasonable. He didn't want to argue.

"I think 'sacrifice' is overly dramatic. They were bootmakers before you came to Cartmel, weren't they?"

She spun to face him. "They made plain boots for common men. They need my help to sell *these* boots."

"Let them go back to making plain boots," he said, getting to his feet because it seemed they were arguing after all.

"They can't! There is no profit in that."

"Well," he fumed, ready to be *very* disagreeable, "even I have a better business sense than that. If they were never turning a profit—"

"They were! The mill provided a living for half a dozen people until the Leather Tax—"

"The Leather Tax?" His knees nearly buckled.

"Yes, Jasper. A tax on leather. The damn nobs thought to pay for the war on the backs of hardworking cobblers, injured veteran bootmakers, saddlers, and…and…"

"Children who need shoes," he said hollowly. He rattled his head, then stomped to the window and faced out. "Bloody hell!"

"Jasper?" Now she sounded more worried than annoyed. "Jasper, what's wrong?"

"I'm one of the damn nobs."

She was quiet for a long moment. "You voted for the tax?"

He exhaled. Inhaled and exhaled. Then he turned. The expression on her face—disappointment. In him. There was no point in claiming his single vote made no difference in the outcome. The point was, he'd voted carelessly and wrongly.

"Vanessa, I'm…I won't ask you to abandon your friends. I'll support you however you need."

Her mouth pursed. "That doesn't change—"

"No, of course it doesn't. It won't make up for anything. I erred and I regret it. But the only thing I can do is learn to do better. I have been trying. I want to be a good man—"

"You are a good man."

"Then a less..." He knew the word. It wasn't fear of being "boring" that haunted him. "A less shallow man. There is so much that I need to learn to understand. Things I never had the cause or opportunity to understand. I-I need your help."

Vanessa's face softened. She came to him and wrapped her arms about his waist, then laid her head on his chest. He lifted her chin and kissed her.

"Do you still want to marry this Tory nob?"

"Surprisingly, yes. I do."

"We should marry quickly. Perhaps a special license?"

"Jasper, I would like to have the banns read." She sounded wistful. He remembered her first marriage had been a hasty elopement. She deserved better.

"Yes, of course. Banns." That would take a month. But it wasn't as though an early babe would surprise anyone. No one imagined they'd been chaste for four years. "Ah, what the devil. They say the first babe always comes in seven months; it's only the rest that take nine."

He meant it as a jest, but her eyes had a stricken look before she managed a smile.

She said, "Your ton friends should be grateful. We are providing them with years' worth of drawing room chatter."

"Yes, quite." That hurt in her eyes bothered him. What had he said wrong? He pressed on more gently. No big ton wedding, obviously. "Would you prefer to be wed here in Cartmel?"

She considered the question.

"No, that wouldn't make sense. It would inconvenience your family. Besides, I don't want to overwhelm everyone here. Imagine what they'll think when I reveal I'm a Culpepper. And that I'm going to be a countess. Jasper, I'm not going to swallow up their enterprise the way my father would, then pay them an unlivable pittance." She crossed her arms over her chest and sighed. "But I wouldn't blame them for thinking that's my intention."

"Focus, love. I merely asked where we should wed."

She gave him a rueful smile. "In Iversley. And I'd like to honeymoon in Binnings, if Crispin permits, but you must promise me you won't fix anything there."

"Binnings?" The deuce. "But you've seen the cottage. It's a hovel. Crispin hasn't the time or the funds to restore it. After all he has done for me, for us—"

"It is hardly a hovel," she interrupted, shaking her head. "It is his own little Eden."

Eden? More likely, Crispin's headache. But Jasper was more than happy to leave it to him. He glanced about the cramped kitchen. Wondering.

"Is this yours? Your little Eden?"

She hesitated before answering, a little sourly, "In a way. But when we wed, it will become yours."

He grimaced. Unfair, perhaps, yet that was the law. Wives could not own property in their own right. She was attached to it, but Cartmel was out of the way and not a particularly charming place to visit. He envisioned the house falling apart like the Binnings cottage. It made more sense to sell it. *But she was attached to it.* And the mill was here.

"Should we keep it?" he asked.

"I'd like to. And hire Bitter and Nan to live here as caretakers."

"Bitter and Nan?"

She started to explain, something about a colony of bootmakers and craftsmen and nursemaids, but he stopped her.

"My love, yes. Whatever you want." He laughed. "I'll wear flowered boots onto the floor of Parliament. But now, we need to return to Binnings. I left Olivia on tenterhooks and Crispin cross as crabs. My coach is in Paxton Downs. Crispin said not to bring it here. Can you pack a few things? We'll send for the rest."

"I haven't much, Jasper. If you go fetch the coach, I'll be ready before you return." She held out her hand. "But come with me for a moment first?"

She looked up from under her lashes rather enticingly. He laid his hand in hers, expecting a tour of the bedroom. But she led him back through her parlor, out her front door, and down the walk. She shushed him when he tried to ask where they were going.

When she pushed open her neighbor's gate, a woman came dashing out of the house. She was young and apple-cheeked—pretty in a common way. No. He kicked himself. She was pretty. Full stop.

Vanessa whispered to him, "She will have seen you enter my cottage. It's cruel to keep her in suspense."

"And who is this?" the woman cried.

Jasper ignored the egregious manners and made a small bow.

"Lord Taverston, this is my dear friend Mrs. Charlotte Gowe."

"I'm delighted, Mrs. Gowe."

"Taverston?" Charlotte said. Her eyes widened.

"Lord Jasper Taverston. The Earl of Iversley," Vanessa explained.

She gaped. "Jasper?"

Vanessa nodded. "With a *J*."

The girl's squeal of delight pierced his eardrums. Oddly, if he wasn't mistaken, it wasn't his title that thrilled her but his *J*.

# Chapter Thirty-One

True to form, Jasper bore the introduction genially: Vanessa knew he would. He kissed the back of Charlotte's hand, then waited for the children to be brought out—to meet an earl!—and squatted down to solemnly shake the little boys' hands.

Charlotte was too much agog at the news of the engagement for any serious conversation, so after Jasper rode off to Paxton Downs to retrieve the coach, Vanessa ran back to the Gowes.' She had a few things to set in motion and hadn't much time.

"We're leaving today, and I'll be gone quite a while." She put the key to the cottage into Charlotte's hand. "Please don't let the food I've left go to waste."

"A gentleman, you said! You never said he was an earl! Lawks, Vanessa! Can I still call you Vanessa?"

"Yes, of course you can." It made her feel a bit green to think people would now call her Lady Iversley.

"But how did you ever meet him? *An earl?* And when?"

She should have prepared for the inevitable questions. Naturally, Charlotte was curious. So would Lydia be. And Mary and Myrtle. She couldn't blurt out the truth—that she'd been the man's mistress and had lied to them all this time. It would hurt more to have her Cartmel friends shun her than the whole of the ton.

"The Earl of Iversley is Captain Taverston's brother. You know that I've kept in touch with Henry's commanding officer." Vanessa tamped down her disquiet. She would say as little as possible. "Iversley and I..." She shrugged. "We were introduced..."

"And fell in love. Oh, Vanessa. It's so romantic. Can I tell everyone? I don't know that I can keep it to myself!"

Vanessa laughed, embarrassed and relieved. "Yes, please, tell everyone. I have to go...meet the rest of his family. We're leaving today, so I won't have time—"

"Oh!" Charlotte's expression changed from ecstatic to crestfallen. "So soon? You won't forget us, will you? You'll come to visit? Will he allow it?"

"Of course, I'll visit! Iversley will too." Charlotte had led her to what she had truly come to say. "Only...oh, I'll have to find someone to watch the place while I'm not here and keep it up, you know, a caretaker. The garden and everything... A young couple would be best, but I can't imagine who would come all the way to Cartmel."

"Nan! Nan and Bitter!"

"Do you think they would? It wouldn't be too much of an imposition?"

Charlotte hemmed. "They couldn't pay much rent."

"Oh, no. No rent, Charlotte. Rather, I'm certain the earl would insist on paying them." Vanessa saw Charlotte's eyes scrunch up and worried the offer might offend. "For looking after the place."

Charlotte burst into laughter. "I see what you're doing. But it does seem to be the best for everyone, doesn't it? Even me. Having Nan right next door when the baby comes...except I don't want you to go!"

"I'll visit. I promise." She hugged Charlotte again.

She would write to Bitter to confirm the details. And to the Comptons. She wasn't deserting them; they mustn't think that. As for what they would think about her marrying Captain

Taverston's brother? She'd let them draw their own conclusions.

>>><<<

Later, Vanessa gazed across the gently rocking coach at her soon-to-be husband. Jasper was sleeping, managing to look peaceful and graceful while folded onto the not-quite-long-enough bench. He'd propped his head on a pillow of clothing, after taking time to redon his drawers. They'd made love amidst leather-and-velvet comfort, and he more than made up for his earlier haste.

As much as she adored watching him sleep—the occasional fluttering of his eyelids, the twitch of his arm, the half-smile curled on his bow-lips—dusk was deepening into night and the fear of highwaymen was beginning to nag at her. His outriders would keep them safe, of course, but she'd feel better if Jasper were clothed.

She cleared her throat loudly. Jasper stirred, then opened his eyes.

"Thank God," he said, smiling. "You're here. I feared I'd dreamed it all. Vanessa..." He stretched his hand out to her. "Sit with me."

"Put your clothes on first."

He laughed and unrolled the pillowed clothing. He pulled on the most wrinkled trousers he had surely ever worn and an equally wrinkled shirt that he did not bother to button before lying back down. He curled sideways, making space for her, so she slipped over to his bench.

"I missed you so much," she admitted, trailing her fingers over his chest. He was not a hairy man but did have a thicket of dark blond curls that were soft to the touch.

"Thank you for giving me another chance."

Next, they were kissing. And shifting about. Jasper lifted her on top of him but made no effort to raise her skirts. After kissing a good long while, she settled her head against his chest with a deep sigh.

"There's something I need to tell you. Something important that I never could bring myself to speak of." She had to tell him. And if it made a difference—better to know now.

"Go on." He sounded wary. His hand stilled on her back. "I'm listening."

"I-I'm looking forward to children. With you." This was not how she meant to start. He stayed quiet. "It's just that…in my heart…there's another child. Henry's baby. Henry's and mine."

Jasper raised her by the shoulders to look into her face.

"I'm so sorry, Vanessa. What happened?"

"I could not carry…him or her, I don't even know. I miscarried. On the retreat to Corunna."

He groaned and repeated, "I'm sorry."

"It was the hardship," she said hastily, nervously. "Lydia said I could have others."

"Vanessa, please, don't fret now about others."

"I know how important it is for you to have a son."

"Do *not* put that burden on your heart. I have two brothers in line after me, both of whom are eminently capable of stepping into the role. And while Crispin may not oblige me with nephews, Reginald and Georgiana undoubtedly will."

"Even so, I thought I should tell you."

"Yes, but not, I hope, not because you thought it might change how I feel about marrying you. Or that I would blame you if God does not bless us with a family."

"No. No, I didn't think that." She hadn't really doubted him. Still, she'd wanted to hear the words. Needed to hear them.

He lowered her down and stroked her back.

"Will you tell me more? If it isn't too private, too painful?"

"I hadn't realized I was carrying. Not at first." The words spilled out. "We were all so tired and hungry all the time, I didn't even know the sickness I felt was from being with child. Lydia saw it first. I didn't want to believe it. I was so frightened."

"Were there women to help you?"

"There were. Babies came, Jasper, despite all our efforts. There were even a few children we took turns carting along. But most died. Oh, Jasper, they were such pitiable little creatures. I couldn't bear to think of bringing a child into that. And yet, I loved that baby so, so much."

Her voice broke. She could still remember how it felt, the baby's quickening, the life beginning inside her.

Jasper held her tighter.

"And then, after months of stagnation and the most intense cold you can imagine, the war accelerated again. Only this time, we heard Napoleon was coming to Spain to take charge himself. Everyone was afraid." She huffed a little. "If we'd had General Wellington to lead us, we'd have fared better."

"Crispin says the same."

"I can't pretend to have followed the minds of the generals the way Crispin does. All I knew was that we were suddenly fleeing, desperate to find refuge, desperate to get out of Spain. The wives broke into smaller groups. We could not run *en masse*. Lydia and I were with five others, still miles from the rendezvous at Corunna." Vanessa squeezed her eyes tight, trying to blot the scene from her vision, trying to hold back her tears. "The baby started coming. I couldn't…"

She wept a long while, with Jasper holding her, smoothing her hair, whispering in a soothing tone. When she had no more tears to cry, she drew a ragged breath and finished.

"Lydia stayed with me. I told her to go on, but she wouldn't. The baby was dead before it was born. I bled a great deal, and I was so tired. Dying would have been easier than…than standing and walking."

"But you did."

"Lydia made me. She buried my baby, then hauled me to my feet and forced me to march. She said it was better to die trying than to give up."

"Thank God for Lydia."

"And for Crispin. Lydia got me to Corunna, but she couldn't have helped me get out of it. They couldn't even evacuate all of the wounded. And with Henry gone, I had no standing at all."

"It's unfathomable." Jasper shifted her onto the bench and sat up. He rubbed his hands over his face. "I'm sorry. Now I can't help thinking about Crispin. No wonder he's become so embittered."

"Embittered? Crispin? But he's so kind."

"Kind? *Crispin?*" Jasper looked—not skeptical, rather just unconvinced.

Crispin had always treated her kindly; yet hadn't he confessed to resentment and mean-spiritedness? What side of himself did he show to his brother?

Jasper wrapped an arm around her.

"Does he know? About your baby?" There was a faint note of hurt in his voice.

"No. Crispin didn't know." Once again, she said, "We were not close then." Then she sniffed and said, "Well, but he's Crispin. Who knows what he knows?"

"Did Henry? I understand he couldn't stay with you. That isn't what I'm implying. I just...I can't imagine how tortured he must have felt."

"He knew. And he was tortured. He was a terrible mix of devastated and absurdly happy. When we parted, oh—" Her voice cracked again, remembering how Henry had broken, sobbing, cursing, utterly terrified for her and their child. "I'm sorry, Jasper." She pressed her fist against her heart. "I can't—"

He kissed her on the temple. "Shh. Don't apologize. I'm not entitled to your memories of Henry."

The coach had been slowing. Now it merely crept along, then turned sharply. They could hear branches and foliage scraping the outside.

"Ah. I think we've arrived." Jasper let go of her and began buttoning his shirt. "I don't mean to be abrupt, but Crispin would find it far too amusing to discover me like this."

OLIVIA WAS WAITING in the drive despite the lateness of the hour. Jasper hopped down from the coach. Before he could hand Vanessa out, Olivia set down her lantern and leaped into his arms. With the door standing open, Vanessa saw it all, though evidently Olivia could not see her in the darkened coach.

"Where is she? What did she say?"

"Is Crispin inside?"

"No, he's gone," Olivia said, displaying an enormously aggrieved pout. "And good riddance. He didn't eat anything in the morning and then he was ill-tempered all day." She sniffed. "You know how he is. Then a letter came, and he disappeared upstairs for *hours*. And then Mrs. Badge burned the rice we were supposed to have, so supper was late. She made dumplings that weren't too terrible, but Crispin wouldn't touch them. I told him he was being rude, and he snapped at me. He was very mean."

She looked more wounded than angry. Then she pawed at Jasper.

"What did Vanessa say!"

"He's gone? Stomped off in a temper over burned rice?" Jasper laughed.

"No, of course not. But he was about to stomp off to the lake after supper and a man came and they argued awhile outside, then Crispin came back in and grabbed his valise and left with him."

"With whom?"

"Crispin didn't say. He just said goodbye. And said to tell you goodbye and good luck." She rolled her eyes. "He treats me like a *child* sometimes."

"Yes, well, he does me too."

Vanessa climbed out of the coach on her own.

"I am here. I said yes."

"Vanessa!" Olivia pushed Jasper aside to greet her. "I wrote to

Alice, she's Georgiana's cousin, she wants boots too. And we're going to be sisters! I can't wait to tell Georgiana. When is the wedding? Will it be in London? I hope not, because Mother and I are still in mourning. We do go to church in Iversley…"

"In Iversley," Jasper said, drawing closer. He signaled to a footman to bring Vanessa's trunk. "As soon as possible. If Crispin isn't here, we may as well return to Chaumbers in easy stages. We'll ask Reg and Georgiana to meet us there."

# Chapter Thirty-Two

*T*RAVEL LIGHT. THAT would be impossible. Vanessa had no choice but to order an entire wedding trousseau; after all, she was going to be a countess. Moreover, if she wanted to make Bitter's boots fashionable, she couldn't arrive back in London in last year's clothes.

*Be prepared.* Three and a half weeks to prepare for this role? Impossible.

Perhaps it was time to set aside Peninsula rules.

The banns were read three Sundays in succession. The wedding was to be held the following Friday—a small family wedding in a quaint, very old, village church.

Chaumbers was not at all what Vanessa expected. That would have been a traditional large country house, beautifully proportioned, perhaps tacked onto a restored medieval keep to lend it character. Or something sweeping and gothic, though that possibility seemed less *Taverstonian* somehow. But Chaumbers was…different. Not gaudy in the way her father's house was. Not ugly. Well, yes, it was ugly. It looked like several unattractive houses pasted together. The grounds were spectacular though.

Jasper had asked if they should invite anyone from Cartmel. Did she want Lydia? Or Charlotte? Or everyone from Cartmel? It was no exaggeration to say they could house the entire village in one wing. But no one in Cartmel could afford to travel a good three-quarters of the way to London for a wedding, a trip that would necessitate losing a solid week of work or more. Inviting them would not be kind; it would be insensitive.

Family only. And Hazard, who was practically family. Vanessa understood why Jasper had asked about inviting someone from Cartmel. She *had* no family.

Olivia was delighted to be asked to stand up with her. Vanessa was a little surprised to discover Jasper had asked Hazard.

"Not your brother? Won't he be hurt?"

"Reg?" His eyebrows rose. "No. That's the sort of slight he won't even notice." Then he'd grumbled, because evidently, *he* was hurt. "I would have asked Crispin, had he deigned to grant us his presence."

She was hurt too by Crispin's absence but mollified by Hazard's arrival shortly after Jasper's request. Hazard was clearly touched to be asked.

It had been a difficult but delightful few weeks. Jasper's mother was not the ogre Vanessa had believed her to be. She didn't apologize. And Vanessa did not allude to her long-ago spurning. Or the reason behind it. They simply started afresh, which was what Vanessa also preferred. Lady Taverston—"Beatrice," but not "Mother," thank goodness—gave her gentle pointers about the quirks of the house and its staff, and then moved quietly to the dower house a week before the wedding.

When Vanessa told her there was no rush, Beatrice said, "The dower house is more comfortable. The memories here…it's too much. Besides, I'll just be a stone's throw away."

Of course, Beatrice's welcome had limits. She assigned Vanessa a guest chamber in a different wing than the earl's apartments.

They respected propriety, despite their impatience to make up for lost time. They made love only once, out at the folly, a pretend medieval ruin a good long walk from the house.

They went out to the folly a second time, but someone had

beaten them there. Fortunately, before they stumbled on the copulating couple, they heard them. Jasper looked shocked. He grabbed her hand and ran, pulling her along. When they were a decent distance away, he said, voice shaking with either horror or laughter, "That was Reg's voice."

"For pity's sake. They're married, Jasper."

"Yes, I know, but you don't understand. That was *Reg*!"

Georgiana and Reginald had arrived the day before, ten days before the wedding. There was no mistaking Georgiana's interesting condition. Vanessa was glad the family's focus turned to her. She wasn't jealous of Georgiana's place in the Taverston family: a duke's daughter, exquisitely pretty, the very definition of respectability, and now the proud bearer of the first grandchild. She wasn't even jealous that Jasper had tried courting Georgiana.

But, ridiculously, she was jealous of the easy-bantering friendship between Georgiana and Hazard. Evidently, even *he* had proposed to her once, which was absurd. In addition to all her other gifts, Georgiana was witty, and it was particularly evident because Hazard was too. Vanessa could appreciate wit, but it was not her own talent.

She confided in Jasper while they were walking in one of the gardens.

"She's wonderful. I love her. I do. But she's so *perfect*. And I don't want to be crabby around her or people will think I hold a grudge because of you."

Jasper laughed. "A ridiculous notion!" Then he'd wrapped his arms around her. "*You* are perfect."

"I'm not—"

"Georgiana is perfect for Reg. You are perfect for me." He gave her a loud kiss.

"Yes," she sighed. "And I do know Hazard likes me, too. I suppose he appreciates seriousness sometimes."

"Ah," Jasper laughed, "he does. But for serious Hazard, you'll have to fight Alice Fogbotham."

"Alice?"

"Georgiana's cousin. She'll be here for the wedding."

She gave him a long look. She didn't mind that Georgiana's cousin was coming but found it a little odd when the wedding was so small.

Jasper cleared his throat. "Actually, I asked Georgiana if I might invite her. To keep Haz company. Draw him out."

"Draw *Hazard* out? What on earth?"

"It's a very long story. Ask me another day. We're out of sight of the house. I'm going to kiss you now."

◆

SUDDENLY, IT WAS her wedding day.

Georgiana, Olivia, and the delightfully clever Alice Fogbotham helped her to dress, two maids hovering in the background, waiting to lend their hands.

When Vanessa was nearly ready, Beatrice appeared in the guest chamber. She was very composed and plainly beautiful in mourning black but with a yellow rose tucked into her widow's cap. She put a sparkling pair of diamond earrings into Vanessa's hand.

"These were a gift from Jasper's grandmother on my wedding day. They were her mother-in-law's before. I'd like for you to have them. You needn't wear them today—"

"Oh, but of course I will!" A little awed by what the jewels represented, she stripped the silver bobs from her ears to exchange them. "Thank you, Beatrice."

"I want you to know how glad I am for Jasper. And for you. You make him happy. I wouldn't have wanted anything different for him than that."

"Thank you. I'll be a good wife to him."

"I know you will. Now I will leave you to the girls. The men have just left for the church. We should follow in a few minutes. It will take us longer to get in and out of our coach."

The moment the door closed, Olivia elbowed Vanessa in the ribs. "I knew she liked you."

"Of course she does!" Georgiana said, reaching out to help fix the clasp on one of the earrings. "Now." She stepped back. "Vanessa, you are stunning."

"So long as Jasper thinks so."

"Let's go," Olivia said, clapping her hands with glee. "I can't wait!"

Georgiana and Vanessa exchanged looks, and then laughed. Olivia was more eager than a bride.

It was a jumble, climbing into the coach, riding the short distance into the village, then climbing out again—all without wrinkling their gowns or snagging their jewelry. A crowd of villagers had already gathered in the churchyard to cheer them after the service ended. The curate, who had been waiting at the church door, escorted the dowager, Georgiana, Olivia, and Alice inside. Vanessa heard voices, excited voices, before the door shut again. The faint sound of organ music began. The curate opened the door.

Reg had offered to walk her down the aisle. Not to "give her away," that would be silly and a bit sad. But she was grateful he'd offered. She'd had no one else to ask since Jasper had claimed Hazard.

Her eyes adjusted to the dim light inside the church. The man waiting, arm crooked, to escort her, was not Reginald. She nearly tripped over her own feet.

"Freddy! Freddy, what are you—"

He grinned at her, a lopsided grin that looked more than a little worried.

"If you want to run, Nessa," he said under his breath, "I'll shoot him."

A laugh caught in her throat. "How did you know?" How had he found her?

He took hold of her arm. "Music, Nessa. Walk with me." They started slowly down the aisle. He leaned his head toward her. "That fellow there." He gestured with his chin. "He told me I'd be welcome. Gave me this, or I mightn't have believed him." He pressed his ring back into her hand. "I hope—I hope I'm not wrong-footed again."

A quick glance showed Crispin, nattily attired in his uniform.
*For the love of God! He'd slipped on that rock on purpose!*
Plotting three steps ahead of everyone else.

Crispin didn't look her way. He was whispering something to a somber-looking stranger who held a curly-haired toddler in his arms.

"Not wrong-footed. Freddy, I'm so happy you're here." Tears welled up, blurring her vision. She was happier than she'd ever been. She clung tight to her brother's arm, and he guided her along.

"Now don't cry, Nessa. Iversley's face is about to crack open with that smile. You can't go up there crying."

"I won't. I'm not."

They reached the front of the church, and her brother released her to the man she loved with all of her heart. The music ceased. The world went silent as if everyone present was holding their breath. Inexplicably nervous, Vanessa glanced at Jasper. Jasper looked calm.

"Vanessa, my love, my world," he murmured, his fingers brushing hers before he turned to face the rector.

Her nerves disappeared.

The rector lifted his book.

"Dearly beloved, we are gathered together here in the sight of God, and in the face of this congregation, to join together this man and this woman in Holy Matrimony…"

## About the Author

Carol Coventry is a born-and-bred Jersey Girl transplanted to Kentucky. A quarter of a century working in the medical field has taught her that, after any tough day, nothing soothes the spirit like a guaranteed happily-ever-after. Escaping to the Regency Era is like a mini-vacation. After spending so much time there, she felt like a native and began spinning her own tales of historical romance.